"I LOVE EVERYTHING ABOUT YOU."

White Fire gently took her by the wrists and laid her down on the blankets. He knelt over her, his lips brushing against her mouth. "I think I fell in love with you all those years ago, Flame, when you flirted with me with those deliciously green eyes and wondrous smile. Yet you were but a mere child. I placed you in the back of my mind until the day you arrived at Fort Snelling on the riverboat. When I saw you, I knew I could never truly love anyone but you."

He kissed her with a meltingly hot passion, his hands releasing her blouse from inside the waist of her skirt. He could feel her shudder of ecstasy as he slid his hands inside the blouse, and their flesh seemed to fuse in the heat ignited between them.

Flame had not expected to go this far when she had come to him this morning, fresh from sensual, sweet dreams of him.

Yet she could not stop what she had started . . .

Also by Cassie Edwards

WHITE
FIRE

CASSIE
EDWARDS

ZEBRA BOOKS
KENSINGTON PUBLISHING CORP.
http://www.kensingtonbooks.com

ZEBRA BOOKS are published by

Kensington Publishing Corp.
119 West 40th Street
New York, NY 10018

All Kensington titles, imprints, and distributed lines are available at special quantity discounts for bulk purchases for sales promotion, premiums, fund-raising, educational, or institutional use.

Special book excerpts or customized printings can also be created to fit specific needs. For details, write or phone the office of the Kensington Sales Manager: Attn.: Sales Department. Kensington Publishing Corp., 119 West 40th Street, New York, NY 10018. Phone: 1-800-221-2647.

Zebra and the Z logo Reg. U.S. Pat. & TM Off.

First published in June 1997 by Topaz, an imprint of Dutton Signet, a division of Penguin Books USA Inc.

First Zebra Books Mass-Market Paperback Printing: March 2017
ISBN-13: 978-1-4201-3672-2
ISBN-10: 1-4201-3672-0

eISBN-13: 978-1-4201-3673-9
eISBN-10: 1-4201-3673-9

10 9 8 7 6 5 4 3 2 1

Printed in the United States of America

With affection I dedicate
White Fire
to my following special friends:

Bettye Inman	*Jane Herron*
Brenda "Nightrose"	*Helen Howe*
Hailey	*Margie Goodman*
Bernice Gardner	*Pat Forrester*
Wanda Fouts	*Marissa Dragoo*
Lois Ellerbee	*Karen Delaney*
Doris Danforth	*Julie Latimer*
Wendi Kozma	*Tammy McCloud*
Vickie Lyons	*Gloria McConnell*

Chapter 1

If ever any beauty I did see,
Which I desired, and got, 'twas
But a dream of thee.

—John Donne

St. Louis, 1820

The cottonwoods whispered in the gentle breeze as the sun filtered through their large, fluttering leaves, onto a fresh mound of dirt. The heart-wrenching military funeral for his father now over, Samuel White Fire Dowling stood over the fresh grave in his stark, jet black suit. Behind him he could hear people talking in polite, soft mumbles as they left for their horses and buggies.

But in *his* mind, White Fire was hearing way more than that: the kind voice of his father who had taught him the morals by which White Fire now led his life.

Morals, he thought bitterly as his thoughts strayed to his mother.

His hands circled into tight fists at his sides when

he thought of how she had betrayed his father. Just prior to his death, his mother had informed his father that she wanted a divorce . . . that she had found someone else she wished to marry.

"Samuel, everyone is gone."

His mother's soft and tiny voice drew White Fire quickly out of his angry reverie. He turned on his heel and gave her a cold gaze.

"Samuel, son," Jania May murmured.

She reached a hand out for him and flinched when he stepped quickly away from her.

She slowly dropped her hand to her side. "Samuel," she said, her voice breaking, "please do not hate me. If I had known your father was going to die in such a way so soon after I told him of my wishes to marry someone else, I would never have told him."

White Fire cringed at how she kept calling him "Samuel." He stood there for a moment, unresponsive, thinking about how he had not yet told her that from now on he was going to use his Indian name, White Fire, to totally distance himself from this life, which had only brought him pain, silent suffering, and degradation.

He was ashamed that he hadn't gone by his Indian name sooner, yet his reasons not to were valid. It was enough that his skin color, his Indian *looks,* had been the cause of him being labeled a 'breed. Using the name White Fire while in school would have only increased the whites' taunts, which he would never forget until the day he died.

"You telling Father about the divorce, about falling in love with another man in such a cold, callous way, is surely what caused his mind to be elsewhere, to be off guard and not realize that he was being stalked by gunmen," White Fire suddenly blurted out, his words bitter as sour grapes as they crossed his tight lips.

He glared at his mother. Then just as quickly his eyes wavered when he saw, as he had always seen when he had looked at her, just how beautiful she was. Born Pretty Cloud into the Miami Indian tribe, his mother's dark, slightly slanted eyes, her smooth, copper skin, and luscious body, and her long, black hair worn to her waist, could intrigue any man. She looked so sweet and innocent. But looks were deceiving.

As were the black veil which hung down over her lovely, copper face, and the black mourning dress she wore today.

All those things were deceitful . . . a *mockery* to the man who lay cold in his grave.

"Mother, just go away," White Fire said, swallowing hard as he turned his back on her.

He still could not believe that she could be such a fickle person.

Yet when he thought of all the social functions that she had managed at their large, two-story mansion, which sat high on a cliff overlooking the Mississippi River, downstream from the hustle and bustle of the St. Louis waterfront, and how she had playfully flirted with the men in attendance, he knew that she surely had been that way since she had discovered how to use her charm on men.

"Son, I *beg* you, *please* do not hate me," Jania May said, her voice breaking. "I am sorry for everything. *Everything.*"

White Fire would not allow her hurt, her apologies to sway him. He turned again and glared at her. "Mother, I doubt I have ever truly known you," he said thickly. "I am certain that even when you were called Pretty Cloud by your people, when you lived with them, you practiced the same sort of deceit that you are so skilled at today."

"Samuel, I have done many things in my life that I am ashamed of, but have I not been a good mother to you?" she asked. "Have I not protected you, heart and soul, when you were taunted as being a half-breed?"

"You did not have to speak up in my behalf when I was able to do it, myself," White Fire mumbled. "I am proud of my Indian heritage. That is why I have chosen now to be called White Fire by my friends and associates, instead of Samuel."

"Yes, I, personally, gave you that name, as well as Samuel, when you were born," Jania May answered. "White Fire was my father's name."

Her eyes dwelled on her son's handsomeness. He was a young man of nineteen, whose skin was the color of copper, whose hair was coal black and hung down to his waist, and whose eyes were as black as midnight.

There was a reason why he showed none of his father's traits. But he would never learn the secret that she had kept from him through the long years since his birth. That, above all else, would infuriate him even more against her. He would hate her forever for such deceit.

Jania May swallowed hard and pleaded with her eyes as she continued to speak. "White Fire," she said, "I went through so much after . . . after . . . the attack on our Miami village those many years ago.

"Most of my Miami people were killed. I . . . I . . . managed to wander off." She cast her eyes downward. "If not for Samuel, your father, I would have died."

"I am certain these past days, before *he* died, he was regretting the very day he set his eyes on you that first time," White Fire said, starting to walk away, stopping only when she reached out and grabbed his hand.

"But he *did* take me in," she said, her eyes still pleading with White Fire. "He *did* marry me. Then you were born to us, ah, such a blessing."

"Yes, Father and I were close," he said, looking away from her. He looked toward the tall bluffs that rose up from the mighty Mississippi on the opposite shore and to where the Jefferson Barracks, a military establishment stood. "I just wish I had been with him when the . . . the . . . outlaws chose *him* to gun down in St. Louis."

Frustrated, he raked his long, lean fingers through his thick, black hair. He gave his mother a look of deep hurt and sadness. "Mother, Father was a military officer who never received even as much as a scratch during his tour of duty,'" he said thickly, "only to then be gunned down by outlaws on the streets. This, only a few days after you told him you were leaving him for another man. After he married you and gave you a wonderful life. What of any of that is fair?"

"Samuel," Jania May said, a sob lodging in her throat as he turned and stamped away from her.

"Samuel! Samuel! White Fire, please stop! Don't leave!"

"Don't pretend you are truly worried about me, Mother," White Fire sarcastically threw at her over his shoulder. "My leaving gives you all the freedom you need to play house with your new husband. Keith Krantz? Isn't that his name? A stockbroker who is going to move you into a house even more grand than the one Father had built for you."

"Please don't go to the Minnesota Territory!" she cried, running after him. "Samuel, I may never see you again!"

"As though you care," White Fire said bitterly.

He truly knew that she cared, but it was hard to think anything positive about her at the moment. In truth, he would never stop blaming her for his father's death. Had his father been more alert, White Fire *knew* that he would have realized that he was being trailed by men who meant to rob, then kill him.

White Fire had longed for adventure these past years, anyhow, and now he was going to follow his hunger into the Minnesota Territory. He was already packed to leave. His heart throbbed excitedly at the thought of riding his sorrel horse into unknown territory.

He was not going to accept any of his mother's inherited money. To pay his own expenses, he was going to use his own meager inheritance. Then when that was gone, he was going to trap and trade his way north.

His throat constricted and he doubled his fists at his sides to think about how much his father had trusted his mother by leaving almost everything to her. He had not had the chance to change his will before he died. He had not had a clear enough mind to think of doing it after being stunned to the very core of his being by the discovery of his wife's infidelity.

"Samuel Dowling?"

A smooth, deep voice caused him to stop and look over at Colonel Frederick Russell, the commandant of Jefferson barracks.

But his gaze did not linger for long on the tall, lanky, middle-aged man. It was the girl standing at his side that drew his quick attention.

White Fire's heart skipped a beat, for never had he seen anyone so beautiful. With her long, flaming red hair hanging in deep waves over her shoulders, and her green eyes smiling at him in a most flirtatious way, her lashes fluttering, he was taken aback and suddenly at a loss for words.

But he quickly reminded himself of the girl's age. He had heard his mother and father discussing the child, remarking how pretty she was, and commenting on how mature and well *developed* she was for her age of ten.

"Samuel, I wish to again extend to you my sympathies for what happened to your father," Colonel Russell said stiffly. "Is there anything I can get you or your mother?"

White Fire was aware of the colonel speaking to him, yet the man's eyes moved as White Fire's mother stepped up beside him. As always, the colonel, whose wife had been too ill to attend the funeral, was openly enjoying looking at White Fire's ravishingly beautiful mother.

White Fire blazed inside as his mother smiled up

at the colonel in her flirtatious way, then lowered her eyes demurely and portrayed the new widow.

Reshelle Russell, the ravishing daughter of the commandant, stood in her tight-fitting green velvet suit, her chin proudly lifted as she continued to smile at White Fire, captivated by him. Not only by his handsomeness, but by the fact that he was a *'breed*.

She entered her own world of pretend as she continued to gaze at him and waited for the discussion between her father and the handsome half-breed to be over. She had heard her parents talking about how Samuel Dowling had the Indian name of White Fire. That was almost as intriguing to Reshelle as the *man*.

She could see herself at age twenty, walking hand in hand with White Fire Dowling along the river, their hearts joined as one. She could even feel what it might be like to be kissed by him. . . .

"Daughter, we must hurry back home now and see how your mother is faring," Colonel Russell said dryly. He took Reshelle's hand and whisked her quickly past White Fire and Jania May.

Just as Reshelle brushed past White Fire, she leaned against him and spoke into his ear. "I am known as Reshelle by everyone," she whispered. "But to you I am *Flame*. When you think of me, think of me as *Flame,* not Reshelle."

The young man was taken aback by her boldness, by her realization that he had been silently admiring her. He watched her walk away beside her father, so straight-backed and confident.

He watched her hair fluttering in the breeze. It was so bright red in color, it looked as though it had been touched by the flames of the sun.

When Flame sent him another smile across her shoulder, White Fire returned her smile.

His smile quickly faded. He felt foolish for having, for even one minute, seen her as someone he might pursue in the future.

Forcing her from his mind, White Fire hurried on in the opposite direction. He saw that his mother was trailing behind him, panting for breath as she tried to keep up with his fast pace.

When he reached his sorrel horse tethered at a post just outside the fort, he stiffened as his mother caught up with him. He could feel her gaze on him. He tried to ignore her. He doubted that he could ever feel close to her again, as he had as a child when he was ignorant of her deceiving ways.

"Son, please don't leave me," Jania May pleaded.

Still White Fire ignored her. He removed his black jacket and shoved it inside one of his saddlebags. He slid into a fringed buckskin jacket, then swung himself up into his saddle.

He turned and checked the blankets rolled up behind him on his saddle. When he saw that they were secure, he checked the buckles of his saddle bags and made sure they were tight.

Seeing that everything was ready for his long travels ahead, he finally turned and gazed down at his mother.

Suddenly he felt sad to leave her. He did love her. He always would. It was just impossible to forgive her for what she had done to his father.

"Mother, whenever possible, I will send you wires and letters," he blurted out. "I assure you, Mother, I am not abandoning you, like—"

He stopped short of saying, "Like you abandoned Father."

"Son, always remember that I have always done what I could for you," Jania May said, a sob lodged in her throat. "Until recently, when I fell in love with another man, everything I did *was* for you."

White Fire gave her a perplexed stare, wondering if she truly believed this. Had she fooled herself *into* believing such nonsense as that?

He sighed heavily, then wheeled his horse around and rode off, concentrating on the adventures that lay before him, leaving all sadness and heartaches behind him.

"White Fire, I love you!" Jania May cried, waving at him as he gave her a quick look over his shoulder. "Samuel White Fire, I shall so terribly miss you!"

Chapter 2

My face in thine eye, thine in mine appear,
And true plain hearts do in the faces rest!

—John Donne

A book of poetry resting on her lap, Flame sat at her ailing mother's bedside, her gaze and her thoughts elsewhere. She was looking through the bedroom window, watching the sky and how the setting sun was sending the most beautiful shades of crimson across the horizon.

Flame could not help but wonder where White Fire might be at this moment. She had heard her father discussing with some of his soldier friends how White Fire had planned to leave today after his father's funeral, to journey alone into the wilderness.

A thrill coursed through Flame to think of how wonderful it would be to join White Fire on his exciting adventure. Although Flame's life was filled with many activities, and she had just discovered the wonders of dancing and enjoyment of the glances from boys her own age, and even of *older* men, she was bored more often than not. She hungered for adventure.

She loved to ride on horseback, feeling the freedom when she rode through the knee-high grasses on her father's broad expanse of land along the Mississippi River.

She wished she were outside *now,* instead of in her mother's bedroom, the bitter smells of medicine wafting up her nose. Ah, how she would, instead, love to be walking amidst swirling, clambering vines and starry flowers!

But now wasn't the time to think of herself. She was there for her mother. She was dedicated to her mother who was ill quite often, with first one ailment, and then another.

"Reshelle, why have you stopped reading poetry to me?" Elizabeth Ann Russell asked, drawing Flame's eyes quickly to her. "Daughter, what's taken your thoughts away? What are you fantasizing about *now?* I do wish you wouldn't wish on things that can never be."

Flame flipped her long, red waves back from her shoulders and forced a smile as she gazed at her mother, when *truly,* looking at her mother only saddened her. Elizabeth Ann was frail and pale, not only because she was so prone to illness, but because she scarcely ever went out into the sunlight, saying that it was bad for her ivory skin.

"Mother, I'm sorry," Flame said softly.

She again opened the poetry book where she had marked the last page that she had read with a pale blue velvet ribbon. "I shouldn't have stopped reading," she murmured, "but, Mother, something happened today that I can't get off my mind."

She closed the book again and laid it aside. She leaned over and straightened her mother's blanket, then smoothed some locks of her mother's auburn hair back from her pale brow.

"I saw a man today, Mother," she quickly said. "I have seen him many times before, but never so close." She sighed. "I shall never forget him, Mother. *Never*."

"Reshelle, Reshelle," Elizabeth Ann said softly, "you are only ten. You shouldn't be thinking of men."

"Perhaps I shouldn't call him a man," Flame said, cocking an eyebrow. "I believe he is only eighteen or nineteen."

"Reshelle, anyone who is eighteen or nineteen is a man and much too old for you to be thinking about," Elizabeth Ann scolded. She turned her head away from Flame and coughed.

"I truly wish you would call me Flame," Flame said, sighing. "Reshelle is such a cold, assuming-sounding name."

Elizabeth Ann turned a slow gaze to Flame again. "The name Reshelle is full of *sunshine*," she said softly. She reached a cold, clammy hand to Flame and patted her on the arm. "Daughter, you shall always be Reshelle to me. Wanting to be called Flame is just another childish notion you will soon get over, just as you will soon forget the young man you saw today."

"A 'breed, mother," Flame quickly interjected. "Mother, he's a 'breed, part *Indian*. Miami, I believe. Isn't that exciting?"

Elizabeth Ann gazed at Flame a moment longer, then slowly closed her eyes.

"Mother, I'm going to marry the handsome Indian

half-breed one day," Flame blurted out. "When I grow up, I will search for him. He will be mine!"

Elizabeth Ann's eyes flew open. "Reshelle, stop that right now," she scolded. "Such talk . . . such thoughts . . . are scandalous."

To soothe her mother's anger, Flame grabbed the poetry book, opened it, and began reading passages. She knew, though, that she couldn't get White Fire off her mind, even though it *was* frivolous of her to think of one day marrying him. And deep down inside she doubted that she would ever see him again.

But it would be a deliciously fun thing to wish for on the stars in the heavens each night!

Chapter 3

It is not while beauty and youth are thine own
And the cheeks unprofaned by a tear
That the fervor and faith of a soul can be known
To which time will but make thee more dear.

—Thomas Moore

The Minnesota Territory, 1828

Her flame-red hair blowing loosely in the wind, Flame stood on the top deck of the *Virginia,* a steamboat that made excursions between St. Louis and the Minnesota Territory.

Now eighteen, and fiercely independent, Flame could hardly wait to arrive at Fort Snelling, a huge fort known as a jumping-off place for Minnesota's explorers, which had been built where the Mississippi and Minnesota rivers converged. A few months ago Colonel Josiah Snelling, the commandant for whom the fort had been named, had been sent to Saint Louis, to be in command of Fort Jefferson Barracks. Flame's colonel father had, in turn, been sent from

Fort Jefferson Barracks to Fort Snelling, where *he* was now in command.

Flame's mother had not moved with her husband to the Minnesota wilderness, nor had she allowed Flame to accompany him there. She had not wanted to leave the security of her home in St. Louis. Nor had her health been good enough for such a move. In time, she had signed divorce papers, giving her total freedom from a husband she had never loved.

Tears came to Flame's eyes when she thought of the recent burial of her mother. Her father had returned home long enough to set things in order and to attend the funeral, then had rushed back to Fort Snelling.

Flame had stayed behind long enough to see to the final sale of the family mansion.

Now she was going to join her father at Fort Snelling and nothing could make her any more excited than the prospect of living in the wilds of Minnesota where she could seek out adventure every day of her life.

Her green silk dress fluttering around her ankles, her waist so narrow, her breasts so generously round, she clung to the boat's railing with her white-gloved hands. She closed her eyes in the same fantasy she had clung to since she had been a young girl of ten falling in love with a 'breed. She had thought of no one since then in a serious way.

Yes, she had attended all of the fancy balls and social functions that St. Louis had to offer. But none of her male escorts had meant anything to her. They were just a means to her having fun. Nothing more.

In her mind's eye she could see White Fire as though his father's funeral were only yesterday. She had never forgotten the intensity of his midnight dark eyes, nor his long and thick hair the color of a raven's wing, nor his muscled body.

A sensual shiver rode her spine. "Nor shall I ever forget the lovely color of his copper skin," she whispered to herself.

How could she have ever forgotten his smile when she had purposely flirted with him? In his eyes she had seen a quiet amusement, yet she felt as though she had possibly seen something more. An appreciation of her.

She opened her eyes and sighed, for she had not found the courage to ask her father if White Fire might be anywhere near Fort Snelling. If White Fire were in the area, she did not want to pique her father's curiosity over her interest in the 'breed. She knew of her father's dislike for Indians, half-breed or not.

Her heart pounded the closer the boat came to Fort Snelling. She had prayed over and over that she just might find White Fire again. Wasn't he headed for the Minnesota Territory all those years ago?

To keep her anxiety to arrive at bay, she concentrated on her surroundings, finding everything so lovely and serene. It was such a beautiful country, with its many high hills covered with pine trees and green grass. The air was fresh and clear, the breeze deliciously warm.

Her eyes widened when she saw mud hens along the sandy shore, and several other kinds of water fowl swooping down to settle in little clusters, rocking on the swells of the river as they waited for some unwary fish for their dinner.

She knew that she would be acquainted soon with

Minnesota's wildlife, for she planned to explore on horseback at every opportunity. Although she was saddened over her mother's death, she could not deny how wonderful it felt to realize the freedom that lay ahead of her in Minnesota. Her father would be too consumed by his duties as colonel to worry about her and what she might be up to every day.

"White Fire, if you are still in the Minnesota Territory, by damn, I vow to find you," she whispered to herself.

Chapter 4

All love that has not friendship for its base
Is like a mansion built upon the sand.

—Ella Wheeler Wilcox

War whoops rang out through the forest and across the muddy waters of the Mississippi River as the St. Croix band of Chippewa, under the command of Chief Gray Feather, forged a hearty attack on a Sioux encampment downriver from Fort Snelling.

Before the Sioux could defend themselves, they were overpowered by the Chippewa.

"*Gee-bah-bah,* Father! *Gee-bah-bah,* Father!" Song Sparrow cried as she fled from one of the Sioux tepees after realizing that the Sioux were surrounded and held at bay by her father's warriors.

Sobbing, she ran up to Chief Gray Feather and flung herself into his arms. "You came! I am no longer *gee-tay-bee-bee-nah,* captive!"

Chief Gray Feather, with black war paint smeared across his thin face, clung to Song Sparrow. "*Gee-dah-niss,* daughter, we have searched for days until we found the Sioux encampment," he said thickly. "Had they harmed you—"

She leaned away and stopped him from saying the words that she knew it pained him to speak. "I am fine, *gee-bah-bah*," she murmured. "They have treated me with the respect due a chief's daughter. It is just that they wanted to use me as a bargaining tool with you. Soon they planned to come and offer an exchange. They have traveled too far from their true home. They do not have much food. Most of their warriors have come down ill with a strange sickness. They have been too ill to hunt. They planned to exchange me for food and supplies."

"*Ah-neen-eh-szheh-yi, on-non-gum,* how are you?" Chief Gray Feather asked, sliding a hand over the delicate features of his daughter's copper face. "You have not come down with the strange ailment?"

"*Gah-ween,* no, nor has White Fire become ill," Song Sparrow said, a sudden excitement lighting up her dark eyes.

"White Fire . . . ?" Chief Gray Feather said, forking an eyebrow. "Why would you mention White Fire? He has been gone three winters now. He was thought to have been killed by a bear or something or someone. All that was found of him when we searched day and night were his clothes."

"That is because the Sioux abducted him and forced him to change into a breechclout," Song Sparrow said, excitedly clutching her father's arm. "*Gee-dah-dah,* he is *here.* He has been held captive by the Sioux these past three summers."

Chief Gray Feather's eyes widened with excitement and his heart thumped wildly when White Fire stepped from a tepee, a breechcloth his only attire.

"*Nee-gee*, friend!" he cried, welcoming White Fire into his arms with a fond embrace. "You are *bee-mah-dee-zee*, alive!"

White Fire clung to the Chippewa chief. He had hoped that once the Sioux ventured this far north from their true home, with the lure of the thick pelts too much for them to ignore, that they would let down their guard and he could return to his wife and family at Fort Snelling.

But even when the warriors became ill, he was watched both day and night. He had hardly been allowed to breathe, the watch on him had been so intense.

Even when the Sioux became hungry and needed someone to hunt for them, they had not allowed him to hunt, knowing that he would take that opportunity to escape.

"*Ay-uh*, yes, I am alive," White Fire said. He was hardly able to believe that his old friend Chief Gray Feather was there, *again*, to save him.

When White Fire had first arrived in the Minnesota Territory, he had become a victim of a trapper's steel-jawed trap. His left ankle was still scarred from the dreadful teeth. Chief Gray Feather had found and released him. He had taken White Fire to his village.

There the young man had stayed, not only until he was well enough to travel again, but for a solid year. He had acquired a profound understanding of the Chippewas' customs and psychology. He had come to know and have a deep respect for them. Not only had he learned their ways, he had shared their food and hardships.

During this time, he had grown close to Gray

Feather, a closeness a son feels for a father. But when White Fire had learned about the fort that was being built downriver from their village, he had left the Chippewa to become a part of the excitement. There he had met Colonel Josiah Snelling, the commandant in charge of the fort, with whom he had *also* become fast friends. White Fire had been placed in charge of building the roads that radiated out from the fort.

In time, he became acquainted with Colonel Snelling's niece, Mary, whose marriage to an abusive husband had torn her confidence in herself. Her French voyager husband had died when his canoe capsized in the river, and she was free to marry again. White Fire had been drawn to her gentleness and sweetness. Their love for one another had never been a passionate one. It was a comfortable relationship. And when they finally married, to them was born a son . . . Michael.

His son had been three when White Fire had been captured by the Sioux while out in the forest mapping out a new roadway. He had been taken far downriver and held captive for three years.

Only recently had the Sioux set up camp closer to the fort, to gather many beaver pelts before returning again to their home. Their mistake, their downfall, was to capture a Chippewa maiden.

"*Mah-bee-szhon,* go with me to my village and again be a part of my people's lives," Chief Gray Feather said, as he stepped away from White Fire. His old brown eyes gazed pleadingly up at White Fire who stood a head taller than him. "It was a mistake for you to leave and join the white world. Your place is with the Chippewa. It is the Chippewa who saved you from the Sioux, not the white-eyed pony soldiers from Fort Snelling. It is the Chippewa, this old chief, who truly loves you as though you are one *with* us."

All around them, the healthy Sioux were being gathered and tied. They would be held at the Chippewa village for a while, then escorted back to their home at their main village. Those who were too ill to travel anywhere, would be brought medicine and food. When they were strong enough to travel, they, also, would be escorted back to their home. Gray Feather did not seek war with them. Only the return of his daughter, and now, also, his friend.

White Fire could feel Song Sparrow's gaze on him. During their captivity, she had told him about how her husband had recently died of a bear mauling, and how she was so saddened by having been separated from her three-year-old daughter.

She had also told White Fire how she still felt about him. She had wanted him for a husband way before he had decided to return to the life of a white man. She had only married one of her own kind because she had given up on having him.

But during their time at the Sioux encampment, she had pleaded with him to marry her when they were set free. She had told him that she had never stopped loving him. And she saw him as someone who would be such a good father to her daughter.

White Fire told her time and again that he was married and had a son. Even so, she had not stopped pleading with him to forget his white wife and child. Be Chippewa! she urged.

Pulled by both Song Sparrow and Chief Gray Feather, and feeling that he again owed the chief a debt for having saved his life a second time, White

Fire was not sure how he could refuse Gray Feather without turning him into a bitter enemy. But he had no choice. He had a wife and son who surely by now thought he was dead. They were his first responsibility.

White Fire placed a gentle hand on Gray Feather's lean, bare shoulder. "My *nee-gee*, friend, I am touched deeply by your words and declaration of love for me," he said thickly. "I am touched to have so good a man as you for my *nee-gee*. I feel the same about you. I feel blessed to have such a bond with you and your people. But I have a wife and son. I must hurry home to them. They have been denied my presence long enough. As did you, when your search failed to find me those long three winters ago, I am certain my family has given up on ever seeing me again."

Song Sparrow stood by her father. In her eyes was a deep hurt and rejection. She turned her eyes to the ground when White Fire looked at her.

"I understand commitment to family," Chief Gray Feather said solemnly, drawing White Fire's eyes back to him. He placed a soft hand on White Fire's shoulder. "I will see to your safe return home."

Gray Feather commanded one of his warriors to bring one of the Sioux horses to White Fire. He mounted bareback as Gray Feather mounted his powerful black stallion.

Gray Feather then reached down and swept Song Sparrow up onto his horse with him. He placed a gentle arm around her waist and held her against him as he rode away with White Fire.

The journey back to White Fire's cabin was one of silence. He regretted the strain that was there now since he had once again turned down the chief's offer to live with the Chippewa.

He had learned while with them that year that adoption of whites and 'breeds was practiced among the varied tribes, especially because much sickness and past warring had claimed the lives of so many of them.

Adoption of those who were not of their tribe was the remedy to keep their populations large enough to defend their villages and to hunt for food.

White Fire had learned that Indians practiced adoption on a large scale, especially those tribes who were friendly with whites. He had discovered that the Chippewa might have been the most friendly of them all. Gray Feather had, in his heart, adopted White Fire, for they shared the same feelings about so many things.

Gray Feather had also admired the young man's strength. His nobility. He had said more than once that White Fire did not seem to have white blood mingling with the Indian blood in his veins. It seemed best to the chief that he live among those whose skin matched his own.

But White Fire was being drawn elsewhere. He could hardly wait to see his son. His wife. He could already envision their reunion. It would be one of joy.

They rode onward through the thick underbrush of the Minnesota forest, and along the winding streams, past the sky-blue waters of many lakes, and then finally beside the mighty Mississippi.

Just as they made a turn at a bend in the river, White Fire caught sight of his cabin a short distance away in a break in the trees.

He turned quick eyes to Chief Gray Feather when

the old chief drew his horse into a sudden shuddering halt.

"*Gee-mah-gi-on-ah-shiq-wah,* we part ways now," Chief Gray Feather said sullenly. "But I will see you again *wi-yee-bah,* soon."

"*Mee-qway-chee-wahn-dum,* thank you, my *nee-gee,* friend, for your kindness," White Fire said, his voice quiet. "I will come soon to your village and have council with you."

Chief Gray Feather nodded and rode away.

White Fire gazed at Song Sparrow when she turned to look at him as her father took her away. His insides stiffened when he saw the utter sadness in Song Sparrow's eyes, and knew that he had again hurt her deeply. He regretted this, but at the moment, he had someone else on his mind.

He wheeled his horse around and rode in the direction of his cabin. Then he grew cold inside when he noticed that no smoke rose from the chimney, and the cabin was overgrown with vines.

An instant fear leaped into his heart when he saw that even the door was crisscrossed by vines. That had to mean only one thing. It had been some time since the door had been opened.

His heart pounding like a thousand drums inside his chest, he rode onward, then drew a tight rein in front of his cabin. When he saw the utter desolation of his home, and saw no one rushing from the cabin to welcome him, he dreaded knowing why.

Chapter 5

She walks in beauty, like the night,
Of cloudless climes and starry nights,
Thus mellowed to that tender light,
Which heaven to gaudy day denies.

—George Gordon, Lord Byron

As the *Virginia* made its way around a bend in the river, Flame's heart skipped a beat when she saw Fort Snelling. It was an impressive sight, perched hundreds of feet above the river on the top of a bluff. Built of stone, with a massive round guard tower, it looked a little like a castle to Flame, who had seen pictures of such things in her father's books.

Outside the walls of the fort, down near the banks of the river, a number of crude structures had been built. Among them she spotted some tepees. This caused an excited shiver to race up and down her spine to know that she would be living this close to Indians.

Again the 'breed came to mind, yet she did not expect him to live like an ordinary Indian. While in

St. Louis, with his military officer father, he had lived a life of affluence.

Yet, she could not help but wonder if perhaps after having become acquainted with the Indian side of his heritage, he might not have become as one with them, more Indian now than white.

She sighed heavily, almost certain that she would never know what sort of life he now lived, for the odds were against her ever seeing him again.

"Ma'am, I think it's best you go to your cabin and prepare your things for departure from the boat," a voice said from beside Flame, drawing her quickly out of her thoughts.

She turned and nodded curtly to a lieutenant who had been appointed her escort to Fort Snelling, a young man with a thick head of blond hair, and a wide-set mouth of flashing white teeth. She had been tempted to flirt with him on the voyage from St. Louis. But his uniform, with its shiny, brass buttons, and the way he stood so erect and stiff, made her think of how he reminded her too much of her father, who was stuffy and boorish in his behavior.

No, she preferred someone whose life was not governed by strict rules and ambition. She preferred—

She pushed White Fire from her mind before he completely took over her thoughts, as he had these past several days while she was traveling to Fort Snelling.

"Thank you, Lieutenant," Flame said, flashing him a tight smile. "I shall go and be sure that I have placed everything in my travel bag."

She lifted the skirt of her dress and brushed past him. Then she stopped and took one last look at the fort that would soon be her home. The Fifth Infantry was stationed there under the command of her father. The post was a way station for traders, soldiers, explorers, travelers, and Indians.

The fort was run by two dozen officers, most of them, like Flame's father, graduates from West Point.

She became lost in thought about the sort of life she would be living. Her father was an autocrat in this northern wilderness. His rule was absolute. He had made his way through the ranks and the command of the Minnesota Army garrison was his ultimate prize.

He had written to her of their home. As in St. Louis, she would be living in a mansion. It had been built for Colonel Josiah Snelling and his wife, Abigail, and their eight children.

He had boasted of the mansion's many luxuries, the fine rugs and beautiful furnishings, many of them imported all the way from Europe. There was even a grand piano, which was often used during the social gatherings hosted by the fort's commander. He had promised to hold a dance in honor of Flame's arrival.

Of course, the three hundred or so enlisted men at the fort would not be invited. They slept in wooden barracks around the massive parade ground. Her father had written that when they weren't out on patrol, they worked hard in the fields outside the fort, growing corn, potatoes and wheat and planting orchards, too. The goal was to make the fort as self-sufficient as possible.

Her father had further boasted that Fort Snelling was the finest fort in the American West!

Anxious to see it, to be a part of this new life,

Flame rushed to her cabin and made sure that she had everything packed.

Then she paused and took a look at herself in a floor-length mirror. She ran her hands slowly over the sleekness of her silk dress, smoothing her fingers over the gentle swell of her breasts.

She ran them lower across her tiny waist, and then across her flat tummy as she turned and looked sideways at herself.

She smiled at her reflection, and how her flaming-red hair hung in long, thick waves down her back. Everywhere she went, men's eyes turned to stare at her. She fluttered her thick lashes over her green eyes, knowing the power she had over men.

Her smile faded and her shoulders slumped. She had wanted only one man these last eight years. She hoped that in time she could forget her foolish notion of seeing the 'breed again. She wished that while she was aboard the riverboat she would have allowed Lieutenant Green to escort her to dinner each evening, and to the ball that the boat captain had given in her honor just this past evening.

But she had preferred staying alone, enjoying the travel, the freedom of it. This was the first time she had ever been away from both parents.

And even though she was soon to be with her father again, she would not allow him to stifle her need of freedom now that she had discovered the wonders, the thrill, of it.

The steamboat's shrieking whistle alerted the passengers that they would soon be docking at the riverbank and brought a wide smile to Flame's shapely, red lips. She lifted her one and only bag. Her father had promised that she could buy a new wardrobe at the fort's commissary. Flame rushed from the cabin.

"When the plank is lowered, ma'am, stay close by me," Lieutenant Green said as he placed a possessive arm around her waist. "There are a lot of ruffians housed along this riverbank."

Flame inched herself free of his arm and stood at the rail, watching the steamboat's slow entry into the port. "It's taking so long," she said, giving the lieutenant a harried look.

"Just be patient," he said, smiling at her. "I'd say it will be another thirty minutes or so before you will set your feet on dry land."

"Why on earth so long?" Flame said, eyes wide.

"The river bottom is much too shallow here," Lieutenant Green said. He clamped his hands on the rail and watched the slow progress of the boat toward shore. "If the captain isn't careful, the boat might run aground. That'd cost him his job, that's for sure."

Flame inhaled an agitated breath, then looked on the opposite shore. She admired the forests, which were composed of towering pines, and the marshes of Minnesota, home to many thousands of deer and bear. They were the trapping grounds of the mink, muskrat, and beaver. It was a place of crystal-clear lakes and streams, the water abundant with fish.

Then she looked past the fort on the near side of the river and saw many neat cabins nestled beneath the trees farther down from the fort. As far as the eye could see there were identical dwellings.

Then, farther away, where the forest had been cleared, she saw the beginnings of a city. Her eyebrows lifted, for her father had not told her about any city within close proximity to the fort. She wondered what city, and what sort of people lived there.

She had been told that in the summer the life of the garrison was sufficiently varied, picnicking and hunting on the shores of Lake Calhoun. It sounded to her like a pleasant variation on the routines of reveille, guard mount, fatigue duty, agricultural labor, dress parades, and five daily roll calls within the walls of the fort.

But never had her father said anything about a city, where other sorts of activities surely could be found.

The boat's whistle emitting another loud screeching blast caused Flame to drop her bag and clasp her hands over her ears.

She groaned when she glanced down at the river and realized that the boat had become somewhat grounded. She now knew that she would be stuck on the boat for a much longer period than she wished to be.

She was so anxious to begin her new life in the wilderness!

Chapter 6

Does there within the dimmest dreams
A possible future shine,
Wherein thy life could henceforth breathe?
Untouchable, unshared by mine?

—Adelaide Anne Procter

White Fire's hands shook from anxiety as he broke through the tangle of vines at the front door of his cabin. The door was slightly ajar, and he held his breath as he shoved it slowly open.

When he saw the utter desolation of the cabin, and the thick cobwebs that hung from the ceiling and from wall to wall, it was as though someone had struck him with a fist in his gut. Finding his wife and child gone was traumatic and frightening.

As he made his way slowly through the cabin, smoothing cobwebs aside as he went from room to room, his heart sank. Everywhere he looked he saw the possessions of his family. That had to mean that when they left, it had been in haste, for they had taken nothing with them.

This puzzled him, for his wife would have needed her clothes, and also their son's. Still there they were, lying neatly in drawers, or hanging on pegs, or on wooden hangers in the chifforobe.

Even his son's crib was still there, cobwebs claiming the mattress.

Stifling a sob in his throat, fearing the worst now, that they might be dead, White Fire gazed at, a tiny wooden horse that he had carved for his son only a few days before his abduction. It lay in his son's crib, just barely visible, where a blanket was turned back at one end.

He picked up the toy and held it to his chest as he went through the cabin again, seeing things as he remembered them.

He saw his wife's knitting basket, with balls of yarn neatly stacked inside it. Tears welled in his eyes as he stared at an unfinished knitted sock that lay across the arm of an upholstered chair.

He went and touched the Bible, where inside were the inscriptions of his wife's parents. He knew that she would have never left it behind. It was the only thing left of her parents after their untimely death in a fire in a cabin outside Fort Snelling.

"Fort Snelling," he whispered, his eyes lighting up with a faint hope. He had to go to Fort Snelling and see Colonel Snelling. Surely Josiah would know where his wife and child were, and why they had left their cabin in such haste.

He spoke a quiet prayer that he would find answers about his family that would not devastate him.

Then he laid the toy aside and looked down at his attire. He grimaced at the sight of the breechclout. He couldn't arrive at the fort dressed in this fashion. At first sight, the soldiers might think he was a full-blooded Indian and not give him quick entrance into the colonel's office.

He went into his bedroom. Then he jumped back when he saw that on the far side of the room, just above the chifforobe, mud dauber wasps were building a nest.

He avoided them and grabbed one of his suits of doeskin. He hurried into the shirt and breeches, which had fringes on the sleeves and across the shoulders, and down the trouser legs. He stepped into his own moccasins and discarded those that the Sioux had forced upon him.

He raked his fingers through his thick, black hair to straighten it, then hurried to the door and went outside. He swung himself onto the horse, again riding it bareback toward the fort.

Just as he arrived outside of the wide gate that led into the fort, White Fire saw the arrival of a steamboat. As he dismounted and led his horse to a hitching rail, he could not get his eyes off the beautiful woman who was just now coming down the gangplank.

As though mesmerized, finding so much about her familiar, White Fire stood for a moment longer and watched the woman being swept away from the gangplank by a soldier, who led her toward the fort.

As she moved past White Fire, too hurried to notice him standing there, he could not believe his eyes, for he had had time to recognize her.

Yes! Surely it *was* the girl he had seen in St. Louis at his father's funeral. She was now grown into a woman. How could he ever forget that flaming red hair, those flirtatious green eyes, or the perfect features of her face? He was very taken by her loveliness, which had been enhanced by maturity.

He was shaken from his reverie when a soldier approached him and stood in the way of his entrance into the fort.

"Sir, what is your business at the fort today?" the uniformed soldier asked, slowly raking his eyes over White Fire.

"I've come to see Colonel Snelling," White Fire said, squaring his shoulders under the soldier's rude, close scrutiny. "My name is White Fire. I'm a close friend of Colonel Snelling. I must see him. I must inquire about the safety of my wife and son."

"If you were such a good friend to Colonel Snelling, you would know that he is no longer at Fort Snelling. That he recently died at Fort Jefferson Barracks in Missouri," the soldier said dryly.

White Fire took a quick, unsteady step away from the soldier, stunned by the news.

"Josiah is dead?" he finally gasped out. "How? When?"

"As I said, if you were such a good friend of the colonel, you would not need to ask," the soldier said, placing a firm grip on White Fire's shoulder, giving him a shove. "Get outta here, Indian. Take your lies back to your tribe. You're going to have to come up with a better story than that to get inside the fort and cause Injun trouble."

Anger rising inside White Fire in heated flashes, he wrenched himself free of the soldier. He glared at him. "I am Samuel White Fire Dowling, who was not only a good friend to Josiah Snelling, but who was also in charge of building the roads in the area until I was abducted three years ago by the Sioux. I have been held captive until today. My Chippewa friend, Chief Gray Feather, came and saw to my release from the Sioux. I hurried home to my cabin and found my wife and son gone. I have come to question Josiah about my family's whereabouts." He swallowed hard. "And then I find that Josiah is dead." He hung his head in his hands and heaved a deep, troubled sigh.

"And who might this be wanting entry into the fort?"

A voice familiar to White Fire, that of Colonel Russell's, which he remembered from his past, drew White Fire's eyes quickly up. He was glad to have someone there who knew him, who would set things right among those who greeted his return to civilization in such an unfriendly fashion. It then suddenly dawned on him, that if Colonel Russell was stationed at Fort Snelling, it *had* been his daughter who had swept past White Fire with her flame of hair, and flying, silk dress.

Ashamed of thinking about her, since he was not yet sure about his wife, White Fire cast her quickly from his mind.

"Samuel? Samuel White Fire Dowling, is that you?" Colonel Russell said, his pale gray eyes widening in surprise. "My Lord, Samuel, it *is* you. I thought you were dead."

"Yes, I would understand why everyone would think that I was," White Fire said sullenly. "I am certain that Josiah searched extensively for me before giving me up for dead."

"Yes, that is what I was told," Colonel Russell said, nodding. He nodded at White Fire. "Come with me. There's much that needs to be explained."

"I hope you are talking about my wife and son,"

White Fire said, walking away from the sour-faced soldier, who continued to glare at him. "I need answers. Do you have them for me?"

"Let's go to my office. Then we can talk about them," Colonel Russell said blandly.

The hesitation in Colonel Russell's voice filled White Fire's heart with dread. He went with the colonel to the familiar house. He had helped with the construction of it and was *almost* familiar with every piece of wood and stone that had been used.

He knew well the interior of the house, especially Colonel Snelling's grand, private study, where Colonel Russell now took him.

Too consumed with worry to feel comfortable, White Fire sat opposite the grand oak desk that once was Josiah's. He watched apprehensively as Colonel Russell eased into the thickly cushioned leather chair behind the desk.

"Wine?" Colonel Russell asked, forking an eyebrow.

"No, I never touch the stuff," White Fire said, his voice tight.

"Cigar?" Colonel Russell offered, holding a cigar out to him.

"Sir, neither do I smoke," White Fire said, his voice agitated, growing impatient with the colonel who was obviously trying to put off telling him the truth he now sorely feared hearing.

"About Colonel Snelling," the colonel said dryly, "he was transferred to Jefferson Barracks. Shortly after his arrival, he died. That's about all I can tell you about Josiah Snelling. The news brought to me of his death was sketchy."

Colonel Russell absently rolled the cigar between

his fingers. "And now about your wife and child," he said, his voice drawn. He gave White Fire a solemn stare. "Samuel, your wife died of pneumonia shortly after your disappearance. Your son? Since he is more white than Indian in appearance, he was adopted by an affluent white family in Pig's Eye. The child is in good hands."

Stunned speechless, White Fire gazed wide-eyed at the colonel.

The colonel cleared his throat nervously. "I suggest you consider leaving your son with this family to be raised as white, rather than allowing him to be known as a 'breed," he said tightly. His eyes locked with White Fire's, a sudden coldness in their depths. White Fire realized that he was most definitely in the presence of a man of prejudice. A bigot.

But it was White Fire's shock over the loss of his wife, Mary, that kept him from thinking more about this man. Courtesy was being paid him only because White Fire's father was . . . a man with ranking in the white world, a man whose skin was white, and who had been deeply admired and respected by all.

"Mary is dead," White Fire gulped out, his heart aching, his insides suddenly feeling empty.

Although he had never truly had a passionate relationship with his wife, he had always felt something warm and special for her.

And his son?

In the three years White Fire had been gone, he had expected many changes in his son's life, but none this severe. His son was being raised by strangers?

It was all too unreal, almost too much to bear or to accept.

"Your wife had a Christian burial in the fort cemetery," Colonel Russell said softly. "Josiah Snelling saw to it for you. He also approved of your son being taken in by a family of *his* own choosing."

His head spinning, his despair so keen and hurtful, White Fire rose clumsily from the chair. "I must go for my child," he said, his voice breaking.

"You might want to think more about that decision once you are past the shock of your discoveries today," Colonel Russell said. He rose and came around, placing a hand on White Fire's shoulder.

He slid the colonel's hand away. "What are their names?" he asked tersely. "Where can I find my son?"

"Your son lives with George and Maureen Greer," Colonel Russell said, his voice drawn. "Once you are in Pig's Eye, all you need is ask where they live and their home will be pointed out to you."

White Fire made a sharp turn and started to leave, then was taken aback when Flame suddenly entered the room.

Their eyes instantly locked.

In her eyes White Fire could see instant recognition. As he had remembered her, she had also somehow remembered him.

He could not help but be taken by her loveliness again. He found her small, delicate, and vivacious.

Flame's face flushed hot from her discovery. Her lips parted in a slight gasp, for she would have never imagined it possible to truly see this handsome 'breed again, and here he was. So close. So real.

And even more now than before, she found him attractive and intriguing.

Yet she knew not to allow her father to see that she recognized White Fire. She knew her father's feelings about Indians. Surely the only reason he had taken White Fire into his private office, which was usually only used for white men, was because of her father's prior association with White Fire's father in St. Louis.

No, she must pretend not to know White Fire. Then she would seek out information about him in a shrewd way that would not cause her father's wrath to come down on White Fire like lightning from the heavens. She knew that her father would never allow her to befriend an Indian, even if he *was* part white.

Feeling as though he was being disloyal to his wife, whom he had just discovered was dead, White Fire gave Flame one last lingering look, then fled quickly from the colonel's office.

He forced himself not to think any more about the lovely lady. Now was not the time to be enamored by a woman. His son!

He must go and find his son.

Her heart racing, and trying to hide her excitement at seeing White Fire after having dreamed of him for so many years, Flame went to her father and gave him a hug.

"And so you have arrived safely to Minnesota's shores, I see," Colonel Russell said, returning Flame's hug. "It's good to have you with me, Reshelle. So very, very good."

Flame didn't waste her time telling him she preferred being called Flame over Reshelle, for he had never once obliged her request.

She hugged him again, then swept away from him. She walked idly around the room, admiring the many shelves of bound-leather books, and other grand appointments.

"And how was your journey up the Mississippi?" Colonel Russell asked, sitting down on the corner of his desk. "Was Lieutenant Green polite enough?"

"Yes, quite," Flame said, her hair whipping around her face as she made a quick turn and smiled at her father. "I love being here, Father. I can hardly wait to go horseback riding."

"You must not get too anxious for that," Colonel Russell said, picking up his cigar, lighting it. "You can only go riding if you agree to an escort."

Flame's eyes widened and she gasped. "Never," she objected, her back stiffening. "I'm much too old to ride with a damned military escort."

"Watch your words or I'll wash your mouth out with soap," Colonel Russell growled, yanking his cigar from his mouth. "Reshelle, I am not only in command of my men here at the fort, but you also must abide by my rules."

"Oh, Father, I had hoped you might have changed since you realized how well I have taken care of things in St. Louis without escorts or someone constantly looking over my shoulder," she said, her voice solemn. "Did I not see to the sale of our home?"

"Yes, but that is much different than doing whimsical things here in the wilderness," Colonel Russell said, going behind his desk and sinking into his chair. "Daughter, you will follow orders, or by damn, I might place you in a convent."

"Oh, Lord, *please,* not that again," Flame said, sighing at the threat she knew so well from her father. Through the years he had more than once threatened to put her in a convent. He knew that she would never stay, even if he tried. She would find a way of escape.

"Well, anyhow, behave, Reshelle," Colonel Russell said thickly. "I've got lots on my mind. I don't need to be constantly worrying about my daughter."

Flame went to the window and gazed out at the courtyard. She was using her usual escape from her father's words by becoming lost in thoughts that were much more pleasant. She stood on tiptoe and stared down from the second-story window at White Fire as he rode from the fort.

"That man that was just here," she murmured, not able to keep totally quiet about her curiosity. "I saw him one other time, Father. I saw him at a funeral when I was ten. His name is White Fire. What is he doing here?"

She paused, then turned and faced her father. "Is he married?" she asked, her voice soft and guarded.

Colonel Russell glared up at her. "The 'breed's wife died a couple of years ago," he said warily. "He only found out today that she is dead and that his six-year-old son is being raised by a family in Pig's Eye."

"A son? His wife is dead?" she said, her pulse racing.

She fought against arousing her father's suspicions of her being too interested in a man she knew he never would approve of.

"And, Father," she said, purposely changing the subject. "Where on earth is Pig's Eye? I have never heard of such an ungodly name for a town."

"Pig's Eye is a short distance from the fort," Colonel Russell said. "I doubt it will ever amount to much."

Flame turned back to the window and gazed from it. She smiled slyly. She had heard all that she needed to know. White Fire was single. And the fact that he had a son made him even more intriguing, for she loved children. She had always hungered for a brother or a sister, but her mother had been too frail ever to have more children.

Her thoughts returned to her father. He was still someone who would try to rule her life. She vowed to herself not to allow it. Since her mother's death in St. Louis, she had learned to enjoy her independence. She had come willingly to the Minnesota Territory with hopes of finding White Fire.

She had also looked forward to experiencing the challenge of living in the wilderness. She loved challenges.

She smiled as she thought of White Fire again.

Now he just might be the biggest challenge of all!

Chapter 7

Coulds't thou withdraw thy hand one day
And answer to my claim,
That fate, and that to-day's mistake—
Not those, —had been to blame?

—Adelaide Anne Procter

White Fire had visited his wife's grave. The very sight of it, the thought of Mary having died at such a young age, leaving behind a son whom she had adored, had given White Fire even more determination to go to his son.

As he arrived at the two-story stone house, where the family of George and Maureen Greer lived, White Fire observed its grandness as it sat back from the dirt road. Inside that house was his beloved six-year-old-son, Michael.

White Fire felt threatened by the apparent wealth of the Greer family, for their home was the best of all those that had been built in the city of Pig's Eye. It stood tall, stately, with open green shutters at each of its many windows on both stories. Chimneys made

of round stones from the river stood two in the front
at opposite ends, and two at the back. On this cool
morning of early September, smoke spiraled slowly
from all of the chimneys.

He gazed at the fenced-in yard, and at the abun-
dance of flowers lining the lane that led to the front
door, and those in the window boxes on the lower-
floor windows.

He looked past the house and saw a grand stable
at the back of the house. He stiffened when he saw a
stable boy bring a horse and buggy from the stable.
He watched, with guarded breath, as the lad took the
horse and buggy to the front of the house.

Shortly after that, a short and squat man, perhaps
twice White Fire's age, came from the house in a
black broadcloth business suit, a valise tucked beneath his right arm.

White Fire watched as the man, who he surmised
was George Greer, took a wide turn in the drive and
directed his horse and buggy down the lane, soon
riding toward White Fire.

White Fire tapped his moccasined heels into the
flanks of his horse and rode onward, making it look
as though he was just another curiosity seeker who
had stopped only long enough to admire the Greers'
fancy home.

White Fire stopped when George Greer left the
lane and traveled onward in the opposite direction
toward the small business district of Pig's Eye.

White Fire wheeled his horse around and rode
back to the lane and in a slow lope up it. He watched
the door, his heart thumping at the thought of his
son coming outside to play. It *was* such a beautiful

day, the sun brilliant overhead, the breeze soft and lulling.

No one came from the house. Even the stable boy had gone back to his duties at the stables

White Fire knew that in a matter of moments he would be with his son again. His heart cried out to hold him and to take him home. But most of all he wished to have things back as they were, that his sweet Mary would be at the cabin awaiting his and Michael's swift return.

It tore at his heart to think back to those lonely moments at the grave. It was then that he knew just how important Mary had been to him. He felt guilty for thinking of how often he had taken her for granted. Yet without question, she had always been there for him.

And although she knew there was never any true passion between them, since their marriage was one more from friendship than true love, she had treated White Fire as though he were the only man on earth.

He knew that even when he did finally marry for love, he would never forget Mary's generous, pure sweetness, and what a good mother she had been to their Michael.

Now in the shadows of the huge, stone house, White Fire dismounted and secured his horse's reins to a hitching post. His knees strangely weak, his pulse racing, he took the three steps that led him to a small porch.

His fingers trembling, he slowly raised his hand toward the door, then doubled his hand into a tight fist and knocked.

Almost dizzy from his anxiousness to see his son

again, White Fire watched the door, waiting for it to open.

And when it did, he was immediately thrust into the company of his son again as Michael stood there, looking up at him with wide, dark and curious eyes. White Fire swallowed a fast-growing lump in his throat.

He stared down at his son, now so grown up at the age of six. He was so flooded with emotions at this moment that he found it hard to move. It was as though his feet were frozen to the porch flooring. He had lost his ability to speak. Suddenly, Michael was whisked from his sight as a middle-aged, tight-lipped lady came and shoved him behind her as she glared up at White Fire from her short height.

"Who are you?" Maureen Greer asked, her voice filled with wariness. "What do you want?"

Still White Fire found it hard to speak. He stared down at the tiny woman, whose brown hair was drawn into a tight bun atop her head, and whose gingham dress, with its high collar, revealed a thick waist and flat breasts.

When Michael peeked from behind the lady, his eyes still innocently wide and filled with a strange sort of wonder, the spell was finally broken. It was at this moment that White Fire knew that his son did not recognize him. In three short years, he had forgotten his own father. He had surely, as well, forgotten his mother.

Yet White Fire reminded himself that he should not be so alarmed. Three years was a long time to a six-year-old.

"Sir, answer my questions, or leave," Maureen snapped, her voice now loud and shrill.

"I have come for my son," White Fire suddenly blurted out. He bent to a knee and held his arms out for Michael. "Michael, come and let me hold you. I have come to take you home."

The color rushed from Maureen's fleshy cheeks. Her lips parted in a loud gasp. She then whirled around, grabbed Michael by a hand, and turned to close the door.

White Fire jumped to his full height and placed a solid hand on the door, stopping her from closing it

"Michael, go to your room!" Maureen cried. "Hurry, son. This man means you harm!"

"Michael, I am your true father," White Fire said as Michael turned to run toward the spiral staircase at the far end of the corridor. "I would *never* harm you."

Michael stopped and turned slowly around. He again gazed at White Fire.

Maureen stepped slowly away from White Fire. "I thought you were dead," she said, a sob lodging in her throat.

"So did everyone else," he said somberly. "But as you can see, I am here, alive, and most certainly Michael's father."

He gazed at Michael as the child inched toward him. Now that he had made this woman believe he was who he was, and his heart was no longer pounding, he found himself horrified at how this woman had clothed his son. Michael was dressed in a black velvet suit with a deep lace collar, with black, patent-leather shoes, his raven-black hair was in long sausage curls which rested on his shoulders. His face

was so pale, White Fire doubted it was scarcely ever
touched by the warm rays of the sun.

It made his heart sink to see his son look so sissi-
fied. Like his father, he should be a child who was as
one with nature.

"I think we need to have a talk," Maureen said,
stepping back and placing a possessive hand on
Michael's shoulder. "Come with me into my parlor."

Michael clung to her skirt as he went with her into
the parlor.

White Fire followed closely, his eyes never leaving
his son, his own arms aching from having thus far
been denied him. He now knew that this was not
going to be as easy as just coming and claiming
Michael as his. It was obvious that the child had close
ties with his adoptive family.

Michael's shying from him cut deeply into White
Fire's heart. Yet he knew that in time this would
change. He would not give up on having his child
back with him.

But White Fire knew to take it slowly and cautiously. He did not want to turn his son against him.
It would take a long time to reacquaint Michael
with him.

Maureen gestured with a hand toward a plush,
thickly cushioned upholstered chair among those
which sat in pairs on each side of the fireplace, in
which a roaring fire burned on the grate.

White Fire nodded a stiff thank-you and sat down
on the velvet-upholstered chair. His eyes never left
Michael as the child squirmed to sit on Maureen's
lap after she sat down in a chair opposite White Fire.

He then glanced quickly around the room and
saw the expensive gilt-framed portraits that lined the

walls, the satin draperies at the windows, and the many pieces of expensive furniture that filled the dark shadows of the room.

A woman coming into the room, dressed as a nanny, caused White Fire's insides to stiffen. He watched without argument as Michael was taken into the thick-waisted woman's arms and whisked quickly from the room.

White Fire realized that, yes, all of this would take time, the return of his son to him, the return of his son's love.

His gaze shifted back to Maureen as she began to talk in a monotone voice, yet working hard to make her point—that she would fight to keep this child whom she now considered her son.

"Michael is happy with George and I," she said, stiffly lifting her chin. "I cannot imagine him living anywhere but here. Sir, from what I know of Michael's earlier years, before we took him to raise as our own, he lived in a small cabin without any comforts whatsoever."

She nodded toward various objects in the room, at the twinkling crystal vases, at the solid gold candlesticks, at the expensive paintings, then smiled smugly at him.

"As you see, sir, we have much to offer Michael," she murmured. "I would hope that you would reconsider the foolishness of trying to have him back with you, to live a life of squalor, when my George and I can offer him everything his heart desires."

She cleared her throat nervously. "Michael's friends know nothing of his background . . . of him being part Indian," she said dryly. She visibly shuddered. "Since his skin is white, he passes as white, not as . . . a savage half-breed."

The way she spoke the words *savage half-breed,* the insult of it, and her actually shuddering when she spoke of Indians, as though they were the lowest form of people on the earth, made an instant rage enter White Fire's heart. And even more than that, he was afraid that his son might have been taught to dislike, to *mistrust* all Indians.

"You bigot, I resent what you said, and what you implied," White Fire said, his jaw tight. "I am proud of my Indian heritage, as will Michael be, once he realizes that he himself is part Indian."

Being called a bigot caused Maureen to sit forward in her chair. "I'll have you know that I am no bigot," she said, her voice trembling. "I-I just don't want Michael to know that he is part Indian. His friends would poke fun at him. He would miss many opportunities in life that a man born *white* is offered. A man who is part Indian, a 'breed, has *much* to endure."

She smiled. "But, of course, you must know that, since you are a 'breed, yourself," she said, her eyes on his face.

"I am a 'breed, yes, that is true," White Fire said, lifting his chin proudly. "And as you know, I chose to be called by my Indian name rather than the name Samuel, which was my mother's choice, since she was so wrong to be ashamed of her Miami heritage."

"That, alone, is cause enough for me to know that Michael is better off being raised here with me and George, than with you—you who cast aside a white man's name as though it is a sinful thing, a *curse,*" Maureen snapped back. "This child I have grown to love must not be faced with such decisions. His name is Michael. He is being raised as white. That is how it must continue to be."

He knew he definitely had a battle on his hands, that he was faced with someone who was determined not to let go without a fight, and it would be too traumatic to just go and grab Michael and abruptly take him away. White Fire decided that now was not the time to make hasty decisions.

Yet even though he saw the prejudice that his son had been forced to live with in his daily life, White Fire still couldn't see taking Michael away from his adoptive family just yet—at least not until he himself had gotten his own life back in order.

"Let me tell you something about my George and myself," Maureen quickly interjected. "George and I have come from Boston to this wilderness of Minnesota. George is a smart, skilled, ambitious man. He sees much hope for this small community of Pig's Eye. He imagines a powerful city rising up from what is now only a few buildings. He wishes to build it. He had seen the possibilities when he heard about the fort being built. He is a trader at heart, having become wealthy from his trading days in Boston. He saw Fort Snelling as possibly one of the better forts used for trading along the two rivers. He sees this as why Pig's Eye will one day prosper as one of the better cities in America. He has even considered renaming it to something like St. Paul."

She stopped and drew in a slow, deep breath, then continued. "Michael is now a part of this wonderful awakening in this wilderness," she said tersely. "As the city grows into something wonderful, so shall Michael's chances to be a part of its powerful future.

And he can only be a part of that if he stays with us, and is given the opportunity."

White Fire patiently listened, letting her have her say, while, in the end, it was all wasted breath, for no matter what, he *would* have his son with him again.

Maureen rose stiffly from her chair. She clasped her hands together before her and stared coldly at him as he slowly rose from the chair.

"We will fight to keep Michael," she said icily. "No matter what you do, he will never be allowed to live in poverty again." Her tone softened and she looked up pleadingly at White Fire. "Can't you see that it would be wrong to take the child away from this life that he has grown to love?"

"Can you not see how wrong it is to keep a son from his true father?" White Fire said, his eyes locked with hers.

He turned and walked out of the parlor.

When he reached the front door, Maureen hurried and stood between him and the door.

"Please don't come back here and confuse the child any more than you already have," she pleaded. 'We have been so happy. *He* has been so happy."

"I doubt that," White Fire said, then placed his hands at her waist and lifted her out of his way.

He went out onto the porch, then turned and gazed at Maureen as she stood at the door. "I will be back," he said thickly. "I want to spend time with Michael. If you do not willingly allow it, you will force me to take him away from you right away, instead of gradually working him into it."

Tears spilled from Maureen's eyes. She gazed up at White Fire for a moment longer, then turned away and slowly closed the door between them.

Strangely empty inside, White Fire stared at the door, then went and uncoiled his reins from the hitching rail.

Feeling eyes on him, he looked up at a second-story window.

His heart almost broke when he saw Michael standing at the window, gazing down at him, his eyes filled no longer with confusion, but with a strange sort of detachment, and . . . resentment just before he was whisked away from the window and Maureen was quickly there, frowning down at White Fire.

White Fire sighed heavily, then swung himself into his saddle and rode away.

It came suddenly to him that if he *was* to get his son back without a fight, he must find a wife, someone who would willingly be a mother to his Michael. For in anyone's eyes, it would not be right to wrench a child away from a true family, to live with only a father.

His spirits low, his shoulders slumped, he could not think of any woman who might be willing to have an instant family, especially in this wilderness where men outnumbered women ten to one.

He was filled with a sudden, deep, bitter hopelessness.

Chapter 8

I sleep with thee, and wake with thee,
And yet thou art not there;
I fill my arms with thoughts of thee.

—John Clare

Restless, and angry at her father for having placed a sentry in the corridor outside her bedroom door, Flame paced the floor.

She couldn't believe that her father could be this overprotective of her! She had experienced his obsession with her while living in St. Louis, but never had he kept her in her bedroom like a prisoner.

But now that she thought about it, she realized that even when she had attended fancy balls and other social functions in St. Louis, one of his military colleagues had always been close by, trying not to be too obvious as he kept an eye on her.

She wondered now, when she had thought she had been alone, free as a bird while horseback riding, if someone had always been there, close at hand, watching her.

"How could he?" she cried, doubling her hands into tight fists at her sides.

She went to the open French doors that led to a small balcony and stepped gingerly out onto it. She circled her hands around the railing, her gaze settling on a small roof that lay just beneath the balcony, where a trellis had been placed, reaching from the ground to the roof. She was glad that roses were not the first choice of flowers for this trellis. Instead it had lovely wisteria vines that had no thorns to tear at her flesh when she escaped from her prison.

"In time he *will* know that he can't hold me back," she whispered, smiling now that she knew that she would have a way to leave the confines of her room whenever she chose to. Let him lock the door and she would escape and have her fun.

Glad to now have a plan, and badly wanting to explore, she decided that tomorrow would be soon enough since she was tired from the long river voyage. Flame went and plopped down on her bed.

Stretching out on her stomach, she rested her chin in her hands as she slowly looked around her room. Her private quarters were, indeed, grand, even as beautiful as those she had at the family mansion in St. Louis.

Her bedroom was large, giving an open feeling that was enhanced by the sunlight streaming through a number of windows, which were graced by beautiful satin draperies.

A fire was burning leisurely in the bedchamber fireplace, casting a soft, golden glow on the rich paneling of the walls. Ceiling beams and crown molding reinforced the sumptuous feeling, with hardwood floors that shined enough to see her reflection in them. Several silver candelabrums stood on various tables in the room, holding numerous tapers. Her bed, with its iron bedstead, was comfortable with its thick feather mattress. A marble-topped washstand stood beside the bed, a china basin decorated with rosebuds atop it.

She gazed at the chifforobe, anxious to make her father keep his promise to allow her to choose a new wardrobe. She closed her eyes and envisioned the hats she would wear for outings on her horse.

"My horse," she whispered, jumping from the bed.

She hurried to the balcony and leaned her head out, to look far to the right, where the stables were. She had brought her steed from St. Louis. She hoped it wouldn't be hard to find it among so many stabled together beneath one roof.

"I shall," she said, stubbornly lifting her chin.

Then she looked past the wall of the fort. Her gaze searched in the distance from cabin to cabin, wondering in which one she might find the handsome 'breed.

Her pulse raced at the thought of beginning her search for him even as soon as tomorrow.

Chapter 9

White Fire awakened with a start when he heard the popping and crackling of a fire in his fireplace. He had not kindled it since last night, which meant that now it should only be simmering coals, or cold, gray ashes.

Remembrances of other times flooded his senses, when he had awakened to the same sort of sound, when his wife, Mary, had risen before him and gotten the fire started.

But this was now.

His Mary wasn't there. Someone else had to have started the fire.

"But who?" he whispered to himself, rushing from the bed.

He scrambled into a pair of fringed, buckskin

breeches and a shirt, then hurried, barefoot, into the living room. Who he saw sitting there caused him to stop with a start.

He stared at Chief Gray Feather, who was even now on his knees before the hearth, placing another piece of wood on the fire.

Then his gaze slowly shifted to the chief's daughter, Song Sparrow, and then to Song Sparrow's three-year-old daughter, Dancing Star.

He didn't have time to wonder more about it, for Song Sparrow had heard him come into the room. She turned and was smiling at him. Then she gently shoved her daughter toward him.

"My *gee-dah-niss,* daughter, Dancing Star, has come to introduce herself to you," Song Sparrow said, giving her daughter another slight shove when Dancing Star hesitated.

Chief Gray Feather rose to his feet and stood with his back to the fire as he watched his granddaughter go to White Fire. Then he watched White Fire intently as he kneeled and reached his arms out for the child.

Knowing of White Fire's gentleness and compassion for children, Chief Gray Feather hoped that he would feel his granddaughter's loneliness for a father.

"Hello, there," White Fire said, taking Dancing Star into his arms and hugging her. "Dancing Star, *nee-may-nan-dum-wah-bum-eh-nawn,* I am glad to see you. It is good to make your acquaintance."

He looked past her shoulder and questioned Gray Feather with his eyes, yet knew, without actually questioning the chief, what was happening here.

Gray Feather wished to sway him into marrying his daughter through the child's affection.

That puzzled White Fire, for Gray Feather knew that he was married and that he had a child. White Fire had not yet had the chance to tell him that things were different, that he no longer had a wife, and in a sense, had lost his child.

He could not help but be touched, though, by the child's tiny arms around his neck, and by how she showed no fear of him, when she had never even known him until now.

He reached his hands up to her long, glossy, black hair and stroked it.

When he looked at Song Sparrow and saw too much in her eyes, caused by his show of genuine affection for the child, fear leaped into his heart that he was giving Song Sparrow false hope.

Gently, he eased the child from his arms. He took her hand and led her back to her mother.

His eyes locked momentarily with Song Sparrow's as she lifted her daughter. Then he turned abruptly from her and went to place his hands on the chief's shoulders with the cordial greeting familiar to them.

"It is good to awaken and find such good company in my home this morning," White Fire said, smiling. He lowered his hands to his sides. "It is always good to see you, Gray Feather."

Chief Gray Feather went to stand at his daughter's side. He placed a gentle arm around her waist and smiled at White Fire. "We came today to have council again about your future, and how it would seem only right that it would be with my St. Croix band of Chippewa, and particularly with my family," he said, his voice a deep rumble. "I have come to ask you again, White Fire, to leave this sort of life behind you. Come and live with people of your own skin coloring."

Gray Feather gestured, making a wide swing as he looked slowly around the room. "This is white man's *en-dah-yen,* home," he said solemnly. "You would be more content in lodge of the Chippewa."

His eyes implored White Fire. "Were you not happy with the Chippewa the time you spent with them?" he asked softly. "Did it not feel only natural that you would awaken in a wigwam instead of this place made of logs?"

The more Gray Feather talked, the more confused White Fire was by how he again pleaded with him to live with his people, when the chief did not yet know about White Fire's discoveries after arriving home from his captivity with the Sioux.

"Gray Feather, please say no more at this time about this that you wish of me," he said quickly, to interrupt Gray Feather before he went further with his pleas which caused only a strain between them. White Fire could think of nothing or no one at this time except for his son and getting him back where he belonged. In his own father's lodge. In his own father's heart.

"White Fire, now that you have no wife, and now that your son has been taken away from you and is living with a white family, it is only right that you leave this life behind and live where you are needed, wanted, and loved," Chief Gray Feather said, himself now interrupting.

White Fire took an unsteady step back from Gray Feather. "How did you know about Mary?" he asked, his voice drawn. "How did you know about my son?"

"I have watched you since your return from your captivity," Chief Gray Feather said. "I have seen you visit your wife's *chee-bay-gah-mig*, grave. I have seen you go to the home in which your son now lives as a white boy. All has been taken from you. I am here to give so much more back to you." Gray Feather gave his daughter a quick glance, then looked at White Fire again.

Song Sparrow stood proudly at her father's side, yet her eyes had never left White Fire since he had come from his bedroom and found them there.

"My *gee-dah-niss*, daughter would make you a good *gee-wee-oo*, wife," Gray Feather said fervently. "You would make a good husband for my daughter. You would make a good father for my grand-daughter." He lifted his chin and squared his shoulders. "You would make a good son for this old man who was never blessed with sons. You would be the heir to all I own!"

Taken aback by the knowledge that Chief Gray Feather was this determined to have him as a part of his family, and had actually followed his each and every movement since his return from his captivity, White Fire was momentarily at a loss for words.

Yes, he had known that their friendship was special. He would never forget the year that he had spent with Gray Feather and his people. It was a unique, special time, which felt normal and right to him while there.

But many things had changed since his farewell to Gray Feather. *He* had changed.

"Do you hear and understand what I say to you this morning?" Gray Feather asked, stepping away from his daughter to place a gentle hand on White

Fire's shoulder. "I offer you way more than you can ever achieve in the world of whites that has given you nothing but heartache. I offer you my daughter's bed. I offer you my *granddaughter,* who would be your daughter, who would take the place of the son you have lost to whites. Besides that, I offer you everything that you enjoyed while living among my people—and even *more!*"

Gray Feather paused, then said, "White Fire, it is time for you to choose your red-skin heritage over the white," he said solemnly. "Is it not obvious that no one is there for you now in the white community to make you happy? Be proud of the red side of your heritage. Live the life of a redskin! Not white!"

White Fire's eyes wavered, for he knew that much of what the chief said was true. He *had* lost much. But none of it was the fault of white eyes! If not for the Sioux, he would be content with his family, rising each morning to his son's laughter, to his wife's sweetness.

Yes, he argued to himself, he never truly loved his wife with the passion he knew was possible between a man and woman. But it was their genuine caring for one another that had mattered. And she had given him the greatest gift of all: a son.

That son would not be denied him now had it not been for the redskins, the Sioux.

No, he would never fault whites for anything, except for only one family, those who now would try and deny him his son. And he was going to change that! His son would again be his!

"Gray Feather, I *am* proud of the Indian side of my heritage," White Fire said, expelling a heavy sigh. "But you must remember, Gray Feather, except for my one year with the Chippewa, and the captive years with the Sioux, I have always lived the life of a white man."

White Fire swallowed hard. He turned his gaze down at the fire and stared into the dancing flames. "And, Gray Feather," he said solemnly, "although my son is not with me at this time, he is still my son, a white son who is true blood kin."

White Fire then turned quick eyes back to the chief. "And I have duties to this son," he said tightly. "I must ready a life for him in the white world . . . in *my* world."

Chief Gray Feather looked sullenly at White Fire for a long moment, then he left the cabin. He went to his horse and reached inside a parfleche bag and removed a long, smooth, gray eagle feather from inside it.

Then he went back inside the cabin and placed the eagle feather on White Fire's kitchen table. He turned weary, sad eyes to the younger man. "This *mee-gwun*, feather, is a gift from Gray Feather to you," he said thickly. "Each time you look at the feather, think of the Chippewa and Chief Gray Feather. Look into the life of the Chippewa as one that would be good to you. As my adopted son, the world of the Chippewa would be *yours*. Would you not be proud to be a central part of my people's lives? Of my family's?"

White Fire didn't get the chance to respond. Chief Gray Feather ushered his daughter and granddaughter from the cabin.

He got to the door just as Chief Gray Feather rode away with his daughter and granddaughter on the same horse.

And when Gray Feather did not turn his gaze back and wave a farewell to him, White Fire could feel the old chief's hurt and rejection deeply inside his own heart.

Sad that he had to disappoint the old chief over and over again, feeling so much for him, as though Gray Feather could be a substitute for his dead father, White Fire watched Gray Feather until he rode completely from sight into the deep, dark shadows of the forest.

A part of White Fire *did* want to go with Gray Feather, to leave behind the sadness that he had found on his return from his captivity. Yet a bigger part of him knew that he must never give up what was rightfully his.

His son!

Chapter 10

The essence of all beauty, I call love
The attribute, the evidence, and end,
The consummation to the inward sense,
Of beauty apprehended from without,
I still call love.

—Elizabeth Barrett Browning

Dressed in her green velvet riding habit, a sheer veil from her hat shielding her green eyes behind it, Flame eased her horse behind a thick cover of brush when she had seen the Indians leave White Fire's cabin. She watched them as they rode away, not catching her spying on them.

It had been by pure chance that they had led her to him. When she had sneaked away from her room just as the sun rose to go horseback riding, she had found such pleasure riding through the forest. Then she had seen the dignified older Indian riding with the woman and child on his horse.

Intrigued by the sight, Flame had followed them, keeping back just far enough so that they would not be aware of her presence. She had felt no threat in doing this. Not while the Indian warrior had a woman and child with him.

When their travel had taken them to a cabin, and they had gone inside without knocking, Flame could not help herself. She was too curious not to continue watching them, especially to see if they lived in the cabin apart from other Indians. It did not seem the norm in the Minnesota Territory that Indians would live like that.

She secured her horse in the woods, then had sneaked up to the cabin and looked into a window. She had watched the Indian warrior build a fire as though he belonged there.

Yet it was the behavior of the woman and child that had made her believe this was not their home. They had stood stiffly, watching the warrior instead of going about their own business. It was as though none of them belonged there.

That had made Flame continue to spy, even though she knew there was a chance of getting caught in her shameful act of voyeurism. She had intended to ride long enough today to possibly find White Fire's cabin. But the intrigue of the Indians had sidetracked her. She would search for White Fire another day.

As she continued to watch the Indians through the window, and then saw White Fire suddenly make an appearance in the room, she had almost fainted. The Indians had unknowingly led her to him.

Upon first seeing him, so handsome even this early in the morning, Flame knew that her heart, as it had been as a child of ten, was truly lost to him. She had thought of him, had *dreamed* of him so often through the years, it was as though she truly knew him.

For certain it was now no fantasy or dream that she was this close to him. It thrilled her to know that she could return another time and talk to him. She could hardly wait for that time.

But for now she had only been able to observe through a pane of glass and wonder what was being said between the Indians and White Fire. When the child had gone to him, and he had taken her into his arms so sweetly and gently, Flame's heart had melted with love for him.

Ah, how *she* longed for children.

And this man, to whom she would give her heart, loved children as much as she. She saw it in his eyes and in the way he held the Indian child.

She had to wonder how he now felt about his son living with someone else and if he had gone yet to see him. Was he going to have a fight on his hands to get the child back from those who now claimed his son as theirs?

Knowing that she must return home before her father caught her gone, and excited about going to choose a new wardrobe, Flame hurried back to her horse. She rode off in a hard gallop toward the fort.

But she would never forget this morning. She laughed softly when she recalled her fright when the Indian warrior had momentarily left White Fire's cabin.

She had moved swiftly to hide at the back of the cabin, yet had managed to still look around the corner of it to see the warrior take an eagle feather from a bag at the side of his horse.

When he had gone back inside, she had crept

back to the window and watched him place the feather on White Fire's table.

Then she had felt that she had taken too many chances by staying so long. She had fled back to her horse and rode off and had hidden just in time not to be caught by the Indian as he had rode away from the cabin.

"I so badly wish I could have gone inside and talked with White Fire," Flame whispered as the fort came into view through a break in the trees a short distance away.

But even now her father could be waiting in her room with words of anger about her escapade this morning; warning her about the dangers *of* it.

She smiled when she recalled her father's habit of sleeping late each morning. While living in St. Louis, he had never risen until around nine, always depending on others to see to the early morning duties at the fort. He was older now. She imagined he might even sleep later.

As she rode out in the open, she glanced at the horizon and saw the sun was now creeping up behind the trees. She knew that it was not yet seven o'clock, and felt safe enough. The sentries at the fort would surely not tell on her for fear of stepping out of line.

Her chin lifted, Flame rode on past them, hurried her horse into the stables. Then, unladylike, she climbed the trellis that led to her balcony, and to the privacy of her room.

When she was finally inside her room, she smiled at the thrill of her discoveries this morning.

"I found him!" she whispered, shivering with ecstasy at the mere thought of having been that close to White Fire again, and especially for now knowing where he lived.

She had to wonder how he would feel if he awakened and found *her* waiting for him some morning, as he had found the Indians this morning.

"No," she whispered, whisking off her riding hat, "I can't be *that* shameful!"

Not yet, anyhow, she thought, smiling mischievously at the very idea of being brazen enough to do it.

Chapter 11

She walks in beauty, like the night
Of cloudless climes and starry skies,
And all that's best of dark and bright,
Meets in her aspect and her eyes.

—Lord Byron

Taking the first necessary step to get his life back in order again, to get his son back, White Fire stood at Colonel Russell's desk.

Colonel Russell gazed up at him. "You say that you need employment," he said dryly, flicking ashes from his cigar into an ashtray.

"Yes, and if possible, I would like to once again be involved in the plans for more road construction in this area," White Fire said. "During the three years I was gone, the population has almost doubled. More than ever roads are needed to help make the settlers' travels more convenient and safe. I believe much more careful planning must be made to see that the roads are not as isolated as before. More trees should be removed. Those who travel the roads should not be made to feel so closed in by the forest on each side of them. Who could not worry about outlaws or Indians if the road is crowded on both sides by dense brush and trees?"

Colonel Russell nodded toward a chair before his desk. "Sit down," he said coldly, resting his cigar in the ashtray.

After White Fire sat down, Colonel Russell leaned toward him. He rested his elbows on his oak desk and placed his fingertips together. "I understand your concern about the roads since you were abducted while involved in building them," he said tightly. "And I am certain that you would have ideas that would be beneficial."

"Most times my duties kept me at the fort," White Fire said, glancing over his shoulder. The office that had been his, when he worked as road commissioner for the fort, was just down the corridor. He didn't expect to be appointed commissioner over who was now working in that capacity. But he would certainly enjoy working with him. "It was only by chance that I was far from the fort the day I was abducted," he continued, his eyes now locked with the colonel's. "I had gone to oversee things after I had been told of a problem. The men under my guidance were having troubles with their measurements. I went there, alone, to remeasure things. My solitude made it easy for me *to* be abducted. Otherwise, I would have been at the fort, safely at my desk, drawing plans."

Frowning at White Fire, suddenly in deep thought, Colonel Russell leaned back in his chair. "I see," he finally said, nervously drumming his fingers on his desk. 'Well, I hope I don't disappoint you when I tell you that I have something else in mind for you."

White Fire's eyebrows forked.

'What *I* have in mind for you would serve me better," Colonel Russell said, slowly nodding. "White Fire, I am in dire need of an interpreter, and since you are, in part, Indian yourself, a *'breed,* and someone who has lived not only with the Chippewa, but also with the Sioux, you are more trained in the art of languages than anyone else I know. I would like to offer you the job of interpreter for the fort. Would you be interested?"

His spine having stiffened at the colonel's reference to him being a 'breed, always having found that word a way to brand someone who was born with dual bloods in his veins, White Fire waited for a moment or two before responding to the colonel's offer.

In truth, had the colonel not called him a 'breed, White Fire would have jumped at the chance to be the fort interpreter. That was something he would thoroughly enjoy. Being an interpreter would be a way to mingle with the Chippewa more often than had he taken on other employment. He *did* enjoy the company of Chief Gray Feather and his people. While with them that year at the village, something awakened inside him that he could not explain. He had felt closer to nature, to life in general, while with them. It was as though somewhere in time he *had* been a part of the Chippewa culture.

Yes, Chief Gray Feather would enjoy his visits, the time of camaraderie that would be created by White Fire being an interpreter.

"Yes, I would appreciate the employment as the fort interpreter," he suddenly blurted out. "When shall I start?"

His eyes danced, truly looking forward to the job of interpreter. It would also give him the opportunity to help keep peace between the different bands of Indians and the soldiers and their families stationed at the fort. He would even enjoy going from village to village, whenever required to, to sit in council.

"White Fire, whenever the need arises, when you are needed to interpret, I shall send word to your cabin," Colonel Russell said, his eyes gleaming. "There is no need for you to set up residency here at the fort."

White Fire stiffened, thinking now that the colonel had, in a sense, just duped him. By assigning him to a job that would only occasionally bring him to the fort, the colonel would be free of White Fire more often than not.

Then he smiled to himself at something that would give him much pleasure, *and* a way to put the bigoted colonel in his place. While sitting in council, being the only one who could interpret the different languages to this bigoted colonel, it would be a way to make the man feel inadequate and for everyone else to see his inadequacies. It could make the colonel look less of a leader in the eyes of all the Indians. This, for a man who thought he was God's gift to mankind, could disgrace him more than disgrace itself.

White Fire rose from the chair, forcing himself to reach out a hand to seal the deal. Then he cringed when the colonel placed his sweaty palm against his as he shook it.

"I appreciate your kindness," White Fire said, trying to keep the bitterness out of his voice.

He eased his hand from the colonel's. Then he turned to leave, stopping and turning around again to gaze in surprise at the colonel when he made an offer that seemed out of character.

"I know that you've been gone for the past three years, and during that time you have had no means to set aside the monies needed to settle into a normal life," Colonel Russell said, rising from his chair. He went to a wall safe and opened it. "I am going to give you an advance on your pay so that you can purchase firearms and food."

He glanced over at White Fire and raked his eyes slowly over him. Then his look turned to one of superiority. "Also clothes," he said dryly. "The commissary will provide you with everything you need. Since my arrival at Fort Snelling, I have made certain that the commissary is well supplied at all times."

White Fire was rendered speechless by this man whose feelings seemed as changeable as a chameleon.

White Fire squared his shoulders proudly. "I need no advance," he said tightly. "I will do just fine."

"I insist. I do not want it *ever* to look as though I am someone who treats a 'breed less kindly than someone else I might hire here at the fort," Colonel Russell said, turning around to thrust a handful of bills toward White Fire. "Anyone who is assigned duties here at the fort who has seen hard times gets an advance on his pay." He frowned and sucked in a deep breath of air. "So, 'breed, do not take this as something special I do for you."

"You know exactly what you are doing every time you are addressing me as a 'breed, don't you?" White Fire said, placing his fists on his hips. "It is meant to put me in my place, to make me remember that my skin color differs from yours." His jaw tightened. "If not for my son, and needing a job to help get Michael back, I would tell you to go to hell and spit in your face," he growled out.

Then his lips quirked into a smug smile. "And there is something more that keeps me here at the fort," he said smoothly. "And it has nothing to do with money, position, or my son."

Colonel Russell eased his hand to his side and clutched the bills. He glared at White Fire. "And that is?" he said tightly.

"A beautiful woman with flaming red hair," White Fire said, laughing bitterly when he saw the colonel's face drain of color.

He ignored the rage that lit the colonel's eyes. He walked to the door and opened it, then stiffened when the colonel was suddenly there, blocking his way.

"I know of only one woman whose hair is flaming red," the colonel said, his teeth clenched.

"Exactly," White Fire said, enjoying toying with the colonel's emotions, yet understanding that there might be some danger in doing it.

But the colonel showed no threat to White Fire. The colonel's hands were tied as far as White Fire was concerned. The colonel had to be aware of what the younger man's position at the fort had been before he had been captured by the Sioux. Although he had never been given any rank in the army, he had been second to Colonel Snelling, admired and liked by everyone.

"You will try my patience one time too many. Then watch out, *'breed*," Colonel Russell snarled, his eyes lit with anger. He leaned his face into White Fire's. "Stay away from my daughter, do you hear?"

White Fire smiled, then turned and left.

He went to his horse and swung up into his saddle. Then he rode in a slow trot from the courtyard, his eyes on the stately Snelling mansion.

His gaze went from window to window, wondering where Flame's room might be. Might she even be there now, watching *him?* He *had* seen in her eyes that she found him intriguing.

Then he frowned as he remembered her father labeling him a 'breed today.

He had to wonder if Flame might look on him as nothing more than a 'breed.

He rode on from the courtyard, his mind elsewhere. He thought about the colonel's offer of money. He smiled as he thought of where he had always hidden his own cache of money. His wife, Mary, had not even known the amount he had set aside, to be used should the need arise.

True, his Mary had been a sweet, compassionate wife, and a wonderful, caring mother. But she was also wont to spend money foolishly. She had seemed to have an addiction, like gamblers who throw their money away at the poker tables.

White Fire recalled the last time he had slipped coins and green bills into the tin box hidden behind a loose stone in the outside fireplace chimney. He mentally counted what he had placed there prior to his abduction. It was more than enough to buy a rifle and ammunition, a knife, food for his table, and some badly needed clothes.

Yes, he would go to the commissary, but the money spent there would be his, not the colonel's.

But first he had a letter to write, to his mother. He could almost envision his mother's face when she realized that he was alive.

He planned to tell her everything that had happened to him—about his time spent with the Sioux, his rescue, and also the kind offer from Chief Gray Feather to live with them as one with his Chippewa people. He had only spoken of the Chippewa a few times in his letters.

His mother would also be told about the chief offering his daughter to White Fire for marriage. That would touch a cord in his mother's heart, since she herself was full-blood Indian, and knew the meaning behind such an offer from an Indian chief. To offer one's daughter was to offer one's own soul.

But most of all, White Fire would write at length about his son and the measures he must take to get his son back. He would tell his mother that a wife would be the true answer.

As he rode toward his cabin, his thoughts went to Flame, then he brushed her from his mind again, for thinking of her brought her father to mind. He would *never* allow himself to forget the hate in the colonel's eyes when he had warned White Fire to stay away from his daughter.

Yet, why *should* he allow such a threat to stand in

his way of doing anything that he wished to do? he thought to himself, smiling. No threat had ever stopped him from pursuing a goal he wished to achieve.

Nor would it now.

Now that he had seen Flame all grown up into a beautiful woman, how *could* he be expected to forget her?

Chapter 12

She seemed to hear my silent voice,
Not love's appeals to know.
I never saw so sweet a face,
As that I stood before.

—John Clare

Ignoring the military chaperon that she had left outside the commissary, yet angry at her father for forcing Lieutenant Green on her, as though she were a prisoner, Flame stood at the back of the room, admiring the beautiful dresses hanging from a rack. Since there were so few women at the fort, there weren't that many dresses, but enough from which to choose a new wardrobe.

She then glanced around her. The dreary room was dimly lit with kerosene lanterns and their smoke-blackened chimneys hanging from the open beams of the ceiling. They scarcely gave off enough light to see by. Even the small windows at the top of the commissary walls did not help much, for they were hazed over with rain-blown dust from the last storm.

She looked then at the far side of the room where the men's clothes and military equipment lay on shelves in vast rows. She tried to make out the features of a man who was going through the arsenal of weapons. She squinted her eyes to see him better, but he was standing too much in the shadows for her to make out his face, or even his build, or what he wore.

Her flame-red hair hung in luscious waves across her shoulders, halfway down to her waist. She was dressed in a demure, pale green chiffon dress, with a floral print skirt and wide embroidered sash. Flame soon forgot the man and began sorting through the dresses. Her eyes devoured the sweeping lines of a two-piece linen outfit with lavishly worked lace insets embellishing the bodice and sleeves. Her fingers nimbly scooted the linen outfit aside.

Her green eyes lingered on the sweeping lines of a velvet cloak. Then she sighed when she saw a white organdy dress with petallike sleeves and hem. As she turned it around, and from side to side, in awe of its loveliness, she felt as though she might never find anything as perfectly right for the ball tonight.

Yet she must make sure something else was not there even more tempting and beautiful.

She looked through the rest of the graceful, deliciously feminine chiffon and organdy dresses. Her fingers moved over moire silks, then she smoothed them over cut velvet and brocade, many of which were intricately trimmed with lace, while others were lush with embroidery.

Quickly, she plucked several dresses from the rack and laid them aside on a table alongside the velvet cloak. Then she stepped over to where many hats were displayed on stands.

Loving them all, Flame clasped her hands and looked from one to the other, from straw hats trimmed with silk flowers to others with voluminous veils of muslin. Finding it too hard to choose which one just yet, she moved onward.

Her gaze swept over fine chemises and petticoats, bracelets, brooches, and purses, stopping on a silk parasol with an ivory-and-green lining.

Then she went to the shoes, sighing at how flirty and feminine they were. She picked up an ivory satin shoe and ran her fingers over its exquisite smoothness.

"I think that would be my choice," White Fire said suddenly from behind her. He had been choosing a rifle and had heard a noise at the back of the room. When he had turned around and saw who was there, he had almost melted in his shoes at her loveliness. It was hard to believe his luck—that he would be at the commissary at the exact time Flame was there.

And now that she had turned and was gazing into his eyes, as though awestruck, he was aware again of how they seemed drawn to one another.

Seeing her the day of his father's funeral came into White Fire's mind's eye, remembering how exquisitely beautiful she had been even then at ten. He had known that she would grow up to be someone exquisite and heart stopping.

Finding White Fire there, being alone with him, made Flame's heart flutter nervously. Had she known it was him standing in the shadows, choosing weapons, she would have been too nervous to continue her own shopping. Her knees would have been too weak with excitement had she known that he was so near; had she known that they were alone in the commissary.

She clutched the shoe to her chest as she continued to look up at him, his midnight dark eyes mesmerizing her as much as they had the first time she had seen him when she was ten and knew even then that she would never forget him.

"Do you truly like the shoes?" she finally blurted out, self-conscious of the blush of her cheeks, their heat proof enough to know that he, too, could see how his presence affected her.

"They seem made for you," White Fire said, picking up the matching shoe, gazing at it, then sliding his gaze again to Flame. "Are you looking for new shoes for a special occasion?"

"Why, surely you've heard," Flame said, thinking that he himself might be at the commissary to look for more than weapons. He had surely come to choose clothes for the ball that was being held this night in her honor.

"Heard *what?*" White Fire said, placing the shoe back on the shelf. It seemed so natural standing with her, sharing small talk, as though they had known each other forever.

And perhaps they *had*. Since their first day of acquaintance, she had more than once plagued his thoughts. Yet knowing their age difference, he had brushed her from his mind.

She looked at him now, as though she had never forgotten him. He could see that she had feelings for him other than just being cordial and polite as she surely was to most men. Yes, there was something more. He knew that fate had drawn them together again, even though she had a father who would rather skin White Fire alive than let him get even a foot near his daughter!

"I'm speaking of the ball tonight," Flame said, finding it so hard to believe that she could be standing there talking with White Fire, as though they were the closest of friends.

Ah, but if he only knew how often he had visited her midnight dreams! To her, he was much more than a friend. For certain, she would see that he soon was, and even more than that, hopefully, her lover.

No matter what she had to do to see him, she would. Her father could not imprison her like a child. She was a woman with feelings of a woman, all stirred up deliciously sweet inside her by this man's nearness!

"Ball?" White Fire said, forking an eyebrow. "No, I haven't heard anything about a ball."

"No, I guess you wouldn't have," Flame said, sighing. "I should have known that my father wouldn't give you an invitation."

"Oh?" he said. "And why not?"

Flame turned her eyes away, angry at herself for having been so open with him, by saying something that could hurt his feelings. She tried to think fast, searching in her mind for a plausible answer as to why her father would not invite White Fire other than him being, in part, an Indian.

But nothing would come to mind.

"Because I am a 'breed'?" White Fire asked, placing a finger to her chin, turning her eyes back around so that he could look into them.

When he saw her eyes lower, he was quickly sorry that he had said what she had purposely failed to say.

"I'm sorry," he said softly, easing his finger from her chin. "I shouldn't have said that."

Her eyes lifted quickly. She gazed raptly up at him. "You were right to," she said, her voice drawn. "For it *is* because of your skin color that my father would not invite you to the ball . . . and . . . because . . ."

She stopped short before telling him that it was because of her feelings for him that her father truly would not invite him to her ball.

"Because of what?" White Fire asked, searching her eyes. "Tell me. Why else would your father not include me in the invitations?"

She stared up at him for a moment longer, then breathless from the feelings assailing her, of wanting to be held by him . . . of wanting to be kissed by him . . . she turned away and plucked first one dress from those she had chosen, and then another.

White Fire cursed himself beneath his breath for having again caused an awkwardness between them by his persistent questioning. She obviously did not wish to answer.

"And so you have chosen a dress to wear tonight to the ball?" he said, trying to again bring lightness to their conversation, to do anything to keep them talking awhile longer, for being near her was like being filled with warm sunshine!

"Yes, I believe I have," Flame said, plucking the special one from the others. She held it out before her. "*This* one."

She was glad that he was still there, instead of being insulted by her having so abruptly turned her back to him.

Her heart pounded as he reached up and ran his fingers over the skirt of the white organdy dress.

When they brushed against her hand, her flesh tingled with aliveness and her breath caught in her throat.

"You will look beautiful in this dress," White Fire said, aware of a huskiness in his voice that he wished she would not hear.

But being so near her, smelling her perfume, and having brushed against her hand, her flesh so warm and soft against his, stirred so much inside him that he could not fight against.

She was gently spoken. She was sweet. She was beautiful. She was radiant.

But having had a loveless marriage, and having been without a woman for so long, and knowing her father's feelings toward him, he saw the danger in wanting Flame so badly. He *must* force himself to forget her.

Yet he could not walk away from her now, any more than the stars could deny the sky on a lovely summer's night. He wanted her. And somehow he would have her, and her father be damned if he tried to come between them!

Flame gazed into his eyes, seeing so much there that told her that his feelings for her were the same as those she felt for him.

Her pulse raced. Her knees grew weak. And at the pit of her stomach she was experiencing such a strange, yet sweet, mushiness.

"You truly believe this is the dress I should wear tonight at the ball?" she murmured, their eyes locked.

"Also the ivory satin shoes," he said, the fire in his loins gnawingly hot.

"Yes, they are quite beautiful," she said, aware of

a strange huskiness in her voice that she had never heard before.

Never had she felt this deliciously queasy before. Oh, Lord, she so badly wished they could dispense with their small talk and confess their feelings for one another! Oh, but if he would only grab her and kiss her!

"I . . . I . . . like the velvet cloak and I also need to choose a couple of hats," she quickly said. She giggled. "But, of course, not for the ball. I need the cloak and hats for my out—"

Her words froze on her lips when she heard her name spoken. It quickly broke the spell between her and White Fire.

"Flame?"

Lieutenant Green's voice came from across the room as he made his way toward Flame. She looked wildly past White Fire at the lieutenant's approach, then back to White Fire.

"You'd best go," she said, her voice quavering with emotion. "Father appointed that . . . that . . . damn lieutenant to keep watch on me today as though I am a mere child. It's best he doesn't see you and me together."

Understanding all too well what she meant, and his hatred for the colonel growing because of it, White Fire placed a gentle hand to Flame's cheek. "I know," he said somberly, "I know."

The feel of his hand on her cheek, so warm, so wonderful, so *gentle,* caused Flame's insides to melt sensually. She momentarily leaned her cheek into his hand. Then she moved quickly away when Lieutenant Green spoke her name again and she knew that he was too close to continue this moment of ecstasy.

She stepped quickly away from White Fire, gathered an armful of dresses, the velvet cloak, the shoes, and rushed away.

White Fire watched her move into the deeper shadows of the room. Then he tightened inside when he saw the young lieutenant place a possessive arm around her waist and whisk her over to the counter where her choices would be recorded in a journal.

White Fire waited long enough for her to leave the building, then he walked stiffly to the men's clothes racks and very determinedly chose an outfit for the ball. He smiled when he imagined the shocked look on Colonel Russell's face when he entered the ball as though he had been invited.

He felt his loins quiver when he envisioned Flame's surprised look when she would discover him there. . . .

He sighed deeply when he envisioned how beautiful she would be in the organdy dress, the red flame of her hair contrasting against the white.

He closed his eyes and envisioned how beautiful she would be as she swirled around the dance floor, the hem of her dress tangling seductively around her tapered legs.

He opened his eyes and sighed. Then he put the clothes back on the rack. What was he thinking about? Although Flame did appear to have feelings for him, surely she did not know what her flirting was getting herself into. He was a man much older than her—a man who even had a son.

No. He *must* force himself to forget her.

Feeling let down and more lonely now than he had ever felt in his entire life, White Fire went back to the arsenal of weapons and chose a rifle and a knife.

His gaze went back to the rack of men's clothes. His thoughts went to Flame.

"Should I?" he whispered.

Chapter 13

O fairest creature, last and best.
Of all God's work, creature in whom excelled,
Whatever can to sight or be formed,
Holy, divine, good, amiable, or sweet!

—John Milton

The moon was high in the sky. Stars sprinkled the heavens like twinkling sequins. The air was caressingly warm and smelled of wisteria from the vines that were thick with their purple flowers on a trellis at White Fire's right side.

As he secured his horse's reins next to the many other horses at a hitching rail, White Fire glanced up at Colonel Russell's personal residence. It brought so much to mind that was melancholy for him. He had visited often with Colonel Snelling and his family in this house.

He looked up at the second-story windows, seeing soft lamplight wafting from each of them. He was familiar with each and every room, for when he had not been talking and chatting with either Josiah

Snelling in his upstairs study, or with Josiah and his wife, Abigail, in their fancy parlor, he was in the children's rooms, often reading them stories at bedtime.

Yes, before he had had a child of his own, he had enjoyed Josiah and Abigail's, realizing then what fathering a child would mean to him.

"I *will* get my son back," he whispered to himself.

In his memory he saw his son dressed in velvet, with curls like a girl lying across his shoulders, and he shuddered and brushed it from his mind. He could hardly stand to know that his son was being treated more like a girl than a young man, who, if he lived among Indians, would be a young brave, practicing and learning the ways of a warrior.

Although White Fire had not had the opportunity to live among Indians growing up, learning the ways of braves and warriors, himself, the one year that he had spent with the Chippewa had shown him how it was done among their boys.

And although he had chosen to live apart from the Indian side of his heritage now, he would take his son to Chief Gray Feather's village often and allow him to learn the ways of the young men his same age. There, among the Chippewa, his son would learn what would make him a man.

"Soon," he whispered. "I must get him back with me *soon*."

He waited before going inside the house. He cringed every time he thought about someone else living there, when he felt it should still belong only to the Snellings.

Yet there *was* someone there that he did wish to see. She, alone, had lured him here tonight.

Hesitant at going where he had not been invited,

White Fire listened to the laughter and the tinkle of glasses drifting from the ballroom to mingle with the sigh of the leaves of the forest, and the cry of a distant loon.

White Fire gazed at the front door of the house, where people were busily coming and going. Although he had only been held captive for three years, he did not recognize anyone. It seemed that when Colonel Snelling was sent to another post, those who had been under his command had left with him.

He looked at how the men were dressed in their fancy black frock coats, with diamonds sparkling in the folds of their ascots.

He then glanced down at himself. Today, while at the commissary, he had decided against buying stiff, uncomfortable clothes, which he had quit wearing after leaving St. Louis to travel. As he had dropped his name Samuel, which identified that white part of his heritage, he had decided against wearing the clothes of a white man.

As now, he wore a fringed buckskin outfit and moccasins. He had acquired a new outfit just prior to being abducted. This would be the first time he could wear it.

Soft, flirting laughter brought his eyes up again. His heart skipped a beat, his thoughts again on his reason for him being there in his new outfit—a girl named Flame!

He sorted through the women standing on the porch, clustered around the door, giggling and chatting amongst themselves, the skirts of their lovely dresses blowing gently in the night breeze.

He saw that Flame was not among them. None

had hair that shone like a brilliant sunset. He waited until everyone had gone inside the mansion, then sauntered toward the porch.

When he heard the music begin again inside the house, White Fire stopped on the porch and listened. He could hear the notes of a piano, joined by violins. The lilting music reminded him of the many parties hosted by Josiah and Abigail, who had often invited him to the mansion. His friends had been such gracious hosts, always careful to be sure each guest felt at home with them.

He smiled as he thought back to those times when the Snellings had given their lavish parties. Abigail always made sure the silver was shined and the furniture polished. She directed the servants to empty out the parlor so it could be used for dancing, while the dining table practically groaned under the weight of the platters of food served to guests. And, of course, there was punch or champagne for the ladies and stronger spirits for the gentlemen. White Fire had such happy memories of those warm, lively gatherings.

Soft laughter drifted from the door, causing White Fire to once again think about Flame. He would never forget her laughter, her flirting smile, the softness of her flesh.

These thoughts, the hunger to see her again, hurried his steps on into the spacious hall of the house. He made a right turn and entered the parlor and mingled with the crowd of onlookers watching the dancers whirling around and around on the floor in time to the music.

Having not been invited to the dance, and realizing that he stood out like a sore thumb among the fancily dressed people, White Fire stayed hidden in the shadows. His eyes searched for Flame among the onlookers.

Not finding her, he looked seriously at the dancers. The women were beautiful in their dresses, which seemed as light as a breeze. Some wore full and floating organza; others wore silks and satins, their feet skimming the floor, their skirts twirling.

White Fire's pulse quickened when he finally saw Flame as she made a graceful, wide whirl on the floor only a short distance from where he stood.

He had never seen anyone as ravishingly beautiful as Flame. His heart raced as he watched at how radiantly she smiled as she gazed up at the man with whom she was dancing. In her white organdy dress with its petallike sleeves, the deliciously feminine skirt bouncing around her ankles as she danced, revealing a glimpse of the sheer lace at the hem of her petticoat, she was a vision to behold.

White Fire smiled a secret smile when he saw that she was wearing the ivory satin shoes he had used as a way of starting their conversation this afternoon.

Then his gaze shifted upward again, at how she wore her hair. White silk flowers pinned above each ear contrasted beautifully against the brilliant red of her hair, which lay in long, lustrous waves across her shoulders, and down her back. Her face was flushed pink with the excitement of the evening, her perfectly shaped, lusciously red lips parted often in soft, gay laughter.

But it was her eyes that held White Fire's gaze. They were suddenly on him. Between laughter and small talk with her dance partner, White Fire had seen her searching the crowd as she made her way around the dance floor. It was as though she had been searching for him, for once she found him, she looked nowhere else.

His loins reacting to her steady gaze, to the intensity of it, White Fire knew now that he had not been wrong to think that she felt something for him. He could tell that she was glad that he had attended the ball.

When she was whisked away by her partner across the dance floor, and too far away now for White Fire to see anything of her but the flowing skirt of her dress, he looked guardedly around the room for Colonel Russell.

His gaze stopped when he found the colonel standing with other officers who had come from the neighboring forts with their wives for this special occasion. They were smoking fat cigars and holding long-stemmed glasses of wine and champagne, while their wives stood in a cluster, gossiping, as they watched the dancers.

A keen sadness crept into White Fire's heart. In his mind's eye he saw Josiah and Abigail standing in the crowd, their smiles beaming as one, and then another would come up to them and chat awhile.

Strange, though, how it felt to White Fire that the Snellings *were* there, their presence absolutely certain in everything that he looked at in the room.

He gazed at the rosewood grand piano that Abigail had taken pleasure in playing. White Fire had to surmise that whatever pieces of furniture belonging to the Snellings that had been left behind were only left because of the hardships of moving them the long distance to St. Louis.

His gaze shifted, admiring now, as he had the first

time he had seen them, the doors inlaid with German silver and bronze, and the gold-and-silver chandeliers. He gazed at the art-glass windows in the walls, and the numerous paintings.

The music stopped, drawing White Fire out of his reverie. His eyes searched for Flame again, stopping and staring at her when her father whisked her from the dance floor, his arm possessively around her waist as he introduced her to his guests.

When her father called her by the name Reshelle, White Fire smiled, for he saw her cringe and understood that she must hate the name.

As Colonel Russell boasted about his daughter, his gaze moved slowly around the room. White Fire stiffened, for he knew that soon he would look in his direction.

Although hidden where the bright candlelight barely reached, White Fire felt that if the colonel saw him, it would cause his mood to darken. It might make it uncomfortable for Flame and ruin the excitement of the night for her.

Quietly White Fire stepped out of the parlor and into the corridor. He looked up the steep staircase. Not only were the bedrooms upstairs, but also the study, where he had enjoyed many a pleasant evening with Colonel Snelling.

He glanced back inside the parlor and saw that Colonel Russell was still holding his daughter "hostage" at his side as he continued to talk about her. This gave White Fire the freedom he needed to go upstairs and sit one last time with Josiah Snelling, or at least with his memory.

Taking the steps two at a time, he hurried to the study. Once inside, he slowly closed the door, then turned and felt the true heartbreak of missing his friend when he looked around the room and saw that nothing had changed since he had last been here. He saw the true haste in which the Snellings had departed the fort. Not only had Abigail's prized piano and their artwork been left behind, but also the colonel's grand oak desk, his many volumes of books lining the walls in oak bookcases, and the hand-carved Palo Verde wood sofa upholstered in red velvet.

Inhaling a deep breath, trying to break free of this melancholy that was overwhelming him, White Fire went farther into the room. He stood over the desk, envisioning Josiah sitting behind it in his leather chair.

Even Josiah's pipe stand had been left on the desk and in it were all the pipes he had smoked from during White Fire's visits. Swallowing hard, so immersed in painful remembrances, he delicately touched one pipe, and then another. Then he gazed at the journals that lay sprawled across the desk. One was open, revealing inked-in entries.

Knowing Colonel Snelling's neat way of writing, he knew that these entries were recent ones, for they were of a handwriting unfamiliar to him. They had been written by Colonel Russell.

Suddenly White Fire sensed a presence in the room. As the feeling became stronger, it was as though someone else was there. Possibly Josiah Snelling's ghost?

White Fire did feel as though that if he chanced to speak aloud to his friend, Josiah would hear and respond.

Footsteps entering the room behind him made

White Fire turn with a start. Discovering who was standing in the doorway made White Fire laugh softly.

"Flame," he said, wondering if she could sense his relief at seeing her there. If she did, she would never expect that relief was because he was not being visited by a ghost of his past.

"I saw you leave the parlor," Flame said, lifting the hem of her skirt in her hands as she moved farther into the room. "I needed a respite from my father, as well as the noise. In truth, I need a breath of air."

"If you needed fresh air, why did you come up here to get it?" White Fire asked, his lips tugging into a slow, teasing smile.

"Because I left the room just in time to see you come up the stairs," Flame said, moving to stand before him. She tilted her eyes up to hold with his. "I have been told of your relationship with Colonel Snelling. I thought you might be here in his study, reliving special moments with him."

"And so you wanted to share them with me?" White Fire said, lifting a hand to gently touch her cheek. He noticed how quickly she took in a breath of air, and how the look in her eyes became soft with passion.

"I wanted to be with you, no matter where, or how," Flame said softly. She lifted her lips in an invitation to be kissed. "I want more than that. I have for so long thought of how it might feel to be kissed by you."

Hardly believing what was transpiring, having never thought that Flame would be this daring, especially when her father could come in at any moment and discover them together, White Fire hesitated.

Then he took her by a hand and took her toward
the French doors that led out on a balcony.

When they were outside in the spill of moonlight,
surrounded by the heady fragrance of honeysuckle
blossoms, and with the doors closed behind them,
White Fire took Flame into his arms.

He brought her supple body against his, and covered her lips with his mouth and kissed her. The
euphoria that filled White Fire's being startled
him. Never before had a woman affected him in
such a way!

His steel arms enfolded her as their kiss deepened.

Flame had dreamed so many times of being with
White Fire, his mouth ravaging hers with heated
kisses, but never in her wildest dreams had it been
this wonderful. The pleasure spreading through her
body was like nothing she could have ever envisioned.

She was not prepared for the intensity that his kiss
evoked. She was weakened by the passion overwhelming her in warm, ecstatic waves. And she could feel
such hunger in the hard, seeking pressure of his lips.

His need matched the need that was spreading
through her, blotting out everything in her consciousness . . . but him.

Although he found himself lost, heart and soul to
Flame, White Fire was aware of the danger of their
being together in such a way. He fought his needs,
his desires, and stepped away from her.

Breathing hard, his heart beating erratically, he
turned his back to her and grasped the rail of the
balcony. He was almost blinded with passion as

he tried to gaze down to the ground spread out below him.

But his vision quickly cleared. He realized that people were departing. The ball was over.

That meant that Flame's father would expect her to stand at the door with him, to say her cordial farewells to the guests.

Just as White Fire turned to Flame, to warn her, to go down and be with her father, the double French doors burst open and Colonel Russell was standing there like the devil himself, his eyes filled with an angry contempt as he glared at White Fire.

"Leave my house at once," the colonel said, his teeth clenched, his hands tight fists at his sides. He looked at Flame. "Reshelle, how could you do this? This man is a 'breed."

"I know what he is, but that does not change my feelings for him," Flame said, placing herself between White Fire and her father. "And, Father, why must you insist on dictating my life? Do you hunger this much for controlling people, even your own daughter?"

"That has nothing to do with this," the colonel bellowed. "I will not have you seen in the company of this 'breed. Do you understand, Reshelle? I absolutely forbid it."

"Oh, Father, *please,*" Flame said, sighing with frustration. But she did not want to create a scene, and place White Fire in danger. She locked her arm through her father's. "But let us not discuss it further now. We have guests awaiting us, Father. Let us go and say our good-byes."

As she led him through the study, leaving White Fire out on the balcony, he sighed heavily. He turned his back to the doors and nervously raked his fingers through his hair. He suddenly realized that the colonel was right to be concerned about his daughter. How could White Fire expect someone as young and beautiful as Flame to be serious enough about him, or enter into a relationship that could lead to marriage and to being an instant *mother*?

"I've got to forget her," he whispered, though the very thought of never holding her again made a slow ache circle his heart.

His jaw tight, and hollow with loneliness, he left the study and took the back stairs past the servants' quarters. Then he went outside and grabbed the reins of his horse.

Without even looking he knew that Flame was standing at the door with her father. He knew that she was watching him as he rode off. He could feel the heat of her gaze on his back.

He could still feel the heat in his loins that her kiss had caused.

He knew then, that no matter how hard he tried, there was no way that he could *ever* forget her now that he had held and kissed her.

Chapter 14

How can I live without thee, how forgo
Thy sweet converse, and love so dearly joined,
To live again in these wild woods, forlorn?

— John Milton

White Fire awakened from a dream that seemed to have continued the entire night—of himself and Flame together making hot. passionate love.

The dream was so real, he leaned up on an elbow and quickly looked over at the other side of the bed to see if Flame had really been there through the night with him. He laughed softly when he saw that, no, she wasn't there, nor had she ever been.

He yawned and stretched his arms over his head, then slid from the bed and pulled on his fringed breeches.

Stretching again, he sauntered into the kitchen and poured fresh water in a basin from a wooden pitcher. Just as he leaned over and splashed water on his face, he heard a soft knock on his door.

Forking an eyebrow, he straightened his back, and

grabbed a towel. As he dried off his face and hands, he gazed at the door, wondering who might be there so early in the morning.

He looked at the gray eagle feather on the kitchen table that Gray Feather had left for him. He looked away when someone knocked at the door again.

Could it be Gray Feather? he wondered, realizing that hardly any time had passed since the chief's last visit. But he knew the chief well enough to know how persistent he could be when he wanted something.

"Or someone," White Fire whispered to himself.

Again someone knocked. He glanced down at himself. He wore no shirt or moccasins, and he hadn't yet shaved.

But the persistent knocking caused him to forget his dishevelment. He tossed the towel over the back of a chair, rushed to the door and opened it. Then he took an unsteady step away from it. He was stunned to see Flame standing there so fresh and beautiful, attired in a green riding habit, her long hair pinned up under her hat, a jeweled riding crop in one of her gloved hands.

Flame was taken off guard when she saw that White Fire was half dressed. She could not help but stare at his smooth, copper chest, and then at the muscles bulging in his shoulders and arms.

He could not help but stare at her loveliness, the dream still lingering in his mind, the remembrances of her soft, silken body against his causing fires to rage inside his loins.

But he managed to shake himself out of the reverie. It was dangerous with her there so close, so alone, so vulnerable to a man who had been with-out a woman for way too long now. He was able to think more logically after forcing his foolish desires from his mind.

And what he suddenly realized made his jaw tighten.

"What on earth is your father thinking allowing you to ride alone in this wilderness?" he said.

Her eyes suddenly widened and her jaw went slack and she stared up at him in total surprise at his brusqueness.

"How can *you* be so daring and foolish to ride alone when you know that I myself was only recently set free from my three-year captivity with the Sioux?" he demanded. "Do you not know that they would not hesitate to steal you away? They only recently abducted Chief Gray Feather's daughter."

Her mind scrambled by his rush of words, and by the anger in his voice, Flame was momentarily at a loss for words.

Then she inhaled deeply and squared her shoulders. "I'll have you know, that after last night, when my father embarrassed me by treating me as a child in your presence, I made it clear to him that I am no longer one, and that the only way he can stop me from doing as I please is to tie me to a bedpost. And he wouldn't *dare* do anything as rash as that." She tilted her chin. "And I am not afraid of the Sioux," she said tightly. "I'm afraid of no one."

White Fire was taken aback by just how stubborn and high spirited she was. And though he was worried about her being so daring, he could not help but admire her.

"Well?" Flame said, straining her neck to look past him. "Aren't you going to invite me in for a cup of coffee?"

White Fire laughed throatily. "I believe you came too early for coffee," he said, unable to stop himself when he thought back to the dream that he had only moments ago awakened from. In truth, he wished to whisk her up into his arms and carry her to his bed.

He had to wonder what her reaction would be if he chanced it.

It was certain that she was not going to give up on their relationship as easily as he had decided to. But that was last night. This was today. He knew that he could never cast her from his mind, or heart.

And though he knew the obstacles that would stand in their way, he would let nothing or no one stop what had begun between them.

"Then I shall make the coffee," Flame said, brushing on past him into the cabin.

In awe of her, and how she so fearlessly trusted him, White Fire closed the door and stood there and watched her as she slipped off her hat, then her gloves, and then the coat of her riding outfit.

The coil of red hair was stunning in the soft sunlight streaming through the windows. The generous swell of breasts was obvious as they pressed against her cotton blouse. Her waist was small where her skirt flared out away from it.

Everything about her threatened to rob him of his senses. He fought to keep sane and to push his hunger to kiss her from his mind.

As she tinkered in the kitchen, preparing the coffeepot with water and coffee, he grabbed a buckskin shirt from a peg on the wall and hurried into it. Nervously, he raked his fingers through his long, black hair. Then he stiffened as she came to him and looked him square in the eyes, with a smile that melted him almost into the wooden boards of the floor.

"Do you truly mind that I am here?" Flame asked, awash with feelings that she had only felt while in the presence of this man.

The dream that she had had last night made her even more determined not to allow her father to keep her from being with White Fire. After their embrace and kiss on the balcony she had gone to bed and dreamed sensual dreams of him the entire night.

She could hardly wait to get bathed and dressed this morning to come to him, to *be* with him.

Now it was like in the dream again as his dark eyes devoured her, telling her more than words could ever say.

"Do I mind that you are here?" White Fire said, holding back from reaching to touch her face, to draw the combs from her hair so that he could see it flutter down across her shoulders. "No." He chuckled softly. "But I must admit, I'm somewhat surprised."

"I had a dream last night," she murmured. "In it, we . . . you . . . you and I . . ."

Finding it hard to be this bold, this daring, she could not say the words.

Instead, she turned and went into his kitchen and grabbed the coffeepot.

Then she went to the fireplace, to place the pot in the hot coals. She sighed heavily and gave him a forlorn look over her shoulder. "There is no fire," she said softly.

"I shall remedy that," he said, rushing to the fireplace. He bent down and placed kindling, small logs, then larger logs across the grate. In a matter of moments, there was a large enough fire with which to brew coffee.

After the pot was sitting at the edge of the flames, White Fire took Flame by the hand and pulled her down on the floor onto a soft cushion of blankets. It had always been his favorite place to lie in the evenings when the fire was cozy and warm.

"Your cabin is nice," Flame said, looking slowly around her, ignoring the cobwebs in the corners of the open-beamed ceiling.

White Fire drew his legs up to his chest and circled his arms around them. He slowly looked around the room, then gazed into the fire. "Everything you see, the curtains, the furniture, the kitchenware, was of my wife's choosing," he said thickly. "When I returned home after my captivity, it was all covered with spiderwebs and dust. I only last night worked hard at getting it back in order."

"Before or after the ball?" Flame asked softly.

White Fire turned quick eyes her way. "After," he said, his eyes locked with hers. "When I first went to bed, I found it hard to sleep. I chose to clean house instead."

"What caused your inability to sleep?" Flame dared to ask, her pulse racing to think she might have been the cause.

"Because of the Sioux, there are many things that are not as they should be in my life," White Fire said solemnly. "They the same as killed my Mary."

"Mary?" Flame said softly. "That was your wife's name?"

He sighed. He gazed into the fire again. "Yes, an angel if I ever saw one," he said, his voice breaking.

"You loved her dearly?" Flame asked, trying not to be jealous of her ghost.

White Fire knew what she was trying to get from him, and understood. He already knew that she loved him. It was in their kiss last night. It was in her persistence to be with him.

"Our love was different than most who are married," he said, turning a slow gaze to Flame. "Mary had an abusive marriage with a French voyager. I found out from Colonel Snelling that he beat her into obedience. He died in a boating accident. She was lonely and scared. I married her."

"You didn't marry her out of love?" Flame asked. "It was out of pity?"

"I would not exactly call it pity," White Fire said, combing his fingers through his hair, pushing it back from his brow. "She was alone. I was alone. Marrying her seemed the thing to do."

He reached a hand out and gently touched Flame's face. "I never felt half as much for her as I do you, and you are but a stranger," he said thickly. "I never truly loved her. I just sort of quietly worshipped her sweetness, her compassion for life. And she gave me the greatest gift of all—a son. Michael. Ah, how I miss my Michael."

"I would love knowing Michael," Flame said, shivering sensually when his hand slid down from her cheek and across her long neck, then down to a breast, where he gently cupped it through her cotton blouse.

She closed her eyes and sighed. "I so badly wish to know *you*—*every*thing about you," she said, her voice filled with deep emotion.

Then her eyes sprang open quickly and she brushed

his hand from her breast. "You must think me shameful," she blurted out. "If you compare me with your Mary, I imagine you see me as too forward—as too shameful—ever to truly love as you surely wish to love a woman."

"I love everything about you," White Fire said. He gently took her by the wrists and slowly laid her down on the blankets. He knelt over her, his lips brushing against her mouth. "I think I fell in love with you all those many years ago, Flame, when you flirted with me with those deliciously green eyes and wondrous smile. Yet you were but a mere child. I placed you from my mind until the day you arrived at Fort Snelling on the riverboat. When I saw you, I knew I could never truly love anyone but you."

He kissed her with a meltingly hot passion, his hands releasing her blouse from inside the waist of her skirt. He could feel her shudder of ecstasy as he slid his hands inside the blouse. Their flesh seemed to fuse in the heat ignited between them.

Flame had not expected to go this far when she had come to him this morning, fresh from sensual, sweet dreams of him. Yet she could not stop what was starting now. Never in her life had she been so brazen with a man as now.

Loving him so much, she could not fight this hungry need that overwhelmed any thoughts that might stop her.

But when he suddenly rose from her and stood over the fire, his back to her, she came out of her passionate reverie and tucked her blouse hurriedly back inside her skirt.

Her face flushed hot, she rose quickly to her feet. "I guess I should go," she murmured, then turned to White Fire. "Come riding with me. It's such a beautiful morning."

Still troubled by how his feelings had gotten out of control with her, having almost gone as far as coaxing her to make love, White Fire breathed hard and could not answer her all that quickly. His fingers tingled from the wondrous softness of her flesh. He had gotten so close to touching her breasts, it made his knees weak.

And, ah, her lips. They had been so soft! The taste had been sweet, like maple syrup made in early spring.

"White Fire, should I leave without you?" Flame asked softly, slipping on her jacket, and buttoning it. "Have I been too shameful this morning? Will you always hate me for it?"

Hearing the concern in her soft voice, and not wanting her to ever feel ashamed of her feelings, he turned quickly toward her. "Do you not know that I could never hate you?" he said, seeing that she was now fully dressed again. "And, yes, I would love to go riding with you this morning."

He paused, then frowned. "But what about your father?" he asked warily. "Are you certain you wish to go against his wishes this much? That you might be seen with me, someone he thinks of as a 'breed?"

"If I worried about my father over such things, I would never be free to love," Flame said softly. She went to White Fire. She framed his face with her hands. "And I love *you*. Father might as well learn to accept that."

He swept his arms around her waist and drew her against his hard body. Holding her in his tight embrace, he lowered his mouth to her lips. Their kiss was frenzied in its fiery passion. Their bodies strained hungrily together.

Then, again not wanting things to get out of hand, at least not yet, he eased away from her. His pulse racing, he slipped into his moccasins, grabbed his rifle, then took her by an elbow and led her outside.

After saddling his horse, they rode off together into the bright sunshine-dappled morning. Laughing and talking, telling each other of their families, and speaking of their wishes for the future, they rode through a thin growth of timber, mostly ash, with some elm, maple, oak, and birch. Wild roses vined up the trunks of the trees and wound along the ground in successions of pinks, whites, and reds.

They rode across a plain of tall, green grass. They rode past an occasional cornfield and cabin.

Fleecy clouds sailed overhead as they rode along the river, the fort a short distance away, where there was much activity as traders came and went in their canoes, and on horseback.

At the sight of the fort, White Fire wheeled his horse to a stop. Flame drew a tight rein beside him.

"I think you should get back home before your father decides to come looking for you," White Fire said, reaching over to take one of her hands.

"I understand that he has hired you as his interpreter," Flame said, smiling. "Before he realized that you and I had feelings for one another, he confided in me that he has tried for months to find someone as skilled and knowledgeable as you in the various Indian languages. I doubt he is eager to be put in the position of finding another interpreter. So he just might look past more than he might have, because you are so important to him."

"I would not get that confident about anything your father feels or says," he said, frowning. He waited a moment before telling her how he really felt about her father, not wanting to upset her.

Yet, by the different things she had said, and by her desire to take her freedom when she wished to, it seemed that she knew the true character of her father.

"In your father, I see such a deviousness," he blurted out. "So be careful, Flame. I truly believe your father might be capable of anything."

"That is why my mother eventually divorced him," Flame said sullenly. "But I believe she made her decision too late. All through their marriage she was ill with one thing or another. I now believe it was because of the strain of living with my father."

"Yet you came to live with him after your mother died?" White Fire could not help but question.

"Only because I saw adventure that I could not deny myself here in the Minnesota wilderness," she said. She smiled slowly and her eyes twinkled. "Nor could I ever forget that you were headed for the Minnesota Territory all those years ago when I first met you."

"You thought you might find me?" he said, forking an eyebrow at her admission.

"I never doubted for one minute that I would," Flame said, giggling.

She sighed, gave him her most winning smile, then rode off. "I shall see you again *very* soon," she said across her shoulder as their eyes locked and held. "I can hardly believe that I *did* find you, and that you *love* me!"

"Fate brought us together again!" he shouted back, waving as she rode on away from him.

His insides soft and mellow with an intense love that he had never felt before, White Fire laughed out loud and wheeled his horse around and rode back in the direction of his cabin. He was ready for that cup of coffee from the pot that she had made for them.

Then he must concentrate solely on Michael.

But he knew that Flame would always be there in his mind no matter what else he pursued while they were apart. He closed his eyes as he envisioned the time when they could both feel it was right to make love.

His cabin only a short distance away, White Fire opened his eyes and wheeled his horse to a stop when he saw a horse tied to the hitching rail just outside his cabin.

Not recognizing the horse, he drew a tight rein and slid his rifle from the gun boot at the side of his pinto.

Riding at a slow lope, he proceeded, his eyes wary, his heart pounding.

Chapter 15

Our state cannot be severed, we are one
One flesh,
To lose thee were to lose myself!

—John Milton

So unsure of who might be waiting for him in his cabin, his three years with the Sioux fresh on his mind, and not trusting that they had accepted his release that easily, White Fire dismounted in the shadows of the trees and tied his horse's reins around a low limb.

His rifle clutched in his right hand, he moved stealthily toward his cabin, his eyes watching for movement on both sides of him. He knew that many Sioux could be hiding there. Although Chief Gray Feather's warriors had escorted their Sioux captives back to their home, which was far from this area, warning them never to return again, White Fire could never believe the Sioux would allow the Chippewa to dictate to them.

Yet he knew that Chief Gray Feather was aware of the other bands of Sioux a day's ride from here. If

Gray Feather had taken *any* Sioux captive, those others who got word of it would rebel. There would be an out-and-out war between the Sioux and Chippewa, and no one wanted blood spilled needlessly.

White Fire reached his front door and saw that it was slightly ajar. He inhaled a nervous breath, then kicked the door open and jumped into the cabin, his rifle poised for firing.

He was quick to lower his rifle when he saw Chief Gray Feather sitting on the blankets before a gently burning fire in the fireplace. Around him on the floor were many tied bundles, and something else that made White Fire's eyebrows fork with wonder.

"You see the gifts?" Chief Gray Feather said, smiling up at him. "They are from me to you."

Very aware of why the chief was there again, bearing many gifts, White Fire smiled awkwardly. He leaned his rifle against the wall, then went and knelt down on his haunches beside the chief.

"When I saw the horse outside, I did not recognize it as yours," White Fire said, trying to ignore the gifts which he knew were Gray Feather's bribe to make him do what he wished—marry his daughter.

"The *bay-bay-shee-go-gah-shee*, horse, was a gift to this old chief from a friend in a neighboring village," Gray Feather said. "I have brought special gifts to *you* from Gray Feather. Take. Enjoy."

"I understand why you have brought the gifts," White Fire said, his voice drawn. "But—"

Before he could finish, Gray Feather interrupted him. "There are blankets, pelts, jewelry," he said, motioning with his hands toward the bundles. Gray Feather rose and stretched out a hand to White Fire.

"Stand before me," he said thickly. "Listen seriously to what this old chief says. It is being said from the bottom of his heart."

White Fire stood up. He swallowed hard when the Chippewa chief placed gentle hands on his shoulders and gazed into his eyes with much warmth and pleading.

"My *nee-gee*, friend, I have come again to ask you to leave this white world behind you and be my daughter's husband," he said. "Be a father for my granddaughter! I would be proud to have you as a son. White Fire, I saw it in a dream! The face of the man sitting at my right side in council was you. You sat there in the capacity of a son."

White Fire was torn by feelings at having to disappoint this wonderful man again, especially since White Fire himself felt so much for him, as though they *were* father and son.

Yes, he could understand the chief's persistence, for the chief's feelings for him had begun before he had left to join Colonel Snelling at the fort. This, perhaps, was why White Fire had felt the urge to leave. He had never joined the Chippewa with plans of staying with them forever. It was just something that he had gotten caught up in. Their magic and mystique had been so intriguing it had been easy to stay with them and learn. Until he had arrived at the Minnesota Territory, he had been denied everything of his Indian heritage. The hunger for it had been fed while living with the tribe.

"Gray Feather, I am honored that you think so much of me that you would wish for me to sit at your right side in council as your son," White Fire said softly. "And I understand the power of dreams. But, Gray Feather, what you had was just that. A *ee-nah-bun-dum,* dream. I cannot go with you to your village. I cannot ever consider marrying your daughter, for you see, Gray Feather, I have chosen another woman, a *white* woman. In time I will marry her."

Gray Feather's hands dropped to his sides. His eyes wavered with disappointment. Hanging his head, he walked toward the door.

Then Gray Feather stopped and gazed back at White Fire. "It is wrong for you to marry another white woman," he said, his voice drawn. "It was meant for you to marry someone of your own skin coloring. My daughter's skin matches yours. So does her daughter's."

White Fire went to Gray Feather. "You have come today bearing gifts, knowing that I have already said that I would not marry your daughter," he said warily. "Gray Feather, please know that I find Song Sparrow beautiful and sweet. Her daughter is as beautiful, but my heart is elsewhere. Nothing can change it. I do not feel it is right for me to keep your gifts," he added softly.

"I brought gifts to you," Gray Feather said, his voice harsh. "They stay with you." He turned and left the cabin.

White Fire went to the door and watched the chief ride away. He felt as though he had done something as bad as betray the chief, yet he knew that there was no reason for him to feel such guilt. He had never once promised to stay with the Chippewa.

And although he felt as though he owed the chief for having rescued him from the Sioux, he just could not allow himself to be coerced into doing something that he felt was wrong, just as a thank-you for having been given back his life. He would find a way to thank Gray Feather, someday, some way. But not like this.

He stared moodily at the horizon.

He paled and gasped when he saw Flame riding in a hard gallop along the horizon, away from the fort.

Fear struck at his heart at her being alone. He wondered what had caused her to leave in such haste, her flight seeming to be one of anger and desperation.

"Her father . . ." he whispered, thinking that her father may have fiercely questioned her about being gone so long on her horse today. If he forbade her to go again, White Fire knew her rebellious nature could have caused this hasty flight, careless though it was.

Closing the door behind him, White Fire ran to where he had left his horse. He leaped into the saddle and rode in pursuit of Flame. He could never get the threat of the Sioux from his mind.

He couldn't understand why she didn't understand the extent of the danger. Was she too stubbornly blind to realize what could happen to her out here, alone?

From the time it took to get to his horse and mount it, Flame had ridden out of sight.

Desperation filling his heart, White Fire searched in all directions, seeing her nowhere. Frustrated, he finally drew a tight rein.

His eyes searched the forest.

Had someone grabbed her? Was she already a captive?

These thoughts sent him into a breathless gallop.

When he still did not find her, he rode to a high bluff, and watched the fort, hoping that he would see her return.

Then he finally saw her riding toward the wide gate, and quickly entering. His shoulders relaxed and he sighed heavily with relief. This time she had made it safely home. But what about the next?

His jaw tight, White Fire knew now that he must not hesitate for too long in asking her to marry him. For certain she would be much safer with him than her father.

He understood how hard it would be to reason with her father about the quickness of their marriage. But haste must be taken, or Colonel Russell might not lose his daughter to White Fire, but to renegade Indians instead!

The thought sent chills up and down White Fire's spine.

Chapter 16

When this life is o'er, love,
With all its joys and jars,
We'll leave behind the wind and fire,
To wage their boisterous wars,

— R. W. Raymond

For the second day in a row White Fire was abruptly awakened from his sleep. Again, someone was knocking on his door.

Recalling Flame having come so early the day before, he wondered if she had come again. He then remembered his concern about her, when he had seen her leave the fort in a frenzied flight on her horse.

He wondered again what might have caused her to leave the fort in such a rush. Her father?

His heart skipped a beat when he thought of who else it could be this morning. The colonel could have sent for him for a talk, if Colonel Russell had learned that she had been with White Fire yesterday.

The knocks persisted at the door, and his jaw tight, White Fire left his bed and dressed quickly in his buckskins and moccasins.

Pushing his long hair back from his face and shoulders, he went to the door. He hesitated before opening it.

Then he swung it open and his heart sank to see that his guess had been right about who might be there.

It wasn't Colonel Russell, but it *was* a soldier from Fort Snelling. The colonel had sent the lieutenant to fetch him.

"Sir, Colonel Russell wants you to accompany me to the fort," Lieutenant Green said, standing square-shouldered in his blue uniform. The saber at his waist picked up the shine of the sun and reflected it up into White Fire's eyes.

Not questioning the soldier as to why the colonel would summon him, White Fire lingered long enough to grab his rifle. Stiffly, he went outside, and saddled, then mounted his horse. Then he rode off with the young lieutenant. "How long have you been at Fort Snelling, Lieutenant?" White Fire asked, trying to ease his anger over being summoned. White Fire expected to be scolded by the colonel like he was some mischievous schoolboy. Today he would make sure this never happened again. He would put the colonel in his place.

And if the colonel saw fit to still try to dictate his life, White Fire would find some other means of employment. He could trap and sell pelts until he made enough money to make a comfortable life for his son. He knew enough about trapping to get rich in six months.

That would also be the way he would provide for his wife, for he *would* marry Flame, no matter how her father might threaten him. Or Flame.

White Fire would protect Flame with his life, especially against a tyrannical father.

She was old enough to know her own mind, her own *heart*.

"I came on the same riverboat that brought Miss Reshelle to the fort from St. Louis," Lieutenant Green said. "I was at Fort Jefferson Barracks for two years, training to live in the wilderness."

"And you prefer the Minnesota Territory over St. Louis?" White Fire asked, watching the wide gate of the fort as they approached it.

"Yes, sir," Lieutenant Green said, smiling. "I hope to stay here for many years."

Lieutenant Green then turned to White Fire. "Your father, Colonel Dowling, is used as an example at Fort Jefferson Barracks," he said, drawing his eyes quickly to him. "He is much admired. He was the epitome of what an infantry officer is about."

White Fire swallowed hard. His eyes wavered as, in his mind, he saw his father in his freshly ironed blue uniform, the brass buttons shining.

As a child, White Fire had followed his father around, eyes wide in admiration of his handsomeness in his uniform, and his square-shouldered way of walking.

"How did you know that he was my father?" White Fire blurted out, riding onto the parade ground with the lieutenant.

"You are a part of the conversation when people speak of your father," Lieutenant Green said, smiling. "Everyone knew how proud your father was of you even if you are a 'br—"

White Fire's insides tightened when he realized that the lieutenant had stopped just short of saying the word that had been like a thorn in his side ever since that first person had called him—a 'breed. He looked away from the lieutenant, and rode on up to the officers' quarters without him.

As he dismounted and tied his reins to a hitching rail, White Fire studied the four horses tied alongside his. He saw markings on the rumps of the horses in the shape of hands. They were markings of the Sioux.

His gut twisted at the thought of coming face-to-face with *any* Sioux now, after having just been released from Sioux captivity.

But realizing that Indians were there surely to meet with the colonel, made White Fire forget about his thought that he might have been summoned because of his relationship with the colonel's daughter. He was surely asked there in the capacity of interpreter.

His right hand clasping his rifle tightly, and with Lieutenant Green again at his side, White Fire glared down the long corridor that led to Colonel Russell's office. He tried to prepare himself for whoever was waiting there, be it a Sioux that he might know, or a Sioux who was a total stranger to him.

A Sioux was a Sioux and his enemy!

The young lieutenant stepped aside and stayed

outside in the corridor as White Fire went into the colonel's office.

When White Fire saw who was there, with three of his warriors standing at the back of the room, their arms crossed, he took an unsteady step backward. It was the very Sioux who had taken him hostage.

White Fire could hardly believe that Chief Shining Turtle had the nerve to return to the area, especially after having been escorted back to his village by Chief Gray Feather's warriors.

It was for certain that the Sioux chief did not fear the wrath of the Chippewa, knowing that, if needed, he could draw the many local bands of Sioux into the fight.

Colonel Russell rose from his chair. He walked from behind his desk and offered White Fire a hand. "I'm glad you came," he said, his voice tightly drawn. "I need you to interpret for me. The Sioux chief came into my office, unannounced. It is obvious he has come for council."

White Fire shook the colonel's hand, then sent a dark frown Shining Turtle's way. "Then you do not know why he is here?" he said, glancing over at the colonel. "It is for certain that you cannot trust this Sioux chief. For three years I was held captive by him. It is ironic that it would be I who would be interpreting for him."

"Will you do it for *me?*" the colonel asked, placing a trembling hand on White Fire's shoulder. "Can we cast aside our own personal feelings long enough to . . . to get this son of a bitch out of my office?"

White Fire looked sharply at the colonel. "It would

be easy for me to walk away and leave you with the problem at hand," he said. "But it would serve no true purpose. Yes. I shall interpret for you."

The colonel started dragging chairs close to his desk. "Tell them to come and sit by my desk, and we shall have council," he said, giving the Sioux chief an uneasy glance over his shoulder.

"They will not sit in chairs," White Fire said, shoving the chairs aside as quickly as the colonel slid them in place. "The floor will suffice."

"The floor?" Colonel Russell grumbled, frowning. "Do you mean I am going to have to sit on the damn floor?"

"If you wish to have council, yes, the floor will have to do," White Fire said, a mischievous gleam entering his eyes.

He waited until the colonel eased himself to the floor, sitting with his legs crossed, his hands resting on his knees. Then, White Fire went to the Sioux and talked to them in their language and told them to come and sit on the floor in a circle with him and the colonel.

His arms folded stiffly across his bare chest, Chief Shining Turtle stared sullenly for a moment into White Fire's eyes. Then he spoke to his companions.

Their breechclouts brushing against their copper-colored, muscular legs, the chief and his three warriors went and sat down in a circle with the colonel. White Fire sat down in the center.

Soon the dialogue began. White Fire knew enough Sioux words to be able to translate their desires to the colonel.

"The recent Chippewa attack on Chief Shining

Turtle's encampment, when Chief Gray Feather came for his daughter, and at the same time freed me from my captivity, robbed Chief Shining Turtle of many of their supplies and warriors," White Fire explained to the colonel. "After they were ushered home by the Chippewa, they found twofold hardships there than when they had left to trap and sell pelts on the banks of the river close to Fort Snelling. They have come to seek your assistance. They need provisions for their children and elderly."

"There are more bands of Sioux than just this one," Colonel Russell mumbled, his knuckles whitening as his grip hardened on his knees. "Ask them why they do not go and pester—no, do not use that word. Ask them why they do not go and seek help from their brothers at the other Sioux villages?"

Seeing the colonel's lack of respect for the Sioux, which meant that he surely lacked the same respect even for the friendly Chippewa, caused White Fire to dislike him even more than before. Yes, it was true that White Fire himself had no liking for the Sioux. But it was not in him to ridicule them, for he knew that the Sioux had learned their manners toward whites after being mistreated by the whites.

He turned toward the Sioux chief. "Why do you not go to your Sioux friends at the other villages and ask them for assistance instead of asking white eyes?" he asked.

"Because my friends and brothers are as poorly as I," Chief Shining Turtle said glumly. "It is not so much because of the recent Chippewa attack on my people as it is because of the *white* eyes that the Sioux are put in the position of begging. And tell this white eyes soldier that it just makes the Sioux hate the white eyes more and more because of being put in this position."

"If you hate them so much, how can you take from them?" White Fire could not help but ask.

"Because we care more for our children, women, and elderly than we do for our pride," Chief Shining Turtle said tightly.

"Do you not feel even the least bit awkward coming and asking this of the white eyes after you kept me, their friend, captive at your village?" White Fire asked, even though he knew that this was not a part of the dialogue expected by the colonel.

"You were a captive, but you are still alive, are you not?" the Sioux chief asked, his eyes suddenly gleaming.

"Yes, that is so," White Fire said warily.

"I will say no more about it, for that should be enough for you," Chief Shining Turtle said, his lips tugging into a smug smile. Then he frowned. "Get answers I need so that I can return to my people."

White Fire sighed, then turned to the colonel. "Are you going to give them supplies?" he asked, his voice solemn.

"What would happen if I didn't?" Colonel Russell said, glaring at the Sioux chief.

"What would happen?" White Fire said, arching an eyebrow. "Do you really wish to test the chief and see?"

"Then you are suggesting I give into his demands?"

"Colonel, although I carry much bitterness and resentment inside my heart for this particular Sioux chief, I urge you to help him. Mainly to keep down hostilities."

"Then it shall be done," Colonel Russell said. He looked from warrior to warrior, then looked into White Fire's midnight dark eyes. "Tell the chief that he will be given as many provisions as he feels are required to ease the hunger and discomfort of his people. Then you, personally, take him to the commissary. Oversee exactly what they do take. Make sure they do not take more than what seems right in your eyes."

White Fire nodded, then conveyed this to the Sioux chief.

Chief Shining Turtle was pleased. He smiled. But he didn't offer any sort of friendly handshake to the colonel. He and his warriors followed White Fire to the commissary.

White Fire stood aside as the Sioux chose food, blankets, and even some white men's clothes.

After these were secured in tight bundles on their horses, White Fire exchanged a lingering stare with the Sioux chief. Then he watched him and his companions ride out of the wide gate of the fort.

Curious as to whether or not the band might travel onward to their village, or make camp for the night and leave on the morrow, White Fire swung himself into his saddle and followed. He kept far enough back not to be seen.

After he traveled for some time, never allowing Chief Shining Turtle to get out of sight, White Fire drew a tight rein, and slid his horse quickly behind a thick covering of brush when he saw many Sioux warriors waiting for the chief.

Some waited on horseback. Others rested on the banks of the river next to their beached canoes.

White Fire knew the Indians in the area well enough. He mentally counted how many Sioux were there waiting on Chief Shining Turtle. There were several Sioux from many bands.

It was at this moment that he realized that by having urged the colonel to give the Sioux the provisions, he had averted an attack on Fort Snelling. It was apparent, by how the Sioux were armed and by how many there were, that they had come together to help the Sioux chief who had lost so much. They had been ready to launch an attack had Chief Shining Turtle returned to them with nothing.

Sweat pearled White Fire's brow to realize just how close the fort had come to becoming the target of the Sioux's anger.

He looked over his shoulder in the direction of the fort, where the woman he loved was trustingly within its walls, unknowing of the threat that lay so close.

He shuddered and looked in another direction, toward Pig's Eye, where his son would have surely died also, had the Sioux become enraged enough to spill white men's blood today.

Loud, mocking laughter brought White Fire's eyes around again. He stared at the Sioux as they opened the many bundles of provisions and showed them to their friends.

His eyes widened when the Sioux laughed even more loudly and mockingly as one by one they ripped up the blankets with their large knives, then spilled the food across the ground and stomped on it.

White Fire now truly knew the danger the people in this area had been in. The Sioux had not truly wanted the provisions! It had been a test. Only a test to see how far they could push the white eyes.

He numbly watched until the Sioux were finished with their fun. He was glad when they all embraced, then departed, traveling in all directions on their horses and in their canoes. For now, it seemed the Sioux had been appeased.

"But for how long?" White Fire whispered, a chill riding his spine.

Chapter 17

I wonder by my troth what thou and I
Did, till we loved? Were we not weaned till then
But sucked in country pleasures, childishly?

—John Donne

White Fire had left the fort after having found just the right pony to buy for his son, Michael. The more he had thought about Michael and how he was being raised in velvet breeches and curls, the more he had known that some of that money that he had hidden in his chimney would be well spent on a way to introduce his son to the "other world" from which he had been kept.

White Fire shuddered inwardly at the thought of his son's face being so pale, which meant that rarely did he go out of doors to play in the sun.

"I will change that and many more things," White Fire whispered to himself as he rode into the outskirts of Pig's Eye.

But things weren't happening fast enough and he hated practicing the art of restraint. Yet he knew that it was best for Michael if things went slowly. He would be less traumatized than being whisked from one family to another. White Fire would work him into it gradually.

When White Fire saw the Greer mansion at the side of the road, he drew rein, and stopped. He winced. He hated having to go and knock on the door like a total stranger when, in truth, his son was in that house.

And he dreaded coming face-to-face with Maureen Greer again. She was cold, and it was obvious that she was going to fight him every inch of the way where Michael was concerned.

When White Fire felt eyes on him, he shifted his gaze to the upper windows of the two-story stone house. His heart skipped a beat when he found Michael standing at a window, holding the curtains aside as he peered down.

White Fire's insides lurched when Michael suddenly left the window, as though someone had purposely grabbed him and yanked him away.

That made White Fire even more determined to get his son out of that house today, if only for a short while. He *would* go horseback riding with him. He would be excited over having a pony of his very own.

His spine stiff, his blood throbbing nervously through his veins, White Fire dismounted. On foot, he led his horse and the pony down the narrow gravel drive.

When he reached the house, he tethered the steeds to the hitching rail. Without hesitation, he went and boldly knocked on the door.

When no one answered, White Fire understood that he was being ignored. This made him even more adamant that he would see his son today, that he would be with him, that he would give him his special gift.

And if Maureen and George Greer were not more gracious about this, White Fire would give up on taking it a day at a time with his son. He would whisk him away today and be in his right to do so. He was the boy's blood kin. No judge in America would deny him the child.

But not wanting to get into a court battle over Michael knowing that it might damage him forever, White Fire stood his ground and knocked until his knuckles grew sore.

Finally the door swung slowly open. A butler dressed in solid black was suddenly there, his eyes cold, his chin smugly lifted.

"Sir, I have been asked to tell you that Mr. and Mrs. Greer are indisposed this fine morning to whoever knocks at the door," the butler said. "So I must bid you good day, sir. Do try another day."

As the butler started to close the door, White Fire placed his hands against it, and with brute force, kept the door from closing.

"You can tell Mr. and Mrs. Greer that I have not come to see them," he said dryly. "They can *stay* indisposed. It is Michael that I wish—that I am *going* to see. And not only *see*. I am taking him on an outing."

"That will do for now, Payton," Maureen Greer said, addressing her butler with a sigh. "I see that the gentleman will not take no for an answer."

White Fire's eyes gleamed into Maureen's as she replaced the butler at the door.

"Why do you persist in coming here when you know that you are not wanted? That, actually, you are trespassing," Maureen said, her face flushing red from anger. "Can't you see that Michael does not want to see you? Wouldn't he be here if he did?"

A voice spoke up from the shadows of the foyer behind Maureen, causing hope to rise within White Fire. He looked past Maureen as his son spoke again, his voice filled with fear.

"I do want to see him . . . but . . . you forbid it," Michael said, tears falling from his eyes.

"Michael!" Maureen gasped, turning sharply to stare at him. "Get back to your room this instant. Do you hear?"

Hearing the hurt in his son's voice and the sternness in Maureen's, White Fire brushed quickly past her.

As Maureen stared in disbelief, he swept Michael into his arms and carried him from the house, outside to the porch.

"Son, I am glad you want to see me," White Fire said, so happy that Michael had spoken up and voiced his wishes. "Son, I could hardly wait until we could be together again."

"I had a dream," Michael said, wiping tears from his eyes. "In the dream I saw you and Mommy together . . . my *real* mommy. Although, I was so little, I *do* remember now so many things that I didn't before . . . before . . . the dream. Father, I remember a toy horse that you carved for me out of wood. I remember sitting on your lap as you carved it."

White Fire was stunned by what his son was saying he remembered.

And it had come to him in a dream?

He smiled, for he did know the power of dreams.

In them, many things of the future *and* past could be seen.

White Fire was thankful for his son's ability to dream. It was because of the Indian side of his heritage. The Indians put much weight in their dreams. They made decisions because of them.

He suddenly recalled Chief Gray Feather's dream: how he had seen White Fire sitting at his right side in the place of a son. He wondered what meaning there was in that dream. But now was not the time to delve into any dreams, except for his son's.

"Yes, I made you the toy," he said thickly. "It is at our home. I found it when I returned there recently. I will take you there soon and give it to you again, so that it will be yours forever."

"That would make me very happy," Michael said, smiling widely. "Father, one day will you tell me about your time away from me? How you lived? How you survived?"

"Yes, one day—" White Fire said, when he was interrupted by Maureen. She came out on the porch and stood stiffly at their side.

"Michael, you shouldn't be out here in the sun without a hat," she said, her hands clasped tightly before her. "You should have a cape around your shoulders!"

"Both the sun and the air will do my son good," White Fire said, glaring down at Maureen. "And today I plan to give him plenty of *both*."

"What do you mean?" Maureen asked faintly, paling.

"Do you see the pony?" White Fire said, more to Michael than to Maureen as he watched his son turn his head to stare at the steed. "I have brought it to you, Michael, as a gift from father to son."

"The pony is for me?" Michael said, scrambling from his arms.

Michael ran down the steps before Maureen could reach out and grab him. He went to the pony and began to stroke its rust-colored mane.

"I won't allow you to take him out on that . . . that . . . creature," Maureen said, puffing as her anger rose within her.

White Fire turned and frowned at her. He made two tight fists at his sides. "Did you not hear my son speak of things past?" he said dryly. "Do you not understand now that he remembers things about his mother? About me, his *father*? Do you not see that I could take him even now, and you could not stop me?"

"You wouldn't," Maureen gasped out, placing her hands to her throat as she took an unsteady step away from White Fire.

"No, I do not plan to change his home that quickly," White Fire said. "Not even if he asks me to. I do see the need in taking him from one household to the other gradually. He has had so much here that he will never have while living with me. I must first make him appreciate the smaller things in life for him to, in the end, truly accept them."

"But please don't take him on that . . . that thing today," Maureen pleaded. "It's so dangerous!"

"Only if I was not with him to see that he will be taught how to ride the pony properly," White Fire said.

Seeing the woman's building grief, realizing how

she would miss the child once he was gone, he softened his tone with her.

"Ma'am, I do understand how you are feeling about losing Michael to me," he said, his voice drawn. "I have been without my son for three years. One never adjusts to losing a son, *ever*, even . . . if that son was never truly theirs to begin with."

Maureen's eyes filled with tears. She stared up at White Fire for a moment longer. Then she broke into fitful sobs and ran inside the house.

White Fire went down the steps and knelt beside Michael. He placed his hands at the boy's shoulders and turned him to face him. "Son," he said, swallowing hard as he ran his fingers over Michael's pale, white face. He lifted his fingers to Michael's curls and cringed as he ran them through the thick tresses.

Then he slid his hands over his son's velvet suit, disgusted at the lace collar that lay around his neck.

"Father, can we go riding now?" Michael murmured, placing a soft hand to his cheek. "Can I ride my pony? I truly love it."

White Fire was touched deeply by Michael's trust in him. If not for Michael having remembered him in his dream, surely he would be frightened of him, for White Fire's appearance showed nothing of his white heritage. Except for those who knew of his mixed blood and saw him as a 'breed, everyone else saw him as an Indian through and through.

"Michael, for now I want you to ride with me on my horse," White Fire said, taking Michael's hand, and leading him over to the larger horse. "We will ride awhile on mine so that you can get used to being on a horse again. Then you can ride your own when I feel you are ready."

He placed Michael in his saddle. He untied the pony's reins and brought the pony up beside his steed. Still gripping the pony's reins, White Fire mounted his horse.

He then handed Michael the pony's reins.

"You hang on to these while we ride for a while on my horse," he said, smiling as Michael took the reins.

White Fire slid an arm around his son's tiny waist and held him in place as he wheeled his horse around and rode in a slow lope away from the Greer mansion. He could feel eyes on him and knew that Maureen was watching them.

He ignored her and absorbed the wonder of being with his son. That his son actually remembered him and loved him. It was sad that Michael could not be as happy about his true mother, for she had been taken from him forever.

One day soon he would take Michael to his mother's grave. That, too, was a part of him growing up and accepting life as it would be for him.

"The air and sun are warm," Michael said, smiling over his shoulder at his father. "It feels good."

"Days like today are made just for little boys like you," White Fire said, making a wide turn toward the open prairie of blowing grasses and wild flowers.

Michael laughed, then turned and gazed at the pony. "Can I ride him soon?" he asked. "Will you teach me how? I remember riding a pony when I was small, before you left and did not come back." He lowered his eyes. "Before Mommy died."

"Yes, before I was abducted by the Sioux and before your mommy died, you had your own pony, and though you were so tiny, you learned quickly how to ride it," White Fire said thickly. "Michael, *son*, turn and look at me."

When Michael turned his dark, trusting eyes up at him, White Fire swallowed hard. At this moment it was as though time was turned back to the day Michael was born, with his midnight dark eyes, and coal-black shock of hair. In his eyes back then there had been the same trust as there was today.

So much love for his child bubbled over inside White Fire that for a moment he could not speak from the joy of being with him again.

"Father, why did you want me to look at you?" Michael asked, his eyes innocently wide. "You suddenly look so sad."

"I am anything but sad," White Fire said, sighing. He smiled. "Son, there are so many things I wish to say to you. There are so many things I wish to teach you. From this day forth I will teach you many things that have been denied you. You have been denied the Indian side of your heritage too long. It is important that you know both sides of your heritage. You are part Indian. Never feel ashamed of that. Michael, Indians are a proud and courageous people. You should be proud to be a part of those people."

"I am proud to be your son," Michael said, turning and wrapping his arms around White Fire's neck. "I am so glad that the dream came to me and made me remember things the way they were."

"Dreams are friends," White Fire said, relishing this moment with his son.

When they came to a stream that wove, snakelike, through the meadow, he drew rein and stopped his horse. "The horses can get drinks here," he said, lifting Michael to the ground.

He slid from the saddle and led both horses to the water. Then he knelt down on his haunches and took Michael's hands. "You truly aren't afraid to ride the pony?" he asked, searching his son's eyes for any signs of fear, and seeing nothing but excitement.

"I have always liked horses," Michael said softly. "But my adopted mommy and daddy forbid them to me, as they forbid the outdoors to me. They treat me like a baby—like a *girl*."

Michael reached a hand up to his hair. "I hate curls," he said, gagging. "I want them cut off!"

"You do not have to cut your hair to be rid of curls," White Fire said, smiling at the boy's dislike of them. "They can be straightened. Then you can wear your hair like mine."

"Yes, I like yours," Michael said, reaching a hand to run it over the smoothness of White Fire's thick mane.

The horses whinnied, drawing Michael and White Fire apart.

"The pony wants me to ride it," Michael said, begging with his eyes to White Fire. "Can I? Now? Please?"

"You are not in the least bit afraid?" he asked, lifting Michael into his arms.

"Well, just a little," Michael said, giggling.

White Fire could feel Michael stiffen as he placed him in the tiny saddle. "Relax," he said softly. "I shall take the reins and lead the pony for a while. Then I will return the reins to you."

Eyes wide, Michael nodded.

As Michael clung to the pommel of the saddle, White Fire walked him back and forth beside the stream.

Then Michael reached for the reins and gave

them a soft yank. "I am ready to do it myself," he said, smiling at his father. "Can I have the reins? Can I?"

"If you truly believe you are ready," White Fire said, hesitating at giving the reins over to the child.

"I am ready," Michael said. "I remember how. I want to do it myself as you allowed me to when I was way smaller than I am now."

"Your memory amazes me," White Fire said, handing the reins to him. "Remembering is a gift. Thank the Great Spirit that he has blessed you with it, that he gave you cause to remember again things of your past."

"The Great Spirit is the same as God?" Michael questioned, lifting an eyebrow.

"Yes, the same as God," White Fire said. Then he stepped aside and watched as his son rode off in a slow lope, looking natural in the saddle. White Fire gazed heavenward and gave a silent thanks for small miracles.

Michael came back on his pony. "Ride with me now, please?" he asked, running a hand over the pony's mane.

White Fire swung himself into his saddle. But before they could ride off together, another horse and rider appeared a short distance away.

White Fire soon recognized the rider. "Flame," he whispered.

Chapter 18

Shall I love you like the wind, love,
That is so fierce and strong?
That sweeps all barriers from its path,
And reeks not right or wrong?

—R. W. Raymond

Flame couldn't believe her eyes when she saw White Fire only a short distance away. When she had gone to his cabin and found him gone, she had given up on seeing him today. She had then sought only to enjoy her momentary freedom from her tyrannical father. He was getting more unbearable as each day passed.

She tried to understand why he was so headstrong about her horseback riding. She *did* know the dangers. But she would not sit idly in her room embroidering or reading. Life was meant to be lived. She would live it.

She gazed at the child. She knew that he was White Fire's son without even being told. Although his skin was white, so many other things about the child resembled White Fire—the set of his jaw, the coal black hair, the dark eyes.

She smiled when White Fire started toward her on his white steed, his son beside him on his pony. She waved, then sank her heels into the flanks of her horse and rode in a hard gallop toward them.

Her heart beating excitedly inside her chest, Flame drew rein and brought her horse to a shimmying halt beside White Fire. He also drew a tight rein, his eyes wide and questioning as he gazed at her.

"White Fire, I went to your cabin," Flame said, before he had a chance to say anything. "I was so disappointed when I found that you were gone." She smiled broadly. "What luck that I found you."

His gaze swept over her. His pulse raced hot and swift through his veins at the very nearness . . . of the very *sight* of her. Today she had on riding clothes that were less constricting and formal. She wore a fully gathered, dark riding skirt made of yards of material, and a white, long-sleeved blouse. Its buttons were undone at the neck, revealing a teasing sight of her deep cleavage. Her hair was free of a hat and worn loose and flowing across her shoulders and down her back. Her cheeks were flushed pink from her brisk ride.

"Father, who is this lady?" Michael said, bringing White Fire out of his momentary trance. "How does she know your name? I heard you say the name Flame when you first saw her. Is that her name?"

"Yes, son, her name is Flame," White Fire said, his eyes now locked with Flame's. "How does she know my name? Michael, we are friends . . . very *good* friends."

"And so this is Michael," Flame said, riding around

to be next to Michael. She reached a hand out toward him. "I'm glad to make your acquaintance, Michael. I hope that you and I can be good friends."

Her gaze raked over him. She was aghast at the boy's attire, and how his adopted mother chose to make him wear his hair. She could not believe that any mother would want to make a boy appear as such a sissy.

Otherwise, up close, yes, she saw again his resemblance to White Fire. If his skin was copper . . .

Michael placed his tiny hand in Flame's, enjoying the feel of her buttery soft gloves against his flesh. He also loved her hair and eyes. Her eyes were so green. Her hair was so red. And if he were an older man like his father, he would fall quickly and madly in love with this woman.

"I would like to be your friend," Michael quickly said, his white teeth shining as he gave Flame one of his biggest smiles.

"Then friends we are," Flame said, laughing softly when she started to remove her hand and he still clung to it.

Seeing how quickly Flame and Michael were smitten with one another, White Fire smiled to himself. Perhaps he *could* expect things to work out for him and his son after all. He now thought that it would be easy to draw Michael into accepting Flame for a mother.

It did not even seem wrong that there were just twelve years between Michael and Flame. That surely would not be a deterrent in how they would get along as mother and son, for it was obvious that they already were drawn to one another.

Then White Fire thought of something else: of last

evening, and Flame's hasty flight from the fort. He must know why.

He felt compelled to scold her again about riding alone so often. She tempted fate too often with her foolhardiness.

He rode around and sidled his horse up next to Flame's. "I saw you at dusk last evening," he said, quickly drawing her eyes to him. "I saw you leave the fort in haste. That concerned me. I tried to follow you. By the time I got my horse, you were already out of sight. I searched, but never found you again. I waited on a knoll until I saw you go back through the gate into the fort."

Flame slid her hand free of Michael's. "Yes, I left home in haste last evening," she said softly. "Because of my father. He badgered and badgered me about where I had been yesterday. I was not about to tell him, for you know how enraged he would have been knowing you and I were together."

"But you *do* know the dangers of leaving the fort and riding off in such a way, especially at that time of evening," White Fire said, realizing how scolding his tone was the minute the words had escaped across his lips.

He saw an instant anger leap into Flame's eyes and knew that she did not appreciate him preaching to her after having just told him how upset she had gotten after her father had scolded her.

"You too?" she said, her eyes wavering. "White Fire, please don't start on me, also, about what I do and don't do. I am my own person. Why can't anyone see that?"

Near tears, she wheeled her horse around and rode away.

White Fire glanced down at Michael, whose eyes were wide from having listened to perhaps his first lovers' quarrel.

"Stay here, Michael," White Fire softly encouraged. "I will be only a moment."

Michael nodded.

White Fire rode after Flame.

When he caught up with her, he reached over and took her reins from her. Her eyes flashing angrily at him, he drew her reins tightly and stopped her horse as he brought his own to a quick stop.

"Give me back my reins," Flame cried, yanking hard and unsuccessfully on them.

"Not until you listen to what I have to say," White Fire said, glad to see her shoulders finally relaxing. "Darling Flame, I was wrong to scold you. It will not happen again."

"Thank you," Flame murmured, her lips quivering into a slow smile when he gave her reins back.

Then she looked past him at Michael. "Can I ride for a while with you and Michael?" she asked softly, the argument forgotten. "I love children. And he seems so special."

"Yes, very," he said, looking over his shoulder at his son.

Then he smiled at her. "You captivated him," he said, laughing softly. "I do believe you now have two men in love with you."

Flame's face flushed hot. "You do believe so, do you?" she murmured. She smiled into White Fire's eyes. "Nothing would make me happier than to be loved by both you and your son."

There was a moment of silence between them, when White Fire wanted so badly to reach over and grab Flame from her horse and onto his lap to kiss her. With innocent eyes of a watching child on them, he instead wheeled his horse around and rode away from Flame.

"Come on," he shouted over his shoulder, "let's go for that ride."

Flame laughed into the wind, then rode off after White Fire.

When they reached Michael, they rode on each side of him, and laughed, chatted, and had a wonderful time.

White Fire's chest swelled with pride to be with the woman he loved and his son at the same time, and seeing that they seemed naturally drawn together. He rode and listened to them having small talk, smiling at his son's true interest in Flame.

"How do you, a lady, know how to ride a horse so well?" Michael asked.

"How?" Flame said, looking past Michael at White Fire, then gazing at Michael again. "I was taught to ride by the master horsemen of St. Louis—the owners of great Clydesdale horses."

"What is a Clydesdale horse?" Michael asked.

"It is a horse much larger than the one me and your father are riding today," Flame said, remembering the thrill of her first time on one of the magnificent steeds. "The Clydesdale horses originated in Lanarkshire, Scotland, near the River Clyde. Not too many people know about them. A dear friend of my father brought four of them from Scotland. I was one of the first to ride them."

"Are they pretty?" Michael asked.

"Very," Flame said. "Their color is usually bay, dark brown, or black. You can recognize them by their white markings and the long hair around their hooves, which people call their feathers. It's quite a thrill to ride on one, up so high above the ground!"

"I would like to see a Clydesdale horse some day," Michael said.

"Perhaps you shall," Flame said, again looking over at his father. "Perhaps sometime in the future you will own one, yourself."

"I would like that," Michael said, beaming.

The more White Fire listened to Flame and Michael talking, the more he could see all of them having a future together. Would she truly not mind becoming an instant mother to a child Michael's age? With her love of freedom, could becoming a mother so quickly be stifling to her?

He would not think of that possibility, for never had White Fire wanted anything as much as he wanted to have both Michael and Flame with him forever.

Flame's eyes wavered as she gazed down at Michael. "I must leave you now," she murmured. "It's time for me to return home. My father has a tendency to worry too much about me."

White Fire rode over and took one of Flame's hands. "I want to see you again real soon," he said thickly. "When can we arrange it?"

"I'll come to your cabin when I get the chance," she murmured. "I just don't want to cause Father to get so angry at my antics that he sends me back to St. Louis. You know that he could do that, White Fire, and there would be nothing much I could do about it." She paused and laughed softly, then said, "Except perhaps dive overboard and swim my way back to you."

"Do you know how to swim as well as you ride a horse?" Michael asked, not understanding that she was just joking.

She looked at Michael. "I'll have you know I can swim as good as any fish in the Mississippi River," she said, laughing again.

"I don't know how to swim," Michael said solemnly, lowering his eyes. Then he looked quickly up at his father. "I am so glad that you taught me how to ride when I was small, so that I could ride with you today." He looked up at Flame. "Can you teach me how to swim someday?" he asked, his eyes innocently wide.

"Why, Michael, I'd love to teach you how to swim and anything else you have failed to be taught by your adoptive family," Flame said. She slid from the saddle and went to him. She reached up and embraced him, melting inside when he wrapped his tiny arms around her neck and returned the hug.

Then she pulled away from him and placed a gentle hand on his cheek. Then she went back and swung herself into her saddle. "I'll see you soon," she said, smiling at White Fire. She then gazed at Michael. "Hopefully you, too, Michael."

Touched deeply by her feelings for his son, almost speechless because of it, White Fire watched Flame ride away at a brisk clip.

"Father, are you going to marry her?"

The question, the seriousness of Michael's voice while asking it, drew White Fire's eyes back around. He smiled at Michael. "Yes, I do believe I am," he said. "How do you feel about that?"

"Am I going to live with you again, Father?" Michael asked.

"As soon as I feel it is in your best interest, yes, you will be living with me again," White Fire said thickly.

"Then I am very happy over your plans to marry Flame," Michael said, his eyes dancing. "That means that I will also be living with her."

"Yes, I do believe that we will all be living together as a family," White Fire said, laughing. "Son, it pleases me clean to my bones that you like Flame so much."

"I do," Michael said. "Very, very much.

"Can I go home now and pack my bags?" Michael then asked, his voice eager.

White Fire was drawn aback by the suddenness of the question. He was at a loss for words.

Then he reached over and grabbed Michael from his horse and placed him on his lap facing him. He placed a hand beneath Michael's chin and lifted it so that their eyes met and held.

"Michael, I so badly wish to have you with me again," he said. "And you *will* be. *Soon.* But things must be right, first, before I can take you from one household to another. My life must be set in order so that *yours* will be in order when you come to live with me again."

"Like what, Father?" Michael asked, lifting an eyebrow.

"It would not be fair to you to bring you to my

house just yet," White Fire said. "After I marry Flame, I will then come for you."

"But why must I wait?"

"Because you need a woman to be a mother, to do mother things that a father does not know how to do," White Fire said in a rush of words. "I plan to marry Flame, but it just can't happen overnight. There are obstacles in the way. Hopefully, we can rid ourselves of such obstacles real soon so that Flame and I can get married."

"I will be patient," Michael said, flinging his arms around his father's neck, hugging him. "Father, I am so glad that you aren't dead. . . . That you came back to me."

"If only I could have returned sooner," White Fire said, returning Michael's hug.

Then he picked Michael up by the waist and put him back on his pony. "We'd better get you back home or I do believe Maureen and George might send out a search party for us," he said, laughing softly.

They rode beneath the sunshine and through the warm autumn air, the air perfumed with the fragrances of the wild flowers that dotted the ground like a colorful patchwork quilt.

When they reached the Greer mansion, White Fire regretted with all of his heart having to give his son back to the care of the Greers. But one thing for sure, Maureen Greer truly loved Michael. It was in the way she grabbed him and hugged him when he dismounted his pony. Her look of desperation showed her intense caring for him.

White Fire could not help but feel something for

the woman, especially a gratefulness for her having taken such good care of Michael in his absence, and for her loving him so much.

He knew now that when he did take Michael away from the Greers, he would still share Michael with them. He would permit them to come for him and have outings with Michael. It would otherwise be heartless of him if he forced them to altogether forget this child they had grown to love these past three years.

Maureen picked Michael up in her arms. As she held him, she turned to White Fire. "Thank you for bringing him home to me," she murmured.

"I shall return soon to be with him again," White Fire said, reaching a hand out to touch Michael on the cheek. "Michael, I will see you again real soon."

"Can I keep the pony with me here?" Michael said, his eyes pleading.

White Fire gazed into Maureen's eyes. Seeing her set, stubborn jaw, he sighed with disappointment. She was still against Michael having the pony.

"Yes, the pony stays here, Michael," White Fire said, feeling just as stubborn as Maureen. He ignored her quick gasp. He leaned over and gave Michael a soft kiss on the cheek, stared at Maureen again, then swung himself into his saddle and rode away.

"Good-bye, Father!" Michael cried. "See you again soon, Father!"

White Fire gave his son a wide smile over his shoulder. "Soon, son!" he shouted back. "Soon!"

He felt as though a piece of his heart was being left behind as he rode away. He didn't dare take another look at his son, for fear that he would turn back and get him.

He rode in a hard gallop out of Pig's Eye, and when his cabin came into sight through a break in the trees, he saw a horse tethered at his hitching rail. White Fire tightened his reins and brought his steed to a quick halt. "Chief Gray Feather?" he whispered.

Thinking it was the chief, he rode on and dismounted and went inside his cabin, stopping short with surprise when he saw who was there, sitting in a chair, waiting for him.

"Colonel Russell?" White Fire said, his eyebrows rising in a question. He feared hearing the reason why the colonel himself was there, instead of a lieutenant sent to summon him to the fort. Surely it was about Flame.

The colonel had come to forbid White Fire to ever see her again.

Perhaps he had spied on Flame and had seen them together even today.

"White Fire, I need your help," Colonel Russell said, rising from the chair. He held a pair of gloves in one hand and nervously slapped them against the palm of his other hand as he gazed with unsteady eyes at him.

"What sort of help?" White Fire asked warily, expecting the colonel to speak Flame's name at any moment.

"As you know, I am aware of your closeness with Colonel Josiah Snelling when he was alive and in command of Fort Snelling," Colonel Russell said, his voice tight and drawn.

"Yes, we became close, *very* close," White Fire said guardedly.

Colonel Russell sighed heavily. His eyes lowered. Then they shot up again and gave White Fire a steady gaze. "Do you believe in the supernatural?" he blurted out. "In ghosts?"

"What?" White Fire asked, his eyebrows rising with surprise. "What do you mean? Why would you ask me such questions as that?"

"White Fire, I am a witness to strange occurrences these past few nights in the Snelling mansion, especially in Josiah's upstairs study," Colonel Russell blurted out. "I . . . it . . . it is as though I feel Josiah's presence there. Also . . . also . . . things aren't always where I have last left them. I can't help but believe that Colonel Snelling's ghost is there. Go back to the fort with me. Go into Josiah's study. Tell me if you notice anything strange."

White Fire scarcely breathed as he thought back to how he himself had recently felt while alone in Josiah Snelling's study. He *had* felt a presence there. He had felt as though Josiah had been there, as though if White Fire had called his name, Josiah would have somehow answered him!

The thought of Colonel Russell now having experienced the same sort of feeling made White Fire's heart race with the wonder of it.

"Yes, I will go with you," he was quick to say.

"*Now,* White Fire," Colonel Russell said, taking him by the elbow, and whisking him back outside to the horses. "Come with me now."

White Fire rode with Colonel Russell to the Snelling

mansion. His eyes were on the upstairs study window as he tethered his horse to the hitching rail.

His heart thudded as he went inside the house and up the stairs that led to the study. He did not even think about Flame and wonder where she might be as he entered the room.

He was filled with all sorts of anxieties, none of which at this moment included a woman.

His eyes wide, his breathing shallow, White Fire and Colonel Russell moved slowly around the study. The colonel's eyes never left White Fire.

'Well?" Colonel Russell softly questioned. "Do you feel anything? Please tell me it is my imagination working overtime."

The scent of pipe tobacco being smoked suddenly wafted up inside White Fire's nose. He quickly recognized the smell. It was quite familiar to him. It was Josiah's own personal brand, which had been brought from France.

He sent the colonel a quick glance. "Have you recently smoked a pipe in this study?" he asked warily. "Like just before you came for me? For I smell the distinct smell of a freshly smoked pipe. I recognize the tobacco. It is Josiah Snelling's own personal brand of tobacco."

Colonel Russell paled. Shaken by what White Fire had said, he grabbed hold of the desk to steady himself. "No, I haven't smoked any pipes in this study," he said, his voice breaking. "Nor have I *ever.* Only cigars."

White Fire stared at the colonel in disbelief, realizing that he was involved with something quite strange here, for he was certainly smelling the scent of Colonel Snelling's pipe tobacco. He recalled the many times when the colonel would enjoy smoking his pipe while White Fire was in the study with him.

Colonel Russell stared at the pipes on the desk. "I wish I had rid this damn office of everything that was Josiah Snelling's," he grumbled. "The pipes especially. Damn it all to hell, I don't like what's happening. I don't like it at all."

White Fire turned to the colonel. "Would you mind leaving the study?" he asked, his voice drawn. "This would give me the opportunity to check things out more carefully." He paused, swallowing hard, then said, "It would allow me some time alone with whatever . . . or whomever . . . might be here, be it a ghost, or whatever."

"Lord almighty," Colonel Russell stammered out, then left the study in a rush of footsteps.

The door closed, leaving White Fire alone. He began walking slowly around the room, his eyes darting here and there, his senses alive, waiting for what might happen next.

After only a few minutes of being alone, his back stiffened, for he was very aware of a lot of strong energy and emotion from the past which seemed suddenly to be in the room.

He took a quick step backward and he gasped when a mysterious white, shimmering light appeared along the far wall, then moved closer to him.

Scarcely breathing, trying to stay rational and alert during this eerie happening, White Fire continued to watch the shimmering light as it approached the old oak desk that Colonel Snelling had personally chosen those many years ago for his study.

White Fire gasped and his knees grew weak from wonder when the light now turned into the face of a man, then his full figure in a cavalry officer's uniform, a pipe clasped between his teeth and pursed lips. There was no doubt that White Fire was being visited by his old friend Josiah Snelling.

Breathless, stunned, White Fire watched as the wavering, hazy likeness of his friend settled into the chair behind the desk.

The likeness of Colonel Snelling rested the pipe he had been smoking on an ashtray and took another pipe from the pipe stand.

In awe, White Fire watched as the colonel lit the pipe and began smoking it.

"Josiah?" White Fire found the courage to say. "I don't understand how this can be happening, but I welcome the opportunity to be with you again."

He could tell by Josiah's wide smile that he was glad to see that White Fire was at the fort, alive and well.

"It was with much regret when I returned from my three year captivity with the Sioux and discovered that you were . . . were . . ." White Fire stammered, unable to say the word "dead."

He watched as the colonel became more absorbed in thumbing through one of his journals, than in listening to him.

"Josiah, I so miss you," White Fire blurted out. "Never have I had, or will ever have again, such a friend as you."

When the likeness of the colonel stayed absorbed in the journal, not responding to White Fire's comments about their friendship, it was then that he

understood that the colonel had come back to him
in this way not to renew their friendship, but to show
him something that was in the journal.

A particular page was found and left open for him
to see. He went behind the desk and started to
read it.

Instead, he was stunned by the quickness in how
the colonel's likeness faded away, leaving no trace
of him having been there . . . except for the one missing pipe. He had taken the pipe with him into his
afterworld. But the smell of the tobacco lingered on.

White Fire looked quickly around the room to see
if the mysterious light might reappear, and with it the
likeness of his friend. But he saw nothing except for
the usual furniture, the rows after rows of books,
and—

White Fire's eyes widened and his heart skipped
a beat when suddenly someone playfully slapped him
on the back. He swung around and saw that no one
was there!

But he knew that he was still not alone. Although
he could not see Josiah, he knew that he was there.
The slap on the back was like those which Josiah had
always playfully given him when they laughed and
chatted together about things of interest to them
both.

"You are still here," White Fire whispered. "I feel
it. I *know* it."

His eyes were drawn quickly back to the journal
when the pages fluttered as though a breeze from a
window had stirred them.

He looked quickly at the windows, and then at the

double doors that led to a balcony, and saw that none
of them were open.

"You are still trying to tell me something about the
journal, aren't you?" White Fire whispered.

He rushed back to the desk and sat down in the
chair. Slowly his eyes pored over the entries, growing
cold the longer he looked and the more he read.

"So now I see why you have come back," White
Fire said, the journal entries showing that Colonel
Russell was spending tons of money to build up the
arsenal at the fort, purchasing many more firearms
than could ever be used, unless . . . the colonel was
planning an attack against the Indians in this area.

"You came to warn me about the arms buildup,"
White Fire said, gazing slowly around the room,
hoping to see the colonel's likeness again. "You, who
kept peace in the area, at all cost, want Colonel
Russell stopped. You want to avert a tragedy for this
entire area."

He understood well enough what this all meant.
The Indian tribes of the Minnesota Territory had
always visited the fort and disposed of their furs
peacefully. They had always been given cause to trust
the white-eyed pony soldiers. They would never
expect an all-out attack on their villages.

For the sake of Minnesota, the red and white skins
alike, White Fire must see that Colonel Russell was
stopped.

White Fire quickly copied the figures from the
pages of the journal onto a piece of paper and
slipped it into his breeches front pocket.

He rose and looked slowly around the room. He
gave a mock salute. "Josiah, all of the Minnesota

Territory thanks you," he whispered. Then he left the room.

He found Colonel Russell pacing just outside the door. He stopped and stared at White Fire. "Well?" he said nervously. "What do you think? Do I have anything to fear?"

"What do I think?" White Fire asked, biting his tongue to keep from speaking up how he truly felt about the deviousness of this heartless colonel.

He found it hard to think that Flame was related to this evil man. Nothing about them seemed alike.

"I think it is all a lot of foolishness," White Fire said. "It's hogwash. You were surely imagining things. There is no ghost." He laughed throatily. "Who believes in ghosts, anyway?"

"Thank God," Colonel Russell said, his shoulders relaxing.

"Send for me if you need me for anything else," White Fire said as he headed for the stairs. He looked at the colonel over his shoulder. "Like interpreting."

Frowning, White Fire hurried outside. He swung himself into his saddle and left right away for Fort Parker, a fort several miles downriver from Fort Snelling. He would meet with Colonel Edwards, who was in command at Fort Parker. He would explain the situation to the colonel and suggest that the colonel send a replacement for Colonel Russell. If not, there would be the massacre of massacres in the Minnesota Territory! Both Indians and whites alike would suffer many losses.

White Fire's thoughts went to his son, knowing that, for his sake, a war *must* be averted!

His jaw tightened when his thoughts went to

Flame. He now knew that he must rush things along with her, for once Colonel Russell realized that he had been duped by White Fire, Flame could be lost to him, forever!

This made him ride at a harder gallop along the riverbank. He must make Colonel Edwards understand the danger of Colonel Russell staying in command. He must. Colonel Russell must be removed immediately.

White Fire would *not* allow anyone else to tamper with his own future ever again, as did the Sioux those long three years!

Chapter 19

Yes! This is love, the steadfast and the true,
The immortal glory which hath never set;
The best, the brightest boon the heart e'er knew;
Of all life's sweets the very sweetest yet!

—Charles Swain

Too restless to return home, Flame had rode for quite a while, exploring some more of the land that she was not familiar with,

Then she had gone to White Fire's cabin to wait for him.

Finding the door unlocked, she wandered inside, as though she belonged there. She wanted to tell him of all of the feelings that were overwhelming her, that the time spent with him and Michael had been wonderful, that it had made her feel as though she belonged to them both.

She wanted to tell him that, adoring children, having always dreamed of having children of her own, she had fallen instantly in love with Michael.

She had a need to tell all of those things to White

Fire, though she was quite certain that he had seen it while she chatted and laughed with Michael.

She scoffed at her father's warning, that she was too young to become an instant mother. She could not help but think that just possibly that gave her father more cause to be upset over the building relationship between her and White Fire than him being, in part, Indian.

"Like he tried with Mother, Father wants to control *me*," Flame whispered to herself. "He sees me only as a possession, not someone he loves from the depths of his heart."

This hurt her deeply, yet she had grown used to knowing this about her father and had lived life as she would live it, ignoring him and the demands he made on her.

Wandering slowly around the cabin as the midday sun poured like satin streamers through the windows, Flame gazed again at White Fire's furnishings. Her gloves removed and thrust inside one of her front skirt pockets, she ran her fingers delicately over the smoothness of an oak table. She then moved her hands over a thickly cushioned chair. It was so pretty and cheerful with its fabric bright with designs of woodland flowers.

She lifted a candlestick and admired it. It was made of wood and she wondered if White Fire might have made it. She set it back on the table and wandered to the window to take a look outside. Shoving the yellowed muslin curtain aside, she was reminded of who had made them. Mary. White Fire's wife, Mary.

Flame had not allowed herself to feel the slightest bit of jealousy that so much inside this cabin had been chosen by his wife. Mary was now just a memory. Flame was real and there for White Fire.

"White Fire, where are you?" she whispered as she peered through the pane of glass.

She could not help but doubt that he would be gone this long with his son, for it was apparent that Michael would tire easily from the long ride, despite the invigorating effect of the fresh air.

But if White Fire was no longer with Michael, she wondered where he might have gone. There were to be no councils held at the fort today between her father and visiting Indians. So there would be no need for White Fire to be there in the capacity of interpreter. Sighing, Flame turned away from the window.

She stopped and gazed at the bedroom that lay only a few footsteps away. Her heart began beating more soundly at the thought of being there with White Fire, of being on the bed, of him kissing her, of him telling her how much he loved and adored her.

Flame closed her eyes as she recalled the one time with him when their feelings had gone further than just an embrace. She shivered sensually and hugged herself as she remembered how wonderful it had felt for him to slide his hand inside her blouse, his flesh hot against her own. Nothing had ever felt so delicious. It had stirred such a feeling of blissful excitement within her very soul.

The sound of a horse approaching brought Flame quickly out of her reverie. She turned back toward the window and gazed outside just in time to see White Fire dismount and whirl his reins around the hitching rail.

She smiled as she saw him stop and look at her horse. She giggled when she saw his slow smile, knowing that he recognized the horse.

As he came inside and gazed down at Flame with his midnight dark eyes, she drifted into his arms. "I could not go home just yet," she murmured, her cheeks flushed hot with excitement. "I didn't think you'd mind if I came here and waited for you."

He wrapped her within his arms. "You know that I would love to always find you here on my return from my outings," he said, his voice husky as his arousal for her could not be denied.

"It seems forever since I first arrived," Flame said, searching his eyes. "What took you so long? Surely you haven't been with Michael this long?"

Unsure of whether or not he should confide in her about what he had just done at Fort Parker, White Fire slipped away and went to stare out the window.

"White Fire?" Flame said, going to his side. She took one of his hands and encouraged him to turn and face her. "Where *have* you been? You seem so troubled."

When he still said nothing to her, but just gazed at her with a strange sort of light in his eyes, Flame became uneasy.

"White Fire, does your behavior have anything to do with my father?" she blurted out.

Knowing that she must know what he had done, regardless of how she might react to it, he framed her face between his hands.

"Yes, it has to do with your father," he said somberly.

He took her by a hand and led her to a chair before the fireplace.

After she was comfortably in the chair, he scooted

another chair over and sat down and faced her. He gazed intently into her eyes.

"Today, Flame, when I returned home from my ride with you and Michael, I found your father here," he said softly. "Your father asked me to go with him to the fort. He asked me to go there for a particular reason."

He proceeded to tell her about his experience with Josiah Snelling's ghost, and Josiah's reason for making his unusual appearance to White Fire.

He even told her about having gone to Fort Parker, to inform on her father to the commandant of the fort. He told her that her father was going to be replaced soon, perhaps even court-martialed, and that haste must be made to avert a tragedy from happening in the Minnesota Territory.

Flame was pale from the knowledge, yet she was not all that surprised. "I have always known the ruthless side of my father," she said solemnly. "That was, in part, why my mother divorced him."

She eased his hands away from her face, then rose from the chair and stood staring into the gray ashes on the grate of the fireplace left from the prior evening's cook fire.

"I . . . I . . . knew that I would have to be faced with my father's ruthlessness when I came here to live with him," she murmured. Then she swung around and gazed down at White Fire. "But I had to chance it," she said, sighing. "I would have chanced anything for the possibility of finding you."

White Fire rose and drew Flame into his arms. Their eyes met and held. "You cared that much for a man you had only met that one time?" he murmured.

"Does that mean that you care twice as much for that man now? Enough to marry him?"

"Yes, oh, yes," Flame said, shivering with delight when his lips came to hers in a powerful, heated kiss.

She clung to him as their bodies strained together hungrily. She was blinded with the rush of need that overwhelmed her. She wanted so much more than an embrace . . . than a kiss. She wanted all of him!

Yet she could not be shameful enough to reveal this need to him by speaking it aloud. She hoped that her kiss, her body pressed hungrily against his, would be enough for him to know that she wanted to make love with him.

Her body was one massive heartbeat as he kissed her a moment longer, then he stepped away from her.

"Flame, should your father discover that it was I who turned him in for his illegal activities, who is to say what he will do?" White Fire said. "For certain he will do everything within his power to keep us apart."

He clasped his hands onto her shoulders. "Flame, marry me," he said huskily. "Marry me *today*, before it's too late."

Flame's lips parted in a light gasp. Her eyes widened. "We can't," she said, her voice quavering with emotion. "Don't you see, White Fire? When Father finds out that we're married, and that we did it behind his back, he will find a way to annul the marriage."

She drifted into his arms and clung to him. "Please wait for just a while longer," she murmured. "I will find a way soon to convince Father how much I love you."

"But there is not much time," White Fire said, placing his hands at her waist, gently easing her away from him. He gazed intently into her eyes. "Who is to say how quickly your father will be ordered from Fort Snelling?" he said. "If he is not court-martialed, or at least arrested, and is, instead free, he will be out for blood. Mine."

"He wouldn't dare harm you," Flame said, her voice tight. "He *won't* harm you."

She twined her arms around his neck and brought his mouth down to hers. She flicked her tongue across his bottom lip, then kissed him with an unleashed passion.

He was unable to stop himself from this need that had eaten away at his gut from that first moment he had seen Flame step from the riverboat when she had first arrived at the Minnesota Territory. Tired of delaying their togetherness, White Fire stepped away from Flame and reached out his arms and swept her fully into them.

Their eyes locked, their hearts pounding, he carried her to his bedroom and started to lay her on the bed, but she clung to him, preventing it.

"Please don't lay me on the bed unless you plan to make love to me," she murmured, her eyes wavering at his as she recalled how he had earlier fought against making love to her. "White Fire, I love you so much. Please show me how much you love *me*."

Not having to be asked twice, his loins on fire and aching with building ecstasy, he gently laid her on the bed. Then he stood up beside it, and as Flame watched, he undressed.

His clothes and moccasins tossed aside, White Fire stood there for a moment to see her reaction to his total nudity . . . to his arousal that was so evident. He could tell by her eyes, by how wide they were as she gazed at that part of his anatomy which pained him so from need, that she had most certainly never seen a naked man before. He was glad that he didn't see fear in her eyes. Instead there was an innocence in that first look at a man's sex.

Flame could hardly control the erratic beat of her heart that seeing him nude caused. His body was so hard, so *ready*. A part of her was afraid of his hugeness. Another part of her could only imagine how such endowment could pleasure a woman.

She had read books her mother had tried to deny her as she had grown up. She had been curious and in need of answers to the strange feelings that were stirring within her body as her breasts had begun to blossom and tiny curls of hair had begun to sprout at the juncture of her thighs. Although she had never seen pictures of a naked man, while feeding her curiosity with the books obtained from other friends, who had obtained them from the hidden drawers of their mothers' bedrooms, she had read about how a man *should* look. Also, while reading the forbidden literature, she had felt the thrill of how it might feel to have a man touch her where she had strangely throbbed.

Now, here it was, instead of being confined to the pages of a book. Flame was aglow with the passion that made her head reel with pleasure.

Without any more undue hesitation, Flame rose from the bed and stood facing White Fire as she slowly unbuttoned her blouse.

She watched the need darken his eyes as she opened her blouse and fully revealed her well-rounded, thick breasts to him.

Her heart pounded as her own desire surged. She

tossed her blouse aside, feeling nothing even akin to shame for being so brazenly bold while in the presence of a man. She reached around and undid her skirt at the back. Then she slowly slid it down past her hips and let it fall to rest around her ankles on the floor.

Breathing hard, her fingers trembled as she finished disrobing then stood square shouldered and still as White Fire's gaze raked slowly, approvingly, over her.

Suddenly he swept her up into his arms again. His eyes locked with hers, he again placed her on the bed. The startling beauty of her naked body had made a fiery fever in his loins.

And now, as her hair spread out like a huge red blossom beneath her, he trembled and knelt down over her.

The white of her skin meeting the copper of his, his lips brushing her throat, she bent under him.

Then he kissed her, hotly, deeply, his hands on her breasts, kneading. His senses swam as he felt the utter softness of her breasts and felt the nipples harden at once against his palms.

Flame abandoned herself to the wondrous feelings that were awash throughout her. There was only now. There was only them. There were only the wonders of touching, throbbing, burning!

But when she felt the velvet tightness of his heat probing where no man had been before, she could not help but grow tense with apprehension. The books she had read had warned of a moment of pain upon the man's first entry into a woman.

White Fire felt her body tighten and her breath catch. He swept his hands up to her face. He gazed endearingly into her eyes. "Trust me," he whispered. "What we are about to share is worth your brief moment of pain."

Eyes wide, her pulse racing, Flame swallowed hard, then nodded. "Hold me," she murmured.

He gathered her into his arms. He held her with an exquisite tenderness, as though she might be a delicate flower whose stem might break. He brought his mouth down on her lips and kissed her.

The press of his lips, so mesmerizing, so warm, made Flame forget why she had only moments before been tense with apprehension. She returned the kiss with a wild abandon. She opened her legs more widely to him when she felt him begin to slowly enter her.

Her whole body quivered and she moaned when the moment of pain grabbed at her consciousness.

Then, when he buried himself more deeply inside her, placing his maleness perfectly within her, he fell into a wild, dizzying rhythm with the slow thrusting of his pelvis. Her heart soared. As he moved within her, she learned quickly that the feelings of ecstasy were intensified if she lifted her own hips and moved with him.

Her spasmodic gasps filled the air as he filled her, over and over again, his powerful hips thrusting, her hips gyrating in rhythm with his movements.

She moaned when his mouth slid from her mouth and his lips moved over one of her nipples, licking, softly biting, then licking again.

Almost wild with the building pleasure, Flame ran her fingers through White Fire's thick, black hair.

She then ran her hands down his muscled, copper back to his thrusting hips.

The feeling came to her all at once, the explosion of ecstasy claiming her so quickly, she was startled by the intensity of the rapture that overtook her.

She clung. She sighed. She rocked with him.

She moaned as White Fire still thrust inside her in steady, heated, deep movements.

She breathed hard as his hold on her tightened and his lips came to hers in a frenzy of kisses. She knew that he was nearing his own release and wondered if it would be as magnificently wonderful as hers.

White Fire covered her mouth with his lips and kissed her hotly, deeply, the explosion of his ecstasy near. He had felt her own spasms of rapture, glad that he had given her such pleasure. But wanting to fulfill his own hungry needs, he held her as though in a vise and plunged over and over again inside her.

The explosion soon claimed him. His body shook and quaked with spasms as he thrust endlessly deeper into her, his seed filling her with an instant warmth.

Afterward, they lay together, their legs entwined. He leaned up over her and tenderly kissed her eyelids closed, then nestled her close at his side.

"Are you all right?" he finally asked when she had yet to say anything since their lovemaking.

Her eyes closed, and still in a state of euphoria, Flame smiled lazily and nodded.

"Flame, I guess you know that I am yours for as long as there will be stars in the heavens," White Fire whispered, then showered her breasts with warm kisses.

"You *are* the stars," Flame said, slowly opening her eyes. "You are the sun, the moon, the wind. You are everything to me."

He kissed her mouth with a lazy warmth. Then he sat up and drew her up to sit on his lap, to straddle him. "You are only eighteen," he said thickly. "Do you truly wish to marry me, an older man, a man who has a son who is six?"

"Darling, I came here today after my outing with you and Michael mainly to tell you how much I love not only you, but also your son," she said, glad to see his eyes take on a glow of pleasure at her words. "I do want to marry you and I *do* wish to be a mother to Michael."

"But you still think we should wait?" he asked, forking an eyebrow.

"I fear my father's wrath too much not to," Flame said, her voice drawn. "I'm going to talk to him. I'm going to make him see reason."

"Do you truly think that is possible where you and I are concerned?" White Fire asked somberly.

"It *has* to be possible," Flame said. She brushed a kiss across his brow, then rushed from the bed. "I've been gone for way too long. Father is surely having fits."

"And you expect to get him to listen to reason?" White Fire said, sour bitterness in his voice. He left the bed and pulled on his fringed breeches. "I doubt he even knows the meaning."

"I must give it a try," Flame said, hurrying into the rest of her clothes.

She ran her fingers through her hair to straighten it. Then she thought not to worry about it. It would just look windblown to her father. He would never think that it had gotten tangled this much while she had been making maddening love with the man she would soon marry.

"My husband," she said, flinging herself into White Fire's arms, hugging him. "Soon you will be my *husband*."

White Fire did not allow her to see his frown, nor know his doubts. He would allow her to have this faith in her father. Soon enough she would discover how wrong she was ever to believe that he would allow her to marry White Fire without a fight.

Chapter 20

Do you ask what the birds say?
The sparrow, the dove, the linnet and thrust say,
"I love, and I love!"

—Samuel Taylor Coleridge

Flame avoided her father's glare as he sat at the far end of the dining table from her. He had met her at the gate when she had arrived from her outing—from her lovemaking with White Fire. He had told her that he was just getting ready to send the cavalry out to look for her.

She shivered even now at the thought of how it might have been had the soldiers arrived at White Fire's cabin in their search for her while she and he were making love.

The soldiers might have surrounded the cabin. She could even envision them firing at the cabin in rapid bursts of gunfire.

Her thoughts so morbid, so frightening, Flame forced them away and again gazed at her father, whose eyes still had not left her. In them there was such a coldness, such annoyance.

"Reshelle, I'm thinking of sending you back to St. Louis," he said, his voice a monotone. "You are out of hand here in the wilderness. You won't listen to anything I say. You ride off on that damn horse of yours at the drop of a hat. All I have to do is look at you crosswise and you are off to only hell knows where."

The threat to send her away was real enough for Flame. She had worried that the strained relationship between herself and her father would make him seek the easiest way out. To be rid of her altogether was his out.

Knowing that she might say the wrong things if she did not take the time to think before she spoke, Flame picked up her fork and began eating the roast pork from her plate. All around her candles glowed from fancy candle holders, wall sconces, and the chandeliers. The large oak table was covered with a lacy, fine linen tablecloth. Goblets of sheer crystal, china from France, and gold flatware from Italy, graced the table, along with piles of rich foodstuffs on fancy gilt-edged platters.

On a side table, cream puffs, cherry and apple pies, and cinnamon rolls covered with gobs of white icing, waited to be chosen for dessert.

"Reshelle, did you hear what I said?" Colonel Russell said, banging the dull end of his fork on the table to draw her attention.

Her hair swirled into a fancy chignon atop her head, with diamond combs glittering from the folds, and wearing a low-swept green satin gown, with rubies sparkling at her ivory throat, Flame looked quickly at her father.

"Yes, I heard," she murmured, her cheeks flushed pink from the strain of the moment. "And, Father, your still calling me Reshelle is only one way of proving how little you care about what I want, or desire. Yes, you can think you might rid yourself of the bother of having me around by sending me back to St. Louis, to force me on some unwilling relative of ours, or by locking me away in a convent. But you know that is not at all what I want."

She placed her fork on the table. Her fingers trembled as she twined them around the stem of a goblet. She slowly turned the goblet around as she gazed with defiance at her father.

"Father, do you truly care about what I want?" she asked softly. "Do you truly care about me at all?"

Colonel Russell's face flooded with color. His eyes narrowed and squinted as he gave Flame a dark frown, the sleek lines of his uniform and the shine of its gold buttons a sight that Flame had grown to resent. The uniform meant authority. That seemed to be her father's guideline in life. He had to be the one who gave orders. He expected everyone to obey them.

"I see that you are having trouble answering my questions," Flame said, sighing heavily. "You know that you would not be able to say what I would like to hear."

"You are wrong," Colonel Russell said, clearing his throat nervously. "I *do* care for you, Resh—er . . . I mean . . . Flame. It's just that I always have so much on my mind I find it hard to show my feelings toward you."

His jaw tightened. "And your behavior warrants
scoldings more than my confessions of how I feel
about you," he was quick to interject.

"Don't you know, Father, that you cause much of
the behavior that you resent?" Flame said, sliding her
hand away from the glass. She fidgeted with the
white linen napkin that lay across her lap. "If you
would just once treat me like . . . like . . . a daughter
instead of the soldiers under your command, I truly
believe I might not be so hasty to—"

He interrupted her. "To go and meet with the
'breed?" he said, his voice low and measured. He
laughed shrewdly. "Of course you weren't going to
say that, were you?" he said menacingly.

Flame rose so quickly from her chair it toppled
over behind her. "You see?" she cried, her voice
breaking. "Just when I thought we were beginning to
have a civil conversation, you have to turn into that
ogre of a man who just . . . who just . . ."

She couldn't find the words she wanted to say
quickly enough. Yes, he was right to accuse her of
meeting with White Fire. Yet it was the way in which
he threw the subject of White Fire in her face which
hurt her to the quick.

Brushing past the fallen chair, Flame rushed from
the room. Blindly, she climbed the stairs that took
her to the upper floor. She then ran to her room and
closed the door behind her.

As she leaned against the closed door, tears flowed
across her cheeks as she thought of White Fire and
how she wished to be with him.

And she hadn't even been able to talk to her father
about their marriage plans.

"But he wouldn't listen, anyhow," she whispered,

brushing the tears from her cheeks with the back of her hand.

Then she thought of what White Fire had told her about her father, about him surely being sent from the fort in the next few days, or perhaps even arrested.

"I have to set things right now, or perhaps never," she whispered.

But then again, she recalled how her father had only moments ago threatened to send her back to St. Louis to live with relatives, or to a convent.

"He can't do that," she sobbed. "He . . . just . . . can't!"

"Reshelle, open the door," she heard her father say outside in the corridor.

When she didn't respond, he tried another approach. "Flame, I'm sorry about having said the wrong things a moment ago," he said, his voice drawn. "Open the door. Let's continue our talk. I promise to keep a civil tongue."

The fact that he had actually called her Flame a second time tonight sent a ray of hope into her heart that just perhaps he *might* listen to reason.

And if he wanted to get rid of her so badly, surely he could see that it could easily be done by her getting married.

"But to a man who is half white and half Indian?" she whispered to herself.

She had already decided that no matter what her father would say about her plans to marry, whether or not he gave his blessing, she was going to marry White Fire.

Holding that thought to keep her nerve up when it came to telling him that she would do as she wished and him be damned, she turned and opened the door.

Waiting, hoping for him to draw her into his arms, not having had that sort of intimacy with her father for so long, Flame gazed into his eyes.

When he stared at her for a moment, then brushed past her and went on into her room, Flame's heart and spirits sank. Somehow, somewhere he had lost all ability to love. He was a stiff, cold-hearted man, whose only thoughts were of himself.

Through the years she had seen his gradual change into this person she scarcely knew. She felt sorry for her mother all over again during moments like this.

"Flame, I just don't know how to communicate with you anymore," Colonel Russell said, turning to face her. "I am a cavalry officer. I sleep, eat, and drink the duties of a colonel. Can't you understand? Don't you see how my work has so overwhelmed me during these past years?"

"Yes, so much that you lost a wife's love, and now you are close to losing a daughter's," Flame managed to get out, although she knew that her father surely had to be hurt at least a little by her words.

"Not because I want it that way," Colonel Russell said. He reached for her hands and twined his fingers through hers. "Flame, I do love you. I just find it hard now to voice it aloud. Tell me you understand."

Tears burning at the corners of her eyes, touched by how her father had finally found the words that she had so longed to hear, Flame flung herself into his arms. She could feel his awkwardness in how his arms hesitated, then moved slowly around her waist and held her tight to him.

"Flame, has my indifference hurt you so badly?"

Colonel Russell said, his voice drawn with emotion. "If so, let me make it up to you."

"Do you truly mean that?" Flame said, inching away from him. She gazed into his eyes. "Father, do you truly wish to make things up to me? Do you wish to see me happy?"

"Parents want only happiness for their children," Colonel Russell said, reaching a hand to her cheek, softly touching it. "Tell me. What would most make you happy?"

At this moment, she hated thinking about the devious side of her father's character, that he was building up the fort arsenal to bring war between his soldiers and the Indians. There was only now and his soft words, his soft hand on her cheek, the look of apology in his eyes.

"Father, you truly want me to tell you what would make me happy?" she asked, smiling at him, believing that he wanted to hear the truth and would give her his blessing, no matter what.

"I want nothing more at this moment than your happiness," Colonel Russell said, his eyes slowly raking over her as she stood there so angelic and sweet before him.

When his gaze lingered longer on her generous swell of breasts than what was appropriate for a father, Flame was taken aback by the boldness of his stare.

Then he slid his hand from her cheek and brushed it against the outside of her breast, his touch seeming deliberate. Flame took an unsteady step away from him.

"Father?" she said, her voice wary.

Colonel Russell's gaze raked, slowly over her again,

and then he gazed into her eyes, suddenly aware of the alarm and question he saw in their depths.

He cleared his throat nervously. "Eh, what were we talking about?" he said, awkwardly running a forefinger around the tight collar of his uniform.

"Father, we were talking about . . . about . . . my happiness," Flame stammered out. Suddenly, there seemed something more to their relationship. She did not want to think of where it had just taken her father. It was too frightening a thought. She would not allow herself to think of it.

"Yes, your happiness," Colonel Russell said, wiping a bead of perspiration from his brow with the back of a hand. "Tell me, darling, what would make you the happiest? I shall see that you get it."

"You shall?" Flame said, again thinking of White Fire, and their future together.

"Speak up, daughter," Colonel Russell said, clasping his hands tightly behind him. "Tell me quickly. I've business awaiting me in my study."

"Father, I want to marry White Fire," Flame blurted out. Then she took a step away from her father when she saw how her words had seemed like a slap across his face.

Weaving, as though he might faint, he grabbed a chair and steadied himself. Then his face flooded with color. His eyes narrowed. His breathing was a low, sharp hiss.

"Never," he growled out.

He turned to leave, but Flame ran to him and grabbed him by an arm. She forced him around to look at her.

"I *am* going to marry him," she said, her voice quavering from emotion. "Please give us your blessing. Moments ago you said—"

"To hell with what I said moments ago," Colonel Russell said darkly. "To hell with White Fire! I forbid you to marry him. Do you hear? Forbid!"

"Forbid?" Flame said, her hands at her throat. "You truly think you can forbid me anything? Never! I didn't want to go behind your back and marry him! I wanted to show you the respect most daughters owe their fathers by telling you of our plans. Now I see that I was wrong to tell you anything. I was wrong to be tricked into thinking that you care."

She shuddered. "To think that only moments ago I was in your arms as though I belonged there," she cried. "I don't! And never shall I hug you again!"

Colonel Russell stepped closer to her. He spoke into her face. "Don't you be foolish enough to think that I will ever allow you to marry that damn 'breed," he hissed out. "Don't you know that Indians, *all* Indians, are a menace and should be killed?"

Paling, seeing her father's hatred for Indians, Flame stared at him for a moment, then ran past him.

She ignored his shouts as she ran down the stairs. She cared not that she was dressed in an expensive gown as she ran to the stables and saddled her horse.

The moon high overhead, she rode from the wide gates of the fort, the soldiers shouting at her to stop.

Chapter 21

Leave all for love;
Yet, hear me, yet,
One more word more thy heart beloved,
One pulse more of firm endeavor.

—Ralph Waldo Emerson

After his tiring day, White Fire sat down on the edge of his bed to remove his moccasins. He stood up again with a start when he heard a knock on his front door. Wondering who might be at his home this late, he lifted an eyebrow.

He doubted it would be Flame. Surely she knew better than to leave the safety of the fort *this* late at night, after darkness had fallen over the land like a black shroud.

Then who else? he wondered as he left his bedroom and walked toward the front door.

When he reached the door, never trusting anyone who might come this time of night, even with a polite knock, he grabbed his rifle. "Who's there?" he called out.

"It is I, Red Buffalo. I have come with a message for you from Chief Gray Feather."

Knowing Red Buffalo, with whom he had been friends when he had lived with the Chippewa, and no longer feeling a threat, White Fire set his rifle aside. Then he swung the door open.

He placed a hand of friendship on Red Buffalo's shoulder. "It is good to see you, my friend," he said. He dropped his hand away and stepped aside. "Would you want to come inside and give me the message by lamplight?"

"Moonlight is ample enough," Red Buffalo said, not offering any smile of friendship, or hand clasp.

"All right, then tell me what you have come to say to me, Red Buffalo," White Fire said, his spine stiffening at the warrior's cold attitude, which was unusual for this man who was known for his humor and lighthearted manner.

"Your woman was abducted tonight as she rode alone in the forest. She is being held captive at my village," Red Buffalo said guardedly, the moon sheening his copper face and revealing his eyes which narrowed as he spoke. "Your woman is being held for ransom."

"What . . . ?" White Fire gasped out, taking an unsteady step away from Red Buffalo. "What do you mean by saying that she is a captive and that she is being held for ransom?"

"My chief says that if you will come to his village and promise to marry Song Sparrow, then Flame will be set free," Red Buffalo said blandly. "If not, the woman with the flaming-red hair will not see another sunrise."

Stunned, and suddenly feeling betrayed by his

long-time friend Gray Feather, White Fire could not find the words to express his depth of disappointment in the chief.

And to think that Flame was surely filled with fear, and that what Gray Feather, an Indian, had done, might turn her against Indians made White Fire feel a desperation he had never felt before.

Ignoring Red Buffalo, White Fire grabbed his rifle and brushed past him in hurried steps.

Almost as quick as lightning, he had his horse saddled and was riding into the forest in the direction of Chief Gray Feather's village.

His thoughts were scrambled as he tried to sort out what had happened, and why. Anger filled him in hot splashes that Gray Feather would think that White Fire could be forced in such a way to marry his daughter. It was hard to understand how the chief would think that they could stay friends after threatening him.

"And Flame . . ." he whispered as he yanked, then slapped the reins as he steered his horse one way and then another around the trees. He was glad when he reached the meadow that would lead him to the Chippewa village.

He rode beside a stream which watered Chief Gray Feather's people and horses.

He sank his heels into the flanks of his horse. He ignored Red Buffalo when he caught up and rode alongside him.

"I saw that this that my chief has done tonight is wrong," Red Buffalo said, drawing White Fire's eyes to him. "But I have tried to understand his logic."

"There *is* no logic in what he has done!" White

Fire said. Yet he was glad to see that he was not alone in his upset over Chief Gray Feather's actions.

"His daughter is the world to him," Red Buffalo said. "*You* are important to him. That year you lived with our people, as one with them? That was when my chief singled you out for a future with his people. Not only as a possible husband for his daughter, but someone who could lead when his body and mind are too weak to lead. In his eyes, you became the son his wives never bore him. He is too old now to have sons by wives. He does not even have a wife. When his last wife died, he laid to rest all feelings of a man inside his mind and heart that would usually belong to a woman."

"I truly am touched over and over again to have someone as great and powerful as Chief Gray Feather think so highly of me, but surely he can see that I cannot be coerced into marrying his daughter and into being his son!" White Fire said, his hold on the reins loosening as his anger waned. He knew Gray Feather well enough to realize that he would never harm Flame.

It was surprising that Gray Feather had tried this tactic tonight—taking a captive—when it was well known to everyone that it was not his practice to do so. He had not even kept Sioux captives after his attack on the Sioux camp while rescuing his daughter from them.

It made White Fire know how much the chief wanted him to marry his daughter, if he would go to such lengths to convince him that he should. It was hard to understand, yet he did recall the chief's dreams about him. There had been more than one dream that told Gray Feather to choose White Fire over others to marry his daughter and to rule at the chief's side as though he was his son. White Fire now understood just how *much* faith the chief put in his dreams!

His jaw tightened. He had to prove to Chief Gray Feather once and for all that he should depend on reality more than dreams to bring a son into his life. He must look elsewhere to fulfill what was lacking in his, and his daughter's, lives.

The reddish-yellow reflection of the outdoor communal fire in the Chippewa village showed in the heavens a short distance away. White Fire glanced up, then sank his heels into the flanks of his horse and rode onward in a hard gallop. He could only hope that Flame would understand that he would not allow anything to happen to her, and that he would be there soon to see that she was released from captivity. And he hoped that she knew him well enough to realize that he would not be blackmailed into marrying another woman—that his heart was hers, alone, forever.

"Be gentle with my uncle the chief," Red Buffalo said as he sidled his horse closer to White Fire's. "You can settle your differences without harsh words or warring."

"I am certain you believe that or you would not allow me to enter the village without aiming your gun at my back," White Fire said, his voice drawn.

"I know you well," Red Buffalo said, a slow smile twitching on his lips. "Have we not hunted together? Have we not sat beneath the stars and wished on them? Are we not the same as brothers?"

"Yes, we are close, you and I, and that is why I was

surprised to see your frown when I opened my door
tonight and found you there," White Fire said.

"It was because I felt pulled between two loyalties,"
Red Buffalo said. "Yours and my uncle's."

Hearing that made White Fire draw his reins
tightly and stop his horse. He took the time to reach
a hand of friendship to Red Buffalo. "Friends always,"
he said.

When Red Buffalo circled his hand around his,
and their fingers tightly intertwined, White Fire
smiled broadly at him.

"Friends always," Red Buffalo said, then eased his
hand to his side. "Let us go now. Soon your woman
will be released. Soon you will ride from my village
without malice in your heart toward my chief or my
people."

They rode on into the village, where wigwams
made of birch bark sat in a wide circle, the large outdoor fire burning in the middle of the circle. Only
a few Chippewa sat outside by the fire. Most were
inside their lodges, as well as their dogs.

But White Fire could feel many eyes on him as
flaps were lifted at the doors and people watched
him dismount and walk, square shouldered, toward
their chief's much larger lodge at the far end of the
circle.

Just as he reached the chief's wigwam, White Fire
stopped suddenly when Chief Gray Feather stepped
outside. A possessive hand was clasped to Flame's
right arm as he forced her outside with him.

"White Fire, help me," Flame said, her eyes on his.

Her soft plea, the fear in her eyes, ate away at
White Fire's heart, for never had she shown this

vulnerable side to him, that things could alarm and frighten her.

He wanted to reach out and grab her from the old chief, but he knew that words would work better now than harsh actions.

"She will be released and escorted home if you make promises to Chief Gray Feather that please him," Gray Feather said in a low rumble of a voice.

"Gray Feather, what you have done tonight could start a war between you and the white eyes," White Fire said, hoping that Flame would understand that he must, at this moment, ignore her and give his full attention to the chief. "Had I gone to Flame's father and told him that she had been abducted, there would be an instant war between the Chippewa and the pony soldiers."

Chief Gray Feather smiled slyly at him. "I knew that you would not go to the white eyes before coming here," he said, laughing softly. "You do not want warring any more than I. Now do we have a bargain? She is set free if you will stay and be a husband to my daughter, a father to her daughter, and a son to this old chief whose dreams tell him that is the way it must be."

"Dreams, dreams, dreams!" White Fire said, frustrated, raking his fingers through his long hair. "You depend too much on your dreams."

"You have said, also, that you know the power of dreams," Chief Gray Feather said, tightening his hold on Flame as she tried to wriggle free.

"Yes, I have dreamed that which has eventually come to pass, but this dream of yours never shall," White Fire said, glancing over at Flame, wishing he could reach out and comfort her. But that would come later. He had the chore of first making the old chief see things which he stubbornly wished not to see.

"'Then you refuse to do as I ask?" Chief Gray Feather asked somberly. "You do nothing tonight to guarantee the freedom of this flame-haired white woman?"

"I cannot do as you ask because my love is for this woman, not your daughter," White Fire said sadly. "Flame is my choice. We are going to be married. Nothing you say or do will change our feelings for one another. Set her free, Gray Feather. Let her come to me. Let me comfort her and tell her that you meant her no true harm. That you are not the sort of Chippewa leader who would provoke the whites into warring over a woman."

Out of the corner of his eye, White Fire saw Song Sparrow inching toward her father on the opposite side from where he held Flame hostage. Feeling Song Sparrow's eyes on him, White Fire turned her way. Their eyes locked and held as she stepped fully to her father's right side.

"Song Sparrow, you would not want to marry a man whose heart belongs elsewhere," White Fire said, feeling the pain that was so visible in her wavering eyes.

He hated hurting her, for she was like a sister to him. Surely she understood now that she could never be anything more to him but that. She had heard.

He prayed that she would speak up and say what she knew had to be said to free Flame without any altercations.

"*Gee-bah-bah*, Father, set her free," Song Sparrow suddenly said, her eyes still locked with White Fire's.

"I no longer want him. Tonight, for everyone to hear, he has openly declared his love for another woman. I would look foolish in the eyes of our people if you still hold the woman as hostage." She lowered her eyes. "I perhaps already look too foolish ever to feel good about myself again."

Flame swallowed hard. She leaned over and gazed at the beautiful Chippewa woman. Although Flame was angry through and through for what had happened here tonight, she could not help but feel a deep sympathy for the woman for whom this had been done. Flame knew how deeply it would hurt her to lose White Fire. She could tell that this Chippewa woman's hurt was as deep; as devastating.

She felt the hand on her wrist drop away. Her heart throbbed wildly within her chest to know that she was free, to know that the Chippewa chief was no longer a threat to her.

Stifling a sob of relief in the depths of her throat she went to White Fire and flung herself into his arms. "Thank you," she murmured, clinging to him. "Oh, Lord, White Fire, thank you. I was never as afraid as I was tonight while alone with the Chippewa!"

"I am sorry that it had to happen," White Fire said, cuddling her close as his gaze moved now to the chief. "You did a wise thing, Gray Feather, by releasing her. But it might be too late. Surely her father is searching for her."

"He would have no reason to search at my village," Chief Gray Feather said, sighing heavily. "During my entire reign as chief, and my father's reign before me, no white captives have been taken. The pony soldiers will look everywhere but here. I imagine, for now, the fault will be laid at the doorstep of the Sioux."

He took a slow step toward White Fire, then stopped and placed a gentle hand on Flame's head. "Child, turn and face me," he said thickly.

He dropped his hand to his side as Flame slowly turned around and gazed at him. "White woman, whose hair is like flames of a fire," he said softly, "it is my sincere apology for having given you such cause to be afraid tonight."

"Yes, I was afraid," flame said, swallowing hard. "But I see now that I was never in any danger. I apologize for showing such fear of you. White Fire has told me nothing but good things about you and your people."

Gray Feather smiled at White Fire. "*Ay-uh,* he would have much good to say because only good came to him while he lived among my people," he said, nodding.

Then Gray Feather's smile faded. "White Fire, please, you and your woman, stay awhile with my people," he said, his voice filled with melancholy. "Eat with my people. Spend the night. Let this old chief have a chance to strengthen our ties again after having weakened them tonight by his harsh, foolish action."

Flame looked over her shoulder at White Fire. They gave each other questioning stares.

Chapter 22

We have walked in Love's land a little way,
We have learnt his lesson a little while,
And shall we not part at the end of day,
With a sigh, a smile?

—Ernest Dowson

Although White Fire knew that Colonel Russell would be fit to be tied over Flame's absence, he felt that he had no choice but to spend the night with the Chippewa. He felt that he needed this time to console Gray Feather over his plan having gone awry, and for learning for certain that White Fire would never live with him, and would never marry his daughter.

White Fire took Flame's hands. He edged her a few feet from the chief so that they could talk in private about what he wished to do.

"We can't stay," Flame blurted out, her eyes wide as she gazed up at him. "My father is already angry over so many things, especially over my having left the fort in such a way."

"And he has a right to be angry," White Fire said, sighing. "You see what happened by you having left the fort at night? You were easily abducted."

"I had to leave," Flame said, yanking her hands free. "Father was so horrible about things when I told him I was going to many you. He . . . he . . . made threats. I ran out on him before he could grab me and imprison me in my room!"

"You can never return to him, you know," White Fire said, his voice drawn. "You will stay with me. We will be married soon. Then just let your father try and interfere. You will be mine to protect. I will protect you with my life."

Feeling so much for him at this moment, seeing the depth of his feelings for her, and realizing the sort of sacrifice he might be making to have her as his wife—that her father's threat would always be there, to haunt White Fire's every move, Flame floated into his arms and hugged him.

"I love you so," she murmured. "And I am so afraid for you. For both of us to be free of my father's wrath, perhaps we should leave the area. We could go and get Michael and go where Father could never find us."

"Your father is an obstacle for only a while longer," White Fire said. "If Colonel Edwards does as he promised, your father will soon be no threat to anyone again."

"But until he does, both our lives are in danger," Flame said, stepping away from him, gazing into his eyes. "Even though I am his daughter, I truly believe he now sees me as no less than an enemy. I fear his wrath so, White Fire. When someone crosses him, he is capable of anything."

"Tonight we are safe from him," White Fire said soothingly. "Let us relax and enjoy this time with the Chippewa."

"I shall try," Flame said, then turned and walked with him back to Chief Gray Feather.

"We both accept your offer to stay," White Fire said, which caused the old chiefs eyes to light up.

But when White Fire looked over at Song Sparrow, and saw a strange sort of emptiness in her eyes, he could not help but be afraid for her. It was not just that he had refused to marry her, it was the way it had all transpired in the presence of her people. She appeared to be totally dejected and ashamed.

When Song Sparrow turned and left, he was glad, for surely when she joined her daughter in the privacy of their lodge, she would realize who was truly the most important person in her life: her daughter. Being a mother, Song Sparrow must know that she must consider her daughter's welfare over her own. Her daughter was solely dependant on her now since she no longer had a father.

"It is good that you will stay," Chief Gray Feather said, taking White Fire by an arm. "Come inside my lodge. Wear the clothes of my people. Let us share tonight what we shared in the past." He nodded at Flame. "Come. Join us."

Flame smiled awkwardly at him. Then she went inside the chief's large wigwam and sat down beside the fire on rich, soft pelts. White Fire and the chief went to the far shadows of the lodge, where the younger man changed from his clothes into a breech-clout.

Trying not to be embarrassed while this was done, Flame centered her attention on other things. She

looked slowly around her. Even though she had
come here as a captive, she was as in awe of it now, as
she had been the first time she had seen it earlier in
the evening.

The lodge was just a single room, built of saplings
which had been covered with woven rush mats and
bark to keep out the cold. Flame noticed that the
bark had been cut in a decorative zigzag pattern, and
more mats on the floor were dyed in bright colors,
giving the whole dwelling a cheerful appearance.

In the center of the lodge, a crackling fire pro-
vided warmth and shed a soft glow over the space. At
the door, a hide had been hung to keep in the heat
during the winter months. Warm blankets, bear skins
and hides were hung from the rafters or arranged
around the edge of the wigwam for sitting or sleeping. It was completely different from any home Flame
had ever seen, but it seemed cozy.

Gray Feather's cache of weapons were in the
shadows at the back of the lodge.

As Gray Feather stood close by, his loose robe
hanging in folds over his left shoulder, White Fire
fastened his breechclout.

"Share body paint tonight with me also?" Chief
Gray Feather asked, holding out a pot of assorted
paints toward him.

White Fire gazed questioningly at the chief for a
moment, then nodded and accepted the paints.

They took turns painting each other's faces in colorful zigzag designs in colors of red, yellow, and blue.

Then White Fire watched the chief remove a long-
stemmed calumet pipe from a sacred bag. Together
they went and sat down by the fire.

Flame gasped when she saw the paint designs on

their bodies and faces. For the first time, ever, she saw just how truly Indian White Fire was, and found it intriguing.

She said nothing, but only watched as White Fire and the chief exchanged smokes from the long-stemmed pipe. It seemed to be some strange sort of ceremony in how the pipe was smoked as the chief lifted it toward the east, the west, the north, and then the south.

She couldn't understand what the old chief was saying as he offered the pipe in all directions, for he spoke the words in his Chippewa tongue.

After the pipe was smoked and set aside, Chief Gray Feather left the wigwam. Flame took this time to scoot closer to White Fire.

"Where is he going?" she whispered.

"To tell the women to bring in some food," White Fire said, reaching a soft hand to her cheek. "Are you all right about everything? You are able to relax?" His lips fluttered into a soft smile. "You have accepted how I look? The paint? The breechclout?"

"I would love you if you wore nothing and you ran around with your body painted black," Flame said, giggling. She leaned closer and ran a finger slowly over his powerful chest. "I think you are so handsome."

"I could paint your face, if you wish," he teased, his eyes dancing into hers. "When we are alone, I could paint your body."

"No, I wouldn't go so far as that in my admiration of the body paint," Flame said, laughing softly. Then she grew quiet and stared at the buckskin entrance flap. "I wish that I could totally relax while being here with you, but I can't get Father off my mind."

"Of course, and who would expect you to?" White Fire said, drawing her into his embrace. He cuddled her closer. "I am sure he will look for you tonight until he is exhausted. Then he will return to the fort. I hope that we can leave early enough in the morning to travel through the forest before he is up again and searching for you."

"What are we going to do in the morning?" Flame asked, shivering at the thought of what her father might do if he found them together. "Where will we go?"

"It would be too risky to go back to my cabin," White Fire said. "Not yet, anyhow. We will establish ourselves elsewhere for a while. We can go to the Indian agent in Pig's Eye. We can seek refuge there until Colonel Edwards sees to your father's dismissal from this area, or better yet, his arrest. Then I will proceed at getting my son, but only after you and I speak vows before a preacher."

"I want nothing but to be with you and Michael," Flame murmured. "I will do anything, go anywhere you say, to achieve it."

"For tonight, let us just forget everything but being together," White Fire said huskily.

He leaned her away from him. He placed both hands at her brow and swept her hair back from her face. "We will be given a wigwam for the night," he said. "You will experience how it feels to live as the Chippewa live. You will experience how it feels to make love in a wigwam."

A sensual shiver raced across Flame's flesh at the thought of being alone in a wigwam with White Fire, making love. It seemed so primitive.

Yes, she concluded. For tonight she would forget

about her father. It served him right to have to worry about her welfare, for in truth, it was only himself that mattered to him.

Perhaps her father might even feel relieved if he never saw her again, she thought bitterly. She had become a nuisance, an obstacle to his peace of mind.

She knew him well, and knew that he needed a clear mind to plan his strategies. A man of no great intelligence, he could only concentrate on one thing at a time.

Gray Feather came back into the lodge. He held the entrance flap aside as several women stepped inside. They carried wooden trays heaping with food and sat them on the floor close to the fire.

Another woman brought in a large brass kettle filled with boiled venison and green corn.

Flame glanced over at Chief Gray Feather. It was as though the Chippewa chief had known there would be a reason to celebrate, that he had known that his scheme to bring White Fire there would work. Much food had been prepared over the cook fires in many lodges.

When the women left, and Gray Feather came and sat down close to White Fire and Flame, he offered them wooden spoons and bowls.

"Eat your fill tonight and then tomorrow there will be more to eat before your departure from my village," the chief said, gesturing with one of his hands toward the food.

Hungry enough, having had only a few bites of food the entire day, White Fire did not have to be asked twice. But first he heaped Flame's plate with different items from the large platters.

As they sat by the fire White Fire sampled all the

dishes they were offered. There was bear meat, which Flame declined, and boiled venison and duck, which she ate daintily with her fingers. They both had bowls of the corn soup, then finished the meal with cups of pine needle tea.

When the platters were empty, Chief Gray Feather gazed over at White Fire; then at length at Flame. Then he touched White Fire gently on the shoulder. "I do understand now why your heart is lost to this white woman," he said thickly. "She is a gracious woman. She is beautiful. And I see much love in her eyes as she looks at you."

"Fate brought us together many years ago just before my departure from St. Louis, as it did again here upon Flame's arrival to the Minnesota Territory," White Fire said, reaching over to take one of Flame's hands in his. "It was written in the stars that we should meet twice, then marry."

"Dreams, *my* dreams, placed you in the arms of my daughter," Gray Feather said sullenly, his attitude cooler. "But in the past, as dreams failed me, so do they fail me now."

White Fire's insides stiffened. "It is with much regret that I am to blame for your dreams proving wrong," he said tightly. "But although I am not marrying your daughter, do you not see that we can still be friends? I still feel a oneness with you and your people. I feel as though I am brother to your warriors, and son to you, their chief."

"A son in my heart is not the same as in truth," Gray Feather said, sighing. "But I do wish for you to still be a part of my life . . . of my *people's*. Come often. Have council. Smoke with me. Hunt with me."

"I will gladly do those things," White Fire said, nodding. "But I have many things to do in my life before I can again sit with you as I sit with you tonight. I must do everything I can to protect my woman against the evil of her father. I must, at all cost, get my son back. These things take time and careful planning."

"I wish you well and much happiness," Chief Gray Feather said. He yawned and stretched. "The hour is late. Go. You will find the lodge that was yours three winters ago still standing. I have not allowed anyone to live in it. It is as you left it when you went to live with whites. I had hoped, even then, that you would return to us. So much inside my heart tells me that you belong here. It is a beckoning of sorts, a whisper in the wind."

Chief Gray Feather rose to his feet as White Fire held Flame's hand and she moved to his side.

The chief walked them to the entrance flap. Then he turned and went to sit by his fire again as they went on to White Fire's wigwam.

Once inside, White Fire and Flame found a fire already burning in the fire pit. They found luxurious rabbit-fur blankets, woven from long strips of cottontail pelts, lying beside the fire.

"The blankets are beautiful," Flame sighed as she sat down on one of them. "They are so *soft*."

"They were made for me when I was an everyday part of the Chippewa's lives," White Fire said, recalling when Song Sparrow had brought them to his lodge and laid them at his feet.

Regret again filled his very soul to have hurt Song Sparrow so deeply by his rejection. But she would have to learn how to accept life as it was, not as she wished it to be. No one had control of their own fate. More than once fate had been unkind to Song Sparrow.

Song Sparrow stood in the dark shadows of night beneath a giant elm tree. As the brisk breeze fluttered the entrance flap that hung at White Fire's lodge's door, she could get an occasional peek of him and the flame-haired lady.

When she saw White Fire cover the white woman with his body and kiss her, she stared for a moment longer, then turned and fled into the forest, sobbing.

"Did you hear something?" Flame asked, drawing her lips from White Fire's.

"Nothing but the thundering of my heart," he whispered against her cheek, his hand sliding up inside her skirt. "Flame, Flame . . ."

Flame soon forgot having heard something that sounded like sobs as White Fire again covered her lips with his mouth and kissed her hard and long, while his fingers stroked her woman's center. All was lost to her now except for the ecstasy that was building within her.

"Undress me," she whispered against his lips. "Let me undress you."

She closed her eyes and shivered sensually as White Fire unfastened her skirt and slowly slid it down across her hips, past her thighs, and then on past her ankles. He tossed it aside.

And before removing her blouse, he bent low and kissed the warm, wet place at the juncture of her thighs, the red tendrils of hair there soft against his lips.

Flame gasped at this forbidden way of loving her.

Chapter 23

Small in the worth of beauty from the light retired.
—Edmund Waller

The eerie cry of a loon sounding across the river outside the wigwam awakened Flame. Everything so unfamiliar to her, she leaned quickly up on an elbow and looked around her.

The soft glowing embers of the fire soon revealed the interior of the wigwam, and then White Fire, who still slept soundly at her right side. His body and face were now washed free of the body paint.

Swallowing back the fear that had crept into her heart upon her first awakening, Flame sighed. Then she stretched out again beside White Fire on the luxuriously soft rabbit-fur blankets. Smiling, deliciously content, at least for the moment, she became lost in deep thought.

It had been interesting the prior night as she and White Fire had lain together after making love. He had opened up to her and told her things about the Chippewa that until now he had not spoken about.

He had told her that the Chippewa called themselves *Anishinabe,* meaning "first or original man."

Each band of Chippewa had its own chief, just as Gray Feather led the tribe that had befriended White Fire. This position was handed down from father to son, along with the example of leadership. If a young man did not show himself to be of good character and good sense, he would never be respected by his people. A chief like Gray Feather, who had no son, would hope to marry his daughter to a worthy candidate. It was no wonder White Fire's friend had tried to convince him to take Song Sparrow as his wife.

Snuggling close, White Fire's flesh warm against hers, Flame knew that he would have made a wonderful chief, for he had all traits expected of a chief and a leader.

Closing her eyes, she relived the sensual moments that they had shared only a few hours ago. He had introduced her into new ways of making love. Some had felt forbidden, yet deliciously wonderful in how they aroused the wild side of her nature.

"I do so love you," she whispered, running a hand down the sleekness of his copper back.

She squeezed her eyes tightly closed and tried to block out the worry of her father and her fear of what would happen if he found her and White Fire together.

No. She would not think about it. She would only think about the wonders of being with White Fire after having thought about him, oh, so often through the years.

She recalled dreams that she had had, in which White Fire would be there, his arms outstretched, his hands beckoning her. She had tried so hard to go to him, yet there always seemed to be a barrier of sorts stopping her.

As she had grown older, the barrier had slowly faded until finally, when she had been seventeen, she had experienced her first sensual dream about her and White Fire together.

She opened her eyes and gazed over at him, smiling at how she had, at that time, felt so shocked at herself when she had awakened from that dream. She had actually slept with him in her dream. He had actually touched her breasts.

But they had not made love, for in her dream she had never seen him totally nude. While in bed with her, he had always worn fringed buckskin breeches.

"You have nothing on now," she whispered, sliding her hand down and across his buttocks.

Daringly, she moved her hand on around and touched the part of his anatomy that could make her soar above the heavens.

Strange how it was so small now.. . .

"And what do you think you are doing?" White Fire suddenly said, flipping over to face her, causing her to jerk her hand away with a start. "My woman is not familiar enough yet with my body?" He laughed huskily. "You wished to explore while you thought I was asleep?"

An embarrassed, heated flush turned Flame's face crimson. She giggled, then sighed with passion when White Fire guided her hand back to him and encouraged her to fill her fingers with his manhood as it began to grow in the anticipation of where this was leading them.

"It's like magic," Flame said, feeling the heat of his manhood as it grew tight and sleek amid her fingers.

"Move your hand on my . . . eh . . . magic," White Fire said, chuckling. He stretched out on his back and spread his bronze, muscled legs apart. "Slowly . . . slowly . . ."

He closed his eyes and sighed as she did as he had suggested. And the more she moved her hand on him, the more the rapture built within him. It was rushing through him in hot waves of bliss, his head becoming dizzy from the intense pleasure.

"You seem so taut and tense all over," Flame said, noticing how his toes were so tightly extended and how the muscles in his arms and legs were so corded. "Are you certain I am not hurting instead of pleasuring you?"

White Fire opened his eyes. He laughed softly. "If only you were inside my body and could feel what I am feeling, you would not question anything," he said huskily. "You would feel as though you were floating above yourself, like an eagle soaring in the heavens."

"I'm so glad that I am capable of giving you such pleasure," Flame said, not feeling at all self-conscious about being there, totally nude with him, touching the part of his body that, until she had made love with him that first time, had been such a mystery to her.

Wanting not to feel selfish in receiving and not giving, he placed his hands around her waist and lowered her beside him on the rabbit-fur blankets.

As he gazed at her with his midnight dark eyes,

and as his hands began to move tenderly, slowly, and caressingly over her body, Flame sighed with pleasure and closed her eyes.

She breathed heavily when she felt his fingers slide down to where she ached with need of him. She threw her head back and gasped with passion when she felt his fingers move slowly on her tight nub of womanhood.

Then she flinched with an even more intense pleasure when she felt his tongue flick over her woman's center.

As he spread her tendrils of hair with his fingers, he licked her until she felt as though she might burst with the building rapture that was flooding her senses.

White Fire saw that she was perhaps getting too close to the brink of total ecstasy. Wanting to join her, he gave her one more long, wet, lick, then moved over her with his body. He paused long enough to take a lingering look at her.

As her eyes opened and she smiled sweetly up at him, he stared at her face, at her perfect features that were crowned by the red flame of her hair beneath her.

Then he greedily absorbed the sight of her breasts. They were soft and pink crested, well-rounded, and heaving—ah, such an invitation for his hands, and for his lips to taste and suckle!

But he delayed his needs a while longer as his gaze swept down across her flat belly, stopping where her red curls framed her wet and warm place.

He could still taste her on his tongue. It was a bittersweet taste. It was her.

Then his gaze burned upon her bare skin as he

moved to the curve of her thighs, and then the soft tapering of her ankles.

Then he looked at her feet, at how straight and perfect her toes were, her toenails as pink as pale pink rosebuds.

"Darling, please . . . ?" Flame murmured, reaching her hands out for him.

She gave him a seductive look through her thick lashes. A trail of fire had been left on her body by the touch of his vision, yet she wanted more.

"I do believe I can give you more pleasure by doing instead of looking," she whispered huskily.

"Yes, I believe so," he said, giving her a steady smile, his eyes glazed and drugged with desire.

Feeling the curl of heat growing in his lower body, White Fire lowered himself fully over Flame. He wove his fingers through her hair and sought her mouth with a wildness and desperation that was new to him.

Their lips met in a frenzy of kisses as he thrust his throbbing member inside her.

Her body a river of sensations, Flame twined her arms around his neck, then lifted her legs around his waist and rode with him as his eager thrusts deepened and became faster.

His kiss now all consuming, his hands now at her breasts, her hard nipples stark against his palms, Flame's happiness bubbled from deep within. Her world melted away as the rapture spread like molten lava throughout her.

Flame's groans of pleasure fired White Fire's passion. He licked his way down to her breasts. Then he flicked a nipple with his tongue as he swept his hands beneath her and locked his fingers into the soft flesh of her buttocks. He lifted her body more tightly against his as he moved rhythmically within her, going deeper with each thrust.

Flame moaned. She sobbed. She thrashed her head back and forth. She could not help but cry out with pleasure as she began to come in waves. She was engulfed in a rush of pleasure so intense she felt as though she might faint. The ecstasy this time had moved her with bone-weakening intensity.

Her pleasure fulfilled, she became more aware then of White Fire's. His mouth rested against the slender column of her throat, and she could feel his rapid breathing. She could hear his guttural groans of pleasure. His eyes were closed as his body moved rigidly in rapid succession, his eager, maddening thrusts almost lifting her from the rabbit-fur blanket each time he shoved into her.

"Flame . . . Flame . . ." White Fire whispered, his cheeks flushed with the building of the heat of his passion.

He rose fully above her again. He wrapped his arms around her and brought her breasts against his chest. His mouth covered hers with a reckless passion as he gave one last shove that brought him over the brink into total rapture.

Flame clung to him as his body spasmed.

Then he rolled away from her and lay on his back, his eyes closed, his chest heaving.

Flame rolled over and snuggled close to his perspiration-laced body. "White Fire, the pleasure was so intense this time, it . . . it . . . somewhat frightened me," she whispered, running a slow hand over his chest. "Did you feel it also twice as much as before? Perhaps even more?"

"The pleasure for me while with you has always

been something that is so ecstasy filled, I doubt it could ever be more intense than what I have experienced . . . or I might not survive it," he said, chuckling.

She slid her hand down his chest and stopped it where she could feel his heart pounding erratically beneath it. "You are still so breathless?" she whispered.

He turned smiling eyes toward her. "Not so much that I could not do it again and again," he said huskily. He grabbed her hand and placed it on his manhood. "All you need to do is touch me there and my blood rushes hot and rapid through it."

She clasped her fingers around him and felt the heat growing against her palm. She did not think she could ever be more than in awe of how this part of his body worked than she was now.

He slid her hand away. "We should not take any more time, though, making love," he said, his voice suddenly serious.

He gazed up at the smoke hole in the ceiling. Stars still flickered like diamonds in the heavens, yet he could see that the sky was lightening somewhat behind them.

He looked over at her. "We must leave," he said. "Now. If we wait until daylight, we might chance running into your father."

"But Chief Gray Feather?" Flame said, reaching for her riding skirt. "He expected us to eat the morning meal with him."

"He will understand when he finds us gone," White Fire said, standing, and sliding on his breeches. "He would not want us to stay for breakfast if it might endanger us, and perhaps even him, for it was he who gave the order to his warriors to abduct you."

He turned to Flame. He framed her face between his fingers. "Your father must never know that Gray Feather abducted you," he said. "You know what would happen. Even before Colonel Edwards got the chance to stop him, your father would attack Gray Feather's village."

Flame paled at the thought.

"Remember, Flame, under *no* circumstances do you *ever* tell your father of Chief Gray Feather's part in your abduction," he said seriously.

Eyes wide, she swallowed hard and nodded. "No, I won't," she promised.

They hurried into the rest of their clothes, ran outside beneath the lightening sky, saddled their horses and rode away into the dawning of morning.

"We may have waited too long as it is," White Fire said, looking heavenward. "It will not be long now until the sun rises along the horizon."

The birds were awakening in their nests. Some, especially the red-breasted robins, were warbling and singing their morning songs. Some were fluttering and leaving their nests for early prey.

A lone wolf howled on a distant bluff.

Chapter 24

Ah! Who to sober measurement
Time's happy swiftness brings,
When birds of paradise have lent
Their plumage to his wings?

—Robert William Spence

The howling of a wolf awakened Colonel Russell. He cringed when he looked around and remembered where he had slept the night. In White Fire's bed in his cabin.

His nose twitched at the smell of coffee brewing over the coals of the fireplace, having given instructions to Lieutenant Green to wake him at daybreak so the search for Flame could continue.

The search had led him far and wide last night, after he realized that Flame was not going to come home. The search had ended at White Fire's cabin.

When Colonel Russell had found White Fire gone and there were still no signs of Flame anywhere, he had concluded that they had left together—that they had more than likely eloped.

Well, Colonel Russell had thought angrily to himself, they had to return. He would be there waiting for them when they arrived at the cabin. Then pity them both!

Grumbling beneath his breath, Colonel Russell eased his legs over the side of the bed. He sat there for a moment and looked slowly around him. The glow of the fire in the fireplace reached just inside the door enough for him to see things. He cringed. He found it hard to understand how Flame, whom had been raised in luxury, could choose this rattrap over what *he* offered her!

"I have even more than that to offer her," he whispered to himself. His eyes took on a devilish gleam and his lips fluttered into a slow smile.

When he had gone back to St. Louis for the burial of his wife, he had seen Flame for the first time in years. He had been shocked at how ravishingly beautiful she was. She had grown up into a lady who drew the eyes of every man who came near her.

He hung his head in his hands as he, at this very moment, could not help but envision her in his arms. He had tried to shake such thoughts from his mind, for they seemed so indecent, even though he was no true-blood kin to her.

He knew now that it had been wrong for her mother to lie to Flame all those years, pretending he was her father, when now, he wanted more than that from her. He wanted her all to himself.

He thought back to when he had met her mother. He had not known until after their marriage that she was pregnant with another man's child. He had tried not to hate her for lying to him.

He had never been able to truly love her. They had seldom shared a bed once he knew the truth about her. He had scarcely taken *any* woman to bed since then.

Now the hunger that had lain dormant for so long had awakened inside him. And only Flame could feed such a hunger!

His jaw tight, and with determination etched on his face, he rushed from the bed and hurried into his clothes.

Fastening a gun belt around his waist, he stamped into the living room. "Out!" he shouted, pointing toward the door as he glared at Lieutenant Green. "We're not waiting here any longer. We are going to search every inch of that forest until we find my daughter."

He felt it wrong now to refer to Flame as his daughter when he knew that if he ever did find her, he would, in time, marry her. When he *did* finally find her, he first would send her to St. Louis. He would send her to a convent until she begged for release and would agree to anything he asked of her.

He would then ask the government to assign him to another fort far from St. Louis and the Minnesota Territory, where no one knew either of them—where it would not look unnatural for them to live as man and wife together.

"And to hell with what some might say about the age difference," he thought to himself. He would look past the stares and close his ears to nasty gossip about him being old enough to be her father.

He chuckled as his thoughts still ran wild on how it would be once he found Flame. Yes, she would have a new husband, but it would not be the 'breed!

Glowering, the colonel left the cabin and waited for his horse to be saddled. He looked heavenward and saw the first signs of the rising sun as shimmering rays of gold fanned across the horizon.

"By damn, I will find her," he whispered. "Pity the 'breed if he is with her!"

Chapter 25

Love not me for comely grace,
For my pleasing eye or face,
Nor for any outward part,
No, nor for my constant heart.

—Anonymous

The sun was up past the horizon just as White Fire and Flame arrived at the Indian agent's cabin. When White Fire saw no smoke spiraling from the fireplace chimney, and no horses in the crude corral at the back of the lodge, his heart sank.

"Isn't he here?" Flame asked, wheeling her horse into a sudden stop beside his.

She could not help but notice the tattered, yellowed curtains at the window. She saw how weeds had grown up knee high around the perimeters of the log structure, even at the door.

"The place looks so deserted," she murmured.

"I had not taken the time yet since my release from the Sioux to come and meet with Neal Geary, the agent," White Fire said, sliding from his saddle. "I should have known something was awry when he did not come and join the recent council with the Sioux at Fort Snelling. I should have known something was wrong when your father placed such an emphasis on finding an interpreter, instead of using Neal's expertise. Neal was fluent in Indian languages. His presence at councils between Colonel Russell and the Indians would have been enough."

"So you knew him?" Flame asked, herself dismounting her horse.

"Yes, before I was forced into captivity by the Sioux, Neal and I were good friends," White Fire said. "Like you and me, he was initially from Missouri."

Flame stepped quickly to his side and went with him through the dew-dampened grass, wincing when a black snake slithered quickly away from them and disappeared beneath the edges of a large rock.

"Do you think my father ordered the agent to leave the premises when he became the commandant at Fort Snelling?" Flame asked, standing aside as White Fire lifted the latch at the door and gently shoved it open.

"Now that I am aware of your father's plans to start a war with the local Indians, yes, I imagine he felt that Neal Geary should be the first to go since he was here in the Minnesota Territory to fight for the rights *of* the Indians," White Fire said somberly.

He reached a hand out for Flame. "Come inside with me," he said softly. "Let's see what we can find."

"Surely nothing that will help us know where he

might be," Flame said, gasping when she stepped into a thick cobweb just inside the door. She fought the cobweb with frantic sweeps of her hands. Then she moved quickly farther into the room to where White Fire was standing, taking a slow look around him.

"I don't like the looks of this," he said warily. He gestured toward a journal that lay open on a desk, as though someone had been disturbed while making entries.

He gazed at the many leather-bound books on the shelves above the desk. "Neal would not have left those behind," he said dryly. "I have never seen a man as proud of books as he was of those you see on the shelves."

He frowned as he looked farther into the morning shadows. "Nor would he leave without his clothes," he said. "See how they are stacked neatly on a shelf? See his boots? His rifle standing against the far wall?"

"No, surely no man would leave those things behind," Flame said, shivering at the chill that crossed her spine, as though an omen of bad tidings. She crept closer to White Fire and looked guardedly around her. "I'm afraid that something has happened to your friend."

A sudden thought caused a sick feeling to grip her insides. "No," she said in a soft moan. She looked frantically up at White Fire. She grabbed his arm, causing him to look quickly down at her with alarm. "White Fire, you don't think that my father could have . . . ?"

She clasped a hand over her mouth, finding it too hard to continue with her suspicions. They were too horrible to say aloud. She didn't want to believe that the man who carried her blood in his veins could have murdered someone and done way with his body as a part of his plot to rid the land of Indians.

But if her father feared that the agent might uncover his devious plot, would not he then have rid himself of such a threat by . . . by . . . doing away with the man?

Her father could never have carried out the plot in the end, making it look as though the Indians were responsible for the blood spilled upon the soil of Minnesota.

Her father would come out of this looking like a hero if he killed the Indians and kept them from slaying whites once the war was started between them. No one but the soldiers under his command would ever know that it was her father who had started the war. Those men would never speak against him, knowing what he was capable of doing to them.

"I believe no one will ever find Neal Geary," White Fire said solemnly. His eyes wavered into Flame's. "And, yes, I believe your father is responsible for his disappearance. Who else would want him dead? The Indians, the Sioux and Chippewa alike, saw him as a good friend. He fought for both their rights. And if a voyager or anyone else, for that matter, had come across this cabin during their journeys and wanted to steal from it, do you think they would have left any of this, especially the rifle and clothes?"

He frowned. "No, whoever came and saw the need to do away with Neal did just that and made sure no one would ever discover his body," he said.

His eyes filled with a sudden rage. Recalling the gentleness of this man who seemed now to have disappeared off the face of the earth, White Fire slammed a fist on a table. "I will find a way to make things right for this man," he shouted. He looked at Flame. "Even if he *is* your father, Colonel Russell will have to pay for this, for I know, without a doubt, that he is responsible."

"I'm sorry," Flame said, swallowing hard. "I'm sorry that I am kin to a man who is so heartless, who would go to any extreme to get what he wants."

White Fire turned to her and placed his hands on her shoulders. "That includes you," he said, his eyes searching hers. "Do you see now why you can never allow him near you? We must find somewhere to hide you until Colonel Edwards—"

He stopped in midsentence. His eyes brightened. His lips quivered into a smile. "Colonel Edwards," he said, dropping his hands to his sides. "We will ride to Colonel Edwards's fort and inform him of our latest find. Also, that is where you will stay until your father is stopped from any more wrongdoings."

"But surely Colonel Edwards is aware already of the agent's disappearance," Flame said softly. "Wouldn't the agent frequent that fort as well as Fort Snelling?"

"Each fort is appointed their own agent," White Fire said. "So, no, he would have no cause to notice Neal's strange disappearance."

Flame drifted into his arms and clung to him. "I'm suddenly so afraid," she said, her voice catching with the fear inside her. "If Father is capable of out-and-out murder, what if he finds us before we reach Fort Parker?"

"Just don't think about it," White Fire said. He held her for a moment longer, then eased her from his arms. "Take Neal's rifle. We need as much protection as possible."

Flame nodded. She grabbed the rifle, then ran from the cabin with White Fire. After mounting her horse, she gripped the rifle with one hand and grabbed her reins with the other. With the skill of a man, she rode off with White Fire, the rifle resting on her lap, her eyes constantly searching around her for any sudden movements.

After they were many miles downriver from Fort Snelling, White Fire sidled his horse closer to Flame's. "Are you all right?" he asked, studying the paleness of her face. "Should we stop?"

"I do feel somewhat lightheaded and dizzy," she murmured. "I . . . I . . . get this way if I don't eat at regular intervals." She laughed awkwardly. "I guess my body is telling me it's time to eat breakfast."

"Can you ride awhile longer, until we find some bushes heavy with berries?" White Fire asked. "Except for animals and fish, there's not much else to eat out here in the wilderness and we don't have time to go on a hunt."

"Yes, I can make it," Flame said, nodding.

She fought the continued dizziness, then was relieved when he pointed to a thick cluster of blackberry bushes that stretched out along the embankment of the river.

The sun warm, the breeze gentle, they dismounted and went and fell to their knees beside the blackberry bushes. Flame placed her rifle on the ground. They both plucked and ate one berry after another, the taste sweet and tantalizing as the juices melted down their throats.

Suddenly there was a commotion behind them.

They scrambled to their feet and turned just in time to see Flame's father and several soldiers step out into the open, their firearms aimed toward them.

"Father!" Flame gasped, paling. "How did you . . . ?"

"We caught sight of you a short while ago," Colonel Russell snarled out, his eyes on White Fire as he talked to Flame. "We waited for the right moment to surprise you." He laughed throatily. "You played right into my hands by stopping. It made it much easier than to accost you while you were on your horses. This way we don't have to make chase."

"Father, why . . . ?" Flame stammered, then winced and screamed when two soldiers ran to White Fire and grabbed him, one on each side, holding his arms in tight grips.

Flame turned and, wide-eyed, stared as White Fire's rifle was yanked from the gunboot at the side of his horse.

Colonel Russell brushed past Flame. He stopped and glared into White Fire's eyes. "You'll be sorry you ever set eyes on my daughter," he barked, placing his fists on his hips. "I arrest you this morning, 'breed, for abducting my daughter."

"No!" Flame cried, paling. She ran to her father and grabbed him by an arm. She yanked hard to draw his attention.

When he turned and glared at her, she pleaded with him with her eyes. "You know he didn't abduct me!" she cried. "You can't arrest him for something he didn't do!"

"You've been gone a full night with this man," Colonel Russell said flatly. "That, alone, is cause for this man's arrest. I'll have him hung for raping you, if nothing else!"

Her knees weakened with fear. She realized now that she was dealing with a man who could be classified as a lunatic. Flame took an unsteady step away from him.

"You . . . are . . . insane!" she gasped out. "Absolutely insane."

"Give me one good reason why I shouldn't arrest and hang this man," Colonel Russell said, flailing a hand in the air. "You've been gone for a full night. Because of this man, you didn't return home. I would never allow anyone to think that you were with him willingly." He lifted his chin and his eyes narrowed. "The utter shame of it, Reshelle."

"Flame!" she screamed. "My name is Flame! And, I'll have you know, I didn't return home because I—"

When White Fire cleared his throat noisily, drawing Flame's eyes to him, she remembered now what he had told her earlier. Under no circumstances should she let her father know that the Chippewa chief had taken her captive. Her father would grab that chance to start his war with them before Colonel Edwards could stop him.

She was torn by what to do or say, for if she didn't tell the truth, White Fire would take the blame.

Yet she knew the true hopelessness of it all, for even if she did tell her father the truth, he would still take White Fire and imprison him, because she had stayed the night with him. That alone seemed all that her father needed to place him in a dungeon before . . . before . . . he was hanged.

"Eh, what were you about to say?" Colonel Russell said, forking an eyebrow as he glanced slowly from Flame to White Fire, aware that something was going on between them by the way they were looking guardedly at one another.

Flame turned quick eyes to her father. "I was about to say that you cannot arrest White Fire for any reason, trumped up, or otherwise, for it is *I* who will stand up before everyone and call you a liar!" she cried. "I was with him willingly! I will proudly announce to the world that I made love with him, not only once, but twice last night!"

She placed her hands on her hips and defied her father with a stubborn, set stare. "You can't stop me, Father," she said, glaring into his eyes. "Even if you tie me to a bedpost, I shall find a way to get loose. I will never allow you to run my life again. Never!"

The colonel was enraged by her impertinence, and by what she had said in the presence of the soldiers about sleeping with the 'breed. He was more enraged at the thought of her being with any man sexually besides himself. Colonel Russell raised a hand and slapped her across the face, not once, but three times.

White Fire growled from the depths of his throat and yanked and strained his muscles in an attempt to get free from those who held him immobile. But no matter how hard he tried to defend his beloved, he was still held fast.

Stunned by her father having slapped her, tears flowed across Flame's cheeks as she stared into his evil, cold, gray eyes. "You'll be sorry," she then managed to say, breathless in her anger toward him.

"You are the one who will be sorry," Colonel Russell said, his teeth clenched, his jaw tight. "Damn it all to hell, Reshelle, you give me no choice but to send you to St. Louis to a convent."

He leaned down and spoke into her face. "And while you are on your way down the river under heavy guard, this 'breed will die not by hanging, but by a firing squad," he said, a crooked smile lifting his lips.

It was as though someone had slammed a fist in her stomach. Flame's breath was suddenly taken away by her father's threats. She turned and gazed at White Fire. Their eyes momentarily locked and held.

When she started to run to him, to fling herself into his arms, Colonel Russell reached out, grabbed her by a wrist and stopped her.

"Take him away!" Colonel Russell shouted, nodding toward White Fire. "Take him to the fort and lock him in chains!"

"No!" Flame cried, yanking at her arm.

But her father's grip was like steel around her wrist. She had no choice but to watch as White Fire was forced onto a horse, his wrists now tied behind him.

Flame's insides turned cold and empty as he was taken away.

She stumbled clumsily when her father finally released her. He shoved her toward her horse.

Lieutenant Green brought the colonel his horse.

Flame glanced down at the rifle that she had left on the ground near the blackberry bushes.

Colonel Russell also looked at the rifle, then gave Flame a slow, taunting stare. "Get on the horse, damn it," he said. "Your feisty days are over."

Flame knew that she had no choice but to do as he told her. She swung herself into her saddle, then turned her eyes heavenward.

Silently she prayed for Colonel Edwards not to wait too long to make things right again at Fort Snelling. Now there was much more at stake here than a war between the soldiers and the Indians. An innocent man was going to be sentenced to die.

As Flame rode off with her father, she could not help but feel guilty for what had happened. Had she not been so foolhardy last evening by leaving the fort in her frenzy of anger against her father, White Fire would be free.

Dispirited, and feeling defeated, Flame knew that no matter how much she blamed herself, it was for naught, for she knew that her father would have found another way, another reason, to eventually imprison White Fire.

"Or just out and out kill him like he surely killed the Indian agent," she thought to herself, shuddering at the thought.

More and more she found it so hard to believe that a man like this could be any kin to her whatsoever, for he seemed evil, through and through.

He seemed soulless!

She did not want to believe that somewhere inside herself there might lie dormant something evil and sinister waiting to surface. If her father could be this horrible, surely she might some day discover that she had inherited some of his traits.

"Lord have mercy," she whispered to herself, tears flowing down her cheeks in small rivulets.

Chapter 26

Love laughed again, and said,
smiling, "Be not afraid."

—John Bowyer Buchanan Nichols

Attired in a lovely green silk dress, Flame sat at a table in the dining room of the riverboat *Virginia,* a heaping breakfast placed before her. Her heart pounded. She had only moments ago been forced on the boat. And as her father had promised. she was not alone. She was being well guarded by two hefty soldier escorts.

Glancing through the windowpane, Flame saw that the boat had not yet started down the river toward St. Louis. She could still see the steep sides of the outer walls of the fort, which faced the river.

She swallowed hard and tears burned at the corners of her eyes to realize that White Fire was being held captive in the dungeon of Fort Snelling, his ankles weighted down by balls and chains.

"Ma'am, it'll be several hours before you get the chance to eat again," Lieutenant Green said as he sat down opposite her at the table. "If you want to keep up your strength, I'd suggest you eat."

She tightened her jaw and glared at the soldier, but the word "strength" stayed in her mind. Yes, she *did* need to eat to have the strength to carry through her plans. As soon as she could get on topdeck again, she planned to do something more reckless than anything else she had chanced to do in her life. She was going to jump overboard and swim to her freedom. Then she would find a way to get White Fire out of her father's clutches. And she must do it soon in order to save him.

She did not expect her father to wait too long before carrying out his devious plan of having White Fire shot by a firing squad, though he had to know that he would be questioned about it by the higher authorities.

Knowing her father, though, he would have answers that would clear him of any crime, just as he would surely have ways to clear himself of what White Fire had accused him of.

"Ma'am, I can't stress enough the importance of you eating your breakfast," Lieutenant Green said, gently shoving her empty plate closer to her. He then lifted a heavy platter of fried eggs toward her. "I'd suggest you start with these eggs, Reshelle. They're mighty tasty."

"Don't call me that name. My name is Flame. Do you hear? Flame!" she said, angrily grabbing the platter and slamming it down on the table beside her plate. She grimaced when several of the greasy eggs slid off the platter and landed on the snow-white linen tablecloth.

"Sorry, ma'am," the lieutenant said, staring at the eggs, their broken yellow centers running along the white cloth.

"Don't sorry me," Flame said, picking up a fork, plunking a large bite of egg from her plate. "Just leave me alone. I *do* see the importance in eating." She smiled slyly at him. "And in keeping my strength."

His eyebrows forked at her behavior and by the look of mischief in her eyes. Then he shrugged and offered her a platter heavy with stacks of pancakes. "Pancake, ma'am?" he said softly.

Flame eyed the pancakes, then the syrup, then smiled a smug, silent thank-you to the lieutenant. If anything could give her strength, the sweet syrup would be more lasting than eggs, bacon, or the butter-drenched toast.

She grabbed the platter of pancakes, shoved several onto her plate, then poured gobs of thick maple syrup onto them.

"My, but you *are* hungry," lieutenant Green said, idly scratching his brow.

"Very," Flame said, chewing big mouthfuls of the food.

When he offered her sausage and bacon, she nodded and pointed toward her plate.

He placed some of the sausage and bacon on it.

She could tell that he was dumbfounded by how eagerly and by how much she ate. She shoved bite after bite into her mouth. But even though she was making a good display of someone who was starved, food was not what was on her mind.

White Fire! She was so frightened for him.

What if her father placed him before the firing

squad even this morning before she had a chance
to go and get help for him?

When she felt a jerking sensation in the floor-
boards of the boat, and heard the boat's shrill whistle, which she knew came just as it moved off from
shore, Flame's heart skipped a beat.

She looked anxiously at the window and saw that
the boat was moving slowly into deeper water. She
didn't have much time. If she waited too long she
would have too far to travel to get help for White Fire.

She started to rise from the chair, but a heavy
hand on her shoulder reminded her of the other
lieutenant who had stayed standing while she and
Lieutenant Green ate their breakfast.

She turned slow eyes up at Lieutenant Hudson,
whose grip was still heavy on her shoulder. "Unhand
me this minute," she said, in her voice a low hiss of a
threat.

"You ain't going anywhere," Lieutenant Hudson
said. "Finish your breakfast, then I'll escort you to
your cabin."

"What you are doing is wrong," Flame said, glaring
from one soldier to the other. "The government isn't
paying you to babysit the colonel's daughter. If you
don't let me go and allow me to do as I wish, I will
turn both your names into the authorities. I will make
sure the President realizes that you are in cahoots
with my father to start a war in the Minnesota Territory."

She smiled slyly from one to the other when she
saw a quick concern leap into their eyes.

"I don't know what you're talking about," Lieutenant Green said, his eyes narrowing.

"I'll make sure the President—you know, the President of the United States—won't believe a word you say," Flame said, laughing haughtily. "Now I'd suggest you both be on your way and forget you had anything to do with keeping me hostage on this boat, or else. . . ."

Lieutenant Green rose from the table and went to her. He placed a solid grip on Flame's upper right arm. "Come with me," he said, almost bodily lifting her from the chair with the hand clasped to arm. "I don't take much to threats, especially from a lady." He sighed. "And I'm damn tired of being the one chosen always to be your escort. I'm in the army to serve my country, not . . . not Colonel Russell."

"Well, then *don't*," Flame said. "Let me go. It's as easy as that."

She flinched when his fingers tightened on her shoulder as he forced her to walk ahead of him. Flame looked around her to see if anyone on board might be looking at her, who might listen to reason and help her.

But the only ones aboard the ship on this early morning voyage to St. Louis were more soldiers. Some sat with wives. Some sat alone. But none of them paid attention to her, for it seemed that all of them had been warned about this colonel's daughter who was too feisty for her own good, and because of her behavior, was on her way to a convent.

Feeling helpless, Flame walked dispiritedly from the dining room. When she stepped out into the fresh air of early morning, and the wind whipped the skirt of her dress up past her ankles, she realized that both lieutenants were taking advantage of seeing the silken taper of her legs, their eyes showing their interest—their lusty thoughts.

For a moment Flame thought she might take advantage of their obvious hunger for a woman and offer herself to them, and take flight from the boat while their breeches were down.

But she was afraid of their brute force and feared that once they got stirred up sexually, they might go ahead and force her to do what she had not planned to carry through with to the end.

No, she thought sullenly to herself. She wouldn't take that approach. There was too much danger in that.

She gazed at the land passing by on either side of the boat. She mentally measured how far the boat was from both shorelines. It was no farther than the length of water she had swum many times in St. Louis. Although her father had always warned her of the undercurrent in the Mississippi River, she and her friends had gone swimming frequently downriver from the family mansion. She had never felt threatened by any undercurrents.

She stared down at the river as the soldiers led her toward her private cabin. She was not familiar with this stretch and how the undercurrents might be, yet she knew that she had no choice but to take her chances in it. She would risk her very life if it meant saving White Fire!

She looked at Lieutenant Green, and then at Lieutenant Hudson. Both of them were now holding her by an arm. Then she again stared at the water.

She gave two hard yanks and managed to get free from the soldiers.

Lifting the hem of her dress into her arms, she broke into a mad run toward the railing of the boat.

Just as she reached it and tried to scramble over the side, her breath was taken away when Lieutenant Green grabbed her around the waist and stopped her.

For a moment things went black inside her head.

Then her vision cleared and she realized that Lieutenant Green had grabbed her in his arms and was now carrying her hurriedly toward her cabin.

When the other soldier opened the door and stepped aside, her heart sank, for she knew now that they would lock her inside.

She felt trapped. Trapped! Surely White Fire would soon die!

Chapter 27

All I imagined musing lonely,
When dreaming 'neath the greenwood tree,
Seeming to fancy visions only.

—John Clare

Chief Gray Feather sat before his lodge fire, eating wild-rice cakes covered with thick, rich syrup. His granddaughter, Dancing Star, had stayed the night with him. She sat at his side, her fingers dripping with syrup, her eyes content as she shoved another piece of cake and syrup into her mouth with her fingertips.

"You eat well this morning," Gray Feather said, smiling down at Dancing Star. "You will grow up and be healthy and strong like your grandfather."

"Where is Mother?" Dancing Star said, glancing toward the door. "Why did she leave me here with you to spend the night instead of having me sleep with her in our own lodge?"

Gray Feather licked his fingers clean of the syrup.

He gave a worried glance toward the entrance flap,
then stared quietly into the lodge fire.

"*Gee-bah-bah-nahn,* Grandfather, where is Mother?"
Dancing Star persisted. She wriggled onto his lap
and faced him as she twined her tiny arms around
his neck. She gave him a steady gaze as he looked
into her eyes. "Do you not think Mother would also
enjoy eating breakfast with us? Should I go and
awaken her?

"*Gah-ween,* no," Gray Feather said, his voice hollow.
"Let her *nee-ban,* sleep."

"But why sleep without me?" Dancing Star asked,
sighing. "And why is she so quiet and strange lately?"

Gray Feather gazed at Dancing Star a moment
longer. Then he lifted her from his lap and rose to
his feet. He went and drew back the entrance flap
and gazed at Song Sparrow's wigwam, which sat not
that far from his own.

"Why is she so quiet and different in personality
lately?" he said softly. "It is because of an *ee-nee-nee,*
man."

"You are speaking of White Fire?" Dancing Star
said, going to Gray Feather, looking up at him again
with her innocently wide, dark eyes.

Gray Feather nodded. "*Ay-uh,* it is because of
White Fire that your mother is so quiet and withdrawn these past few days," he said thickly. "But in
time, she will be her usual, cheerful self again."

He dropped the flap and went to bend low over a
washbasin of water. He sank his hands into the water
and sloshed them around until they were clean of
the syrup.

He then went and picked up Dancing Star and
brought her to the water. "Wash your hands and then

we will go and awaken your mother," he said. "We will take her a platter of wild-rice cakes."

"With lots of syrup on them?" Dancing Star said, putting her hands into the water, enjoying splashing them around in it.

"*Ay-uh,* yes, with lots of syrup on them," Gray Feather said, laughing throatily. "She loves sweet things, especially *geen,* you."

"Am I sweet?" Dancing Star asked, smiling softly up at Gray Feather.

"Better than all of the syrup in the world," Gray Feather said, placing her to the floor as she lifted her hands from the water and shook them free of drops.

He grabbed the platter of wild-rice cakes.

Dancing Star picked up the wooden bowl of syrup.

They left the wigwam and walked out into the bright sunshine. When they reached Song Sparrow's lodge, Gray Feather stopped and looked up at the smoke hole. There was no smoke spiraling into the sky. That had to mean that his daughter was still fast asleep.

He hesitated waking her, then shrugged his shoulders. It was a beautiful morning. It would do her good to wake up to the songs of the birds and the laughter of her daughter and to the warmth of the sun.

"Hold the flap aside for me," Gray Feather said, nodding at his granddaughter toward the buckskin flap.

Dancing Star held the bowl of syrup with one hand and slid the flap aside with the other. She waited as her grandfather entered the lodge.

She then went inside, herself, and stood, wide-eyed, staring down at where her mother's blankets had not been rolled out for her to sleep upon.

Then she smiled. "Mother is already awake," she said. "She is down at the river bathing."

Dancing Star set the syrup down on a bulrush mat and ran from the wigwam. "Grandfather, I will go and bathe with Mother," she shouted over her shoulder.

Gray Feather set down the platter of wild-rice cakes on the bulrush mats beside the syrup. He kneaded his chin thoughtfully as he gazed at the cold ashes in the fire pit. It was not usual for his daughter to leave her lodge without first starting her fire, which would last the entire day for the preparation of her meals for herself and her daughter.

He again gazed at the blankets and pelts that were so neatly rolled up at the sides of the lodge. "I do not think she slept in them at all last night," he suddenly said aloud, a sudden fear leaping into his heart.

He thought back to the previous evening and at how moody his daughter had been; how quiet and withdrawn. Even when she had asked if Dancing Star would spend the night with Gray Feather, he had felt that something was amiss.

"Chief Gray Feather! Chief Gray Feather!"

A voice filled with panic and alarm outside the lodge drew Gray Feather quickly outside. When he saw his nephew, Red Buffalo, standing there holding Song Sparrow in his arms, her body lifeless and limp, her eyes locked in a death stare, everything within Gray Feather went cold with despair.

His daughter was dead! The mother to his grand-child was dead!

"I found her hanging by her long hair . . . from . . . a limb of a tree," Red Buffalo stammered out. "She wrapped a long coil of her hair around her neck and hung herself with it!"

Chief Gray Feather felt too numb to move. He could do nothing but stare at his daughter.

She was gone! This quickly she was gone from this earth. He would not hear her laughter again. And he would not see her sadness.

"*Gee-mah-mah,* Mother!" Dancing Star screamed as she came running toward them. "*Gee-mah-mah!*"

The child's voice brought Gray Feather out of his trance. He looked at Dancing Star as she stopped and became quiet as she stared at the lifeless body of her mother.

"*Ah-bee-no-gee,* child, come to me," Chief Gray Feather said sadly. He bent to a knee, his arms outstretched for Dancing Star.

When she went to him, her body suddenly racked with tears, he held her tightly to him.

As he stared across her shoulder at Song Sparrow, anger filled his very soul at why his daughter had become so distraught that she lost her will to live.

"White Fire . . ." he whispered, the name a low hiss as it crossed his pursed lips.

But Gray Feather had done everything within his power to make the man his daughter loved her husband. And because Gray Feather loved his daughter so much, he had gone beyond what he would normally do to bring the man she loved into her life.

Only now did Gray Feather truly know just how *much* his daughter had loved White Fire!

Oh, but if only White Fire could have returned the love with the same sort of strength, with the same sort of passion, Gray Feather would have not lost his daughter in such a way—in total disgrace.

Chapter 28

*To her is only known his faith that from the world
is hidden.*

—Nicholas Breton

His granddaughter on his lap, Chief Gray Feather
reined in his horse in front of White Fire's cabin.

Somber, and feeling the stark weight of the emptiness in his heart that the death of his daughter had
left, Gray Feather held Dancing Star snugly against
his chest as he slid from the horse, then placed her
tiny moccasined feet on solid ground.

His upper lip stiff, Gray Feather gazed at White
Fire's cabin. He saw no smoke rising from the chimney. Then he looked around for his horse. He saw no
horse.

"He is not here," he whispered to himself.

But Gray Feather would wait for White Fire's
return, *that* was for certain. He was there with a mission and he would not leave until White Fire understood how it must be now that Song Sparrow was

dead. White Fire was free of his daughter, but not Gray Feather's daughter's child!

"*Mah-szhon,* go to the door and open it," Gray Feather said, nodding at his granddaughter as she turned her soft, questioning eyes to him.

He slung his reins around the horse's hitching rail, then went to stand over his granddaughter. He placed a gentle hand on her shoulder. "Open the door, grandchild, for this is now your home," he said sullenly. "You have a right to go and come as you please. As do I, your grandfather."

Gray Feather folded his arms across his bare chest and set his jaw firmly as Dancing Star placed her tiny hand on the door latch and slowly opened the door.

When she turned questioning eyes up at him again, Gray Feather frowned down at her. "Go inside," he said flatly. "I will follow."

Dancing Star nodded and looked as though she was going to enter. But instead she turned and flung herself against Gray Feather's legs and desperately hugged them.

He understood her fear, her sadness, her feeling of loss. Her mother's burial was not so far behind her and the mourning in the village was continuing. Gray Feather placed a gentle hand on Dancing Star's head.

"You are so small, so dear to me," he said emotionally. "But because of how your mother died, I must sever my ties with you."

He bent down and swept his arms around the child, lifted her up and held her close as she snuggled against his chest, sobbing.

"My child," he whispered, caressing her long, thick, black hair, "I do love you still. I shall evermore love you. But I cannot keep you with me. Seeing you every day would be a reminder of what your mother did . . . how your mother *died*."

Dancing Star leaned away from him and gazed intently into his eyes. "Tell me again how she died," she said, her child's voice so soft, the words intelligently said for a child of such few years.

"It is not a pleasant thing to talk about," Gray Feather said, his spine stiffening. "You had to be told the truth once, but never will I repeat it to you. In time, I hope that it will fade from your heart so that you can remember your mother with respect and love."

"I love her now," Dancing Star said, her lower lip quivering. "Just because she . . . she killed herself, how could that make *you* love her less? Do you not see how sad she must have been? Do you not hurt for her, Grandfather, as I hurt for her?"

"Gray Feather hurts so badly for your mother that it is hard to think of anything or anyone else," Gray Feather said sadly. "So you see, I, also, have much to get through before I can face life again as I faced it before your mother chose to die such useless a death."

Dancing Star laid her cheek against his chest. "I will never die such a death," she said, her voice innocently sweet. "I will never hurt you in such a way."

Knowing that these might be his last private moments with his granddaughter, because he saw no other way than to give her to someone else, Gray Feather stood there for a moment longer in the morning sunshine. He held her close, oh, so near and dear to his heart. And at this moment, he almost turned and took her home with him again.

But having been taught all of his life that suicide was not only a cowardly way to end one's life, but also a mortal sin, he had no choice but to leave his granddaughter to be raised by someone besides himself. In his heart he saw the child, his precious grandchild, taking part of her mother's sin.

And thinking White Fire responsible for Song Sparrow's death, since she had killed herself over him, Gray Feather knew that her child was now White Fire's responsibility.

"Will I call White Fire 'Father'?" Dancing Star suddenly blurted out, as she gazed at Gray Feather with questioning eyes. "Will he call me 'Daughter?'"

"It will be chosen between you and White Fire what you will call one another," Gray Feather said, taking slow steps toward the open door. "In time, *ay-uh,* I do hope that you will become his daughter in all respects and that you will be a sister to his son."

"He has a son?" Dancing Star said, her eyes wide as Gray Feather stepped inside the lodge.

"*Ay-uh,* he has a son and that is partly why he would not take your mother to a marriage bed with him," Gray Feather said somberly.

He did not speak of the woman who was the cause of White Fire's rejection of Song Sparrow, yet he knew that Dancing Star surely remembered the flame-haired woman who had been a captive for a short while at their village.

But he also knew that Dancing Star was too young to understand why White Fire had come and spoken on the white woman's behalf and took her from the village, no longer a captive. The child was too young to understand that this flaming-haired woman had won White Fire's heart over her mother.

His jaw tightened as he thought further of Flame. Would *she*, when she became White Fire's wife, treat Dancing Star as a mother would treat a daughter? Or would she resent Dancing Star for being part of White Fire's life? Would Flame be able to accept a son and a daughter as soon as she spoke her marriage vows? Would the beautiful, young white woman be able to accept an instant family?

Gray Feather's eyes narrowed, thinking that in a sense, Flame was to blame for Song Sparrow's death as much as White Fire, and it was only right that she, also, would have to care for Song Sparrow's child.

Knowing White Fire so well, Gray Feather did not doubt that he would see that Flame and everyone else would treat Dancing Star with respect.

And who could not love his Dancing Star?

Ay-uh, Gray Feather saw the flaming-haired woman as soon taking Dancing Star into her arms and loving her as she would her very own flesh-and-blood daughter.

It was evident that Flame did not look at the Chippewa as people beneath her, that she did respect them even though she had been taken captive for a short time, and that their skin color differed. She had fallen in love with someone of such skin color. She would surely love this child as much!

They entered the cabin and Gray Feather instantly saw that everything was quiet and damp, without a fire burning on the grate.

Dancing Star trembled with a chill and twined an arm around her grandfather's neck and clung to him.

"It will be all right," Gray Feather said, his voice breaking. He studied the cold ashes beneath the grate, knowing now that White Fire had not been there for some time. He could not help but wonder where he had gone when he had left the village, if not here, his own home?

Then his eyes narrowed as he thought about the surly, evil colonel who had become a threat to both Flame and White Fire. Perhaps they had hesitated to return to the cabin, thinking to avoid the colonel's wrath.

Yet he could not see White Fire as being the sort who would run from such a fight. And Gray Feather knew how much White Fire loved his son. That, also, would be why he would not leave the area.

"Where is White Fire?" Dancing Star asked, now walking slowly around the room, looking closely at everything.

"I do not know," Gray Feather said somberly as he knelt before the fireplace. He placed small twigs on the grate, and then larger logs. "But this is now your home. We will stay until White Fire returns."

Dancing Star moved slowly into the bedroom.

When she saw the child's crib against the far wall, she went to it and stared at it. Her gaze settled on a small horse that had been carved from wood. She inched her hand toward it, then stopped when Gray Feather came and stood beside her.

"'That crib belonged to White Fire's son when he was a smaller child than he is now," Gray Feather said. He saw his granddaughter's interest in the tiny wooden horse. "The horse also belongs to his son, but I am sure the child would share it with you if he were here and he saw your interest in it."

He picked up the toy and handed it to his grand-daughter; then he led her back into the living room.

"How long will we have to wait before White Fire

comes home?" Dancing Star asked as Gray Feather sat down on the blankets before the fire, then gathered her onto his lap and held her.

"As long as it takes for him to return," Gray Feather said sullenly as he took a quick look toward the door.

When he heard the cry of an eagle outside, not that far from the open door, a chill rode up and down his spine.

He could not help but think that the eagle's cry was some sort of an omen. Perhaps White Fire had run into trouble after he had left the village.

Yet there was no proof of that except that he was not here in his lodge. He could not send out his warriors to look for him on such a foolish notion as that. Surely White Fire was all right. He would arrive home safe and would embrace Dancing Star as his birth daughter.

"Tell me again how you came to know White Fire," Dancing Star asked, gazing up at Gray Feather. "He is not Chippewa, so why do you care so much for him?"

Gray Feather sighed. "There is so much about the young brave that reminds me so much of myself when I was his age," he murmured. "And too often I have dreams that set him at my right side in council, as though he is my son by birth. Our hearts became as one almost the moment I set eyes on him when he came to our village in friendship." He swallowed hard. "And your mother loved him."

"You did not have a son, only a daughter," Dancing Star said, a sadness entering her eyes.

"No, I did not have a son, and now I do not even have a daughter," Gray Feather said.

He gazed into Dancing Star's eyes and could not find the words to tell her that he no longer even had a granddaughter. The moment Song Sparrow had placed the coil of her hair around her neck and chose the cowardly way out of life; she had yanked Dancing Star from Gray Feather's arms and heart.

"I will always love you, Grandfather," Dancing Star murmured, as though she had read his thoughts.

Taking these last moments with her, before he left her to live separately from himself and his people, Gray Feather hugged her tightly to him. "No matter what I feel forced to do, I will always love you, too, Granddaughter," he said, his voice breaking.

When she kissed him softly on the cheek, that part of his heart that had been left intact after the discovery of his daughter, broke into shreds.

Chapter 29

She bid me take life easy,
as the grass grows on the weirs;
But I was young and foolish,
and now am full of tears.

—William Butler Yeats

His wrists and ankles raw from the chains and the weight of the balls holding them down, White Fire hung from the stone wall, the bars on three sides of him a crude reminder of what his fate might soon be.

Stripped of all his clothing, and with welts on his wrists from trying to get free of the chains, he stared up at the window at the highest point of his cell.

The sky was blue with only a few puffs of white clouds sailing past. He could hear the activity in the courtyard, reveille having been sounded some time ago.

His stomach aching, he fought against his mounting hunger, for there were more important things on his mind at this moment than food; than even his own welfare. Flame.

He wondered where she was now. All that he knew was that she was being sent upriver to a convent.

And then there was Michael. White Fire hung his head and sighed as in his mind's eye he saw his son and the trust that he had finally gained from him, which had been torn asunder by Michael's adopted parents during White Fire's absence.

"All of this is gone from me now," he whispered to himself.

He saw no hope of getting free. No one but Flame and the soldiers at Fort Snelling knew that he was incarcerated. The soldiers would not dare go behind the sadistic colonel's back and release him, though they all had to know that he was wrongly imprisoned.

And he knew that Flame would be watched so carefully that she could not come to him and help him escape.

"And Chief Gray Feather would have no way of knowing. . . ." he said.

He gasped when a fat rat came scurrying by, stopping long enough to place his twitching nose at White Fire's bare toes.

"Scat!" he said, wiggling his toes.

He sighed with relief when the rat scrambled on past him and left through the open spaces of the bars.

When he heard voices, White Fire strained his neck to see whose they were. The door was closed between his cell and the outer room where guards were stationed day and night. No one had even come and spoken to him since his incarceration, or he might have tried convincing them of the wrong that was being done here.

He sighed heavily, for it seemed even that orders had been given not to feed him. Perhaps he would not die by hanging or by a firing squad after all. Colonel Russell might let him slowly starve to death.

He lowered his head again, his chin almost touching his chest. "Flame . . ." he whispered. "Flame . . ."

Chapter 30

Birds in the high hall-garden
Were crying and calling to her,
One is come to woo her.

—Alfred Lord Tennyson

Having heard the two soldiers talking about wanting more morning coffee, and knowing that only one of them was outside the cabin door, Flame took the opportunity to set her plan of escape into motion. She opened one of her travel bags and removed one of her most lightweight skirts and a white blouse.

Her heart beat quickly. She must dive overboard soon or they would be too far downriver for her to get help for White Fire quickly enough. Flame removed her beautiful silk dress and hurried into the skirt and blouse.

She stared at her bare feet. It would be best for her not to have shoes on during her swim. Yet knowing that she could travel shod much more quickly once she reached dry land, she stepped into a soft pair of flat shoes.

Then she searched through another valise and found the letter her father had given to her to deliver to the head nun at the convent where she was to stay until he sent for her.

"Obedience, *ha*," she said sarcastically as she pulled out the letter. "I'll show him a thing or two about how to teach me obedience."

Grasping it in one hand, Flame went to the cabin door and tapped on it. "Lieutenant," she said, loud enough for him to hear her through the closed door. "Will you please come in my cabin for a moment?"

She looked around the room for something with which to bang him on the head.

She quickly thought better of resorting to that sort of violence and stepped back from the door and smiled wickedly up at Lieutenant Green as he opened it and came into the cabin. She was glad that it was him, for she knew that he had the other letter—the one that was the exact copy of the one she carried.

Lieutenant Green's gaze swept quickly over her and he noticed her change of attire. Then he looked guardedly at her, his eyes squinting into the soft rays of the sun as it poured in velvet, golden streamers through the one cabin window.

"Well?" he said, placing his fists on his hips. "What do you want this time?"

"Do you see this letter?" Flame said, giving him a wicked smile as she held the envelope out before her.

"Sure, I see the letter," Lieutenant Green said, forking an eyebrow. "Why? What about it?"

"Do you know what the letter is all about?" she

asked, slowly opening the envelope, and just as slowly removing the letter from inside it.

"It's a letter to the supervising nun at the convent," Lieutenant Green said. "I'm to see that you, personally, place it in the hands of the nun."

"And what if I don't give it to the nun?" Flame taunted, waving the unfolded letter before his eyes. "What if I tear it up instead?"

As his eyes widened, she did just that. She tore the letter in half, and then continued to rip it into shreds.

"Now what are you going to tell my father when you tell him that you didn't stop me from tearing up this important letter?" Flame said, laughing mockingly.

He didn't know that she knew about the duplicate letter. She had seen her father palm it into his hand, looking slyly over his shoulder to make sure Flame didn't see.

She had turned her eyes away quickly enough so that he had not caught her witnessing his action. She had known the true purpose of a second letter. He had expected her to tear up the one he gave to her.

She now waited anxiously for Lieutenant Green to pull an envelope from his inside jacket pocket, to show her that he had a backup for the one she tore up.

Lieutenant Green laughed throatily as he looked away from her long enough to slip one of his hands inside his jacket pocket for the letter.

The moment he turned his eyes away from her, Flame stepped quickly around him and ran from the cabin. She closed the door behind her, and then ran over to the boat's railing.

She didn't take the time to stare down at the swirling, muddy water of the Mississippi River, fearing she might have second thoughts about the dangers of the undercurrents.

But she did take the time to look around her, to see if there was anyone who could quickly tell the soldiers how she had escaped. She smiled when she saw no one. Not even a crew member. Everyone was still leisurely enjoying morning breakfast and coffee in the dining room.

With a racing pulse, Flame climbed over the railing and jumped, feet first, into the water.

With the wide, powerful strokes that she had learned swimming in the Mississippi River back at St. Louis, she swam toward the shore. She prayed that the soldiers wouldn't think to look in the river for her escape, but would instead start searching the hidden passageways of the boat, where someone could hide for the duration of the voyage.

She could hear the steady swishing sound of the large paddlewheel churning the water as it took the boat downriver.

Flame then smiled when she saw the riverbank only a short distance away. She thanked her lucky stars that the undercurrent had not been all that strong. Only once or twice had she felt it sucking at her legs and feet, and then she would swim free of the threat.

Panting, water dripping from her hair, her skirt and blouse clinging to her like a second skin, Flame finally reached the shore. Her feet slipped and slid on the muddy bottom as she made her way toward the rocky embankment.

Once there, she stopped and turned and stared at the riverboat as it floated farther and farther away from her.

Smiling, she pulled her fingers through her hair and drew it back from her face, to hang in long, wet ringlets across her shoulders and down her back.

"'Bye, 'bye," she whispered to the soldiers, giggling. "Now what are you going to tell my papa?"

Not wanting to waste any more time gloating over her escape, Flame rushed up the embankment and stepped into knee-high grass.

Trying to get her bearings, to ascertain how far she was from civilization, she stopped and looked into the distance, then looked from side to side.

Frowning, she saw that she had traveled too far downriver to go to Fort Parker to ask for Colonel Edwards's help in getting White Fire set free.

But she knew that she was within walking distance of Chief Gray Feather's village. It was not that far through the thick trees. The river would be visible to her again where it made a wide turn before it straightened out and ran on past Fort Snelling.

"Yes, Gray Feather is my only chance to get White Fire free," she murmured, hoping that her father would not be too hasty in his desire to see to White Fire's end.

Flame gazed heavenward. "Lord, please let me be in time," she prayed. "Oh, please help me find someone to help me get White Fire free. Please let it be Chief Gray Feather."

She lifted her skirt and ran into the forest. Yet something that White Fire had warned her about came to her so suddenly, she stopped and wondered if she was right to go to the Chippewa chief after all.

White Fire had warned her that it was not wise to get the Indians involved in anything that might draw them into a war with the soldiers at Fort Snelling.

If Gray Feather helped set him free, would not that give Flame's father all the reason he needed to set his plans in motions to start a war with the Chippewa, and then the Sioux, until all of the Indians in the Minnesota Territory were annihilated?

Then she thought of Colonel Edwards's role in this. If Colonel Edwards had taken what White Fire had told him seriously enough, surely Colonel Edwards would soon move against her father and stop any warring before it got started.

"He's got to have believed White Fire," she whispered, a shiver racing up and down her spine as her worries for her beloved mounted.

Desperate, Flame broke into a mad run through the forest. She stopped only long enough to get her breath when her side began to ache from her incessant push to get to the Indian village.

"I'll never make it in time at this rate," she said, a sob lodging in her throat. But she was not going to give up that easily. She *would* reach the Indian village. She *would* get the chief's help.

Several warriors could go to the fort and get White Fire out of that damnable prison where chains and balls held him hostage.

It was a horrible thought to know that what was done to him now was far worse than what had happened to him at the hand of the Sioux during his three-year captivity with them.

"And to think that my father is the cause!" she cried to the heavens.

Then she stopped with a start and her eyes widened

when she saw a cabin through a break in the trees up
ahead. Her heart pounded like a thousand drums
inside her chest as she also saw a small barn at the
far side of the cleared yard at the back of the cabin.

"If only I had a horse," she whispered, edging her
way closer to the clearing that led to the cabin and
barn. But she had never stolen anything. Could she
now? Or should she go and ask those who lived at the
cabin for help?

No, she could not take that chance. She had no
idea who lived there, whether it was a family, or a
lonely trapper who might take advantage of a lone
woman.

"I have no choice," she whispered. She *had* to steal
a horse, if one was available.

As she got closer to the back of the barn, she
scarcely breathed while looking guardedly from side
to side.

When she saw no one, she rushed to the barn and
placed her back flat against it. She waited long
enough to get her breath, then crept along the back
of the barn until she could look around a corner and
get a full view of the cabin.

Smoke spiraled from the chimney. But still she saw
no one. She didn't see any movement through the
windows, for the sun was reflecting against them,
making the pane of glass look like a shield of orange
fire.

Then her eyes widened and she turned an ear in
the direction of the cabin when she heard the strum-
ming of a guitar and a man's voice as he began
singing.

Flame smiled. The man inside the cabin would be
too occupied with his music to notice what might

happen outside. The music would even drown out the sound of a horse being stolen.

"Let there *be* a horse," Flame whispered, knowing that some of the trappers in this area owned only mules, which were too often stubborn to move but an inch at a time along the trail.

Holding her breath, her eyes watching the door of the cabin, Flame ran around the edge of the barn and headed toward the open door.

Once inside, she sighed with relief when she saw a great roan standing in a stall, idly nibbling on hay, its big brown eyes trustingly watching her approach.

Flame smiled at her luck when she saw that whoever the horse belonged to had not removed its saddle.

"Whoa, boy," Flame whispered as she approached the roan. "I'm a friend. Do you hear? A friend. You and I are going to take a ride this morning."

The horse softly whinnied and shook its heavy mane playfully as Flame untied the reins from around a rail. She knew that she had made a fast friend of the animal. Smiling, she led the horse from its stall.

To be sure she had the horse's full trust, she stopped long enough to run her hands along its withers, then allowed it to nuzzle her hand.

"We're pals, right?" she whispered, again patting its withers. "You're going to get me to the Indian village real quick, aren't you?"

Feeling comfortable enough now with the horse, and fully trusting it, Flame led it over to the door of the barn. She stopped and stared at the cabin once again.

She listened intently and smiled when she heard that the man was still too involved with his music to know that he was soon to lose a valuable horse to a lady.

"I'll get it back to him whenever I can," she whispered. She hurriedly led the horse from the barn.

She walked into the shadows of the forest, then swung herself into the saddle and rode off at a fast gallop.

When she heard a man loudly cursing behind her, she knew that the thievery had been discovered. But the man had no way to catch her. She had stolen his swiftest mode of travel.

Feeling guilty for being a thief, Flame frowned. Then she leaned low over the horse and forgot everything and everyone but White Fire.

Her hair flying in the wind, she imagined White Fire in balls and chains. Her father had taken her into the dark, dank dungeon where White Fire had been incarcerated. Her father had forced her to see how he was being held there, unclothed and helpless.

She would never forget her father's evil laughter when he saw her distress over White Fire's mistreatment. That laughter, the harshness of it, made Flame vow that somehow, some way, she *would* set her beloved free.

She rode hard through the forest, and then made her way along the Mississippi River, knowing that she should soon reach the Chippewa village. She was now familiar enough with the terrain around their village to know when she would be getting near. She was seeing much now that was familiar to her.

When she saw the wigwams a short distance away through a break in the trees, Flames's heart soared. Her plan to set White Fire free would work! Surely all she had to do was ask the old chief and he would find a way to spring White Fire from his imprisonment. Had he not rescued White Fire and his daughter from the Sioux?

Keeping that thought, taking hope from it, Flame rode in a hard gallop into the outer perimeters of the Chippewa village.

Then she saw the bitter, sour glares as she drew the roan to a shimmying halt. She wondered why she would draw such antagonistic stares from those who had recently been friendly toward her.

Then she noticed how quiet the village was. It was as though someone had died.

Oh, Lord, she hoped that someone wasn't Chief Gray Feather! As far as she knew, he was the only member of the St. Croix band of the Chippewa who cared deeply enough for White Fire to help him in his critical time of need!

Chapter 31

How should I your true love know
From another one?

—William Shakespeare

Trying to ignore the cold stares, struggling with everything within her to keep her fears at bay, Flame rode onward through the village, then drew a tight rein before Chief Gray Feather's large wigwam.

Just as she slid out of the saddle, she found herself surrounded by several Chippewa warriors, their faces dark and unfriendly. Her eyes moving in jerks from one to the other, she slowly backed away from them.

Then she turned, and without asking permission, darted inside the chiefs dwelling.

Once inside, she stopped and looked slowly around her. No one was there. Cold ashes lay in the fire pit.

There was a strange, muted silence, not only inside the lodge, but outside where everyone had seemed to have stopped all of their normal activity.

Realizing now that something must have happened

at the Chippewa village, and feeling as though she had stepped into a lion's den, Flame was torn with what to do.

It seemed that much of the Chippewas' anger was focused on her. But why? she wondered, trying to think of what she might have done to cause such anger. When she had last been here, it had been on friendly terms with their chief after she forgave him for taking her hostage. Something had to have happened since then to bring on such hatred and resentment.

She stepped farther into the wigwam. Then she turned with a start when she heard someone behind her.

Eyes wide, her heart thumping, she stared up at Red Buffalo, whose midnight black eyes were narrowed, whose jaw was tight.

"You are not welcome here," Red Buffalo said angrily. He gestured. "You do not belong in the chief's lodge. *Mah-szhon,* go. Do not come to our village again, *ever.*"

Stubbornly deciding that she would not leave until she had answers, Flame stood her ground. "Why are you being so unfriendly toward me?" she asked softly.

She looked slowly around the wigwam again, then gazed into the tall Indian's eyes. "And where is Chief Gray Feather?" she murmured. She swallowed hard. "Has something happened to him?"

"Not to our chief, but to my cousin, our chief's daughter," Red Buffalo said solemnly.

A warning rushed through Flame, especially at how the mention of Song Sparrow had seemed to make more anger leap into Red Buffalo's eyes.

"What about Song Sparrow?" she found the courage to ask, but speaking only faintly.

"She is gone from us," Red Buffalo said, angrily folding his arms across his chest. "So many of our people see you as partially the cause of her death."

Flame paled. She took an unsteady step away from him. "She is dead? And you see me as the cause?" she asked, placing a hand to her throat. "Why would anyone blame me for Song Sparrow's death?"

"She died because of having lost White Fire's love," Red Buffalo said sullenly.

"Do you mean to say that she . . . she killed herself?" Flame said, feeling more threatened by each new discovery.

"*Ay-uh*, that is how she died," Red Buffalo said.

He took a slow step toward her.

She took a quicker one back from him.

"If not for you, she would not have died," Red Buffalo growled out. "In time White Fire *would* have married her."

"White Fire never loved her," Flame said.

She then wished she had not so openly spoken her mind when she saw the warriors face redden with rage.

"He would have learned to love her, for Song Sparrow was sweet and lovable," Red Buffalo said. "She had no enemies except the love she felt for a man who scorned her."

He then gestured toward the entrance flap. "You are in our chiefs lodge without his permission," he said in a monotone. "You are in our village without an invitation. *Mah-szhon, go.* Go while you can."

"What . . . do . . . you mean by saying go . . . while I can?" Flame asked, swallowing hard. "How can I make you understand that I am not to blame for anything?"

"Too many will never believe that," Red Buffalo said. He went to the entrance flap and lifted it. "Go now."

"But you haven't told me where I can find Chief Gray Feather," Flame murmured, inching toward the flap, her eyes never leaving the warrior's. "I need his help. *Please* tell me where I can find him."

"You are an interference in the lives of the Chippewa," Red Buffalo said, glaring at her. "Why would I tell you where our chief is, or why he is there? None of my people's lives are your concern, especially not our chief's."

Frustrated, and fearing that as each moment passed White Fire's life was more at stake, Flame impulsively grabbed Red Buffalo by an arm. She sank her fingers into his copper flesh.

"I desperately need to know where I can find your chief," she said, begging him with her eyes. "White Fire is in trouble. He needs your chief's help."

The fact that White Fire was in trouble caused Red Buffalo to be somewhat taken aback. Flame searched his eyes, trying to understand his feelings.

Then she thought of why there was such anger toward her today. Surely these people had the same anger toward White Fire, for it was he who had turned his back on Song Sparrow's love. The Chippewa must hold him responsible for her death!

"You also blame White Fire for Song Sparrow's death, don't you?" she gasped out. "You no longer see him as a friend . . . as a brother?"

Red Buffalo's lips became tightly pursed together.

He offered no further comment as he continued to glare at Flame.

"If anything happens to him, don't you know that you will be partially responsible?" Flame said, her voice rising in pitch. She felt almost hysterical now that she saw that she would not have the help she had sought here at the Chippewa village.

"How can you stand there so cold and unfeeling toward White Fire when you know that he is not responsible for anything but being your friend—your ally?" she half screamed. "Your chief loves him as a father loves a son!"

She paled and dropped her hand to her side. "Oh, no," she said, her voice breaking as a cold splash of fear grabbed her in the pit of her stomach. "Your chief *does* hold White Fire responsible for his daughter's death, doesn't he? Lord, he would not have helped him if he were even here. Even if I begged, do you think he would ignore the danger White Fire is in?"

She could see Red Buffalo's eyes waver somewhat. Then she saw his gaze wander over her, seeming suddenly aware of her disheveled clothes and hair. It was obvious to anyone who looked at her that she had been in the river.

By that, the warrior must know then that she had also faced danger. That would surely tell him that she had come out of desperation to seek help from his chief. From his people.

But Red Buffalo still offered no kindness, no sympathy. Instead he held the flap open more widely with one hand, while gesturing with his free hand toward it. She knew that nothing she had said, or would say, could make him change his mind about how he felt about things today. Perhaps the death of the Chippewa maiden was too fresh in his heart to care for anyone else, especially a white woman and a 'breed who had no blood ties at all with the Chippewa.

Inhaling a quavering breath, finding the courage to say just one more thing to this stubborn Chippewa warrior, Flame went and stood before him. Her eyes held his as she glared at him. "If White Fire dies, I, personally, *will* hold you responsible," she said flatly. "I *know* that if Chief Gray Feather knew that he was in mortal danger, he would go to his rescue. He just can't hate someone so quickly whom he has loved so dearly. Not even because he has lost a daughter!"

When she saw how that made Red Buffalo's eyes soften, and how it made him take a long, slow swallow, she knew that she had hit home. This warrior absolutely knew that his chief *would* defend White Fire, at all cost.

Yet he still stood there, making no attempt to go to his chief and tell him the bad news about White Fire. Nor did he offer her the information of where Gray Feather was.

Stifling a frustrated sob behind a hand, Flame ran from the lodge.

Ignoring that everyone still stood around, staring at her, she quickly mounted the horse.

When no one budged, she sighed deeply. Then she gazed at the crowd with rage-filled eyes as they edged closer, giving her no escape route.

"If you don't give me space to ride from your village, by damn I shall *make* space!" she cried. "I will trample anyone who gets in my way beneath the hooves of this horse!"

She knew the chance she was taking by talking so angrily and threateningly to these people, yet she felt a desperation seizing her heart to know that if she hadn't found help here for White Fire, where could she find it?

Yes, she knew that she could go to Fort Parker and Colonel Edwards would leave immediately for Fort Snelling. But the ride was so far to the fort! She would not be able to get there before nightfall.

Then it might be too late.

Exhausted and dispirited, she rode off through the Chippewa as they backed off and stood on two sides, allowing it.

Tears poured from her eyes as she rode free of the village. "What am I to do now?" she cried, lifting her gaze to the heavens as though trying to find answers from a God who for now seemed to have abandoned not only her, but also White Fire.

"Can't you do something for me, Lord?" she cried. "Can't you give me some sort of direction? You know the goodness of White Fire! Please don't allow him to die needlessly!"

She found no release from her cry of panic toward heaven. Nor did she have any response. She was in this by herself. Never had she felt as alone!

The sun had reached the center point in the sky, and was now drifting toward what Flame thought might be three o'clock. She rode hard along the banks of the Mississippi River.

Her thoughts were scrambled, unsure of even where she should go for help. Hunger pangs ate away at her insides. Her legs and back ached from the hard ride.

She felt that if she could just stop and take a rest and get a bite to eat, she could think more clearly.

Perhaps she could think of someone who might have the power to go against her father and his faithful soldiers. Again Colonel Edwards came to mind.

Again she remembered how far downriver his fort was. But it was the last chance.

She rode onward, her shoulders slumping in her building tiredness. She felt dizzy from hunger. She was dying from thirst. And she itched all over from having been in the muddy river. Her clothes had dried rough and scratchy against her flesh.

She knew of one place she might go, at least for a momentary reprieve from all that ailed her. Her father would have no cause to go there once he heard of her escape. He would not think that she might be that stupid, to go somewhere so close to the fort that he could almost sneeze on it from the lushness of his private office.

"Yes, for now I shall go and rest in White Fire's cabin," she whispered to herself. She sighed heavily. "I'll grab a quick bite. I'll rest my weary bones, and then, by God, I'll go into Pig's Eye and find someone *there* who will be willing to help me."

A keen sadness overtook her when she thought of Neal Geary, the Indian agent, and how he was no longer available to offer assistance to those who might need it in this wilderness.

She was almost certain that her father had had a part in the agent's death, as he would in White Fire's, if she didn't find a way to stop him.

So weary of not only traveling, but also thinking, Flame was glad when she caught sight of the cabin through a break in the trees a short distance away.

Her eyes widened. She gasped.

She drew rein and wheeled her horse to a quick stop when she saw smoke spiraling slowly from the stone chimney at the side of the cabin.

"White Fire?" she whispered, forking an eyebrow.

A quick hope swam through her, that perhaps her father had changed his mind about White Fire and had set him free. Surely her father had thought it over and realized how much trouble he could get in if the government discovered that he had wrongly imprisoned and killed an innocent man.

And perhaps her father no longer saw White Fire as a threat as far as Flame was concerned, thinking that Flame would be hidden away in some convent where he would never find her.

"Lord, let it be true," Flame softly prayed as she sank her heels into the flanks of her steed and rode in a hard gallop toward the cabin.

Chapter 32

Dozing, momentarily awakening, then dozing again, White Fire's eyes sprang quickly open when he heard the loud whistle of the riverboat outside as it drew closer to the pier.

His heart leaped at the sound. He could not help but wonder about the return of the riverboat, when it had only a few short hours ago left for St. Louis!

Aboard that paddle wheeler had been Flame. Colonel Russell had bragged to White Fire, he had taunted him, about sending Flame where no one could ever find her.

He had known that Colonel Russell would have only been this open with him, because he knew that White Fire would never have the opportunity to go and release her from her imprisonment, because he would be dead.

He gazed up at the window and listened as the

boat let out another sharp whistle as it came to a stop at the pier. White Fire's pulse began to race, knowing that Flame was near again. He fought against the chains that held him in bondage. He struggled to get his ankles free.

All that his efforts gained him was more blood running from the wounds that the irons had inflicted on his wrists and ankles from him straining against them.

Yet White Fire could not help but think that with Flame's return came just a slight ray of hope for his release . . . for his life. Perhaps the boat had returned solely because of her!

With her willful stubbornness, perhaps she had convinced those who accompanied her that White Fire was wrongly imprisoned by her madman father.

Just perhaps someone would come soon and release him.

But he knew that he was only reaching for a miracle in all that was bleak.

He hung his head and again slipped into a troubled sleep. He had not been fed. He had not been given water.

His body throbbed from being held up flat against the cold stone wall, his legs spread wide, his arms stretched out on either side.

"Flame . . ." he whispered in his sleep. "Flame . . ."

Chapter 33

My face turned pale as deadly pale,
My legs refused to walk away,
My life and all seemed turned to clay.

—John Clare

Breathless, Flame dismounted, then stopped suddenly when she found someone besides White Fire standing at the door of the cabin.

"Chief Gray Feather," she gasped, her eyes wide with questioning.

Chief Gray Feather stared at her, then looked past her, his eyes searching for White Fire. Then he gazed at Flame again.

"Where is White Fire?" he asked, raising an eyebrow.

His gaze swept over her and saw her disarray. He gazed into her eyes once again. "When I last saw White Fire he was with you," he said guardedly. "Why is he not with you now? Your clothes. Your hair. They are in such disorder. Why?"

Flame's heart sank to learn that White Fire *wasn't* there. He was still in that damnable cell, unless . . .

Fear brushed her insides in cold splashes to think that, to *know* that, her father could take away White Fire's life at any moment, if he hadn't already.

She rushed to Gray Feather and frantically gripped one of his arms. "White Fire was taken away by my father and . . . and . . . placed in the fort's dungeon," she said in a rush of words. "My father sent me away on a riverboat. I jumped overboard. I went to your village to seek your help. I . . . was—"

"*No-gee-shkan,* stop. Tell me more slowly what happened, and why," Gray Feather said, placing a gentle hand to her elbow. "Come inside. Sit down. Take a deep breath. Tell me everything. Then I will determine what must be done for White Fire."

"What must be done?" Flame cried. "We must go and save him! That's what must be done."

Then she recalled how she had been treated at the Chippewa village.

Could she trust this chief to really listen and care about anything she had to say? Did he not care about White Fire any longer? Or did he blame both of them so much for the death of his daughter that he could never forgive them?

When Gray Feather said nothing more, but instead led her inside by a gentle hand on her elbow, Flame was glad to have time to get her breath. She knew that she must have some rest before heading out again to save her beloved. She even had to eat something, or else she would not have the strength to do what was required these next few hours.

When she got inside the cabin, she stopped and gaped openly at the child who was on a chair in the darker shadows. She was curled up, fast asleep, a wooden, carved horse clutched in her right hand.

She quickly recognized the child. It was Dancing Star, Song Sparrow's daughter.

She looked quickly at Gray Feather again. "Why is she here?" she asked softly, trying to keep her voice low enough so that she would not awaken the child.

"I have brought her to White Fire," Gray Feather said sullenly. "She is now his responsibility." His eyes narrowed as he looked intently at Flame. "You said that you were at my village. While there, were you told of my daughter's death?"

Flame slowly nodded. "Yes, I know of your daughter's death," she murmured. "I am so sorry, Gray Feather. So very sorry."

"You know why she died?" he said flatly. "How she died?"

She nodded. "Yes, I know both things," she said, swallowing hard. She had a desperate need to flee, for she knew not what to expect next from this powerful Chippewa chief. If he was toying with her . . .

"Then you know why my grandchild is here," Gray Feather said, giving Dancing Star a soft glance.

"No, not really," Flame said, scarcely breathing as Gray Feather went and leaned over and swept Dancing Star into his arms.

When the child awakened and smiled up at him, Flame saw the affection, the undying love each had for the other.

This made it hard for her to understand why the chief would be compelled to give her up so easily to be raised by someone not of their village. Not of their blood.

"Why *is* this child now White Fire's responsibility?" she blurted out.

"Because my daughter took her own life," Gray Feather said, his voice breaking. "She died in *sin*. My granddaughter is a part of that sin. And because White Fire is the cause of my daughter's death, he must now assume responsibility of my daughter's child."

Trying so hard to understand everything, Flame's head was spinning.

And she knew that the longer they stood there discussing things other than White Fire's release, the chances grew slimmer that he would be alive.

"You are White Fire's chosen woman," Gray Feather said. He took the child over and held her out to Flame. "That makes my grandchild also *your* responsibility. She will be raised as your daughter."

Stunned speechless by what he was saying, and by his reasoning, Flame stood there fore a moment staring at Dancing Star. Then when she saw that Chief Gray Feather was serious, she saw no other choice but to take the child.

When Dancing Star moved easily, trustingly into her arms, Flame's heart went out to her. Her heart was melted by the child's sweet smile and by how she snuggled into her arms, as though she belonged there.

"Now tell me everything about White Fire," Gray Feather said, taking Flame by an elbow, and leading her to the blankets spread on the floor before the fireplace. "I see that you need rest before we leave again to do what must be done for him. While taking the time to rest, tell me everything."

So glad to be off her feet, and still holding Dancing

Star in her arms, Flame blurted out the story of when she and White Fire were surrounded by the soldiers.

"You *are* going to help him, aren't you?" Flame questioned, when she saw that hearing everything had caused the old chief to go quiet, his eyes now watching the dancing flames of the fire.

When he still said nothing, fear began to flow into Flame's heart that he might have decided against putting his people in danger by helping one man escape from Fort Snelling. Was he thinking that White Fire was not worth the chance it would take to get him from the soldiers? Did he see that a war between his people and the soldiers might be started?

"If we can't get White Fire free without a fight, there *might* be a war between your people and the soldiers," Flame blurted out. "I know this and I hate to think it might happen. But we must chance anything and everything to set White Fire free. He doesn't deserve to be deserted in such a way. He doesn't deserve to die."

Still Gray Feather said nothing.

Anger—a bitter rage—entered Flame's heart to think that this chief was going to ignore everything that she had said, and abandon a man who was the epitome of kindness.

"Do you now hate White Fire so much that you would allow him to die needlessly?" she said, her voice drawn. "Because of your daughter, will you allow him to die?"

She picked Dancing Star up and held her out for the chief. "Here," she said, her voice breaking, "she belongs with you. Not with me. Without White Fire, the child—"

Chief Gray Feather looked quickly over at Flame.

"Keep the child," he said, his voice a low grumble. His eyes were flashing angrily. "She *is* yours *and* White Fire's, forevermore."

More confused by the comment, Flame's eyes wavered. "But if you do nothing to help him, how can the child be his?" she murmured.

"Did I say that I would do nothing to help him?" the chief growled out.

"No, but you haven't said you would help him, either," Flame said, sighing. "Which is it, Chief? Are you going to help me get him free? Or not?"

"Are you rested enough now so that you can ride with me to my village to get my warriors?" Chief Gray Feather said, placing a gentle hand on Flame's shoulder. "Are you strong and brave enough to join the fight to set White Fire free?"

"I am both of those things," Flame said, boldly lifting her chin. Then her eyes wavered again. "But I don't think your warriors will want me riding with them. While at your village, I was made to feel very unwelcome. I was told that I was, in part, responsible for your daughter's death. I was told never to enter your village again."

"Whoever told you that spoke out of turn," Gray Feather said, rising to his feet. He held out a hand for Flame. "*Mah-bee-szhon,* come."

"But, Chief Gray Feather, I was told not to enter your village again," Flame said, holding the child as she moved slowly to her feet.

"I, alone, am my people's voice," Gray Feather said, folding his arms across his bare chest. "Only I say who can and cannot come and go from my village. I tell you now, white woman with flame of hair, you are always welcome at my village, for you are

White Fire's choice, and he is like a son to me. When you become his wife, you will become a daughter to this old chief."

"Yet you give up your granddaughter so easily?" Flame asked, stroking her fingers through the child's long, black hair.

"She is not being given up," Gray Feather said, placing a gentle hand to the child's cheek. "Will she not be still my granddaughter when she lives with you and White Fire?"

"Yes, she will always be your granddaughter," Flame said, cuddling Dancing Star closer. "And I will love her as though she were my very own child."

Then Flame's eyes widened. "What are we to do with her while we go to the village for your warriors?" she blurted out.

Gray Feather took Dancing Star from Flame. He held her and spoke into her face. "Granddaughter, you must stay here in this cabin while your grandfather and Flame leave for a while," he said thickly. "You can reach the bolt lock at the door. After we leave, lock it. Let no one but us or White Fire back inside the cabin. Do you understand?"

Eyes wide and devoid of fear, Dancing Star nodded.

"After you lock the door, sit in this chair close to the fire and we will return as soon as we can," Gray Feather said, placing Dancing Star in an oak rocking chair. He glanced over at a large bowl of fruit on the kitchen table. "Leave the chair only long enough to lock the door and to get fruit when your belly tells you that you are hungry. There is a pitcher of water on the table. That will quench your thirst."

Seeing the fruit made Flame remember her own

hunger. She hurried to the table and picked up two apples. She thrust one in each of her skirt pockets. Then she went and kneeled on one knee before Dancing Star. "We will be bringing White Fire home to you soon," she murmured. "He will be so glad to see you here, waiting for him."

Dancing Star smiled, then clutched the wooden horse in her hand. "My friend and I will wait," she said softly.

Flame leaned closer and gave Dancing Star a deep hug. Then she rose quickly, turned, and ran to the door with Gray Feather.

Seeing how soon darkness would be falling over the cabin like a shroud, Flame took the time to light one kerosene lamp. Then she ran outside and mounted her horse and waited for Gray Feather.

"Dancing Star, come now to the door," Gray Feather said, beckoning with a hand toward the child. "Lift the bolt. Slide it in place after I close the door. You will be safe until we return."

Dancing Star placed Michael's wooden horse on the chair, then slid from it, and went and stood looking trustingly up at her grandfather. When she was left alone and the door was closed, she slid the bolt lock in place.

She ran to the window and stood on tiptoe. The sky darkening, Dancing Star squinted her eyes as she watched Flame and Gray Feather ride into the dark shadows of the forest.

After they were fully out of sight, Dancing Star went and stood on tiptoe and grabbed a banana from the bowl of fruit. Then she ran back to the rocker and climbed on it.

After the small wooden horse was on her lap, and the banana was peeled, Dancing Star began slowly rocking back and forth as she nibbled at the banana and stared into the hypnotic flames of the fire.

Slowly her eyelids became heavier and heavier.

Soon she was fast asleep again, the banana peel on the floor beside the rocker, Michael's horse snuggled against her.

Chapter 34

Cry! Speak once more—thou lovest!
—Elizabeth Barrett Browning

White Fire dozed off and on again, his head bobbing as he would awaken for a short while. Then he would drift off asleep again. When he was awake, he found it hard to concentrate. Without having eaten for so long, and still not having been given even water, he felt dehydrated and weak, so weak that he could no longer successfully fight to stay awake.

Voices now awakened him. Slowly he opened his eyes.

When he saw lamplight approaching, he tensed, for except when Colonel Russell had brought Flame to see him, this was the first time anyone had come into his cell after he had been left there, surely to die.

"Because of you she is now dead!" Colonel Russell shouted as he stepped up to the bars and glared at White Fire.

"Who . . . is . . . dead?" White Fire asked, his thick,

dry tongue sticking first to the roof of his mouth, and then to his parched lips. He tried to make out the colonel's face, but all that he could see in the lamp-light was a blur.

"Who *do* you think I would be talking about?" Colonel Russell shouted, banging a fist against one of the bars. "Reshelle, by damn! Reshelle!"

"Reshelle?" White Fire said, finding it hard to concentrate, to make sense of anything the colonel was saying.

"Flame, you idiot!" Colonel Russell shouted. "Flame is missing! Because of you, I'm sure she is dead!"

Cold fear splashed inside White Fire's heart as he comprehended what the colonel was saying. "What . . . happened . . . to Flame?" he gasped out. "Where is she?"

"While traveling on the riverboat, she leaped overboard," Colonel Russell cried. "That's the only logical thing that could have happened to her. Every inch of the boat was searched when she came up missing. She wasn't there! Lord a'mighty, she is surely sucked to the very bottom of the river. I'll never see her again!"

A remorse overwhelmed White Fire, so keen that he cried out as though someone had stabbed him in the heart. "No!" he cried. "No! Not Flame!"

"You are going to die for this," Colonel Russell hissed out. "I was contemplating freeing you and having you escorted far from the Minnesota Territory. But now? By God, at sunup you will be standing before a firing squad. I will laugh as I watch bullets riddle your copper body. You damn, worthless *'breed*."

White Fire's insides turned cold to realize that he had not only lost Flame, but that, he, too, would soon join her in death.

But perhaps that was the only place they could ever be together peacefully, he thought—walking hand in hand on the road of the hereafter. . . .

Chapter 35

That I, in whom the sweet time wrought,
Lay stretch'd within a lonely glade,
Abandon'd to delicious thoughts,
Beneath the softly twinkling shade.

—Coventry Patmore

As she wheeled her horse to a shimmying halt, Flame could hardly believe her eyes as she stared at Fort Snelling. There was a solid wall of soldiers standing guard on all sides, except for the one wall that was part of the rocky cliff.

Flame gazed with a building anger at the tall, closed gate. She could see soldiers standing guard on the walkway atop it, the moon reflected on their rifle barrels.

"He's more demonic than I could ever have imagined him to be," Flame whispered to herself. A shudder ran through her whole body as she thought of what her father was doing to keep anyone from saving White Fire from certain death.

"I have never seen the fort protected in such a

way," Chief Gray Feather said, sidling his horse closer to Flame's. He glanced over his shoulder at his warriors, prepared to attack the fort at his command.

Then Gray Feather gazed at Flame. "We do not have enough men to go against such odds as these," he said sullenly. "There can be nothing done in secret with so many eyes watching."

"Yes, I know," Flame said, her hope to save White Fire all but gone.

"There is one more thing I can do," Gray Feather said, glaring at the fort. "I can send warriors to all the neighboring bands of Chippewa. We will ask for their assistance."

"There isn't enough time for that," Flame said, frustratedly raking her fingers through her thick, red hair. Her eyes wavered as she gazed into the old chief's eyes. "And, anyway, no other band of Chippewa would risk what you are willing to risk to save White Fire." She swallowed hard. "And he would never approve," she murmured. "He would rather die than bring your people into war against the soldiers."

She sighed deeply, so bone weary, so sad, she found each moment now a struggle to stay atop the horse, to even stay awake. Yet she could not give in to her weariness. She had to think of some way to get past the soldiers.

Of course, all that she herself had to do to get past them, was to ride up and announce that she was returning to her father.

But she, alone, was not enough to stop what her father planned for White Fire. Her presence there might even hasten his death.

No, there had to be another way.

"I should have gone to Fort Parker," she said, swallowing hard. "By now they could have arrived and . . . and—"

The sound of horses arriving somewhere close by made her words fall silent on her lips and her eyes widen as she searched through the darkness for whoever was approaching. The hour was late. She knew enough from her years of living the military life that no one came in the middle of the night unless it was an emergency. Late visitors threw soldiers out of their beds, their firearms quickly readied for whoever was coming, unannounced.

"We'd best take quick cover," Flame said, giving Gray Feather a frightened glance.

Her thoughts went to the Sioux Indians. What if they had decided upon an uprising? They were not as peaceful as the Chippewa.

And the Sioux had been forced from this part of the country too often—if not by the Chippewa, then by the white soldiers. They carried much hate inside their hearts for both their white-skinned enemies, *and* red.

Chief Gray Feather raised his rifle over his head and made a quiet motion with it for the men to retreat into the cover of the forest.

Flame followed them. Then she stopped suddenly when she caught sight of just who was arriving. She recognized Colonel Edwards. He was leading a contingent of cavalry directly toward the fort.

She wheeled her horse around and watched as those at the fort saw the approach of the soldiers on horseback. She held her breath as she waited for Fort Snelling's soldiers' reactions.

But she was not close enough to hear what was

being said when voices lifted in the air from the fort as Colonel Edwards stopped and conversed with the Fort Snelling soldiers.

Frustrated, Flame could not just stay back and not know what was going on between the two factions of soldiers. She had to know exactly why the colonel was there. At all cost, even at the chance of being shot as she rode free of the trees, she had to seek Colonel Edwards's help.

And she must do it before he got inside the walls of the fort. He must know that an innocent man was held prisoner there, soon wrongly to die.

A thought sprang to Flame's mind. Could the colonel have come because of what White Fire had warned him about?

But surely not. Not this time of night. It had to be something else.

She gave Chief Gray Feather a quick look. "I must go and speak to Colonel Edwards," she cried, "before he gets inside the fort."

"I shall go with you," Gray Feather said, his jaw tight.

"No, it would be best if I go alone," Flame said. "IF the guards see me riding with an Indian, they might not stop to ask why. We might both be targets for their itchy trigger fingers!"

"But you will be so vulnerable alone," Gray Feather argued.

"Thank you for caring," Flame said, touched deeply by his concern for her—a white woman—a woman he still, in part, blamed for his daughter's death.

She gave him a last, lingering look, then sank her heels into the flanks of her horse and rode off in a hard gallop toward the soldiers, who were just drawing a tight rein behind Colonel Edwards. Colonel Edwards was still speaking to those guarding the gate of the fort.

"Colonel Edwards!" Flame shouted as she rode toward the soldiers.

She was aware of a quick silence and saw the soldiers spin their horses around to look at her. The soldiers at the fort gawked, slack-jawed at her, their colonel's daughter coming in out of hiding.

Colonel Edwards, in his full military attire, the brass buttons of his blue uniform shining in the moonlight, rode toward Flame as his soldiers parted and made way for him.

Panting, her face flushed, Flame tightened her rein and drew her horse to a stop as the colonel stopped beside her.

"Reshelle Russell?" the colonel asked, leaning to take a closer look at her, the moon bathing her face with its sheen of white. "What are you doing out here alone this time of night?" His gaze swept over her and saw her disarray. "Lord, girl, what happened to you?" he said, his eyebrows arching. "Does your father know—?"

She interrupted him. "Colonel Edwards," she blurted out, "thank God you are here. I only hope you are in time."

"In time for what?" he said.

"White Fire!" she cried. "My father has him locked up in a cell! I'm afraid he's going to kill him."

Colonel Edwards's eyes widened. "What?" he gasped out. "Why would he imprison White Fire?"

"It's too long a story to explain it to you now," Flame said. Her breath caught in her throat as she asked, "Why are you here this time of night? Surely it's not because of what White Fire told you about my father. You wouldn't have come at this late hour to check out things. Why are you here?"

She looked past him and at all of the soldiers with him.

Then she gazed into his eyes. "Why have you brought so many men?" she asked guardedly. "Have you received word that there is trouble here? It's obvious you don't know about White Fire's incarceration or you wouldn't have acted so surprised when I told you. So why are you here?"

"It's the damndest thing," Colonel Edwards said, his eyes narrowing as he leaned closer to Flame. "I was asleep. I was awakened with a start. Damn if I didn't feel some sort of presence in my bed chamber. My wife awakened. Even she felt it."

"Presence?" Flame said, eyeing him curiously. "What sort of presence?"

"I find it hard to tell," Colonel Edwards said, laughing awkwardly. "Some would say I was ready for the loony bin."

"Tell me," Flame said softly. "Please tell me."

"Well, you see, Reshelle, Colonel Josiah Snelling and I were the best of friends," he said. "When he left for Missouri, I felt as though my right arm had been severed from my body, for Josiah *was* my right arm. His beliefs were the same as mine. We both joined peace councils with the local Indians. We spent many a night drinking and smoking and talking of our childhood adventures. When he left, there was such a strange void left in my life I don't know how to explain it."

Feeling a slow desperation rising inside her, that

too much time was passing, Flame edged her horse closer to the colonel's. "What does Colonel Snelling have to do with you being here tonight?" she asked, trying to hide her impatience.

"I feel that I was visited by Josiah tonight in my bed chamber," Colonel Edwards said, his voice guarded as he watched for her reaction. "I was awakened from a sound sleep by . . . by a presence in my room. I . . . looked around, then saw it—saw him. Of course, it was only a shimmering faint light that showed his likeness. But it was no less Josiah Snelling!"

Flame paled. She recalled White Fire telling her about his moments alone with Colonel Snelling's ghost, and why the colonel had appeared to him in such a way. To reveal to him what her father was planning.

Tonight Colonel Snelling must have appeared to his friend to warn him of something that was about to happen. He had surely tried to warn him about the danger White Fire was in.

"Why are you here?" she asked again.

"The whole time he was there, Josiah pointed toward Fort Snelling," Colonel Edwards said, his voice drawn. "I was quickly reminded of what White Fire had told me about your father. But I thought it had to be more than that that would bring Josiah to my room in such a way. And, by God, now I know. He was warning me about White Fire being imprisoned!"

"Can you get him free?" Flame asked, grabbing him quickly by the arm. "Can you?"

"Most certainly," Colonel Edwards said, easing her hand from his arm, then holding it. "I will look forward to hearing later what has happened to you tonight—why you are out here, instead of inside the fort."

"Yes, I will tell you, but for now, let us concentrate on freeing White Fire," Flame said, easing her hand from his. She looked over her shoulder and could feel Gray Feather's eyes on her, waiting for her to motion for him to come to her.

But she still felt that it was best that he and his warriors stay out of the fracas. All that was required to set White Fire free was right there with Colonel Edwards.

"Come on and let's set things right," Colonel Edwards said, nodding toward Flame, drawing her eyes back to him. "And once White Fire is set free, I'll take care of that other matter that I have delayed doing for too long, it seems."

"You mean sending my father away from Fort Snelling?" Flame asked, riding alongside him toward the gate of the fort.

"No, I mean to arrest him, to see that he is *court-martialed*," Colonel Edwards said, his jaw tight. "And not only because of him having wrongly incarcerated White Fire, but because of how he has schemed to cause a massacre in this area. He will take White Fire's place in the cell, but not here. At Fort Parker."

His eyes wavered as he gazed at Flame. "I'm sorry that things have turned out this way for your father," he said thickly. "I can't imagine how you must be feeling about all of this."

"No one could ever know," Flame said, her eyes burning with the need to cry.

But she fought back the tears. She had to look

strong. She had to feel strong to save the man she loved and to be able to watch her father arrested.

Although she knew that her father deserved no less, she could not help but feel a deep, gnawing sadness over what he had become—a ruthless, worthless man.

Flame rode straight-backed and square-shouldered beside Colonel Edwards as they headed toward the gate.

The soldiers under Flame's father's command soon saw that they were outnumbered by Colonel Edwards's men and didn't hesitate at opening the wide gate.

Flame rode on inside, then stiffened when her father came from the mansion only half dressed, his hair mussed, his eyes heavy with sleep.

"Colonel Edwards, what's going on here?" he asked, paling when he looked over at Flame. "Reshelle, thank God you are all right. But good God, look at you. And why are you with Colonel Edwards?"

"Arrest that man," Colonel Edwards said, nodding to two of his soldiers as they slid quickly from their saddles. He looked at several of his other soldiers. "You! Go and find where White Fire is being held. Release him."

"You can't do this," Colonel Russell cried, trying to yank free of the soldiers as they grabbed each of his arms and held him firmly between them. "You have no authority here, Colonel Edwards. You have no right to do this to me. Nor do you have the right to release White Fire."

"I am taking charge here until Washington sends a replacement," Colonel Edwards said, dismounting.

He went and stood before Colonel Russell. He placed his fists on his hips. "How did you think you'd get away with all of this, Colonel?"

"I almost did, didn't I?" Colonel Russell said, laughing fiendishly. He glared at Flame as she dismounted and went to stand before him. "My own daughter betrays me. Reshelle, why? Why?"

"How can you ask me such a question as that?" Flame said, fighting back the urge to cry. "Father, you have turned into someone I no longer know."

She then turned from him.

When she saw White Fire being held between two soldiers as he walked toward her, a blanket wrapped around him, she gasped at how weak he looked, and at how gaunt he had become even during his short time of imprisonment.

"White Fire!" she cried, then broke into a mad run toward him. When she reached him, she eased into his arms.

Sobbing, she hugged him. "It's all over now," she murmured. "You are safe, darling. You are safe."

She heard the arrival of many horses behind her. She did not have to look to know that Chief Gray Feather had decided to come into the courtyard to see if his assistance was needed.

As White Fire hugged Flame, he looked over her shoulder and gave Colonel Edwards a smile of thanks.

He smiled at Chief Gray Feather as the old chief nodded toward him. Then his gaze shifted and he glared at Colonel Russell.

Suddenly his eyes were drawn somewhere else.

He saw curtains being drawn aside in an upstairs window of the Snelling mansion, in the study where he had been visited by Colonel Snelling's ghost. He blinked nervously to see if he was truly seeing the apparition again, or if, in his weakness, he was imagining things.

The likeness of Colonel Snelling smiled down at him and tipped his hat, and then slowly faded into the night shadows. White Fire knew that it most certainly hadn't been his imagination. His friend had been there again.

"White Fire, you won't believe what happened tonight at Colonel Edwards's house," Flame said, easing from his arms. "Darling, Colonel Snelling appeared to Colonel Edwards. He pointed a hand toward Fort Snelling. He is why Colonel Edwards knew to come tonight. He saw the ghost. He understood the meaning of his sudden appearance!"

"Yes, I would believe it," White Fire said, still watching the window. "I owe Josiah. I most certainly owe him."

Chapter 36

Graceful and useful all she does,
Blessing and blest where'er she goes,
Pure bosom'd as that watery glass,
And Heaven reflected in her face.

—William Cowper

Flame stood beside White Fire as her father was taken away to be incarcerated at Fort Parker. Colonel Edwards had assigned one of his most trusted men to stay behind at Fort Snelling, to see to things until a replacement for Colonel Russell arrived.

Chief Gray Feather and his warriors had left as soon as the chief had seen that White Fire was all right, having taken only enough time to give him a hearty hug and to invite him to his lodge soon for council.

"This has been a night of nights. I shall never forget it," Flame said, placing an arm around White Fire's waist as she slowly led him up the stairs toward the front door of the Snelling mansion. "I was so afraid that I wouldn't get to you in time."

"When I was told about your escape from the riverboat, a part of my heart died at the thought of possibly having lost you," he said, grunting from the energy it took him to take the last step that led him to the porch. His knees trembled from weakness. His tongue and lips were so parched he could hardly speak.

"Come on inside," Flame said softly. "I shall have Lorraine, my maid, prepare you a bath. While you are bathing, I shall go to the kitchen and find us something to eat. I've hardly eaten, myself, since you were taken away by my father."

Then she remembered how she had poked breakfast down herself while on the boat, and she gave White Fire a mischievous stare.

"What is that look for?" he asked, arching an eyebrow.

"Well, there was this one time that I ate like a pig," she said, giggling. She proceeded to tell him how much she had eaten, and why.

"But that was then," she said, sighing. "And now I feel as though I haven't eaten in days."

Clutching the blanket about his nude body, White Fire smiled down at Flame as she held the front door open for him. "The whole nightmare is over. *All* of it," he said. "Now we can truly begin the rest of our lives without interferences from men like your father."

"Yes, he can no longer cause either of us any trouble," she murmured, fighting the sadness that crept into her heart whenever she thought of him.

She wanted to hate her father. But the part of her that had loved him when she was a small child would not allow her to totally loathe him.

"I am so tired," White Fire said. He stumbled as he moved into the dim light of the foyer, the candles almost having burned out in their sconces along the walls. He licked his lips. "God, I am so thirsty. I'm so hungry."

A middle-aged lady came down the stairs in a wool robe, her hair bundled up beneath a sleeping cap. Flame looked up at her. "Lorraine, hurry and prepare a bath in my room for White Fire," she said. "Please hurry."

Lorraine reached the floor. She stopped to place a gentle hand on Flame's cheek. "I prayed that you would be all right," she said, a sob lodging in her throat. "My prayers were answered."

She gazed past Flame and through the open door, then looked again at Flame. "I watched through the window as your father was taken away," she said, her voice drawn. "Why, Flame? Why was he taken away by soldiers from another fort? It looked as though he was arrested."

"He was," Flame said flatly. "Lorraine, please go and wake the others of the household. Ask them to help you. Have my copper tub brought to my room. Heat the bathwater and prepare the bath. I shall tell you everything later."

Lorraine dropped her hand to her side, nodded, then shuffled away in her heavy slippers across the oak hardwood flooring.

"Come with me," Flame said, steadying White Fire with her arm around his waist. "I know it might be hard to take the steps. But once you are upstairs and in my room, everything else will come easy enough for you."

He placed a trembling hand on the staircase railing. He pulled himself up one step at a time. Finally they reached Flame's bedroom.

She helped him down onto the bed and sat beside him as the tub was brought into the room. Soon steaming water filled it to the brim.

Once alone, Flame helped White Fire up from the bed. She was near tears, finding it so hard to accept how her father's treatment had so weakened White Fire. Flame slid the blanket from around his shoulders.

When she got a look at his wrists and ankles, and saw the bloody, dried wounds left there by the chains, she paled. "Lord," she gasped, running a slow hand along one of his wrists, "I find it so hard that my father is capable of such . . . such . . . cruelty." She placed a hand to his cheek and gazed into his eyes, her own wavering. "Does it hurt so badly?" she whispered.

"Nothing hurts now that I am with you," he said, sliding his arms around her waist, drawing her into his embrace.

She lifted her lips to his. Their kiss was lingering, soft, and sweet.

Then she felt his body give somewhat and his knees almost buckle beneath him. She stepped away from him and held him by an elbow as she led him to the water.

White Fire stepped into the tub and sank into the warm water.

Flame kneeled down beside the tub and picked up a piece of soap and began lathering him across his shoulders, and chest. He slid farther down into the water and rested the back of his head against the tub.

As he closed his eyes, she studied him more closely. Her heart ached to see his gauntness and his parched lips. She dropped the soap into the water and rushed to her nightstand, where she grabbed a pitcher and poured water into a glass.

She took this to White Fire. He took the glass and swallowed the cool, refreshing liquid in fast gulps.

Then remembering him speaking of being hungry, and dying of hunger, herself, Flame sat the glass down on the floor. She bent low and brushed a kiss across White Fire's lips.

"I won't be gone long," she said. "When I return, I shall have brought us a feast from the kitchen."

As she rushed down the stairs, something came to her like someone had hit her in the abdomen with a fist. "Dancing Star," she whispered, her eyes wide as she stopped on a step. "Oh, Lord, I have absolutely forgotten about Dancing Star."

She turned and looked up the stairs. She realized that no one had yet told White Fire the news about Song Sparrow, nor did he know that he had another child to father.

She realized that they couldn't spend much time at the mansion. Once White Fire was dressed and fed, they had to return to his cabin.

"I won't tell him about the child until we get there," she whispered, rushing on again to the kitchen.

After getting a large platter of cheese, cold roasted chicken, and slabs of beef, and also grapes, bananas, and apples, Flame hurried back up the stairs.

When she arrived at her room, she found White

Fire finished with his bath and dressed. She stopped with a start when she saw the clothes he wore.

"I went to your father's room and borrowed a pair of his breeches and a shirt," White Fire said. He raised up a pant leg high enough for her to see the black-leather dress boots. He chuckled. "A tight fit, nevertheless a pair of shoes until I go home to get into my moccasins."

His mention of "home," and again thinking of who was there awaiting their arrival, made Flame's inside tighten. They had to get to his cabin soon, for Dancing Star had been there alone for way too long as it was.

But she still thought it was best to tell White Fire about her later. He had been through enough for now.

Yet it did not seem right to wait and tell him just after he discovered Dancing Star at his house. He would have to be told in front of Dancing Star about Song Sparrow's death. That could be too traumatic for the child to hear it all over again, and to see White Fire's reaction to the knowledge.

"What's wrong?" he asked, seeing how quiet Flame had become, and how she seemed to be worried about something. He went to her and took the tray of food and set it on a table beside the bed.

Then he took her hands and gazed into her eyes. "Tonight has been almost too much for you, hasn't it?" he asked softly. "Seeing your father taken away like that . . . Seeing me in such a mess. And you. How did you live through the ordeal in the river?"

"Yes, tonight, today has been quite something," Flame said, laughing softly. "But it's easily forgotten now, for the whole reason for everything that I did was to set you free. You are free. We are together now and nothing ever again will come between us."

He drew her into his arms and kissed her. Then he eased away from her and pulled two chairs up to the table where the food awaited them.

They ate and ate.

Lorraine brought in a bottle of wine, that Flame had asked for before she returned to the bedroom. That was consumed until both Flame and White Fire were comfortably full and relaxed.

"Your feather mattress is going to feel good tonight," White Fire said, reaching over to run a hand over her mattress. His eyes twinkled into hers. "I think I have enough renewed strength now to take more from this bed than only a night of sleeping."

Flame smiled softly at him, her pulse racing at the thought of how wonderful it would be to sleep with him there tonight, making love over and over again.

Yet there was someone else to consider now—Dancing Star.

"I would love nothing more than to go to bed here tonight with you," Flame said, setting her empty wineglass aside. She reached over and took White Fire's hands in hers. "Darling, I have something that needs saying."

"Has something happened you haven't told me about?" White Fire asked, seeing the seriousness of her expression.

"Yes, something else has happened," Flame said, swallowing hard. "It's about Song Sparrow and Dancing Star."

A quick fear leaped into his dark eyes. "What about them?" he said, his eyes searching hers. "I see that what you are about to tell me is not good or you would not look so guarded and be so hesitant about telling me."

He brushed a hand through his thick hair. "Do not tell me that both Song Sparrow and her daughter are dead," he said.

"No, not both of them," Flame said, swallowing hard. "Only one."

"The child?" he said, a quick panic leaping into his eyes.

"No, the child's mother," Flame quickly corrected.

White Fire's breath caught in his throat. "Song Sparrow is dead?" he breathed out.

"Yes," Flame said, hesitating at telling him how. Then she blurted it out to get it over with. She saw how knowing the way that Song Sparrow had killed herself made him cringe.

"But there is more that I haven't yet told you," she rushed out, knowing that she had no choice but to tell him about Dancing Star now.

"What else can there be to say about it?" he said, sighing heavily.

She hurried through the explanation about Dancing Star, and how the child had been given to him to raise.

"Chief Gray Feather did that?" he gasped out. "He gave up his granddaughter to me?"

She further explained about why the chief had made his decision to leave Dancing Star with him.

White Fire rose from the chair and went to a window, drawing back a curtain to stare out into the darkness. "I can hardly believe the chief's logic, but, by damn, I will gladly take the child," he said, his voice drawn. "And tomorrow? I will go for my son."

He turned and went back to Flame. He took her

hands and drew her from the chair. "Does any of this change how you feel about our plans for marriage?" he asked, searching her eyes.

"Why would it?" she asked, her eyes innocently wide.

"You will be marrying a man who has two children," he said softly. "When it was just my son, you were willing to marry me. Now that there is also Dancing Star, and you will be the mother of two children instead of one, does that make you hesitate at all about marrying me?"

Flame flung herself into his arms. "Nothing could ever change my mind about marrying you," she murmured. "I shall be the best mother ever to the children. I love children."

"Tomorrow we shall find us a preacher and speak vows that will make us a true family," White Fire said. He wove his fingers through her hair and drew her lips to his.

Then they pulled apart from one another. "Let us go now to my home," White Fire said, offering a hand to Flame. "I believe someone awaits us there."

Flame took his hand. Without looking back at the comforts that she would be leaving behind forever, she went down the stairs and outside into the moon-splashed night.

Again without looking back, she went with him to the stables and chose one of her most favored horses. It was a gift from her father last Christmas—a black stallion with white spots on its ears. She saddled it and handed the reins to White Fire.

"My gift to you," she murmured. "For all the trouble my father has put you through, please take this gift and know that I am giving it to you from the bottom of my heart."

He stepped up to the horse and ran his hands down is withers. "A lovely bridegroom price, I would say," he said, laughing softly as he glanced over at Flame.

"Yes, a lovely bridegroom price," she said, her eyes locking with his.

They floated into one another's arms and shared a long and sweet kiss.

Then they rode from the fort, leaving so much unhappiness behind them.

But White Fire could not help but look over his shoulder and take one last look at the study where he had shared so much with his friend Josiah Snelling. He wished there was a way to thank the colonel for what he had done for him tonight.

Josiah, more than anyone else, had saved White Fire's life.

Chapter 37

Oh, could the Fair, who this does see,
Be by this great example won,
And learn but thus to smile on me,
As they smile on the kissing sun!

—Richard Leigh

Soft kisses being feathered across her brow, and then her cheeks, awakened Flame. She sighed and lay there for a moment longer enjoying that it was White Fire who was giving her such soft, sweet kisses; that it was White Fire who was all right, and that he was with her now, for always.

When she felt his hands touch her naked breasts, her nipples quickly hardened against his palms, igniting all of Flame's senses. She inhaled a quick breath of instant pleasure.

Fluttering her eyes open, she smiled up at White Fire, then gasped with rapture when one of his hands moved lower and he began to stroke the tender flesh where her desire was centered.

"I love you so," she whispered, reaching her hands

up to cradle his face in her hands. "Darling, kiss me. Please . . . kiss . . . me."

She brought his face down to hers. Her lips trembled beneath his mouth as he gave her a meltingly hot kiss, his nude, bronze body sliding over hers. His swollen manhood heavy against her right leg, she was in awe again at its length and firmness.

As he moved his heaviness against her leg while his fingers continued to stroke her woman's center, she writhed in response, soft moans repeatedly surfacing from inside her.

Drawing a ragged breath, she twined her arms around his neck and clung to his rock hardness. She gave herself up to the rapture as he continued kissing her with a fierce, possessive heat born of having thought for a while that they had lost each other forever.

The raging hunger built inside Flame. With the portion of her mind that was not stolen away by the heat of her passion, she thought of how wonderful it was to be there when it could have been so different. Had Colonel Edwards not arrived in time the prior evening. . . .

No. She would not think of the possibilities.

She would only think of the wonders of having seen White Fire and Dancing Star together when they had arrived home. It had taken awhile to stir Dancing Star awake, so she could unlatch the door.

But when she had finally opened the door, White Fire's and the child's eyes had met. Then Dancing Star had so trustingly held her arms out for him. Nothing could have kept them apart.

White Fire had grabbed the child in his arms and held her as though she were a precious jewel.

Then later, when Dancing Star had fallen asleep in White Fire's arms, Flame watched him place her onto the soft blankets and pelts on the floor before the gentle flames of the fire. Flame had known then that things would be all right.

And today he was going to get his son! Today there was going to be a wedding!

Extremely happy from the promise of the future, Flame's thoughts merged now with her passion that was growing into a heated inferno. When she felt White Fire's manhood probing her hot, moist place, she opened her legs more fully to him, and clung to him as with one insistent thrust he was inside her.

His mouth slid from her lips and fell over one of her breasts. As he rolled her nipple with his tongue, and he plunged deeply into her, withdrew and plunged again, she became mindless with bliss.

Again he sought her lips with his mouth. His hands took in the roundness of her breasts, gently stroking. He kissed her with an easy sureness, his hips rhythmically moving as he brought her closer and closer to a mind-exploding release.

His tongue brushed her lips lightly. Then he kissed her again. His body was on fire with the building ecstasy. He groaned in whispers against her lips.

Cradling her close, his steel arms enfolding her, White Fire felt Flame's hunger as she twined her fingers through his hair and brought his lips down hard on hers again.

As the pleasure built inside him, he fought to bring his breathing under control. He could tell that her cresting pleasure matched his by the way her fingers bit into the corded muscles of his shoulders.

Trembling, he reached a hand between them and

found her warm and secret place. As he moved rhythmically within her, he caressed her damp valley, her woman's center tight and large against the tips of his fingers.

Becoming almost crazed from the intense rapture that was overwhelming her, Flame ran her hands slowly down White Fire's back, then clasped her fingers onto the taut muscles of his buttocks. She pressed him closer to her as she lifted her hips and met every demanding stroke.

A sensual tremor went through her body. It suddenly exploded in spasms of desire.

He buried his face between her breasts as his thrusts speeded up and went deeper and deeper.

She clung and rocked with him when she could tell that he had reached his own final throes of passion.

Then he kissed her again, his tongue parting her lips, the pulsing crest of their passion sought, found, and now subsiding.

Their tongues met and leaped together. His hands cupped her breasts. Their perspiration-laced bodies strained together.

Breathless, they finally broke apart and lay side by side, their eyes closed.

"If this is the way I will be awakened every morning, how can I sleep all night from anticipation?" Flame asked, turning to stretch out on her stomach. She rested her chin in her hands and gazed at White Fire. "Today everything will finally come together for us," she murmured. "You are going to go and claim your son. We are going to be married. I can hardly believe it. It is too much like a dream since there were so many obstacles in the way of where we so badly wanted to be."

"Yes, but nothing else can stand in our way," he said, reaching over, stroking the soft flesh of her bottom.

"Dancing Star and I will wait anxiously for your return with Michael," Flame said, shivering sensually when his fingers crept around and he stroked her where she was still wet, warm, and tender from lovemaking.

She closed her eyes. She giggled.

"But if you don't stop that," she said, her voice husky with need. "I doubt I shall ever let you out of this bed today."

"Let's go and see if our little darling is still asleep," White Fire said, hopping from the bed.

Flame rolled from the bed and slipped into a loose dress, all the while watching White Fire's exuberance as he finished dressing. She could see that he was accepting this new fatherhood with an open, loving heart.

She had worried about what his reaction would be that he had been given the child, and for what reason she had been handed over to him as though she were born of his flesh. Seeing his instant acceptance of Dancing Star, Flame realized just how much he loved children. She saw a future with him of many children. She had been too alone as a child. She saw the importance of the bonding of brothers and sisters.

Together, hand in hand, they tiptoed from the bedroom and went and knelt down beside the pallet on which Dancing Star still soundly slept.

"Doesn't she look like an angel?" White Fire said,

reaching over to gently slide locks of hair from Dancing Star's eyes. "It's so awful about her mother."

"We will give the child so much love," Flame whispered. Then she smiled at Dancing Star as the child awakened and found them both hovering over her.

Dancing Star wiped sleep from her eyes, then slowly rose from beneath the blankets. She moved almost automatically into White Fire's arms and twined her tiny arms around his neck.

Flame winced when she saw tears splashing from Dancing Star's eyes. She knew then that the child had not accepted her fate yet. She obviously sorely missed her mother, and the father taken from her not so long ago.

"Things will be all right," White Fire said, softly stroking Dancing Star's back through her buckskin dress. "Flame and I both love you, Dancing Star. And so will Michael."

"Michael?" Dancing Star said, leaning back so that she could gaze into White Fire's eyes. "Your little boy Michael?"

"Yes, my little boy Michael," he said, laughing softly. "I am going to go and bring him home with me today. He will be your brother, Dancing Star. Would you like that?"

Dancing Star scrambled from his arms and reached down and grabbed the little wooden horse. "This is Michael's," she said, stroking the sleekness of the carved wood with her tiny fingers. "Do you think he will care if I share it with him?"

"Michael will be glad to share it with you," White Fire said softly.

While he still talked and held Dancing Star, Flame got a good fire going in the fireplace. She then went to the kitchen and went through the food supplies and soon had breakfast ready for them.

After breakfast was over, White Fire gave them both a hug and left to go on another mission of the heart.

His strength fully regained, he rode toward Pig's Eye. He would not take no for an answer today. He would not wait another day to have his son with him. Of late he had seen how quickly things in life could change. If he did not take the opportunity now to have his son with him, he might never have it.

As he rode beneath the bright sunlight, the breeze soft on his face, he thought back to the experiences of the past several days. Time and again Chief Gray Feather had proven his love for him, even after losing his daughter in such a traumatic way!

And this thing with Josiah Snelling! No one would ever be able to convince White Fire that it had not happened, that he had not come face-to-face with the ghost of the colonel.

He smiled as he recalled how Flame had said that even Colonel Edwards had been visited by Colonel Josiah Snelling's ghost.

"Yes, he was here all right," he whispered to himself. "But now maybe he can have his final, true rest, knowing that the massacre has been stopped—that Colonel Russell has been stopped!"

His thoughts were brushed aside when he rode into the outskirts of Pig's Eye and the majestic Greer mansion came into view.

His insides tightened to think of having to face them again and argue for his rights to his son. But he would go to hell and back if it meant getting Michael in the end!

He slowed his horse to a slow lope as he turned onto the narrow lane that led to the Greer house. His eyes searched the windows for any signs of Michael, and he was disappointed when he saw him nowhere. He rode onward, then drew a tight rein before the house and dismounted.

His spine stiff, his throat dry, he swirled the reins around the hitching rail, then sucked in a deep breath for confidence and took the steep porch steps that led to the front door.

He did not even have to knock. The door opened suddenly.

Michael stepped out onto the porch and hugged White Fire's legs.

Before he could reach down and take his son into his arms, Maureen Greer was there, a small valise in her right hand.

"He's cried every day since your visit," Maureen said emotionally. "Why didn't you come sooner? We've been waiting."

"You've been waiting?" White Fire said, forking an eyebrow. He gazed down at the valise, then into Maureen's eyes. "I would have come sooner but things interfered."

"Father, take me home," Michael said, pleading up at White Fire with his dark, brown eyes.

"Yes, home," White Fire said, sweeping his son into his arms, holding him close as Michael wrapped his arms about his neck.

He was stunned by how simple it was to take his son. Michael was being handed over to him so easily!

"Here's some of his clothes," Maureen said, tears streaming from her eyes. "Of course, I didn't pack everything. There is too much. But I have packed his favorite things."

White Fire gazed at Michael's velvet suit, the white lacy collar hideously clinging at his throat, then he gazed down at the valise. "I don't think we'll be needing the clothes," he said softly.

"But they are his favorite—"

"I doubt that," White Fire said, chuckling.

Maureen set the valise down and stepped out onto the porch. She held her arms out for Michael. "Michael, please let me hold you one last time," she said, her voice breaking. "Please give Mommie a hug."

Michael turned his soft, wondering eyes at Maureen. Then he reached his arms out for her.

White Fire almost hesitated to allow his son to go to Maureen. Deep down inside he was afraid that she might change her mind.

But seeing her sincere hurt, he relinquished Michael to her this one last time.

As Maureen held and hugged Michael and whispered softly into his ear, White Fire looked past them and realized that George Greer had already left for work. And perhaps that was best. This way he would not have the sad, final farewell to Michael to work through. Such a good-bye caused a deep hurt, one that was too final.

Michael squirmed free of Maureen's grip and jumped to the floor. He looked up at her with a soft pleading look. "I want to take my pony with me," he said. "Please let me have my pony."

White Fire looked quickly from one to the other,

stunned that the child seemed to be begging for
something that was already his.

"No," Maureen said, stiffening her upper lip. She
clasped her hands together before her. "I can't allow
you to have that . . . that . . . wild thing. I won't be responsible for anything that might happen to you
while riding it."

"But it's mine," Michael cried. "It is a gift from my
true father."

White Fire's lips parted, stunned that this woman
could be so nice and cooperative one minute, and so
ugly and stubborn the next.

"The pony belongs to Michael," he said sternly. "I
will go to the stable. I shall get it."

"No, I can't allow that," Maureen said sharply.
"Now if you want to take Michael with you, you'd best
do it now, or by God, I will change my mind and fight
you all of the way. But I won't allow him on that . . .
that thing. Do you hear? I won't allow it."

White Fire wanted to snap back at her and tell her
how stupid she was being, for did she not know that
he would just go and purchase Michael another
pony?

Michael would be allowed to ride. To learn to
shoot. To learn to hunt.

"Father, tell her that you are going to take my
pony anyway," Michael pleaded, grabbing his hand,
and jerking on it.

"Let her have it," White Fire said, sweeping
Michael into his arms. He whispered into his ear.
"Son, we will go where there are many horses to
choose from. You will have your pick of them."

"Where would that be?" Michael whispered back, his eyes wide.

"At the Chippewa Indian village," White Fire said, stroking Michael's back.

"At an Indian village?" Michael gasped, his eyes wide.

His father smiled and nodded.

Michael clung to his neck as White Fire carried him to his horse. He gave Maureen a cold stare. Then he placed Michael comfortably on his saddle and swung himself up behind him. He heard Maureen gasp.

White Fire glared at her. "My son will know the joy of riding horses," he said calmly.

An arm around Michael's waist, holding him securely in the saddle before him, White Fire wheeled his horse around and rode away.

He ignored the woman's sobs behind him. Had she not been so stubborn by not allowing Michael to have his pony, White Fire would have offered her and her husband occasional visits with Michael, so that they would not be totally parted from the child they had grown to love.

His jaw tightened. He saw their sort of love as harmful to his son, for it was based on selfishness.

"Can I see Flame soon?" Michael asked, turning to gaze up at White Fire. "Daddy, I liked her a lot."

So pleased that Michael remembered Flame, and with such fondness, White Fire smiled down at him. "You liked her, did you?" he asked, his eyes gleaming.

"Very much," Michael said, nodding.

"And you want to see her very soon?"

"Yes, soon."

"I think that can be arranged," White Fire said, chuckling.

He sank his heels into the flanks of his horse and rode off in a hard gallop toward his home. He felt so content he thought he might burst from the feeling. He had everything.

And even more . . .

Chapter 38

Search I the shade to fly the pain.

—Thomas Lodge

As White Fire rode up to his cabin, he gazed in wonder at the door. He had expected Flame to open it as soon as she heard him approaching on his horse. By her not doing it, he wondered now if she had not been so excited after all about him getting his son. Perhaps, she didn't like the idea of becoming an instant mother after all—not only to Michael, but also to Dancing Star.

Had his absence given her time to reconsider? Had she thought it over and decided that this was not what she wanted out of life after all?

Was her love for him not strong enough to give her the courage to step into motherhood so soon?

"This is your home?" Michael asked, turning to gaze up at his father.

White Fire glanced quickly down at him, wondering if Michael regretted returning to a very different life from the one he had grown used to the past three years. It was obvious that he had forgotten this home. But being only three, yes, it would be hard to remember it.

"This is *our* home," White Fire said cautiously, watching his son's expression, hoping to read in it his true feelings. "I built it, Michael, even before you were born."

Michael turned slowly back to the cabin. "This is where my real mother lived," he said, in almost a whisper. Then he turned quick eyes back up to White Fire. "Tell me again how she died?"

"In my absence, while I was being held hostage by the Sioux, your mother became weakened by pneumonia," White Fire said softly, while looking at the cabin again. Flame had still not opened the door.

His heart sank to think that she had left him to raise the children alone, to be heartbroken by her decision not to marry him.

He turned slowly to the hitching rail. He felt instantly cold inside when he saw that her horse wasn't there. That had to mean that she had left. He tried not to reveal his sudden despair and disappointment to his son.

"She then died from pneumonia?" Michael said, stammering clumsily over the word "pneumonia," finding it difficult to pronounce.

"Yes, that is what claimed her life," White Fire said.

His jaw tightened and anger flashed through him now, replacing his sadness over Flame. He had trusted her! How could she have disappointed him in such a way? How could she have lain there this morning with him in the bed and told him more than once that she loved him, and talked of being so excited about him going for Michael? And of marrying him today?

"Father, moments ago you looked sad," Michael said, placing a gentle hand to White Fire's cheek. "But now you suddenly look angry. Why were you sad? Was it because you were speaking of Mother? What has made you angry? Also speaking of her and how she died?"

Seeing that his son picked up on his feelings too easily, White Fire tried to force his emotions, all except for the happiness at having his son with him again, behind him. He had faced many disappointments in life and had conquered the demons that would try to defeat him at such times. He would conquer such demons again.

"Everything is fine," he said, bringing Michael into his arms to hug him. "How could it not be? I have you with me again."

"I love you, Daddy," Michael murmured. "I'm glad to be with you again. I'm so glad you came and got me. Life with my adopted parents was nice, yet they did not allow me to act like a boy. I am so anxious for the pony you said you would get for me at the Chippewa village."

Michael suddenly eased from White Fire's arms and gazed with wonder into his eyes. "Daddy, if you were captured by Indians, how could you still be friends with Indians?" he asked, lifting an eyebrow. "You said that you would take me to an Indian village. That is where you plan to get my pony. How could you be friends with people like that, who took you away from Mommy and me?"

"As there are differences in white men, there are differences in men with skin the color of mine,"

White Fire said. "The Sioux and the Chippewa are two different tribes of Indians. They have different beliefs and ways of doing things. I am friends with the Chippewa and enemies with the Sioux, for it was the *Sioux* who abducted me, not the Chippewa. The Chippewa befriended me long ago when I first came to the Minnesota Territory. In fact, Michael, I lived one entire year of my life with them."

"Did Mother live with them with you?" Michael asked softly.

"No, that was before I met your mother," White Fire said, then gazed at the door again.

Now all hopes of Flame being there had been shattered. In the time spent talking with Michael, Flame would have surely opened the door had she been there.

Again he stared at the empty hitching rail. He felt a spiraling of despair over not seeing her horse still there. Yes, she was gone.

Why?

He doubted that he would ever know.

"Let's go inside, Michael," White Fire said, forcing a smile as he leaned over and lowered Michael to the ground. He slid out of the saddle, then took Michael by a hand. "I've someone I'd like for you to meet."

"Flame?" Michael said, smiling up at him as they walked toward the door.

His spine went stiff. "No, I don't believe she is here after all," he said sullenly.

"Where did she go?" Michael asked, his eyes innocently wide as he stared up at White Fire. "I thought she was waiting on us. Didn't you tell me that she was here? That you were going to be married today?"

"Sometimes things change," White Fire said, his

jaw tight. "But there is someone waiting for us. It is someone who will be raised with you as your sister."

"A sister?" Michael said, surprise leaping into his eyes.

White Fire stopped and knelt before Michael. "She has skin the coloring of mine," he said softly. "She is Chippewa, Michael. Her mother died recently. Her mother was a friend. I have taken the child in, to raise as mine."

"I will like having a sister," Michael said, beaming. "Is she older or younger?"

"She is younger," White Fire said, sighing deeply to know that Michael had such a giving heart. That he was willing to take Dancing Star into his life as quickly as his father had accepted her. "But she is old enough to enjoy things that you enjoy. She does not yet know how to ride a horse, though. Michael, will you help teach her?"

It was so hard talking calmly while his heart was aching over Flame's absence.

"Yes, I will help teach her," Michael said, smiling proudly. "Will she get a pony, also, from the Chippewa?" He spoke the word "Chippewa" awkwardly, finding it also hard to pronounce.

"Yes, she will also get a pony from my friends, her relatives, the Chippewa," White Fire said, drawing Michael into his arms and hugging him. "Now let us go and tell Dancing Star to open the door. I am certain that when Flame left, she instructed the child to lock the door until we arrived. Everyone has to be careful in the wilderness. Doors must be locked at all times against intruders. Do you understand that if I am ever called away, that you will also make sure the door is locked?"

Michael nodded.

White Fire rose slowly to his feet and went to the door and knocked on it. "Dancing Star, it is I, White Fire," he said, his eyebrows rising when she didn't come immediately to the door and open it.

White Fire asked her three more times to open it, and fear began to ebb its way into his heart when she still didn't come to the door.

"Where is she?" Michael asked softly.

"I am not certain," White Fire said.

He hurried to the window and gazed through the pane. His heart skipped a beat when he saw Dancing Star sitting on the floor against the far wall, visibly shivering, her eyes wide with fear.

He knew then that something had happened while he had gone to get Michael.

It came suddenly to him that just perhaps Flame had not made her own decision to leave! Perhaps someone had come and forced her. Only that could explain the child's obvious fear.

White Fire rapped his knuckles against the windowpane. "Dancing Star!" he shouted. "Open the door! You have nothing to fear! It is I! White Fire!"

Finally he saw her stir. Their eyes then met and held.

Then she leaped to her feet and ran to the door.

White Fire hurried to the door just as it was opened.

As he knelt down on one knee, Dancing Star flung herself into his arms. "A man came and took Flame away!" she cried, sobs wracking her body. "He forced her! He . . . half . . . choked her when she fought against him!"

White Fire's heart sank at the thought of someone

forcing Flame in such a way. Then guilt washed through him at the thought of his having so quickly doubted her.

He placed his fingers on Dancing Star's shoulders and gently held her away from him so that their eyes could meet. "Dancing Star, did the man mention his name?" he asked slowly, trying to break through her fear to get answers from her. "Did Flame say his name as he took her away?"

"No, no name was said!" she cried. "It was a man wearing dirty clothes. He wore no shoes! His hair was black. His eyes were gray and cold!"

Disappointed that he couldn't get a better description of Flame's abductor, knowing that could fit any criminal in the area, White Fire sighed and looked away from the child.

Dancing Star flung herself into his arms again. "I was so afraid!" she cried. "But the man did not take me! He only wanted Flame!"

White Fire again held her away from him and gazed into her eyes. "When the man came to the cabin, did Flame seem to know him?" he asked slowly. "Or did he seem to be a stranger to her?"

"When she opened the door, she gasped and took quick steps away from him," Dancing Star said, her sobs subsiding. "It was as though she knew him, yet the man tied something about her mouth too fast for her to be able to speak."

Stunned, finding it hard to think of who might come with the sole purpose of taking Flame away, White Fire rose slowly to his feet.

Michael came to him and tugged on his arm.

White Fire gazed down at him and saw that he was staring at Dancing Star.

White Fire made quick introductions. Then before they turned to go inside the cabin, a soldier from Fort Snelling rode up.

Lieutenant Green dismounted and walked stiffly to White Fire. "I have come for two reasons," he said. He took an envelope from the inner pocket of his blue uniform and handed it to White Fire. "A wire arrived at the fort today for you."

Forking an eyebrow, White Fire took the envelope, then he nodded. "Yes, I am certain it is from my mother," he said, recalling having sent her a letter not all that long ago. "Why *else* are you here?" he said, slowly taking the wire from the envelope.

"I have some disturbing news," Lieutenant Green said, clasping his hands tightly behind him.

"What sort?" White Fire asked, gazing into the lieutenant's eyes.

"Colonel Edwards sent word to us at Fort Snelling that Colonel Russell has escaped," he said blandly. "Colonel Edwards says to tell you a search party did not find him."

The blood rushed from White Fire's face. "Colonel Russell escaped?" he gasped out. Like a blow to his gut, he now realized who might have abducted Flame. Her crazed father. The black hair. The gray eyes. The anger.

Yes, more than likely she had been abducted by her very own father!

"I was told that whoever left Colonel Russell after he took him food did not lock the cell well enough when he left," Lieutenant Green said dryly. "Colonel

Russell left the cell, knocked a guard in the head and killed him. I don't know how he managed to get across the wide courtyard without being spied, but he did. He seems to have waited and hid behind supplies left just inside the fort walls. While Colonel Edwards's men were busy taking in more supplies from St. Louis" Colonel Russell slipped away into the forest. He wasn't missed until the next meal was taken to him. So he had a good head start before it was noticed he was gone."

"And you say a search party has been sent out?"

"Sent out, and all but now given up."

"Colonel Edwards gave up that easily on finding him?"

"He'll show up in time. There aren't many places a man can go, barefoot and dressed in prison clothes, without someone recognizing him as an escaped prisoner. Someone'll turn him in."

"In the meantime he is left free to wreak his havoc?" White Fire said, his voice rising in pitch as his anger toward Colonel Edwards grew.

"What can Russell do?" the lieutenant asked, idly scratching his brow. "He's barefoot, penniless, and weaponless."

"He stole his daughter, that's what!" White Fire shouted, his face beet red from anger.

"He did what?" the soldier asked, paling.

White Fire set his jaw. "You go back to the fort and tell Colonel Edwards that he gave up his manhunt too soon," he said. "You tell him that Flame—Reshelle—is out there somewhere in the wilderness at the mercy of her crazed father!"

"Yes, sir, I'll go and tell him," the lieutenant said,

nervously shuffling his feet. "I'll go and tell him right away, sir."

"You just do that," White Fire said, his eyes narrowing.

As the lieutenant rode off, White Fire's thoughts scrambled as to how he could go about finding Flame, himself.

His gaze fell on the gray feather on the table.

"Chief Gray Feather," he whispered, his eyes brightening. "Gray Feather's warriors! They know the land! They are good at tracking!"

"Flame is gone?" Michael asked, tugging on his sleeve. "Her own father took her away, like you would have taken me away had my adopted parents not allowed you to have me?"

"Yes, her own father took her away, but not in the same way I would have taken you, had you not been given back to me when I asked for you," White Fire said, stroking his fingers through his son's thick, black hair. "This man, Flame's father, is an evil man. Flame is not safe while with him. I must go and find her, Michael."

Dancing Star took Michael's hand. "We will help you," she said, her eyes innocently wide. She looked at Michael. "Won't we, Michael?"

"I am certain you would like to do that, but it would be too dangerous," White Fire said solemnly. "I'll take you to stay with the Chippewa while I go with many Chippewa warriors to search for her."

He suddenly remembered the wire. He went into the cabin. The children came in behind him. He started to lay the wire aside, to read later, when he returned from his search for Flame.

But something told him to read it now. His mother

sending her response to his letter with a quick wire, instead of a leisurely letter, told him that something must be wrong. Perhaps her new husband wasn't treating her well. Perhaps she had seen someone else she desired more. He could hardly believe his mother's fickleness.

Taking the wire from the envelope, he opened it and began reading. His eyes widened and his heart pounded like distant thunder the more he read.

He saw that his mother was fickle even as a younger woman.

The wire revealed to White Fire the truth of who his father truly was.

And he was not white.

All these years, when he had been taunted for being a 'breed, he was being wrongly labeled, for both his mother and father were Indian. One was Miami. The other was Chippewa.

"Chief Gray Feather?" he whispered, staring blankly at the truth as it lay there before him in black and white.

Chapter 39

Words from my eyes did start—
They spoke as chords do from the string.

—John Clare

The wire from his mother tucked inside his front breeches pocket and both children on the saddle before him Dancing Star more on his lap than in the saddle, White Fire rode in a gallop toward the Chippewa village. He was glad to see it was now only a short distance away. He knew that as each moment passed, Colonel Russell could be taking Flame farther and farther away from him. There was even a chance that White Fire might not even ever find them.

That thought, that possibility, tore at his heart.

And then what he had discovered in his mother's wire was clinging to his mind with every heartbeat. The man he had always thought was his father wasn't? A man he would have never guessed to be his father was? Irony of all ironies, that it was someone he had grown to love as a father.

Chief Gray Feather.

Chills rode up his spine as he recalled the many times Chief Gray Feather had said that he was drawn to him as a man is drawn to a son. And the chief had dreamed that he *was* his son.

And White Fire *was*. All along he had been the son of this proud, peace-loving chief.

Michael looked over his shoulder at White Fire. "I see Indian houses. Is that the Indian village where I am going to get me a pony?" he asked, drawing White Fire out of his reverie.

He smiled down at his son. "Yes, that is the Chippewa village where we will get both you and Dancing Star ponies," he said. His smile faded. "But first I have things to do that will take me away from you for a while," he said. "Will you mind being left with the Chippewa as I go with many warriors to search for Flame?"

Michael beamed. "It will be fun being with Indians," he said, his eyes dancing. His gaze swept slowly over his father's face. "Will their skin color be like yours? Are you part Chippewa, Father?"

White Fire's lips parted, then they quivered into a proud smile. "Yes, in part, I am Chippewa," he said. "I am part Miami and Chippewa."

Dancing Star turned and gave White Fire a questioning stare. "I did not know that you were Chippewa," she said, cocking an eyebrow. "Mother did not tell me that you were of our same tribe,"

"That is because I did not know until today that I was," White Fire answered, his voice breaking with emotion.

"Does Grandfather know?" Dancing Star asked.

"No, and do not tell him, Dancing Star," he said. "I wish to tell him, myself. But I won't have time until I return from my search for Flame."

"Flame is pretty," Dancing Star said softly. "I like her red hair." She reached up and ran a hand through her long, thick, black hair. "I wish mine was red."

"Do not ever wish to be what you are not," White Fire said, reaching around to place a gentle hand on Dancing Star's shoulder. "Be proud of your heritage. Your hair is beautiful, Dancing Star. It shines and it is smooth as a bird's wing."

"I like birds," Dancing Star said, smiling widely.

As White Fire led his stallion into the outskirts of the village, he became quiet. His jaw tightened as he gazed past everyone who stood aside and watched their arrival. He looked at the chief's lodge, his heart pounding at the thought of his very own father being inside the large wigwam. He so badly wished to go to him and embrace him and call him "Father," but time did not allow it.

Flame. He must concentrate on finding Flame.

Then he would sit in council with his father and tell him what White Fire knew would please the old chief.

By the time he arrived at Gray Feather's lodge, the chief was standing outside, watching with a curious eye, his eyebrows raised.

White Fire wheeled his horse to a quick halt. He set first Dancing Star on the ground, and then Michael. Then he slid from the saddle and placed a hand behind each of the children's heads and led them over to the chief.

"Why have you come?" Chief Gray Feather asked,

looking slowly from child to child, his eyes lingering the longest on Michael.

Then he gazed into White Fire's eyes, awaiting an answer.

White Fire found it difficult to speak, for this was the first time he had ever stood face-to-face with Gray Feather, knowing that he was his true father.

Tears threatened to reveal the secret he must hold within him until Flame was found and was safe. If the tears did spill from his eyes, it would be impossible not to explain why. He fought them back.

He squared his shoulders and tightened his jaw as he gently shoved the children toward the chief. "I must ask two favors of you, Gray Feather," he said, his voice drawn. "That you please keep the children safe with you, and that you please allow many of your warriors to go with me to search for my woman."

"Your woman is missing?" Gray Feather asked, finding this all too familiar since his daughter had not so long ago been stolen away. "The Sioux? They are the cause? They abducted your woman?"

"*Gah-ween*, no, not the Sioux," White Fire said bitterly. "Her father took her away."

"Colonel Russell?" Gray Feather said, his eyes widening. "I saw him taken into custody by the white pony soldiers at Fort Snelling. Did he escape them?"

"*Ay-uh*, yes, he escaped and he abducted Flame right before the eyes of Dancing Star," White Fire said in a rush of words. "Thank God, at least he didn't harm the child."

"I will care for the children and *ay-uh*, take as many warriors as you need to search for the flame-haired woman," Gray Feather said. "I like that woman. She has spirit and she also has a kind heart."

"*Ay-uh,* yes, she is one of a kind, that is for certain," White Fire said thickly, his heart paining him anew to think he might never see her again.

Gray Feather knelt before the children. "Dancing Star, take Michael into my lodge while I see to it that many warriors are sent out to search for Flame," he said, embracing one, and then the other. "I shall return to my lodge in a matter of moments. We will sit by the fire and tell stories until White Fire's return."

"That will be fun, *gee-bah-bah-nahn,* Grandfather," Dancing Star said, clapping her hands excitedly. Then she grabbed Michael's hand and, in a skipping run, led him into the wigwam.

Soon many warriors were on horseback, and armed—some with rifles and some with bows and arrows. Gray Feather stood back and watched White Fire and his warriors leave. Then he went inside his lodge and looked at the children who were sitting by the fire, giggling and chattering like magpies.

His gaze fell on Michael, feeling a strange sort of bond with him, the same that he had always felt for Michael's father.

He inhaled a shaky breath, then went and sat down with the children.

They instantly crawled over and sat down before him.

"Grandfather, tell us about how the skunk got its white stripe, please?" Dancing Star begged. "I love that story."

Gray Feather patted first one head and then the

other, then began the story that he had so often told his granddaughter. It was good to have her with him again. He now knew that he had been wrong to give her away so easily. Yet he could tell that she would be content in her new home, for there she would have a brother to grow up with, and a father who would be the best of fathers!

Chapter 40

Come, come, my love!
—John Clare

Flame glared at her father as he cooked fish over a campfire. The moon reflected into the Mississippi River on one side of them; the shadows of the forest were on the other.

"How could you do this?" Flame asked, her eyes flaming angrily as she glared at her father. "How can you think you can get away with it?"

"I swore that I would never allow you to live with a 'breed," Colonel Russell said flatly, slowly turning the stick on which the fish had been skewered, the fire browning it.

He gave Flame a cold, menacing stare. "And did you think I would allow myself to be penned up in prison like some mad, raging lunatic? A dog?" he grumbled. "I deserve better after all I have done for my country."

"Yes, you've been a dedicated soldier, but you got

too power hungry," Flame said, scratching a mosquito bite on her left arm. "If you had been allowed to start an Indian war in the Minnesota Territory, the government would have done more than court-martial you. You would have been shot by a firing squad."

She swallowed hard and her eyes wavered. "Just like you planned for White Fire," she said, tears swimming in her eyes at the thought of how White Fire must feel now that he knew that she had been abducted.

"He deserved to die," Colonel Russell said in a hiss. "He is a worthless son of a bitch. I don't know how I was ever stupid enough to hire him as my interpreter. I should've known that would backfire on me."

He glowered at her. "And it did," he said dryly. "It brought you two together."

"No matter what you would have done, whether you hired him or not at the fort, we would have found ways to be together," Flame shot back heatedly. "I have loved him since I was ten. I would have searched for him forever until I found him. The Minnesota wilderness was the first place I would look. If I hadn't found him there, I would have sought him everywhere."

"I raised you better than that," Colonel Russell said. He pinched off a piece of the fish and took a bite, to see if it was cooked thoroughly enough.

He licked his fingers. Then he glared at Flame again. "I raised you with class, baby," he said, his teeth clenched. "*Class.* Not to be manhandled by a 'breed. Especially not to live in a damn rickety cabin. You were used to so much more than that."

"And now what do I have?" she taunted. "A father

who is wearing rags, no shoes, and who is hunted by the cavalry?" She laughed. "Yes, you've done quite well for yourself, Father," she mocked. "It's laughable."

"How can you show me such disrespect when it was I who gave you so much through the years after I married your mother?" he said. "You weren't born yet. She tricked me. I'm not your father."

Flame was so stunned by what he had just said, about him not being her real father, she found it hard to comprehend it. Even her mother had betrayed her by never having told her that he wasn't her father.

Then so many things began to make sense to her: How she had so often felt a strange sort of detachment from this man. How she had often wondered how she could be related to someone who was so evil, so cold-hearted and depraved.

She, on the other hand, had always had good feelings, so much compassion for everyone.

So had her beloved mother. Yes, it was all falling into place now, yet knowing it didn't make it any easier to understand. To *accept*, yes. But not to understand.

"You aren't my father?" she finally said.

"Everyone thought your father died of natural causes, but, in truth, I hastened his death after I saw your mother and wanted her," Colonel Russell said, laughing throatily. "When your father got pneumonia and was placed in the hospital at Jefferson Barracks in St. Louis, I just so easily slipped a pillow over his head and—"

"Don't say any more!" Flame cried, feeling as

though she might throw up from the vision evoked by his words. She scrambled to her feet and slowly backed away from him. "You are even more sick than I thought," she said warily. "How could I have ever had any feelings for you, and I *did,* when I was a child?"

"But of course you would," Colonel Russell said, laughing. "I was your 'daddy', wasn't I? Daughters worship their daddies."

"I never worshipped you," Flame said, her voice catching. "I thought I loved you, yet I doubt that I ever did. How could I love someone like you? How could my mother?"

"It was so easy to sway her into loving me," he said, laying the cooked fish on a rock.

He rose slowly, then inched his way toward Flame. "I was so gentle and kind to her while she was getting over the death of her husband," he said, cackling. "Why, darling, I swept her clean off her feet. She married me two months after your father was buried."

"Lord," Flame gasped, her hands at her throat.

"Just the same as I'm going to sweep you off your feet once you've gotten over the shock of hearing all of this," he said.

He quickly grabbed her by an arm and yanked her to him. "Darling daughter," he said, "when we reach Canada, you will become my *wife.*"

"How disgusting!" Flame said, shuddering. "Never will you be allowed to lay one hand on me. I'll kill you first."

"When you grew up into a woman, I knew I'd have you," he said, ignoring what she had said. "One way or another."

His eyes narrowed. He took on a dark and sinister look as he glared at Flame. "Then White Fire interfered," he said tightly.

Then he chuckled. "Well, he won't get the chance to interfere again," he said.

He gazed up one direction of the river, and then the other. "Voyagers are known to stop here and camp on their travels along the Mississippi," he said. "That is why I chose this spot for our camp. Before midnight I am certain voyagers will stop here. We'll steal their large canoe. We'll get quickly out of this area, then head for Canada."

"Over my dead body!" Flame screamed, yanking her arm free. She turned and began to run into the dark shadows of the forest.

She gasped and sobbed when she heard the twigs breaking behind her, realizing that her father—no, not her father—*the fiend* was gaining on her.

"Please, God, don't let this be happening!" she cried. "White Fire, where are you? Please save me!"

She almost fainted with fright when two men jumped out from behind bushes and stood in her path, stopping her. She immediately knew that they were trappers. One was holding the reins to a mule heavily laden with pelts. The other one had a pistol aimed at Flame.

The aim quickly changed. Flame turned with a start and watched the one trapper shoot the man she had always thought was her father. She screamed as Colonel Russell grabbed at a wound on his chest, blood curling from between his fingers. She paled and gasped when he crumpled to the ground, dead.

"Got him!" the one trapper said, chuckling.

As the trapper kneeled down over the fallen victim, Flame turned and jumped the man who was preoccupied watching his friend rifling through the dead man's pockets.

Her heart pounding, knowing that her life depended on her own clear head and swiftness, Flame grabbed a knife from the man's sheath and sank the blade into his chest before he could stop her.

She stepped quickly away from him as he fell to the ground, his eyes locked in a death stare.

Trembling, aghast at having just killed a man, Flame stood over him. Then she screamed when she felt arms of steel grab her around her waist. The man yanked her so roughly against his hard body, that it not only took Flame's breath away, but also jarred the knife from her hand.

"You bitch!" the man hollered, staring wild-eyed down at his dead friend. "You killed my partner!"

He grabbed Flame by the hair and yanked on it as he forced her to turn around and face him. "You are going to pay," he snarled. "First I'm going to rape you. Then I'll enjoy watching you die as I strangle the breath from inside you."

Frightened speechless, Flame stared into the man's dark eyes. Then she found her voice again, at least enough to scream as he half dragged her away behind thick forsythia bushes.

As he shoved her to the ground and ripped at her clothing, Flame's past life flashed before her eyes. . . .

Chapter 41

Is there within thy heart a need
That mine cannot fulfill?
One chord that any other hand
Could better wake or still?

—Adelaide Anne Procter

White Fire's insides splashed cold when he heard a
frightened scream through the trees.

"Flame?" he gasped.

His jaw tight, his pulse racing, he wheeled his
horse to a stop and turned and stared in the direction of the scream. Knowing that was surely Flame,
he dismounted and grabbed his rifle from the gunboot.

The Chippewa warriors followed White Fire's lead
and also dismounted. Then with weapons in hand,
they followed him through the thick brush.

As White Fire stepped into a clearing, he saw that
it was Flame. His heart froze. She was with a man on
the riverbank behind some forsythia. The whiskered

man was easing over her, ready to mount her, his breeches resting around his ankles.

An instant rage filled White Fire. Heated anger flooded his senses. He raised his rifle and took steady aim; then decided against shooting the man. He felt that the trauma of the man falling on Flame, dying atop her, might be too much for her to bear.

Instead, White Fire raised his rifle and fired into the air to frighten the man away.

White Fire's eyes danced and he smiled devilishly when the man tried to scamper to his feet, not succeeding very well as he desperately yanked on his breeches to get them back on. His eyes were wide with fear as he turned and saw the Indians standing there, their weapons drawn on him.

When the trapper tripped and fell and rolled away from Flame, his breeches twisted about his knees, Flame shoved her skirt down to cover her nudity. Then she scurried to her feet and ran toward White Fire.

She screamed and stopped dead in her tracks when an arrow whizzed through the air, just missing her by inches, and settled into the chest of the trapper.

Eyes wild, the trapper grabbed for the arrow and tried to dislodge it. Then unable to, fell over backward into the river.

A hand covering another scream behind it, Flame watched the current grab the man. The lifeless body of the trapper bobbed up and down in the water as he was carried downriver by the swiftness of the current.

White Fire dropped his rifle to the ground. He ran to Flame and took her into his arms. He felt the desperation in her hug as she held him tightly to her.

"Thank God," she sobbed. "It's been so horrible, White Fire! So horrible!"

"You are safe now," he murmured, stroking her back. "You are safe."

Flame clung to him for a moment longer. Then she eased from his arms and gazed up at him. His copper face was bathed in moonlight. His eyes were filled with love and emotion as he looked down at her.

"The man who I thought was my father wasn't my father after all," she blurted out. "White Fire, he abducted me for reasons you will never believe!"

"What do you mean he wasn't your father?" he asked, aware of how he also had only a short while ago discovered that *his* father wasn't his true kin!

"He married my mother when she was pregnant by my true father," Flame blurted out. She looked past him, where Colonel Russell now lay dead. "My life was a lie." She gave White Fire a look of desperation. "My mother never told me the truth!"

He had much to tell her, too, about his own discoveries. But he decided the time was not now, not while she was still trying to sort through her own truths and make some sense about them.

"My father—I mean, Colonel Russell, planned to take me to Canada," she said, her voice breaking. "Once there, he planned to marry me. Can you believe that, White Fire? The man who raised me as his daughter had sexual feelings for me? He actually thought I could be persuaded to return such feelings and marry him?"

She swallowed hard. "He's dead," she murmured. "One of the trappers killed him."

Stunned by the knowledge that the colonel was not

her father, White Fire gasped. Then he again drew
her into his arms to comfort her.

"It is all over," he said softly. "Try to push this all
from your mind. We have the rest of our lives ahead
of us."

He gently framed her face between his hands.
"The children are waiting for us," he said, gazing into
her eyes. "Let us go now and show them that you are
all right."

Flame swallowed back the urge to give in to tears
all over again, but this time it was from happiness,
not from the trauma she had just gone through.

"Yes, let's go to the children," she said, wiping
tears from her eyes with the back of a hand.

"They are at Chief Gray Feather's village," White
Fire said. "I felt they would be safer there."

"Then you were able to get Michael from the
Greers?" Flame asked, stepping away from him.

"Actually, Michael was waiting for me," White Fire
said, proudly squaring his shoulders. "Maureen even
had his clothes packed, for she saw that Michael
could never be happy with them. Not when he knew
that his father was alive and well, and wanted him."

They locked hands. Their fingers intertwined,
they walked toward the waiting Chippewa warriors.

"And Dancing Star?" Flame asked, gazing up at
White Fire. "Will she and Michael get along?"

"They are already fast friends," he said, stepping
up to his horse, and grabbing the reins. He turned
and smiled at Flame. "The last time I saw them, they
were sitting beside Chief Gray Feather's fire and
giggling and talking. Gray Feather had promised to
tell them stories."

He looked over his shoulder at the warriors as they

mounted their steeds, touched deeply to know that he was, in truth, a part of them by heritage. His gaze moved to one warrior in particular, a warrior he now realized was his cousin.

He then looked at Flame. "I have much to tell you," he said, his voice low and measured. He placed a gentle hand to her cheek. "You see, I have also discovered something quite unique about my *own* father."

"About your own father?" Flame said, lifting an eyebrow. "You mean you have discovered something about Samuel Dowling that you never knew before?"

"Yes, something that shook my innermost faith in my mother," White Fire said sullenly.

"What on earth could do that?" Flame asked, searching his eyes.

"Let me tell you about it on our way back to the Chippewa village," he answered. He placed his hands at her waist and lifted her onto his horse.

He then went and got his rifle, sliding it inside the gunboot at his horse's flank. Then he swung himself into the saddle behind Flame.

As they rode off, with the Chippewa warriors following them, White Fire told Flame about receiving the wire from his mother, and about the news of who his true father was.

"Gray Feather is your father?" Flame gasped out after listening intently. She was awestruck to hear how both she and White Fire had at almost the same time discovered the lies they had been living.

"I am Chippewa!" White Fire proudly declared. He lifted his chin and shouted it for the warriors to hear. "I am Chippewa!" he proudly cried.

He could feel a commotion behind him and as he

looked over his shoulder, he saw the wonder in the warrior's stares.

He smiled at them. "I *am* part Chippewa," he said. "Your chief is my father!"

Gasps reverberated through the warriors.

Red Buffalo then rode up next to him. "What do you mean?" he asked, his voice filled with shock. "Has Chief Gray Feather, my uncle, said that you are his blood kin, his son? That you are my cousin? He has just said that in his dreams you sit by his side in the capacity of a son. Dreams are not real."

"This dream seems to be," White Fire said. "But I know it's hard for you to understand. You and Gray Feather, as well as all of your people, will soon know how this can be."

He smiled broadly at Red Buffalo. "All those times that you and I hunted, practiced shooting bows and arrows, or just sat around and talked of life, we were acquainted, Red Buffalo. Ah, but if only I had known then what I know now."

Red Buffalo was rendered speechless, but knowing that White Fire was not one who spoke a false tongue, he quickly reached over and clasped a hand of love on White Fire's shoulder. His eyes locked with his for a moment, then Red Buffalo swung his horse away and fell back again to ride with the warriors.

"I am touched deeply by Red Buffalo's reaction to knowing the truth," White Fire said, tapping his horse's flanks with his heels to urge him into a faster lope. "You see, since my father has no sons, it would have been Red Buffalo who would have been next in line to be chief for his people. His father, who has been dead for many years now, was my father's brother. He is my father's nephew, my cousin."

"Would he have cause to resent you?" Flame asked softly. "Are you going to be chief, not Red Buffalo?" She was not sure what she wanted to hear from White Fire. She wasn't sure if she was ready to live in an Indian village and be a part of their way of living.

To live outdoors? To cook over a fire in the floor? Perhaps to almost freeze to death in the winter in a wigwam?

No, she wasn't sure if she was ready for that sort of radical change in her life.

"I have not thought that far ahead as to how my life will be changed by knowing that I am a full-blooded Indian," White Fire said softly.

His eyes met and held with hers. "Does knowing all of this about me make things different for you?" he asked guardedly. "Can you still love me knowing that I am a full blood?"

"White Fire, darling, you are you," Flame murmured, turning to embrace him. "How could you ever doubt my love for you?"

He held her close and sighed.

Chapter 42

Come live with me, and be my love,
And we will all the pleasures prove
That valleys, groves, hills or fields,
Woods or steepy mountains, yield.

—Christopher Marlowe

Flame strolled along the river hand in hand with Michael and Dancing Star as White Fire opened up his heart to his true father. Flame looked around her, at the wigwams, and at the people coming and going from them, and at the work the women were busy at.

Yes, after much thought, she could see herself there, as one of them.

And before White Fire had gone to meet with his father, he and Flame had talked at length about their future. White Fire had promised to build her a cabin, one which would hold many children instead of their trying to live in a wigwam.

Yes, they were going to move to the Chippewa village, so that Gray Feather and White Fire could become totally acquainted as father and son, which had been denied them since his mother had chosen to keep White Fire's true birthright a secret.

Flame gazed at the larger wigwam in which her beloved sat with his father, revealing truths to him. She smiled and wished that she could be there to see Gray Feather's expression once he realized that he had a son, and that son was White Fire!

But she had wanted to give them the privacy they deserved.

"Let's find pretty shells," Dancing Star said, yanking on Flame's hand to get her attention. "Can we, Flame? Can we find pretty shells and make a necklace of them?"

"Yes, that would be fun," Flame said, laughing softly. "Let's see who can find the prettiest shells."

She watched Michael and Dancing Star scamper on ahead of her along the rocky shore, occasionally dropping to their knees to search through the various shells.

Again Flame turned and gazed at the larger wigwam. "God bless, my darling," she whispered, blowing a kiss toward the dwelling.

Chapter 43

I love thee freely, as man strive for Right;
I love thee purely, as they turn from Praise,
I love thee with the passion put to use,
In my old griefs, and with my childhood's faith.

—Elizabeth Barrett Browning

White Fire sat on plush pelts beside his father before the lodge fire. He gave Gray Feather a steady gaze.

"This wire arrived today from my mother," he said, handing it to Gray Feather.

"You know that I cannot read white man's scribblings," Gray Feather said, yet slowly unfolded the paper anyway, gazing down at it.

"I know, and I will explain what the words on the page say," White Fire said, folding his legs before him.

His knuckles became white from his tight grip on his knees as he began explaining, bringing everything into the open that had been kept secret since his mother had discovered that she had a tiny seed growing inside her womb that had not been planted there by her Miami Indian husband.

"Gray Feather, do you recall a time many years ago when you went to a huge council of various Indian tribes in Kentucky?" White Fire asked. "Do you remember attending that council that was held at a Miami Indian village?"

Gray Feather squinted. His breathing became shallow as he was momentarily lost in thought.

Then he gave White Fire a steady stare. "*Ay-uh*, I remember being in that council in Kentucky," he said in a low voice. "I was only in Kentucky once at that Miami village. The stay became a lengthy one. Many councils were held, not only one. Much was achieved in those councils."

"Do you remember something that happened while you were there, besides sitting in council?" White Fire asked guardedly. He leaned somewhat forward and his heart began to race when he saw a melancholy look suddenly appear in Gray Feather's fading brown eyes.

"*Ay-uh*, more was achieved while in Kentucky than mere talks in councils," Gray Feather said, nodding. His lips quivered into a slow smile as he looked over at White Fire. "There was an *ee-quay*, woman."

"I know," White Fire quickly interjected.

Gray Feather's shoulders tightened. He stared with questioning at him. "How could you know?" he asked softly.

"Because this woman was my mother," White Fire said, his words coming slowly across his lips as his gaze tried to capture all of his father's expression as the knowing was slowly being revealed to him.

"Your . . . *gee-mah-mah*, mother?" Gray Feather gasped out. "How could you know that I knew your mother? That I fell in love with her? That she—"

His words stopped short of revealing his hidden affair to someone after having held it inside his heart, a secret, all of these years. Gray Feather had never forgotten the woman.

At night he still dreamed about holding her, about loving her, about begging her to leave her betrothed and return with him to his Chippewa village!

He had so badly wanted her as his own woman, a woman he would have cherished forever.

He had ached for years over her rejection of him.

"That she rejected you after you had trysts with her behind her husband's back?" White Fire blurted out. "You wanted her, but she only used you. She made love with you because she was that sort of woman—one who would be unfaithful to her husband for the excitement of doing it."

When White Fire saw how what he had just said made his father go so pale, he regretted revealing to his father that his mother was a loose, uncaring woman.

"Husband?" Gray Feather gulped out. "She was married? She was not betrothed, but instead married?"

"I should not have told you," White Fire said, reaching over to place a gentle hand on his father's shoulder. "But, you see, I know all about my mother's affair with you, and that she is capable of deceits that I hate to even think about."

"Your . . . *gee-mah-mah*, mother?" Gray Feather gasped out, his chin trembling as his emotion rose within him.

"*Ay-uh*, yes, my *gee-mah-mah*, mother," White Fire said, slowly easing his hand away from his father,

"Pretty Cloud. Did not my mother tell you that she could not go with you to this land of sky-blue waters because she was betrothed to a powerful Miami chief and feared a war might erupt between the Chippewa and Miami if she turned her back and heart on her betrothed?"

"*Ay-uh,* that is what she told me," Gray Feather said softly. "And she lied? She was married? I joined the woman in her sin against her husband?" Gray Feather held his head in his hands. "The shame of it," he said, his voice breaking. "I am a man of honor. Never would I have laid down with a married woman."

"Do not despair so over having done it," White Fire said. He stood up, then knelt down directly at his father's left side. "For had you not, I would not have been born."

Gray Feather raised his face up in jerks. He stared in disbelief at White Fire. "What did you say?" he gasped. out.

"While you were with Pretty Cloud, she slept with no one but you, for she no longer loved her husband and would not share his blankets with him," White Fire slowly explained. "When you slept with her, you made a child with her. That child is this man who has grown to love you as a father. *You* are my father, not the white man my mother married just after she left her Miami husband."

For a moment all that Gray Feather could do was stare at White Fire, his lips parted, his eyes brimming with sudden tears.

Then he reached out and placed a gentle hand on his face. "My son?" he said, his voice breaking. "My dreams were real? They tried to tell me what was truly real, that you are my son?"

"*Ay-uh*, your son," White Fire said. Then he felt warm and wonderful inside as Gray Feather enwrapped him with his powerful arms and held him close.

"My son," Gray Feather said, over and over again.

They embraced for a long while. Then Gray Feather eased away from White Fire. "This is a day I shall cherish forever," he said thickly. "I have for so long wanted a son. When you suddenly appeared in my life, I felt drawn to you. I puzzled over it for so long, then accepted it. I knew that you were meant to be a part of my life. I knew it. But I just did not know why." He smiled. "Ah, what a wonder it is to have you here with me like this, to know that through my years of pining for your mother that something good came out of our short time together."

White Fire sat down beside his father. Gray Feather turned and sat directly before him so that their eyes could meet.

"Tell me about your mother," Gray Feather said thickly. "Who her husband is now? And what sort of life does she lead. For you see, after I left Kentucky and knew that I could not have her, I found another woman, yet none as fine and beautiful as my Pretty Cloud. Pretty Cloud has stayed in my heart forever. She has been a part of my dreams, oh, so often in my arms in my dreams, telling me how much she loved me."

"It is good that you have held such good memories about her, as though she is a woman worthy of such memories, for in truth, she is an unlikable, deceitful woman," White Fire said sullenly. "She has turned

her back entirely on her Miami people. She lives
the life of a white woman. She is married again. She
scarcely waited for my father's body, or should I say
the man I thought was my father, to get cold in the
grave before she married another wealthy, affluent
St. Louis man."

"In your voice I hear much disrespect when you
speak of your mother," Gray Feather said, searching
his eyes. "Tell me why."

"My disrespect for her began even before I was
born, it seems," White Fire said, running his fingers
through his hair in frustration. He could not get over
how his mother had lied so often to him about how
she had happened to be alone when she was found
wandering in the forest by Samuel Dowling. She told
White Fire that she was there because there had been
an attack on her village. The lies! She knew so well
the art of lying.

"After you left," White Fire continued, "and it was
discovered that my mother was with child, and that it
could not have possibly been her husband's since she
no longer shared her blankets with him at night, her
husband banished her from the tribe. It was then,
only then, that everyone knew that she had wronged
her husband, and how."

"How did she meet the man she married after she
left her village?" Gray Feather asked softly. "The
white man who raised you as his son."

"The man, who until today I thought was my
father, was a trapper," White Fire said. "He found
Mother wandering alone in the forest. And as you
know, she was beautiful and intriguing. She came up
with some sort of lie that convinced him about why
she was alone in the forest, without telling him the

truth of her shameful banishment. He took her in and married her. When he discovered that she was pregnant, he thought the child was his."

"And from that time on she turned her back totally on her heritage?" Gray Feather asked solemnly. "She lived the life of a white woman?"

"*Ay-uh*, as a white woman." White Fire nodded. "From that time on she went by the white name Jania May and cast aside her Indian name as her Indian people had cast her aside. When I was born, with all my features Indian, she convinced her white husband that that happens, and he never doubted that he was the father to her son."

White Fire's jaw tightened. "All my life I was taunted as a 'breed, while all along I did not deserve such a degrading title!" he said, his teeth clenched. "I was Indian, through and through!"

He clasped his hands to his father's shoulders. "Father, I am proud to say that I am part Miami, and part Chippewa. I am proud to be your son."

Gray Feather slid White Fire's hands from his shoulders. He then embraced him long and hard. "My *ningwis*, son," he said, a sob lodging in his throat.

Then he held White Fire away from him and grinned widely. "And that means that I also have a *go-shee-shay*, grandson!" he said, his voice lifting in pitch in his excitement. "Your son, Michael, is my *grandson*."

White' Fire returned his broad grin. "*Ay-uh*, that is so," he said, chuckling. "Today your family has grown in leaps and bounds."

"My heart is filled with so much joy I cannot even express it. It runs so deep and wonderful inside me," Gray Feather said, wiping tears from his eyes.

"I have talked of Mother to you today and shown less than respect for her in my explanations of her, but I can say that I am thankful that she finally found the courage to be truthful with me about my birthright," White Fire said, swallowing hard.

"What prompted her to tell you now, when in the past she has kept it all locked up inside her heart?" Gray Feather asked, forking an eyebrow.

"You or I may have never known the truth except for the panic that my mother must have felt upon reading my last letter to her," White Fire said. "In my letter I spoke of you and your daughter's interest in me. Fearing that I might marry your daughter, who was, in truth, my very own sister, my mother had no choice but to open up truths to her son that she wished never to tell anyone. She could not allow my marriage to my very own sister."

White Fire's heart skipped a beat. "My sister," he said, his voice breaking. "I had a sister and did not even know it. Things could have been so different. Had I but known that Song Sparrow was my sister, she would have never foolishly fallen in love with me. She would have never had cause to take her—"

Suddenly Gray Feather slid a hand over White Fire's mouth, silencing him. "Do not say the words that are a torment to us both," he said thickly. "Let us put it behind us, for nothing will change it. The past is the past. Let it rest there."

"*Ay-uh*, let it rest there," White Fire said. He sighed heavily. "The future, Father, is so bright for us all. It is a future we shall now share as father and son!"

As Flame lifted the entrance flap and she saw Chief Gray Feather and White Fire embrace, she stifled a sob of happiness behind a hand, for the sight was such a beautiful one to witness!

"Grandfather!" Dancing Star cried as she ran on past Flame. "You are as happy to see White Fire as I am."

Michael ran after Dancing Star and sat down beside his father and Gray Feather.

Gray Feather turned to Michael seeing him for the first time as his grandson. His hand trembled as he reached over and placed it on Michael's face and slowly moved his fingers over his features.

"My grandson," he said, his voice filled with pride. He then looked over at White Fire. "My son," he said, his eyes filling with joyful tears.

Chapter 44

Thou art my own, my darling, and my wife;
And when we pass into another life,
Still thou art mine.
All this which now we see
Is but the childhood of Eternity.

—Arthur Joseph Mundby

Three years later—

Father Sun was at the centermost part of the sky, sending his rays down upon a great celebration that was in progress.

The Chippewa women had been cooking for days for the feast that was now spread out on platforms. Dancers dressed in fancy attire swayed in rhythm around a huge, outdoor fire as the drums beat their cadence.

Dressed in a buckskin dress and moccasins, and with flowers woven into the strands of her hair, Flame sat on a pelt-strewn platform with her husband.

She was proud to be a part of the celebration of the Chippewas' lives.

Especially today she was exceedingly proud, for Michael was being adopted into the tribe, as one with them.

Today's celebration was just a small part of Michael's initiation ceremony. He had even chosen a name by which he would be called from this day forward-Black Shield. The name had been chosen for the black shield that his Chippewa grandfather had given to him early this morning, just prior to the start of the day's celebration.

White Fire sat beside her on the platform. His chieftain father was on a platform next to them. Flame gazed at her husband. The past three years had been magical. Being White Fire's wife was something she would have never imagined.

Not even when she was ten and she had fantasized about being with him. Her fantasies had been the best a girl could conjure, but were never as wonderful as it was in real life. Now, as his wife, she awakened every morning in his arms. As his wife, she went to sleep every night being held by him after they shared such sweet lovemaking.

They never raised their voices to one another, nor did they to their three children.

The thought of the children made a sweet peace swim through Flame's consciousness. She turned her gaze and watched her youngest at play, as Dancing Star watched over her, the doting sister.

Yes, Zoe, born of Flame and White Fire's love, was now two and as feisty and pretty as she could be with her black, raven-colored hair, green eyes, and her smooth copper skin. Flame knew that when her daughter grew up into a woman there would be men clamoring for her attention.

She looked again at Dancing Star. She also was an eye-catcher with her features so much like her mother's, which were nothing less than vivacious. Yes, Flame and White Fire would have a fight on their hands when both their daughters grew into women and men began noticing them.

Flame's gaze shifted again.

Ah, yes, there was Michael, who was still only a child, but who had adapted well to living among the Chippewa, in the Chippewa tradition, for it was his father's.

And it was good that Michael would be living under the protection of the Indians. If he still lived among the whites, all of the white boys would call him a 'breed. He would have to suffer the same insults his father had when he had lived among whites. He would be tormented by those who knew no better than to behave as their parents, who were for the most part prejudiced against anything and everything Indian.

The drumming suddenly ceased. Chief Gray Feather rose from his platform and went and stood in the midst of his people, who circled around him, watching him, their pride for him in their eyes and smiles.

"Today we have come together as one heart and soul to celebrate my grandson's initiation into our tribe, required because, in part, he is white, born of a white mother," Gray Feather said, the many colorful feathers of his headdress fluttering in the gentle breeze. His bare, copper chest shone from a fresh bear greasing. His fading brown eyes danced, his pride revealed to everyone in his gentle smile.

He looked over at Michael, who was dressed in only a breechcloth. "Grandson, come to me," he said, gesturing with a hand toward him. "Come and stand with your grandfather so that everyone can see you. My grandson, Black Shield, today you make this old grandfather so proud."

Barefoot, his glistening black hair now worn to his waist and drawn back from his brow by a colorful, beaded headband, Black Shield walked proudly to his grandfather and stood at his side. He smiled broadly at his father, and then at Flame, whom he saw now as his mother.

Then he laughed softly when someone suddenly came to him and held her arms up, silently begging to be held. "Sweet Zoe," Black Shield whispered, grabbing her up into his arms. She snuggled against his bare chest, laying her cheek against it.

Flame gave White Fire a quick, questioning look, wondering what should be done about Zoe.

"I am certain that her sister will get her when it is time for our son to go to the river," White Fire whispered, reaching over and giving Flame's hand a soft squeeze. "Is not it a beautiful sight to see Zoe caring so much for her older brother?"

"She is like an angel fallen from the heavens into our son's arms," Flame whispered back.

They grew quiet and listened as Gray Feather gave a long speech about his feelings for Black Shield, and then his son, White Fire.

His old eyes then turned to Flame, whom he spoke of as though she were his daughter, born of his flesh.

Tears spilled from Flame's eyes to feel this loved, to feel so at peace with her life with these wonderful people. She wished that everyone could trade places with her for only one day so that they could see how wrong they were about the Chippewa—about all Indians, in general.

In truth, they were filled with more love and understanding than most whites that Flame had known while living in the white world. The Chippewa were as one with nature and their Great Spirit. They were a spiritual people who sought only to live in peace and harmony with everyone.

Gray Feather turned to Black Shield and clamped his fingers on his shoulders. "It is time now for you to go to the river," he said thickly. "There we will finalize the ceremony. You will then be Chippewa through and through."

Without having to be told, Dancing Star went and took Zoe from Black Shield's arms. And before turning to leave him, she stood on tiptoe and kissed him on the cheek.

Black Shield watched his cousin walk away, having found such a good friend in her. They were almost inseparable. He knew that he would protect her with his life.

"Come," Gray Feather said, placing a gentle hand on Black Shield's elbow.

Black Shield gave his mother and father a wide grin as they stepped down from their platform and followed closely behind him and his grandfather. Then he smiled again at Dancing Star as she walked beside Flame, Zoe still nestled comfortably in her arms, and clinging around her neck.

The whole village went and stood along the

riverbank. Everyone was quiet as the true initiation began.

Flame had taught Black Shield how to swim, and he was not afraid to plunge up to his waist in the river. He stopped and turned to face the witnesses to his change into a Chippewa.

Then three young maidens came to him in the water. He knew that it was a part of the ritual when they began scrubbing him briskly with bars of soap. He had been told that this was required, that by this ritual, every drop of his white blood would be washed out of him . . . that then he would be Chippewa forever and ever.

When the maidens left the river, Chief Gray Feather entered the water and went and stood before Black Shield. He lifted a hand and held it over Black Shield's head as he spoke in a soft, but carrying voice for all to hear.

"Grandson, you are adopted into a great family of people," Gray Feather said, gazing intently into Black Shield's eyes. "By the power given to me as chief of our band of Chippewa I say to you, grandson, that you are now one of us by an old, strong law and custom."

Loud shouts rose into the air. Women began to sing. Again the drums began to play as Black Shield gave his grandfather a large, warm hug.

They then waded out of the water.

One by one the people came and hugged Black Shield.

And after receiving his congratulations from everyone but his family, Black Shield broke free of the crowd and went to his father. Their eyes locked for a moment. Then Black Shield hugged White Fire, and then Flame.

"Son, I am so very proud of you," White Fire said as Black Shield stepped away from him, his eyes filled with the excitement of the moment.

"So am I," Flame said, flicking tears from her eyes. "So very, very proud."

She gave White Fire a quick, mischievous smile, then took Black Shield by the hand. "Come with me," she said, her eyes dancing. "We have a special surprise for you, Michael—I mean, Black Shield. It is a gift of congratulations for being initiated into the Chippewa tribe."

"What *is* it?" Black Shield asked, then gasped when Red Buffalo suddenly appeared from behind a wigwam, leading a horse toward him by the reins.

Black Shield let out a loud yelp of glee as he ran and took the reins. He gazed with wide eyes at the horse as he ran a hand along its withers. "Mine?" he said, giving White Fire and Flame a look over his shoulder as they stood, watching.

"Yours, *all* yours," Flame said, twining her fingers through White Fire's.

Black Shield ran to them and embraced them. "Thank you," he said, swallowing hard. "Thank you!"

Black Shield then turned and smiled at Dancing Star. Zoe asleep in her arms, Dancing Star was now standing before Black Shield, her eyes filled with her own excitement for him.

"Take me for a ride, Black Shield?" Dancing Star asked, taking Zoe and sliding her into Flame's arms.

"*Ay-uh,* let's take a ride!" Black Shield said. He

grabbed Dancing Star by a hand and led her to the horse.

White Fire went and lifted her onto the horse's bare back, and then helped his son up behind her. "Be careful," he said, then wished he hadn't when Black Shield looked embarrassed by the reminder. "Have fun," he hurriedly interjected. Then he stepped back to Flame's side. Together they watched Dancing Star and Black Shield ride off, giggling.

Flame then gazed down at Zoe, smiling to see that none of the excitement about the gift had awakened her.

Flame then smiled up at White Fire. "I'm going to take Zoe to bed," she murmured. "I think she's had enough excitement for one day."

"I shall go with you," he said. He slid an arm around Flame's waist and led her through the crowd of people who were readying themselves for many more hours of dancing and eating. The celebration was planned to go into the wee hours of morning.

Flame stepped inside her cabin and walked softly across braided rugs until she came to Zoe's bedroom.

After she placed Zoe in her bed, White Fire drew a soft patchwork quilt up to their daughter's chin.

They stood for a moment watching their daughter sleep. Then White Fire surprised Flame by hoisting her into his arms and carrying her to their own bedroom.

"My darling, are we going to have our own private celebration?" she murmured and giggled as he placed her on their bed.

"We will not be missed," White Fire said. "But perhaps I should still close the door to secure privacy."

After he closed the bedroom door, he stood beside the bed and removed his clothes.

Nude, his copper body gleaming in the soft splash of the sun's rays as it bled though the windowpane and sheer curtains at the sides of the bed, he reached a hand out for Flame.

"Come to me," he said huskily. "Let me undress you."

Flame rose from the bed. Her pulse raced as he removed her soft, buckskin dress, that was beautifully decorated with beads that she had sewn on herself.

When she was finally undressed and his eyes slowly drank in her nakedness, she could hardly stand the waiting. Her desire for him was no less now than the first time they had made love. In fact, it grew with each day, with each kiss, with each embrace.

She felt, ah, so blessed, to be married to such a wonderful, caring man. They had lived in the Chippewa village since the very first day of their marriage.

Although Flame had told him that she would make do in a wigwam, he had still wanted to make things as easy on her as possible since she had known only rich comforts while growing up.

Soon White Fire had built her a large, comfortable cabin with a bedroom for each of their children, and for themselves.

The kitchen was well designed for her use, and their parlor was filled with plush furniture that he had shipped in from St. Louis.

"My woman," White Fire said huskily, taking her hands, and yanking her against his hard, ready body.

His lips came down on hers in a hot, lingering kiss. His hands went to her buttocks. He clasped his fingers into her soft flesh and drew her closer to his heat, to his building need of her.

Delicious shivers of desire floated across Flame's flesh as he ground his hardness against her body. She slid her mouth away from his lips. "I need you," she whispered, her face aflame with her building need. "Now, White Fire. Oh, darling, *now*."

He lifted her into his arms, lying her down across the bed. Then he moved onto the bed with her.

As he kissed her again, his tongue delving through her lips, touching hers, he thrust his throbbing manhood deeply inside her warm and wet place.

Flame opened her legs wide to him and lifted them around his waist and rode with him as he moved rhythmically within her.

She clung to him as he pressed his lips to her throat, and then slid his mouth down to flick his tongue around first one of her nipples, and then the other. Her nipples grew hard at once beneath the wet assault.

Flame's breath quickened as he swept his arms around her and enfolded her with his solid strength, his hot and hungry mouth on her lips again with an all consuming kiss.

His lips drugging her, she was so close, oh, so close to the ultimate pleasure, which she had only known while with her husband.

She sought his mouth with a wildness and desperation. She cried out against his lips as he shoved his sex more deeply into the yielding silk of her folds, and thrust over and over again into her in a more demanding rhythm. She clung. She sobbed. She floated.

White Fire held her tightly as over and over again he drove in swiftly and surely, the heat building inside him, the pleasure mounting.

His fingers pressed urgently into her flesh as he felt himself drawing close to his release. He gasped. He groaned. He kissed her wildly as he took her mouth by storm.

And then he made one last leap inside her and shuddered his seed into her as a searing, scorching flame shot through him.

He smothered her outcry of passion with his mouth as she, too, reached the peak of her passion.

Afterward, he lay beside her, his face snuggled into her round, thick breasts, his warm breath stirring shivers along Flame's flesh.

She stroked her fingers through his sleek, black hair. "Darling," she murmured. "My darling White Fire, I did not know that happiness could be so complete."

He leaned up on an elbow. His eyes swept over her, and then he gazed into her eyes. "I knew not the meaning of the word 'happiness' until I knew you," he said softly, then twined his fingers through her hair and brought her lips to his again.

She moaned throatily as he once again began to spin his golden web of magic around her.

Don't miss any of Cassie Edwards's
stirring historical romances.

Coming soon,

Wild Embrace!

Desire untamed . . .

Raised in luxury in San Francisco, exquisite
Elizabeth Easton thought Seattle a raw, rough
frontier harbor. But when the noble Suquamish
warrior, Strong Heart, sweeps her into his flight
back to his people, Elizabeth discovers what true
wilderness is. For deep in the breathtaking forests
of the great Pacific Northwest, Strong Heart is
free from intolerance and injustice. Elizabeth is
free from her controlling businessman father.
And both she and Strong Heart are unbound
from the prejudice that keeps them apart in
the white world. Soon the handsome, sensitive
man becomes her guide to ecstasy . . . and
she resolves to defy anything—and anyone—
that tries to end their undeniable love . . .

Praise for Cassie Edwards

**"A sensitive storyteller who always
touches readers' hearts."**
—*RT Book Reviews*

**"Cassie Edwards captivates with white hot
adventure and romance."**
—**Karen Harper**

**"Edwards moves readers with
love and compassion."**
—*Bell, Book & Candle*

Connect with

Visit us online at
KensingtonBooks.com
to read more from your favorite authors, see books
by series, view reading group guides, and more.

for sneak peeks, chances to win books and prize packs,
and to share your thoughts with other readers.

facebook.com/kensingtonpublishing
twitter.com/kensingtonbooks

Tell us what you think!

To share your thoughts, submit a review,
or sign up for our eNewsletters, please visit:
KensingtonBooks.com/TellUs.

Books by Bestselling Author
Fehr Michaels

Available Wherever Books Are Sold!
Check out our website at **www.kensingtonbooks.com**

More by Bestselling Author
Hannah Howell

__Highland Angel	978-1-4201-0864-4	$6.99US/$8.99CAN
__If He's Sinful	978-1-4201-0461-5	$6.99US/$8.99CAN
__Wild Conquest	978-1-4201-0464-6	$6.99US/$8.99CAN
__If He's Wicked	978-1-4201-0460-8	$6.99US/$8.49CAN
__My Lady Captor	978-0-8217-7430-4	$6.99US/$8.49CAN
__Highland Sinner	978-0-8217-8001-5	$6.99US/$8.49CAN
__Highland Captive	978-0-8217-8003-9	$6.99US/$8.49CAN
__Nature of the Beast	978-1-4201-0435-6	$6.99US/$8.49CAN
__Highland Fire	978-0-8217-7429-8	$6.99US/$8.49CAN
__Silver Flame	978-1-4201-0107-2	$6.99US/$8.49CAN
__Highland Wolf	978-0-8217-8000-8	$6.99US/$9.99CAN
__Highland Wedding	978-0-8217-8002-2	$4.99US/$6.99CAN
__Highland Destiny	978-1-4201-0259-8	$4.99US/$6.99CAN
__Only for You	978-0-8217-8151-7	$6.99US/$8.99CAN
__Highland Promise	978-1-4201-0261-1	$4.99US/$6.99CAN
__Highland Vow	978-1-4201-0260-4	$4.99US/$6.99CAN
__Highland Savage	978-0-8217-7999-6	$6.99US/$9.99CAN
__Beauty and the Beast	978-0-8217-8004-6	$4.99US/$6.99CAN
__Unconquered	978-0-8217-8088-6	$4.99US/$6.99CAN
__Highland Barbarian	978-0-8217-7998-9	$6.99US/$9.99CAN
__Highland Conqueror	978-0-8217-8148-7	$6.99US/$9.99CAN
__Conqueror's Kiss	978-0-8217-8005-3	$4.99US/$6.99CAN
__A Stockingful of Joy	978-1-4201-0018-1	$4.99US/$6.99CAN
__Highland Bride	978-0-8217-7995-8	$4.99US/$6.99CAN
__Highland Lover	978-0-8217-7759-6	$6.99US/$9.99CAN

Available Wherever Books Are Sold!

Check out our website at
http://www.kensingtonbooks.com